全国英语等级考试(PETS)

综合阅读全面突破

(第2级)

主　编	清华大学英语系	李华山
副主编	萧晓红　欧阳瑾	钟海燕
编　者	肖嫦娥　罗小荣	阳碧云
	王希勇　刘莹欣	朱礼清
	王注明　王拥军	杨　琛
	赵　育　郑重辉	朱志平
	杜　华　李坤琳	罗　阳
	李建泉　阳惠楚	李春良
	刘　迪　邓云霞	丁　宁

科学技术文献出版社

Scientific and Technical Documents Publishing House

北　京

（京）新登字 130 号

内 容 简 介

　　阅读理解能力（包括完形填空，即在有障碍的情况下进行阅读和理解的能力）是英语学习者必须掌握的一项重要能力，也是 PETS 各级考试中最重要的考核内容。而且事实上 PETS 其他各个部分的考试中也不可避免地涉及到了这一能力，因此阅读理解水平的高低关系到考生能否顺利通过考试、能否拿到合格证书。

　　本书从 PETS 考试中完形填空与阅读理解两种题型的出题点、出题方式、问题类别等方面对不同题型的答题思路、方法、应该注意的地方等进行了详细而准确的分析和指导，并佐以大量典型而具有趣味性、能寓教于乐的例题和强化练习，使考生能在掌握综合阅读技巧理论的基础上对这一考试中的完形填空与阅读理解两种题型有更直观和更透彻的把握，因此是顺利通过 PETS 考试并获得高分的必备考前专项辅导用书。

　　科学技术文献出版社是国家科学技术部系统惟——家中央级综合性科技出版机构。我们所有的努力都是为了使您增长知识和才干。

前　言

　　全国英语等级考试体系(Public English Test System,简称 PETS)是教育部考试中心设计开发和推出的一种开放型英语考试,它以我国全体公民为对象,构筑了一个全国性的英语能力考查和测试平台。

　　为了帮助广大考生提高自己的英语水平并轻松通过这一考试,我们组织了清华大学等高校中部分经验丰富的英语教师,根据教育部颁发的《全国英语等级考试大纲》精心编写了这套 PETS 考试辅导丛书。本书即是严格按照考试大纲编写的专项指导和提高用书——《PETS-2 综合阅读全面突破》。

　　阅读理解能力(包括完形填空,即在有障碍的情况下进行阅读和理解的能力)是考试中所占分值最大、而考生普遍反映失分较多的题型。究其原因,主要是因为阅读是外语学习的基础,同时阅读本身也是一种高度综合的思维和判断过程,需要考生具备相当扎实的语法、词汇基础,并且能够自如地运用各种诸如快速阅读、细读、略读、回读、归纳、分析等等阅读技巧,还要能做到不被形形色色的干扰项所迷惑,才能准确找到答案。此外,任何考试都有时间的限制,如果在规定时间内不能够顺利、熟练地完成所有试题,必然造成失分。

　　《PETS-2 综合阅读全面突破》正是这样一本旨在帮助考生在较短时间内尽可能克服以上种种难点的、针对性很强的考前辅导用书。在编写体例和内容上,本书具有如下特点:

　　一、大纲规定,PETS 第 2 级笔试中英语知识运用部分有单项填空、完形填空两类题型,阅读理解部分只有多项选择一类题型。由于完形填空是在对篇章进行阅读与理解的基础上考查考生的词汇、语法和表达等知识,所以本书也对这一题型进行了较为详细的讲解。因此,本书所指的"综合阅读"实际上包括了这一级别考试中的完形填空和阅读多项选择两种题型。

　　二、为便于考生从整体上了解PETS-2这一级别的考试,本书首先对考试大纲进行了简单解读，主要是考试形式和试卷结构，分析大纲对这几种题型的能力要求与具体的考查角度，让考生不必购买考试大纲即可从整体和全局的角度对这一考试的特点进行把握。

三、本书综合了近年的一些实考真题，从中归纳出各种题型的命题规律和相应的答题技巧，并从备考的角度对各种题型的知识与技能储备进行了适度分析，紧扣原文和一般性阅读技巧，不但能够帮助考生提高应试技巧，而且做到了使其知其然，也知其所以然。

四、语言的学习是一个逐步加深、完善、熟能生巧的过程。仅仅听老师讲解或者看看书上的几道例题显然是不够的，还需要大量的针对性的练习才能将语言技巧真正转化成自己的能力。本书的主体部分就是在分析讲解真题的基础上，严格按照 PETS 考试的形式、长度、难度和出题特点，为考生准备了大量的强化型习题。每道习题后均有详细的分析，包括出题点、解题思路、排除干扰项等等。本书最后还给出了难度与实考真题相当的模拟试题与参考答案，考生可以在学完本书后进行综合性的自测。强化训练与模拟试题都可作为老师在进行 PETS 考试辅导时的随堂练习。

五、本书的另一特点是所有强化训练后都附有高质量的准确译文。初级、中级英语学习者的英语应用水平一般是有限的，在阅读过程中往往不能够完全深刻地把握原文的全部含义，遗漏、曲解和只看表面、忽视深层次意思等都是普遍现象。而在做完习题后，用自己熟悉的母语阅读译文，重新回到原文，找到自己理解和答题出现问题的地方，往往具有事半功倍的神奇效果。

总之，我们认为，这是一本针对 PETS 综合阅读的颇具特色和实用价值的考前辅导用书。如果考生能够系统地按照本书进行训练，阅读能力一定会在较短的时间内有较大的提高。而且，这种提高不仅会表现在这一级别考生的应试水平上，更重要的是会表现在考生整体英语运用能力的提高上。

在本书的编写过程中，我们参考了大量相关文献和资料，限于篇幅，在此不一一列举，谨致谢意。当然，由于编者水平有限，错误和疏漏在所难免，希望广大读者和同行对本书提出宝贵意见。

目　录

第三章 综合阅读·实战经典

第四章 综合阅读·模拟考场

第 1 节　PETS-2 应试须知

一　PETS-2 笔试概述

PETS 第 2 级考试笔试时间为 120 分钟，满分 100 分。

1. 关于答题卡和登分卡的使用

PETS 第 2 级笔试采用特别设计的、用于光电阅读器（OMR）评分的答题卡 1 和用于人工阅卷（阅读器登分）的答题卡 2。答题卡的种类如下表所示：

部　分	答题卡种类
听力	答题卡 1
英语知识运用	
阅读理解	
写作	答题卡 2

2. 关于答题时间

PETS 第 2 级考试笔试的答题时间分配如下表：

部　分	听力	英语知识运用	阅读理解	写作	总计
时间（分钟）	20	25	35	40	120

3. 关于笔试试卷的题量与采分点（原始赋分）

PETS 第 2 级考试笔试各部分的题量与采分点（原始赋分）如下表所示。除特殊情况外，原则上每题 1 分。

部　分	题量	原始赋分	备　注
听力	20	20	
英语知识运用	35	35	
阅读理解	20	20	
写作	10+1	35	第 2 节原始赋分满分为 25 分。
合计	86	110	

4.关于分数权重

　　为了处理好考试中题目数量、赋分与各种技能的考查关系,PETS第 2 级考试笔试采用了分数加权的办法,即对各部分题目的原始赋分分别给予不同的权重,使之能够平衡各种技能的考查关系。

　　PETS 第 2 级考试笔试中各部分所占分数权重如下表所示:

部　分	听力	英语知识运用	阅读理解	写作	合计
权重(%)	30	20	30	20	100

　　考生得到的笔试成绩是其各部分所得原始分分别经过加权处理后的分数总和。如:

　　某考生听力部分原始得分为 15 分,经加权处理后的分数应为 22.5 分(15÷20×30=22.5 分);

　　其英语知识运用部分原始得分为 20 分,经加权处理后的分数应为 11.4 分(20÷35×20≈11.4 分);

　　其阅读理解部分原始得分为 15 分,经加权处理后的分数应为 22.5 分(15÷20×30=22.5 分);

　　其写作部分原始得分为 25 分,经加权处理后的分数应为 14.3 分(25÷35×20=14.3 分)。

　　该考生未经过加权处理的原始总分为 75 分,各部分经过加权处理后的总分应为 70.7≈71 分。

二 笔试试卷内容和结构

　　PETS 第 2 级考试笔试的全部试题都在 1 份试卷中,包括听力、英语知识运用、阅读理解和写作 4 个部分。

　　PETS 第 2 级考试笔试内容如下表所示:

部分	节	为考生提供的信息	考查要点	题型	题目数量	采分点
听力*（接受）	第1节	5段短对话（放一遍录音）	简单的事实性信息	多项选择题（三选一）	5	5
	第2节	5段短对话和独白（放两遍录音）			15	15
英语知识运用（接受）	第1节	15个句子或对话	语法和词汇	多项选择题（四选一）	15	15
	第2节	1篇文章（180～210词）	词汇	完形填空多项选择题（四选一）	20	20
阅读理解（接受）		5篇文章（共约1000词）	总体和特定信息	多项选择题（四选一）	20	20
写作（产出）	第1节	1篇文章（约100词）	改错	改错题	10	10
	第2节	中文提示信息	简短文章	指导性作文	1	25
总计					85＋1	110

＊ 问题不在录音中播放，仅在试卷上印出。

第2节　综合阅读的具体考试形式

一　完形填空部分

　　完形填空是给出一篇180～210词的短文，在文中留出20个空白，要求考生在对应每个空白处给出的4个备选项中选出最佳选项补全短文，使补全后的短文意思通顺、结构完整。共20个小题，每题的原始赋分为1分，共20分。

二　阅读理解部分

　　在考试形式上，PETS第2级笔试中阅读理解部分由五篇短文组成。平均每篇短文约有200词，短文后的题目数量为3～5题，要求考生根据文章内容，从每题所给的4个选项中选出正确的一项，并且在答题卡1上作答。五篇短文共给出20道题，每题1分，共计20分。一般完成这部分的时间为35分钟。绝大部分考生对这样的题目形式已经非常熟悉了,所以在此不再赘述。

第3节 综合阅读的能力要求

一 完形填空部分

PETS第2级英语知识运用部分的测试内容涉及到《全国英语等级考试第2级考试大纲》中所规定的词汇和基本的语法知识,重在考查考生对基础语言知识的掌握情况、运用能力和对语篇的理解分析能力等方面。这部分对考生的能力要求简单说来包括以下几点:

1. 能够熟练掌握大纲规定的2 000左右词汇,熟悉常见词语的搭配及其习惯用法,并要求能在特定语境条件下熟练运用,对于近义词、同义词等易混淆词汇具有一定的辨析能力。

2. 能够熟练掌握和运用大纲列出的基础语法知识(具体的语法项目请参考我们编写的《全国英语等级考试笔试题型全解与高分突破(第2级)》中的相关内容)。

3. 具有较强的阅读能力及语篇分析能力,能灵活运用归纳、判断、分析和推理的方法,快速领悟文章主旨,把握文章的篇章结构和内在逻辑关系等。

4. 具有较强的交际能力,熟悉英语表达方式,如习语、固定搭配和日常对话等。

二 阅读理解部分

阅读理解部分在各类英语考试中占有相当大的分量。在PETS-2考试中,阅读占笔试试卷权重的30%,与听力部分所占的权重相同,是笔试试卷中所占权重最大的部分之一。可以说,阅读理解关系到一场英语考试的成败。

大纲指出,PETS第2级考生应能读懂通知、简单的介绍和广告、通俗易懂的英文书刊或报纸。具体要求如下:

1. 理解文章的主旨要义

考生应能掌握文章的主旨大意及相应的细节,对短文的主要内容及中心思想、段落大意和细节描写有较为准确的领会和把握。

2. 能够准确理解文中具体信息

短文所包含的具体信息主要为叙述事件、说明细节、推理论述。要求考生能够对事件的时间、地点、人物、事情发生过程,事物或理论说明的细节,论述的人、物、例的各方面信息有全面和准确的捕捉和理解。理解这些重要的具体信息是 PETS 第 2 级考试要求的重要阅读技能。

3. 能够根据上下文推测生词的词义

考生应能对文章中具体词汇进行准确理解,对某些具有多种意思的词语、固定短语、口头语及习语能够理解到位,进而把握句子及段落的意思。

4. 能够作出简单判断和推理

考生应当能够在理解文字表面意思的基础上,理解其深层次含义。通过文章个别词汇、句段、语气语调、明确信息及基本常识,能对文中信息进行合理的判断、推理、联想和引申,以得出未明示的细节、结论、事情发展趋势等,体察作者的“弦外之音”。这是对考生认知能力、理解能力和思维能力的综合考查。

5. 能够理解文章的基本结构

考生应能掌握文中各单句之间、各段落之间的逻辑关系,进而理清文章的脉络和作者的行文思路。这种能力是阅读大篇幅书面文献资料的需要,也是 PETS 第 2 级考试的重要考查方面。

6. 能够理解作者的意图和态度

考生应能理解作者的写作目的,把握作者的观点和态度。作者通过短文表达对某事件、新闻时事、社会现象的观点和态度,考生应对其有准确的拿捏。作者写此文章的目的和意图,考生应对其有准确到位的体会。

以上要求包含了大纲中考查考生对英语“接受能力”的各个方面。阅读理解部分的试题也是本着此宗旨对以上所述的要求进行细化的测试。

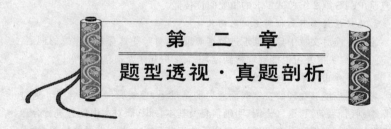

第 二 章
题型透视·真题剖析

第1节　完形填空部分

一　完形填空命题规律

完形填空部分主要考核的是考生对英语这门语言的综合运用能力以及考生的语篇分析能力。

通过对历年考卷的分析来看,PETS-2考试选择的完形填空材料,在体裁上多为记叙文或者带有一定的记叙成分的议论文,几乎没有出现过说明文。材料难度一般低于普通高考中的英语考试。而从题目的设置上来看,也呈现出一定的规律:首先,短文的首句一般不会设置选择项;其次,短文每句话中留的空格数一般不会多于2个,空格与空格之间的距离多在6个单词以上;第三,选择项的设置多是单个的词,并且实词较虚词出现得多;第四,题目着重考查考生能否通过对材料上下文的理解找出正确的选择项,而单纯考查英语语言和语法知识的题目非常少。

二　完形填空答题要点

1. 快速通读全文,把握文章主旨

首先要重视首句,开篇明义。从历次PETS-2的实考试题可以看出,完形填空首句一般是不设题的。文章的首句是整篇文章的起点,它决定文章行文的方式和方向。认真阅读短文第一句,有利于准确地预测和推断短文的主旨。所以考生应充分重视首句的启示作用,使它成为解读全篇的一个突破口。

快速通读全文时,考生的主要任务是:抓住文章线索,了解文章大体结构,把握文章中心意思。阅读过程中一定不要急于看选项,要把注意力集中在文

章的主线上,同时尽可能多地捕捉到一些关键信息。比如说一篇故事性文章,关键信息就往往是时间、地点和人物等,抓住了关键信息就抓住了故事的线索,理解起全文来就非常容易了。先快速将全文浏览一遍是非常必要的,因为如果一开始就边看文章边选答案,非常容易误选失分。进行这个步骤时要控制好时间,对于一篇210词左右的文章,其最佳通读时间应控制在2分钟左右。读得太快或太慢的考生,都要在平时的训练中有针对性地调整自己的浏览速度。

2.细读全文,推断选项

(1)抓住文章结构及行文逻辑

完形填空是一篇被人为切断的语篇,考生的任务就是选择词语将其贯通,所以只要考生依据自己对文章的理解使语文的思路通顺了,大多数答案也就显而易见了。因此,在细读时,我们要紧抓文章线索,理清文章思路。

(2)以语义为主,以词句知识为辅推断选项

考生在答题时,首先要对空格前后句子作较深入的分析,确定空格在句中的意思。然后选择在意思上相符的答案,此时要注意整个句子语法(词性、语态、语气、时态)是否正确、语义是否合理。有时如果填入空白处在语义和语法上都没有问题的选项不止一个,就要看哪个选项在逻辑上最为合理。有些题目还需要结合生活常识来进行判断,如有关地理历史、文化背景、风土人情等的材料中往往会出现根据常识来确定选项的题目。

(3)学会跳读

在完形填空中,常常出现所谓的"后提示性"题,这样的题其答案的线索或信息就隐藏或者明示在下文里。遇到这样的题目时,考生如果在第一次快速浏览时没有抓住下文提示,即使停下来死抠,也很难选出正确答案。因此,在做题过程中,如果碰到暂时没有头绪的题,完全可以先放下,运用跳读的方法,从容地继续阅读下文中的语段,甚至是整个语篇。

3.复核全篇,调整答案

考生在答完题后,如果还有足够的时间,要再回过头去将文章通读一遍,检查短文意思是否通顺,上下文衔接是否合理;检查所选答案是否符合逻辑,有无语法或搭配错误。如果在复核的过程中发现还有不畅通的地方,就应该重新进行判断。但是对于重新判断时仍拿不准的个别选项,建议考生坚持自己的第一感觉。

最后要注意,做完形填空时,一定要很好地控制时间,总的时间应控制在15分钟以内。

三 完形填空答题技巧

1. 利用词句知识进行选择

缺失的词语与其所在句子所表达的意义之间是存在着一定的语义联系的。有时候根据语境能大体上确定缺失词语的意义,但此时各备选答案的词很可能就是同、近义词,或是意义及用法容易混淆的词。这时候考生要充分调动自己的语言知识对各词进行比较,才能从备选答案中选择既符合语境意义和词汇特点,又可以使句子结构完整的词。利用句子语境可以大体上确定空格处应填入词的意义的题大致可以分为以下三种情况:

A. 词汇(包括短语和搭配)辨义。这类题目只要求考生能了解选项中每个词(或短语、搭配)的确切含义,根据它们所表达意思的不同进行选择,所以要做出这一类型的题,把词汇知识掌握好是关键。例如:

A land free from destruction, plus wealth, natural resources, and labor supply — all these were important   1   in helping England to become the center of the Industrial Revolution.

1. [A]cases   [B]situations   [C]factors   [D]reasons

选项中 case 是"事例,案例",situation 的意思是"形势,状况",factor 意为"因素",reason 是"原因"之意,而文中句子的意思是"……所有这些都是使英国成为工业革命中心的重要____?",显然填"因素"是最合适的,故答案就是[C]factors。再如:

But all of us are called   1   daily to make a great many personal decisions.

1. [A]out   [B]up   [C]for   [D]upon

四个选项都能用在动词 call 后与之构成固定搭配。call out(出动,唤起)、call up(召集,动员)和 call for(邀请,请求)都不合文意,只有 call upon sb. to do sth.(要求某人做某事)能使意思通顺。

这类题要从词语的习惯用法和固定搭配上着手,选择一个不仅在语意上贴切,而且在搭配上和用法上也合乎要求的词语。

B. 根据词汇和句法功能确定待选项。例如:

Even those who had   1   or no training in science might not have made their inventions if a ground work had not been laid by scientists years before.

1. [A]much　　　[B]few　　　　[C]little　　　　[D]some

由句意可知空白处应填与 no 意义相近的不定代词,在四个选项中,只有 few 和 little 的意思是"几乎没有",又因为后接不可数名词,所以 little 符合题意。

C. 结合句子结构与词汇辨义来确定选项。需要分析句子结构才能看出所填词语的成分的题目也常常出现。这种情况通常出现在一个长句中设空时,由于设空密度的关系,很可能整句话中设有多个空。这时候就要从简单着手,先易后难。比如说下面这个例子中,第二空比较容易确定,就可以先选择,把选得的词填入句子,这样整句话就只有一个空白了,分析起第一个空来就会相对简单些。例如:

That "something special" was men — ___1___ individuals who could invent machines,find new ___2___ of power,and *establish*(设立) business organizations to reshape society.

1. [A]creative　　　[B]generating　　　[C]effective　　　[D]motivating
2. [A]origins　　　[B]discoveries　　　[C]bases　　　[D]sources

这是个长句,其中设有两个空,先分析句子结构。"who could . . . "是定语从句,修饰 individuals(个体),而空格上要填的词正是 individuals 的定语。第一空的选项中,creative 是"创造性的"之意,generating 指"生产的"、effective 指"有效的",motivating 指"有动机的"。根据后面定语从句的内容,可以推断出,creative 是最佳选项。而第二空处,origin 指"起因,由来",如 the origin of a river(河流的源头);discovery 指"发现";base 指"基础";sources 意为"来源,根源",如 sources of power(能源)。所以 sources 正合题意。

2.利用上下文语境
先看这段短文:

James sat outside the office waiting for the interview. He felt so ___1___ that he didn't know what to do with ___2___. The person who had gone in ___3___ him had been there for nearly an hour. And she looked so confident when she went in. ___4___ James. He felt ___5___ that she had already got the ___6___. The problem was that he wanted this job ___7___. It meant ___8___ to him. He had ___9___ it such a lot before the day of the interview. He had imagined himself ___10___ brilliantly at the interview and ___11___ the job immediately. But now here he was ___12___.

He couldn't __13__ all those things he had __14__ to say. At that moment, he almost decided to get up and __15__ .

1. [A]confident   [B]careless   [C]nervous   [D]healthy
2. [A]the situation   [B]himself
    [C]the woman   [D]the managing director
3. [A]before   [B]with   [C]by   [D]after
4. [A]Not like   [B]Do like   [C]So did   [D]Do as
5. [A]astonishing   [B]doubtful   [C]sure   [D]angry
6. [A]first   [B]reward   [C]prize   [D]job
7. [A]so much   [B]hopelessly   [C]naturally   [D]easily
8. [A]happiness   [B]everything   [C]difficulty   [D]nothing
9. [A]learned of   [B]talked about
    [C]dreamed of   [D]thought about
10. [A]explaining   [B]answering   [C]performing   [D]writing
11. [A]being offered   [B]asked for
    [C]being asked for   [D]offered
12. [A]crazy   [B]terrible   [C]probable   [D]excited
13. [A]afford   [B]depend on   [C]believe in   [D]remember
14. [A]planned   [B]kept
    [C]been taught   [D]been supplied
15. [A]prepare   [B]practice   [C]leave   [D]go in

　　通读全文可知,这是一篇记叙文,主要描写了James在办公室外等候应聘面试时的心理活动。由于体裁的特点,这段文章中的题目大部分都需要根据上下文的信息才能得出答案。有的是利用上文的某些信息推断出下文未知信息,这样的题称为"前提示题",要确保从上文推断出的信息准确无误,就必须注意上下文连贯顺畅。有的得通过下文所提供的信息进行反向推断,得出前文信息,我们称这样的题为"后提示题",此时需要借助某些逻辑性强的连词进行严谨的逆向逻辑判断,才能得出答案。还有的题需要同时利用上下文的逻辑性综合推断出所需信息,这类题我们称为"前后提示题"。

　　答案: 1.[C]   2.[B]   3.[A]   4.[A]   5.[C]
　　　　　6.[D]   7.[A]   8.[B]   9.[D]   10.[C]
　　　　　11.[A]   12.[B]   13.[D]   14.[A]   15.[C]

其中第5、10、11、15属于前提示题，第4、6、12题属于前后提示题，第1、2、3、7、8、9都是后提示题。对于第1、2题，通读全文后可知全篇以James的紧张、忧虑为主线。于是可以推断出James很紧张，自己不知如何是好，所以第1题选[C]，第2题选[B]。至于第3题，由于下文有 for nearly an hour 和 ... an hour earlier，所以选[A]before合适。对于第4题，由于上文说"she looked so confident when she went in"，而从下文又可以看出James与女应聘者很不同。对于第6题，我们从上下文中可以看出这是应聘一份"工作"。对于第7、8两题，由于下文" ... such a lot before the day of the interview. He had imagined himself ... "等说明了James对于应聘这份工作很重视，很想得到这份工作，所以应该选择 so much 和 everything。而第9题，由于下句说"He had imagined himself ... "，即他在想像，所以应选 thought about。而第10题的选项中，explaining，answering，writing都是只表示单个的具体动作，只有 performing 可以表示应聘面试时总的表现情况，所以答案就是它。第11题是前提示题，想像的是"被给工作"时的情景。对于第12题，由于前面有 but 表示转折，说明现在的感觉完全不同于前一天的想像，而后文又说他忘了准备要说的话，所以选 terrible(糟糕的)。第15题是说他几乎要站起来"离开"，而不是"进去"，顺着前文的思路就可以推出来。

可以看出，这种体裁的文章要从整体上将文章的结构理清了，把握住行文线索，根据上下文给出的提示信息才能得到准确的答案。

除以上总结的两点外，有些时候还可以利用褒贬语气等进行判断，因为多数完形填空文章是有一定的褒贬性的，这种褒贬性直接反映了主人公的态度和写作意图，因此注意文章的褒贬语气，并利用它进行判断，也可以帮助我们做出正确的选择。

真 题 剖 析

 Example 1　　　　　　　　　　　　　　(*2006.9*)

阅读下面短文，从短文后所给各题的四个选项([A]、[B]、[C]和[D])中选出能填入相应空白处的最佳选项，并在答题卡1上将该项涂黑。

　　Sisters are often alike but they are never exactly the same. In many ___36___ , one sister is often called "the pretty one" and the other "the __37__ one" when they are still babies. Even young children think __38__ is more important than brains.

"I envied my sister's looks. She had long __39__ hair and nice clothes and the most __40__. I hated her so much that I decided to __41__ her. One day when the roof of the house was being repaired, I __42__ a brick out of a window __43__ she was underneath. Thank God it __44__!" says one ashamed near-murderer. "I must have been about ten at the time, and she was eight years old. __45__ she tells me that she always felt __46__ beside me in school because I was a __47__ student and she was weaker __48__ school work. But when you're fourteen or fifteen, you __49__ attention and praise and you need boyfriends; good exam results don't __50__ a fair exchange."

Life is particularly __51__ for someone who wants to __52__ in the footsteps of a famous sister. Dee Dee Pfeiffer wants to be a film star like her sister, Michelle. "When we were children, Michelle was the beautiful one and I was the __53__ one," says Dee Dee. "I have been trying to lose weight for years to achieve a __54__ which is as good as hers. In Hollywood, everyone __55__ you critically, and compares you with your famous sister."

36. [A]houses   [B]families   [C]places   [D]times
37. [A]shy   [B]active   [C]ugly   [D]clever
38. [A]body   [B]mind   [C]beauty   [D]height
39. [A]dry   [B]yellow   [C]fair   [D]thin
40. [A]interest   [B]time   [C]money   [D]attention
41. [A]kill   [B]beat   [C]attack   [D]defeat
42. [A]got   [B]left   [C]placed   [D]dropped
43. [A]as   [B]when   [C]though   [D]where
44. [A]failed   [B]hit   [C]missed   [D]hurt
45. [A]So   [B]Then   [C]But   [D]Now
46. [A]pretty   [B]proud   [C]sorry   [D]stupid
47. [A]good   [B]popular   [C]serious   [D]lucky
48. [A]about   [B]with   [C]at   [D]for
49. [A]want   [B]receive   [C]gain   [D]give

50. [A]stand for　　　[B]seem like　　　[C]lead to　　　[D]turn into
51. [A]boring　　　　　[B]hard　　　　　[C]easy　　　　　[D]exciting
52. [A]develop　　　　　[B]follow　　　　　[C]walk　　　　　[D]keep
53. [A]difficult　　　　[B]smart　　　　　[C]young　　　　　[D]fat
54. [A]figure　　　　　[B]result　　　　　[C]standard　　　　[D]success
55. [A]looks at　　　　　　　　　　　　　[B]talks about
　　 [C]thinks about　　　　　　　　　　[D]points at

> **underneath** *ad.* 在下面
> **a fair exchange**：一次公平的交换
> **(follow) in the footsteps of sb.**：步某人的后尘，效仿某人
> **critically** *ad.* 批剔地

 **答案与分析**

36.[B]。考查名词辨义与上下文理解。由于文章谈论的是姐妹之间的长相问题，故与之相关的是"家庭"(family)而不应是"房屋"(house)、"地方"(place)或者"次数"(time)。

37.[D]。考查形容词辨义与上下文理解。由下面一句的意思(小孩认为外表比有头脑重要)可知这里是将姐妹分成两类，一是外表好看(pretty)的，二是有头脑的，故这里选 clever 才符合上下文文意联系。shy 腼腆的；active 活跃的；ugly 丑陋的。

38.[C]。考查名词辨义与上下文理解。参见上文解析。body 身体；mind 精神；beauty 美丽；height 身高。

39.[C]。考查形容词辨义与习惯表达。由前面一句可知她的头发很好，故 dry(干燥的)不对。thin(瘦的)不用于形容头发。容易混淆的是[B]、[C]两项。yellow(黄色的)用于指颜色，但指头发的金黄时不用它，而用 fair。

40.[D]。考查名词辨义与上下文理解。interest 利益，兴趣；time 时间；money 钱。这三项都与前文描述的她的外貌毫无联系。attention 指"注意(力)"，这里指她因外表漂亮而吸引大家的注意，符合逻辑。

41.[A]。考查动词辨义与上下文理解。由下文的描述，特别是其中的 near-murderer 一词可知这里叙述者是想"杀死"(kill)比她漂亮的妹妹，而不只是想"揍"(beat)、"袭击"(attack)或者"打败"(defeat)她。

42.[D]。考查动词辨义与上下文理解。由空格后的文意可知这里指她

往窗外扔下砖头,故选 drop,与 out of 构成搭配,指"扔出…"。get out of 出来;leave out of 离开;place out of 放在…外。

43.[D]。考查句子结构与连接词。由句子结构可知空格后是一状语从句,表示的是地点,故选连接副词 where。

44.[C]。考查动词辨义与上下文理解。由本句中的 Thank God(感谢上帝)及后文中的 near-murderer 可知砖头并没有砸中妹妹,故选 missed(未击中,错过)。fail 失败;hit 击中;hurt 伤害。

45.[D]。考查上下文理解。由本句使用的现在时态可知叙述者说的是现在的事情了,故应用副词 now,表示时间转换。so 表因果,then 表顺承,but 表转折,用在这里都不合逻辑。

46.[D]。考查形容词辨义与上下文理解。由这一句后面的内容可以看出,妹妹的成绩不如姐姐,因此其感觉只能是自己"蠢"(stupid),而不会是"骄傲"(proud)、"漂亮"(pretty)或者"抱歉"(sorry)。

47.[A]。考查形容词辨义与上下文理解。参见上题解析。popular 受欢迎的;serious 严肃的,认真的;lucky 幸运的。

48.[C]。考查固定搭配。be good/weak at 是固定搭配,指"在某方面做得好,擅长/不擅长于…"。这里用的是比较级,其后省略了 than。

49.[A]。考查动词辨义与上下文理解。由空格后表并列关系的 and 与动词 need 及上下文文意可知应填入与 need 同义的 want(想要)。receive 收到;gain 获得;give 给。

50.[B]。考查搭配辨义与上下文理解。stand for 代表;seem like 看起来像;lead to 导致,引领;turn to 转向,求助于。由上下文不难看出,叙述者的意思是考试成绩好似乎并不会像漂亮那样能为她换来别人的注意、表扬与男朋友,故选[B]最恰当。

51.[B]。考查形容词辨义与上下文理解。由下文所举的例子可以看出,仿效自己出了名的姐妹需要付出很大的努力,所以只能选 hard(困难的)。boring 无聊的,乏味的;easy 轻易的;exciting 令人兴奋的。

52.[B]。考查固定搭配。follow(in)one's footsteps/follow(in)the footsteps of sb. 是固定搭配,指"效仿某人"。

53.[D]。考查形容词辨义与上下文理解。注意本题与第37题不同,此处后文叙述的是自己的体重问题,所以不再是将"美丽"与"聪明"对立起来,而是将它与"胖瘦"对立,应选 fat(胖的)。difficult 困难的(不用于指人);smart 机灵的;young 年轻的。

54.[A]。考查名词辨义与上下文理解。figure 体形;result 结果;standard 标准；success 成功。由空格前的 lose weight（减肥）、表目的的 to 及常识可知[A]是正确答案。

　　55.[A]。考查搭配辨义与上下文理解。look at 看；talk about 谈论；think about 考虑；point at 指着。由常识可知，一般说人们用一种什么样的眼光看待某人，而不会当面谈论，故用 look at 最恰当。

　　姐妹们长得一般都很相像，但永远不可能完全一样。在许多家庭里，当两姐妹还是婴儿时，其中一个就经常被称作"漂亮的"，而另一个则被称作"聪明的"。即便是小孩子也认为漂亮要比聪明重要得多。

　　"我很嫉妒我妹妹的外表。她有长长的金发、漂亮的衣服，得到大家最多的注意。我很恨她，以至于决定杀了她。有一天家里在修缮房顶时，我把一块砖头从窗户扔了出去，而她那里正在窗户下面。感谢上帝，没有砸中她！"这位险些成为杀人犯的姐姐一脸羞愧地说。"那时我一定有十岁左右了，她八岁。现在她告诉我说，她那时在学校与我在一起时常常感到她自己很愚蠢，因为我是优秀学生，而她的成绩差一些。但是在十四五岁的时候，你需要别人的注意、表扬，还需要男朋友；考试成绩好似乎并不能换来这些。"

　　生活对于那些想要仿效自己出了名的姐姐或者妹妹的人来说尤其艰难。Dee Dee Pfeiffer 想要成为一名与她姐姐 Michelle 一样的电影明星。"我们还是小孩子时，Michelle 就是漂亮的那个，而我是胖乎乎的那个，"Dee Dee 说。"我多年来一直努力减肥，以达到与她一样好的体形。在好莱坞，每个人都会用挑剔的眼光来看待你，来比较你和你那出了名的姐姐。"

Example 2　　　　　　　　　　　　　　　　　（2006.3）

　　阅读下面短文，从短文后所给的[A]、[B]、[C]三个选项中选出能填入相应空白处的最佳选项，并在答题卡 1 上将该项涂黑。

　　I began to register on Monday by picking up registration forms, completing them, and then turning them in with my photo. On Tuesday when I ___36___ to pay my fee, the lady at the fee desk ___37___ me to the line of ___38___ registrants because the university's computer refused to ___39___ my forms. Even after standing in line for an hour, I

___40___ to see the humor in the ___41___ when the little man at the desk told me that I did not have a good ___42___ for not living in a school dormitory. However, he ___43___ to let me register when I asked him to note the ___44___ of my being a girl and the university's all-boy dormitories. He asked me to come back the next day, at which time my ___45___ would have been through the computer again. When I came back on Wednesday and ___46___ Tuesday's experience, I began to ___47___ my sense of humor. Almost to my ___48___ I was not sent to the line of problem registration on Thursday. ___49___ the lady at the fee desk ___50___ my computerized fee receipt and announced that I ___51___ Green College $ 100. When I questioned her about the ___52___ of registering for fifteen hours a week for that small fee, she answered that the computer ___53___ that I was a full-time teacher. Early the next morning, Friday, I visited the registrar, who was able to ___54___ the problem, and then went to the Fiscal Office where I paid the additional fee. As I wrote the check, I congratulated myself on ___55___ registration at Green College in only five days.

36. 〔A〕returned   〔B〕remembered   〔C〕desired   〔D〕continued
37. 〔A〕directed   〔B〕invited   〔C〕waved   〔D〕presented
38. 〔A〕special   〔B〕part-time   〔C〕problem   〔D〕regular
39. 〔A〕recognize   〔B〕accept   〔C〕admit   〔D〕notice
40. 〔A〕began   〔B〕happened   〔C〕managed   〔D〕decided
41. 〔A〕situation   〔B〕place   〔C〕condition   〔D〕scene
42. 〔A〕record   〔B〕chance   〔C〕quality   〔D〕reason
43. 〔A〕refused   〔B〕attempted   〔C〕promised   〔D〕agreed
44. 〔A〕fact   〔B〕advantage   〔C〕difference   〔D〕role
45. 〔A〕turn   〔B〕forms   〔C〕questions   〔D〕correction
46. 〔A〕discovered   〔B〕reported   〔C〕repeated   〔D〕expected
47. 〔A〕lose   〔B〕have   〔C〕enjoy   〔D〕improve
48. 〔A〕knowledge   〔B〕surprise
    〔C〕expectation   〔D〕disappointment
49. 〔A〕Instead   〔B〕Still   〔C〕So   〔D〕Otherwise
50. 〔A〕offered   〔B〕collected   〔C〕found   〔D〕included

51. [A]owed   [B]paid   [C]used   [D]received
52. [A]explanation   [B]possibility   [C]judgement   [D]reality
53. [A]thought   [B]arranged   [C]checked   [D]doubted
54. [A]face   [B]stop   [C]deal with   [D]pick up
55. [A]completing   [B]experimenting
    [C]experiencing   [D]passing

> **register** v. 注册   **pay one's fee**：付费
> **the Fiscal Office**：财务办公室

答案与分析

36. [A]。考查动词辨义与上下文理解。return 返回；remember 记得；desire 希望；continue 继续。由上下文及注册的常识可知，作者是在填完表格交上去后第二天再回来交费，故只能选[A]。

37. [A]。考查动词辨义与上下文理解。direct 指导；invite 邀请；wave 挥（手）；present 出现，展现。由上下文文意与语境可以看出，这里指工作人员让作者去排队，所以选[A]最恰当。

38. [C]。考查上下文理解。由本句中 because 后解释的原因可以看出，作者的注册信息出了"问题"(problem)。其余三项都与此形不成因果关系：special 特殊的；part-time 业余的；regular 常规的。而后文中明确出现了 the line of problem registration 这个词组，因此答案只能是[C]。

39. [A]。考查动词辨义与上下文理解。recognize 认出，辨认出；accept 接受；admit 承认；notice 注意到。由于句子的主语是 computer(计算机)，而后面三个动词都不用于机器，所以答案是[A]。

40. [C]。考查动词辨义与上下文理解。四个选项都可跟不定式：begin 开始；happen 碰巧；manage 设法做到；decide 决定。由下文可知作者指尽管站了一个小时队，但还是感到很幽默，故选[C]。

41. [A]。考查名词名词辨义与搭配。situation 指"局面，情形"，常与 in 搭配，合乎文意。place 指"地方，位置"，它与 in 连用时多指"位置"；condition 指"条件，状态"，一般与 under 连用；scene 指"场景"，它多与 on 搭配。

42. [D]。考查名词辨义与上下文理解。由空格后表原因的介词 for 可知应选 reason(原因，理由)。record 记录；chance 机会；quality 品质，质量。它们都不符合文意。

43.[A]。考查动词辨义与上下文理解。由后面一句的句意可知工作人员仍然没有让作者注册,即拒绝了她,故选 refused。

44.[A]。考查名词辨义与上下文理解。fact 事实;advantage 好处,优点;difference 区别,差异;role 角色,作用。作者指出的是"她是一位女性而学校宿舍都是男生宿舍"这样一个事实,只能选[A]。

45.[B]。考查上下文理解。前面说过学校的计算机读取不了作者的注册表格,那么此处当然是说第二天她的表格可能被电脑读取了。

46.[C]。考查动词辨义与上下文理解。discover 发现;report 报告;re-peat 重复,复述;expect 期待。这里指作者重复了前一天的经历,所以才开始生气,故选[C]。其余三项都不合逻辑。

47.[A]。考查动词辨义与习惯表达。lose one's sense of humor 指"不再有幽默感",即不耐烦了。

48.[B]。考查习惯表达与上下文理解。to one's surprise/disappointment为习惯表达,指"让某人吃惊/失望的是"。由下文可以看出,这天作者没有像前两天那样被派到有问题的注册队伍中去,令她惊讶,故选[B]。

49.[A]。考查副词辨义与上下文联系。由上下文文意可知,工作人员没有把作者派到有问题的注册队伍中去,而是又指出了另一个问题,所以选表"代替,相反"的 instead。其余三个副词填入都不合逻辑。

50.[A]。考查动词辨义与上下文理解。offer 提供,交给;collect 收集;find 发现,找到;include 包括。由上下文与常识可知,这里应当是指工作人员将收据交给作者。

51.[A]。考查动词辨义与上下文理解。owe 欠(债);pay 付款;use 使用,利用;receive 收到。由下文的描述可知,作者仍没有完成注册,说明这里仍是一个问题,最有可能的是她欠学校钱,故选[A]。

52.[A]。考查名词辨义与上下文理解。explanation 解释;possibility 可能性;judgement 判断;reality 现实。本题较难,需仔细分析句子意思。首先,空格前的 question 在此指"质疑";其次,registering for fifteen hours a week for that small fee 指的是作者注册的是每周 15 个小时的(课程)却只要那么一点点钱。综合这两方面可以看出,作者质疑的是这种情况如何解释,故选 expla-nation。[C]、[D]两项可以较易排除,但[B]项 possibility 不能用在此处是因为作者质疑的已经不是一种可能性,而是已经发生的(错误)事实。

53.[C]。考查动词辨义。think 认为;arrange 安排;check 检查,审核;doubt 怀疑。电脑只能是"审核"。

54.[C]。考查动词辨义与上下文理解。face 面对;stop 阻止;deal with

处理;pick up 挑选,捡起。由上下文及宾语 problem 不难看出应选[C]。

55.[D]。考查动词搭配与上下文理解。complete 完成;experiment 实验;experience 经历;pass 通过。指"完成注册"用 pass registration,注意不能按中文意思用 complete registration。

同
步
译
文

　　我在周一开始注册,领取注册表格并填写完毕,然后与照片一起交上去。周二我回来交费时,收费台的一位女士让我去有问题的注册者队伍中排队,因为大学的电脑不能读取我的注册表格。尽管站了一个小时的队,但当坐在桌子那里的那个小个子告诉我说我没有充足的理由不住在学校宿舍里时,我还是觉得很好笑。然而,当我请他注意我是一个女生而大学里全是男生宿舍这个事实后,他仍拒绝让我注册。他让我第二天再来,那时我的注册表也许可以让电脑再次读取了。周三我返回来,却与周二的经历一样,我开始感到不耐烦了。周四时,令我惊讶的是并没有派我去有问题的注册队伍。相反,收费台的女士把电脑打出的费用收据给了我,并说我欠格林学院 100 美元。我向她质疑如何解释注册每周 15 个课时只收这么一点点费用时,她回答说电脑查出我是一个全职教师。第二天,周五一大早,我拜访了能处理这一问题的注册主管,然后去财务办公室交完了其余的费用。在填写支票时,我庆贺自己"仅仅"花了 5 天时间就完成了在格林学院的注册。

🔊 *Example 3*   (2005.9)

　　阅读下面短文,从短文后所给的[A]、[B]、[C]三个选项中选出能填入相应空白处的最佳选项,并在答题卡 1 上将该项涂黑。

　　A businesswoman got into a taxi in midtown. Because it was rush hour and she was in a hurry to catch a ___36___ , she suggested a quick way to ___37___ it. "I've been a taxi driver for 15 years!" the driver said ___38___ . "You think I don't know the best way to go?"

　　The woman tried to explain that she hadn't ___39___ to annoy him, but the driver kept ___40___ . She finally realized he was too annoyed to be ___41___ . So she did the ___42___ . "You know, you're ___43___ ," she told him. "It must seem ___44___ for me to think you don't know the best way through the city."

     __45__ , the driver glanced at his rider in the rearview mirror, turned down the street she __46__ and got her to the train on time. "He didn't say another word the rest of the ride," she said, "__47__ I got out and paid him. Then he thanked me."

When you find yourself __48__ with people like this taxi driver, you will always try to __49__ your idea. This can lead to longer arguments, lost job chances and __50__ marriages. I've discovered one simple __51__ extremely unlikely method that can prevent a disagreement or __52__ difficult situation from resulting in a disaster.

The __53__ is to put yourself in the other person's shoes and look for the __54__ in what that person is saying. Find a way to __55__ . The result may surprise you.

36. [A] train   [B] taxi   [C] bus   [D] plane
37. [A] choose   [B] reach   [C] find   [D] pass
38. [A] jokingly   [B] curiously   [C] anxiously   [D] angrily
39. [A] meant   [B] expected   [C] supposed   [D] decided
40. [A] apologizing   [B] shouting   [C] asking   [D] driving
41. [A] normal   [B] blamed   [C] reasonable [D] practical
42. [A] unreasonable [B] unbelievable [C] unnecessary [D] unexpected
43. [A] right   [B] clever   [C] honest   [D] helpful
44. [A] strange   [B] stupid   [C] wrong   [D] terrible
45. [A] Worried   [B] Annoyed   [C] Surprised   [D] Disappointed
46. [A] came   [B] found   [C] wanted   [D] lived
47. [A] until   [B] because   [C] after   [D] since
48. [A] stopped   [B] helped   [C] needed   [D] faced
49. [A] stick to   [B] turn down   [C] give up   [D] point out
50. [A] broken   [B] destroyed   [C] divided   [D] suffered
51. [A] which   [B] but   [C] that   [D] though
52. [A] its   [B] this   [C] those   [D] other
53. [A] problem   [B] importance   [C] key   [D] result
54. [A] fact   [B] truth   [C] expression [D] meaning
55. [A] agree   [B] argue   [C] explain   [D] escape

midtown *n.* 靠近市中心的地区，市中心附近
the rearview mirror：汽车的后视镜
disaster *n.* 灾难
put yourself in the other person's shoes：设身处地，将心比心

答案与分析

36.[A]。考查上下文理解。由第三段第一句后半部分中的 got her to the train 可知应选[A]。

37.[B]。考查动词辨义。choose 选择，挑选；reach 到达；find 发现，找到；pass 通过。由文意可知这里指尽快到达车站，所以选 reach。

38.[D]。考查副词辨义与上下文理解。由后文中出现的 annoyed（生气的）与 annoy 及出租车司机说话的语气与用词可知应选 angrily（生气地）。jokingly 开玩笑地；curiously 好奇地；anxiously 焦急地。

39.[A]。考查动词搭配。not mean to do 为习惯搭配，指"无意做某事，不是故意做某事"。其余三项后都可跟动词不定式，但含意不合本题：expect（希望）与 suggest（建议）用于否定时，一般都是否定不定式的内容；decide（决定，决心）后的不定式一般指尚未发生的动作。

40.[B]。考查动词辨义与上下文理解。由上文可知司机生气了，所以不可能"道歉"（apologize）。而 ask（问）与 drive（驾驶）在此不合语境。故只能选 shout（嚷嚷，喊叫）。

41.[C]。考查形容词辨义与用法。四个选项中，normal（正常的）与 practical（实用的，实际的）一般都不用于人；blamed（受责备的）用在此处不合逻辑；只有 reasonable（讲道理的，明事理的）可用于人，且符合上下文语境。

42.[D]。考查形容词辨义与上下文理解。这里是"the＋形容词"表示一类人或事物的用法。unreasonable 不讲道理的，不明事理的；unbelievable 不可信的，令人难以相信的；unnecessary 不必要的；unexpected 出乎意料的。由后文第四段中的 extremely unlikely method（最不可能的方法）可知这里强调的是女士所用方法的不常见与令人意外，故选[D]。

43.[A]。考查习惯用法与上下文理解。you're right 是常见用语，指"你是对的"，即肯定上文中司机的话。说司机"聪明"（clever）、"诚实"（honest）或者"有帮助"（helpful）都不合上下文逻辑。

44.[B]。考查形容词辨义与上下文理解。strange 陌生的，奇怪的；stupid

愚蠢的；wrong 错误的；terrible 可怕的。由下文可以看出，女士在这里强调自己建议的不恰当，以平息司机的怒气。[A]、[D]两项明显不对，而 wrong 用在此处与前面的 seem 及后文逻辑不合。

45.[C]。考查形容词辨义与上下文理解。这里是用分词作状语。worried 担心的，焦急的；annoyed 生气的；surprised 惊讶的；disappointed 失望的。由前文中的 unexpected 及后文的 extremely unlikely 等词及上下文语境可知司机肯定是很惊讶，故选[C]。

46.[C]。考查动词辨义与上下文理解。由句子结构可知 she ＿＿ 是作 street 的定语，而前文中说女士 suggest a quick way，所以这里应选 wanted（想要）。其余三项在词义上都不合文意。

47.[A]。考查句型与上下文理解。由文意可知这里指女士下车付钱时司机才说话，故选 until，与前面一句引语中的 not 构成 not ... until ... 这一句式。注意不要被中间的插入语 she said 所干扰。

48.[D]。考查动词固定搭配。face with 为固定搭配，指"（使）面对"。stop 与 help 后跟 with 时，表示的是伴随或者方式，with 后的部分是状语。need 后不跟 with。

49.[A]。考查固定搭配辨义与上下文理解。stick to 坚持；turn down 调低，拒绝；give up 放弃；point out 指出。由后面一句（This can lead to ...）可知应选[A]。

50.[A]。考查形容词辨义与搭配。四个选项都是分词作定语：broken 破裂的，打破的；destroyed 破坏的，毁灭的；divided 分开的，分裂的；suffered 受苦的，忍受的。marriage（婚姻）一般用 broken 修饰。注意前面的 lost 也是用分词作的定语。

51.[B]。考查上下文联系。填入的词应连接两个形容词：simple（简单的）和 extremely unlikely（极不可能的），由这两个词的词义之间可以看出有转折含意，故选 but。which 和 that 都是关系连词；though 表示的是让步关系，含有否定后者的意思，也不合文意。

52.[D]。考查限定词。由于修饰的是单数可数名词 situation（情形），故 those 肯定不对。its 与 this 都是特指，也不对。other 指"其他的"，符合文意与语法。

53.[C]。考查名词辨义与上下文理解。problem 问题；importance 重要（性）；key 关键；result 结果。由后面表语的句意可知应选[C]。

54.[B]。考查名词辨义与上下文理解。fact 事实；truth 真实，真相；expression 表达（法）；meaning 意思，含意。由空格前的 look for（寻找）及空格后的介词 in 可知应选 truth。

55.[A]。考查动词辨义与上下文理解。agree 同意，达成一致；argue 辩论，争辩；explain 解释，说明；escape 逃脱。由上下文文意可知，这里指理解别人话语的真正含意，找到达成一致意见的方法以平息争端，故选[A]。

　　　　　　　　一位女商人在市中心附近上了一辆出租车。由于是交通高峰期，她又急于赶火车，所以她建议司机走一条去车站的近路。"我当了 15 年的出租车司机了！"司机生气地说。"您是认为我不知道去那里的最佳路线吗？"

　　那位女士试图解释自己并非有意冒犯，但那司机仍不停地嘟囔。最后她意识到他太生气了，无法和他讲道理。于是她做了一件令人意想不到的事。"您知道，您是对的，"她对他说。"认为您不知道穿过市区的最佳路线，我看来一定很愚蠢。"

　　司机很惊讶地从后视镜里看了他的乘客一眼，然后转向了她要求走的那条街道，准时将她送到了火车站。"在剩下的那段路上他没有再说一句话，"她说，"直到我下车付钱给他。然后他感谢了我。"

　　当你发现自己面对的是像那位出租车司机一样的人时，你总是会试图坚持自己的观点。这会导致长时间的争论、失去工作机会、导致婚姻破裂。我发现了一个简单，但一般人不太可能用的方法，可以防止使意见上的分歧和其他困难情形导致灾难性的后果。

　　关键是让自己设身处地地为别人着想，寻找别人话语里的真正含义。找到达成一致的办法。结果之好也许会让你感到惊讶。

Example 4　　　　　　　　　　　　　　　　　　　　（2005.3）

　　阅读下面短文，从短文后所给的[A]、[B]、[C]三个选项中选出能填入相应空白处的最佳选项，并在答题卡 1 上将该项涂黑。

　　　　The mystery around the disappearance of the famous crime writer Agatha Christie in 1926 was almost as ___36___ as any of her exciting stories. At about 11 o'clock on the evening of Friday, December 3rd, Mrs Christie had got into her car and taken a drive without saying ___37___ she was going. She didn't return.

The next morning her car was found without __38__ at Newlands Corner, Surrey. It was __39__ put on record that the Surrey Police did not find __40__ until 11:00 that morning. People __41__ that she might have killed herself. __42__ as the days went by, it was suggested that she was __43__ . The press and the public naturally took great interest in the __44__ , with at least one newspaper offering a reward to anyone who could find the __45__ writer.

Of course the police did their best to __46__ her. But, sadly, after a week's __47__ they had made no progress. In the end they decided that Agatha must __48__ the area.

Agatha finally made __49__ on Tuesday, December 14th, when she was reunited with __50__ at a hotel in Harrogate, North Yorkshire. It was said she had been staying at the hotel for the past ten __51__ under the name of "Mrs Theresa Neele". Her husband said, "She has suffered from the most complete loss of __52__ and I do not think she knows who she is."

Agatha Christie hated __53__ . She seldom met reporters and made no __54__ this time. The only __55__ she made was that she had lost her memory, although with the help of a doctor she did manage to remember some of what she had done during her disappearance.

36. [A]important   [B]great   [C]terrible   [D]sad
37. [A]how   [B]when   [C]why   [D]where
38. [A]her husband   [B]her doctor   [C]the driver   [D]the policeman
39. [A]later   [B]then   [C]so   [D]now
40. [A]an explanation   [B]a murderer
      [C]the car   [D]Agatha
41. [A]imagined   [B]realized   [C]knew   [D]feared
42. [A]But   [B]Thus   [C]And   [D]Still
43. [A]arrested   [B]murdered   [C]hospitalized   [D]followed
44. [A]cause   [B]case   [C]report   [D]adventure
45. [A]alive   [B]strange   [C]missing   [D]staying
46. [A]treat   [B]find   [C]catch   [D]persuade
47. [A]research   [B]interest   [C]review   [D]search

48. [A]have left   [B]have disliked
　　[C]have visited   [D]have found
49. [A]an offer   [B]an announcement
　　[C]a story   [D]a re-appearance
50. [A]her husband   [B]her neighbor
　　[C]Theresa   [D]the Surrey Police
51. [A]hours   [B]days   [C]weeks   [D]months
52. [A]wealth   [B]memory   [C]senses   [D]imagination
53. [A]driving   [B]public attention
　　[C]her family   [D]the city
54. [A]mention   [B]effort   [C]acceptance   [D]exception
55. [A]explanation [B]guess   [C]record   [D]reason

---

mystery *n.* 悬案, 悬疑
crime *n.* 犯罪。注意 a crime writer 指"罪案作家"。
reward *n.* 悬赏, 报偿

答案与分析

36. [B]。考查形容词辨义与上下文理解。important 重要的；great 伟大的，了不起的；terrible 可怕的，糟糕的；sad 悲伤的，伤感的。由同级比较结构 as ... as 及后面的 exciting(引人人胜的)可知应选 great。

37. [D]。考查关系词的用法。由空格后的 she was going 可知这是 saying 的宾语从句，且从句中缺少状语，指的又是地点，故选关系副词 where。

38. [C]。考查上下文理解。很明显，这里指的是车里没有 Mrs Christie 本人，故应选 the driver，因为前文说她是自己驾车出去的。

39. [A]。考查副词辨义与上下文理解。later 后来；then 然后；so 因此；now 如今，既然。由后文中的 that morning 可以看出，这里指的是时间上的先后，故选 later。

40. [C]。考查上下文理解。前面一句说找到了车，车里并没有人；而后文又说失踪者到十几天后才出现，所以这里仍是说警方记录找到车的时间，故选[C]。

41. [A]。考查动词用法与上下文理解。imagine 想像；realize 意识到；know 知道，听说；fear 害怕，担心。由宾语从句所用的虚拟语气可知这里是指人们对她的失踪的推测，故选[A]。

42.[A]。考查上下文联系。前面一句指的是人们的一种想像,这一句提到的是另一种猜测,后者是对前者的否定,两者之间有明显的转折关系,故选 But。

43.[B]。考查动词辨义与上下文理解。arrest 逮捕;murder 谋杀,杀害;hospitalize 使住院治疗;follow 跟随,尾随。由全文文意可知这里指人们猜测她被人谋杀了,故选[B]。

44.[B]。考查名词辨义与上下文理解。cause 原因,事业;case 案件,情况;report 报告;adventure 冒险,探险。由文意与 police(警方)、reward(悬赏)等词不难选出与此有关的 case。

45.[C]。考查形容词辨义与上下文理解。alive 活着的;strange 奇怪的,陌生的;missing 失踪的;staying 停留的。全文都在围绕 Mrs Christie 失踪一事,所以这里肯定应选[C]。

46.[B]。考查动词辨义与上下文理解。treat 对待;find 找到;catch 抓住,赶上;persuade 劝说。全文谈论的是 Mrs Christie 失踪、警方寻找她的经过,故这里当然是指警方尽力去找到她。

47.[D]。考查名词辨义与上下文理解。research 研究;interest 兴趣,利益;review 复习;search 搜索,寻找。由前文的 find 可知应选与之对应的 search,指警方搜索了一周。

48.[A]。考查动词辨义与上下文理解。前面说警方搜寻未果,所以断定她不在这一地区了,故选表示"离开"的[A]项。dislike 不喜欢,厌烦;visit 访问,拜访;find 找到,发现。它们填入题中都不合上下文逻辑。

49.[D]。考查名词辨义与上下文理解。由这一段后面的内容可知这里指 Agatha 出现并与丈夫团聚了,所以选[D]项,make a re-appearance 指"重新露面"。make an offer 指"提供,提出条件";make an announcement 指"声明";make a story 指"编故事"。

50.[A]。考查上下文理解。由后文内容、空格前的 reunite(使团聚)及常识可知她是与丈夫而不可能与其他人团聚。

51.[B]。考查上下文理解。由前文指出的她失踪的时间(12 月 3 日)到重新露面的时间(12 月 14 日)可知她失踪了 10 天,故选 days。

52.[B]。考查名词辨义与上下文理解。wealth 财富,财产;memory 记忆;sense 感觉;imagination 想像力。由空格后的"I don't think she knows who she is"(我想她不知道自己是谁)可知这里指失去了记忆。

53.[B]。考查上下文理解。由后一句的意思"她很少会见记者"可知这里指她不喜欢媒体报道,当然也就是不喜欢被公众注意了,故选[B]。

54.[D]。考查固定搭配。make no exception 为固定搭配，指"不例外"。mention(提及)与 acceptance(接受)都不与 make 构成搭配；make no effort 指"没有努力"，也不合文意。

55.[A]。考查名词辨义与上下文理解。explanation 解释；guess 猜测；record 记录；reason 原因。由后文的意思可知这里是她对自己的失踪作出解释，所以选 explanation。

同步译文

　　1926 年著名罪案作家阿加莎·克里斯蒂失踪的悬案就像她写的那些引人入胜的小说一样离奇。12 月 3 日，星期五晚上大概 11 点钟，克里斯蒂夫人钻进自己的车子，没有说她要去哪里就开车走了。她没有回来。

　　第二天上午，她的车被发现在萨瑞的新地角，车里的司机却不在。后来萨瑞警方的记录上说直到那天上午 11 点才发现那辆车。人们猜想她可能自杀了。但随着日子一天天过去，又有人说她是被人杀害了。报纸和公众自然对这个案子很感兴趣，至少有一家报纸悬赏寻找这位失踪的作家。

　　警方当然也在尽力寻找她。但是令人沮丧的是，搜寻了一个星期后他们没有任何进展。最后他们断定阿加莎已经离开了那个地区。

　　最后在 12 月 14 日星期二，阿加莎终于重新露面，在北约克郡哈罗盖特的一家旅馆里与她的丈夫团聚了。据说她以"瑟瑞莎·尼尔夫人"的名字在该旅馆里度过了过去的 10 天。她的丈夫说："她患上了严重的失忆症，我想她并不知道她是谁了。"

　　阿加莎·克里斯蒂讨厌被公众注意。她很少会见记者，这次也不例外。她给出的惟一解释是她失去了记忆，尽管在医生的帮助下她确实记起了一些在失踪期间所做的事情。

Example 5　　　　　　　　　　　　　　　　　　　　　(2004.9)

　　阅读下面短文，从短文后所给的[A]、[B]、[C]三个选项中选出能填入相应空白处的最佳选项，并在答题卡 1 上将该项涂黑。

　　　　I usually don't take the subway to get to my office, but it's a good thing I did last Tuesday. I __36__ a man sitting opposite me who __37__ to be extremely nervous. He was __38__ wide-eyed at one of the advertisements in the car. Then his hands started to ___39___ . I took my medical bag and ___40___ to him.

"Well，what ___41___ seems to be wrong with you?"I asked.

He pointed at an advertisement ___42___ the good qualities of a ___43___ kind of shirt. It ___44___ ："It will not wilt，shrink，crease，or wrinkle."

"Well. ___45___ about it?"

"I'm going ___46___ ,"he said."I can read it to myself，but I can't say it out ___47___ ."

"My dear man,"I comforted him,"you can say it. Of course you can. You're ___48___ a little nervous. This is just a nervous attack. You must not ___49___ . You must try and say it. Now say it."

"It ... it will not wilt，crink，wack，or shrinkle,"he said，and with a groan he ___50___ his face with his hands.

"Now come. ___51___ me,"I told him,"and learn how perfectly simple the whole ___52___ is."I continued in a firm voice："It will not wink，shink，wack，or cinkle." Oh, my God! I ___53___ several times，each was wrong in a different way.

The man ___54___ , and appeared completely recovered. I was ___55___ . The man was cured. Of course，I had been putting on an act.

36. [A]cured [B]met [C]taught [D]noticed
37. [A]turned [B]appeared [C]pretended [D]meant
38. [A]admiring [B]screaming [C]pointing [D]staring
39. [A]move [B]shake [C]touch [D]wave
40. [A]came back [B]went on [C]rushed over [D]looked over
41. [A]generally [B]exactly [C]usually [D]naturally
42. [A]telling about [B]showing off
    [C]calling for [D]dealing with
43. [A]common [B]regular [C]famous [D]certain
44. [A]admitted [B]said [C]proved [D]called
45. [A]what [B]how [C]talk [D]think
46. [A]crazy [B]ahead [C]angry [D]back
47. [A]loud [B]alone [C]freely [D]completely

48. [A]truly　　　[B]really　　　[C]simply　　　[D]particularly
49. [A]stop　　　[B]give in　　　[C]hurry up　　　[D]look
50. [A]covered　　[B]turned　　　[C]hid　　　　[D]touched
51. [A]Talk to　　[B]Allow　　　[C]Listen to　　[D]Show
52. [A]advertisement　　　　　[B]problem
　　[C]situation　　　　　　　[D]thing
53. [A]tried　　　[B]spelled　　　[C]spoke　　　[D]explained
54. [A]was anxious　　　　　　[B]was nervous
　　[C]laughed　　　　　　　[D]shouted
55. [A]interested　[B]delighted　　[C]worried　　[D]astonished

---

subway *n.* 地铁　　　　　　　**advertisement** *n.* 广告
wilt, shrink, crease, or wrinkle：下垂,缩水,打折或起皱
groan *v.* 呻吟

答案与分析

36.[D]。考查动词辨义与上下文理解。cure 治愈；meet 遇见；teach 教，教会；notice 注意到。由下文可知作者与那个人并不相识,因此选 notice。

37.[B]。考查动词辨义与上下文理解。由前文的 notice 可知这里是作者对那人进行观察所得的印象,故选 appeared(看起来)。turn 转向；pretend 假装；mean 意思是,意欲。它们虽然都可跟不定式,但在意思上都不合文意。

38.[D]。考查动词辨义与上下文理解。admire 钦佩,崇敬；scream 尖叫；point 指着；stare 瞪着,凝视。由后面的 wide-eyed(眼睛瞪得大大的)可知应选与之对应的 staring。

39.[B]。考查动词辨义与上下文理解。move 运动,移动；shake 颤抖,抖动；touch 触摸；wave 挥动。由后文他们之间对话中的 nervous(紧张的)及常识可知,人一紧张手肯定是"颤抖",所以选[B]。

40.[C]。考查固定搭配辨义与上下文理解。come back to 回到；go on to 继续；rush over to 急速跑向；look over 检查,查看,从⋯上看过去(它一般不与 to 连用)。由上下文可知[C]最合文意。

41.[B]。考查副词辨义与上下文理解。generally 通常；exactly 准确地,全然地；usually 通常,惯常；naturally 自然地,天然地。其余三项放在此处都不合逻辑,因为作者问的是那人的情况,exactly 在此有强调意味。

42.[D]。考查动词搭配辨义与上下文理解。tell about 可以指"说明,显示",但 tell 后应当跟宾语;show off 炫耀,卖弄;call for 要求,呼吁;deal with 涉及,论及,处理。由上下文可知,这里指广告所涉及的内容,故选[D]。

43.[D]。考查形容词辨义与上下文理解。common 共同的,普通的;regular 规律的,定期的;famous 有名的;certain 某种的,某一的。由于上下文并未提及衬衫的牌子和具体质量,所以这里应是泛指某种衬衫。

44.[B]。考查习惯用法。指广告、文章等"表达"某种内容时一般用 say 和 read 等动词。admit 承认;prove 证明;call 叫,打电话。

45.[A]。考查习惯用法。what/how about 是习惯用法,用于询问、征求意见及提出建议,其区别在于后跟名词或者代词时,what about 指"怎么回事",是询问,而 how about 指"怎么样",一般指征求意见和提出建议。由于这里是询问,故选 what about。

46.[A]。考查习惯用法与上下文理解。go crazy 指"发疯";go ahead 指"往前走";go angry 指"生气,发怒";go back 指"回去"。由下一句的意思可知那人因为自己读不出那句广告语而情绪激动,故应选[A]。

47.[C]。考查副词辨义与上下文理解。由下文的描述可知,那人不能流利、正确地说出那句广告语,所以选 freely(自由地)。loud 响亮地;alone 独自地,单独地;completely 完全,全部地。

48.[C]。考查副词辨义与上下文理解。truly 真正地;really 真正地,确实;simply 仅仅,只;particularly 特别地,尤其。由下文可以看出,作者在这里是安慰那人,所以应是说他只是有点紧张,选[C]。

49.[B]。考查动词(搭配)辨义与上下文理解。stop 停止,停下;give in 屈服,让步;hurry up 赶紧;look 看。由上一题的分析可知作者是在安慰那人,而由下一句可知作者的意思是要那人不能轻易放弃,故 give in 最恰当。

50.[A]。考查动词辨义与上下文理解。cover 盖住;turn 转向;hide 藏住;touch 触摸。由空格后表方式的 with his hands(用手)及常识可知应选 cover,指"用手捂住脸"。

51.[C]。考查动词(搭配)辨义与上下文理解。talk to 跟…说话;allow 允许;listen to 听;show 展示,表现。由后面一句可知这里作者是让那人听作者说那句广告语,故选[C]。

52.[D]。考查名词辨义与上下文理解。advertisement 广告;problem(需要解决的)问题;situation 形势,情况;thing 事情,东西。由上下文及常识可以看出,作者在此是指读出那句话很简单,而并非说那个广告很简单,所以应选 thing 来指代"读广告语"这件事。

53.[A]。考查动词辨义与上下文理解。try 尝试；spell 拼写；speak 说（某种语言），讲；explain 解释。由前文可知作者是在"读"那句话，故只能用 try 来替代这一动作，而不能用其他动词。

54.[C]。考查上下文理解。anxious 焦急的；nervous 紧张的；laugh 笑；shout 喊，叫。由后一分句的意思（他完全恢复了）及常识可知，那人听到作者也读不出那句话后应当是"笑"了而放松了，所以选[C]。

55.[B]。考查形容词辨义与上下文理解。四个选项都是动词的过去分词转义为形容词：interested 感兴趣的；delighted 高兴的；worried 担心的；astonished 惊讶的。由后文可知，作者治好了那人，所以当然是感到高兴。

同步译文

我不常坐地铁去办公室，但上个星期二我坐地铁却是一件好事。我注意到坐在我对面的一个人看起来似乎极为紧张。他正瞪大了眼睛看着车厢里的广告。然后他的手开始发抖。我拿起我的药箱，急忙向他走过去。

"噢，你这是怎么了？"我问道。

他指了指一则宣传某种衬衫质量好的广告。广告上说："它不会下垂，缩水，打折或起皱。"

"哦，那又怎么了？"

"我都快疯了，"他说。"我能默念出来，却不能流利地读出来。"

"我的老兄，"我安慰他说，"你能读出来。你当然能。你只是有点紧张而已。这只不过是一种紧张症状。你不能放弃。你得试着去把它说出来。现在就说。"

"它……它不会下垂，细皱，打击或起瘦，"他说，然后呻吟了一声，用手捂住了自己的脸。

"现在来吧。听我读，"我对他说，"看看这有多么简单。"我继续用坚定的声音读道："它不会下睡，宿水，打击或起绐。"哦，天哪！我试了好几次，每次都是不同的方式出错。

那人笑了，看起来完全恢复了。我很高兴。那人治好了。当然，我那样做都是装出来的。

第 2 节　阅读理解部分

一　阅读理解命题规律

对历次 PETS-2 考试的阅读理解部分进行研究后,编者发现该部分的命题呈现出如下规律:

1. 文章选材广泛

阅读短文的选材所涉及的知识面非常广,包括人物小传、故事、史地知识介绍、新闻报道、科普小说明文、产品等的说明书,社会政治、经济、文化现象,书信、广告、通知等各方面。这些材料很大程度上是来自于对一些英语书刊杂志的摘选和改编。

2. 文章体裁多样交替

阅读短文的体裁常为记叙文、说明文、应用文、议论文,一般交替出现。其中出现最频繁的是记叙文和说明文,所以这两类文章也是考生要重点练习的。

3. 题目的设计灵活

题干是一个针对该篇短文内容的问题或不完整的句子。考生在仔细阅读过短文的基础上,从出题者给出的四个选项中,选出一个可以用来回答问题或补全句子的最佳选项。对比许多其他类型的英语水平考试中阅读理解部分的试题,PETS 在题目的设问上思路非常灵活,设问技巧很高,能准确考核出考生实际的英语阅读能力及水平。所以只有考生能很好地把握短文的主旨大意,能捕捉到短文中主要事实,能理解短文中内在的逻辑关系和基本结构,能根据上下文正确判断生词或短语的含义,能在看懂短文的字面意思的同时推断出短文中隐含的深层含义,才能准确答出短文局部的细节问题及总体内容上的问题,并且理解作者的写作意图和态度。

4. 题目的类型丰富

(1)细节题,如直接问答、判断是非题等。

(2)词句理解题,如猜词义、猜单句意思题等。

(3)主旨题,如归纳中心思想、概括段落大意、给短文起标题等题型。

(4)推理判断题,如阐述文章寓意、作者的态度或意图等题型。

二　阅读理解备考要点

1. 养成良好的阅读习惯

在考生中普遍存在着或多或少的一些不良的阅读习惯,这些习惯都极大地阻碍着阅读水平的提高。主要有下面几种情况：

（1）一目一词

"一目一词"包括用手指指着读、默读或出声读等。

英语中的一个单词，翻译成汉语往往是一个有完整意思的词语，而不是单个的字，所以很多人以为，英语只要按一个个单词来读就可以。那么这种想法对吗？我们知道，在阅读中文文章的时候，如果细读的话，的确可以一个个词语来读，我们会很自然地把这一连串词语连成短语和句子，并且能轻松理解句子的意思。可是由于英语组成句子的方式跟汉语大不相同，如果也一个一个词读下去，我们就会得到一串用我们自己的习惯方式很难理解的信息。所以，"一目一词"地读英文是肯定不行的，不仅会大大减慢阅读的速度，还会影响对句意的理解。而如果能按一个个意群来读的话，问题就解决了。

比如说这句话：

When I was in the army /I received an intelligence test /that all soldiers took,/ and against an average of 100,/ scored 160.

全句有 23 个单词，将它们划分成 5 个意群。阅读读后，得到这样一串信息：当我在军队服役时，/ 我曾接受过智力测试/所有战士都参加的，/与平均分100分相比，/得了160分。稍加整理，句子结构、意思就清晰明了了。而且我们只需要注视五遍就能完成整句话的阅读，速度也提升了好几倍。

（2）过分依赖词典

有许多考生在阅读过程中只要碰到生词就查词典，这样做使整个阅读的过程不能一次完成，不但会影响阅读的速度，还会影响对文章信息的整体把握。PETS-2 大纲中规定，阅读理解文章中出现的生词都会给出相应的注释，并且会严格控制其数量。所以，考生在练习时如果总碰到生词，很可能就是自己的词汇量还达不到大纲要求。掌握好了大纲的词汇后，在阅读中碰到的少量生词，我们也常常可以通过上下文来确定词义。

（3）惧怕长句

长句理解困难历来就是个普遍存在的问题，特别是在接触英语时间相对较短、英语水平相对较低的考生中是一只不折不扣的"拦路虎"。这就造成了很多考生惧怕长句、逃避长句，比如说碰到长句就跳过去；还有的考生则一遇到长句就犯晕，哪怕翻过来覆过去地读上五六遍也不一定能理解句意。这种习惯严重影响对文章的理解。这个问题的根源在于阅读技巧了解不到位，对语法知识掌握不够。要克服这一困难必须做到：加强对语法知识的学习；多做阅读练习，掌握一定的阅读技巧。在练习中碰到长句时，不要再回避问题，只有迎难而上，才能将困难克服，将问题解决。

(4)翻译式阅读

这一现象在考生中也不少见。对于英语初学者来说,用母语释义是很普遍的途径,随着接触英语的时间越来越长以后,他们可以慢慢学会摆脱母语,最终学会用英语思维。可有些考生却不是这样做的,他们从一开始学习阅读时就对母语释义产生了依赖,于是就养成了只要阅读就必须先翻译成中文的习惯。这样就大大减慢了阅读的速度,而且更重要的是,这种习惯会制约自己整体英语水平的提高。所以学会用英语思维是非常必要的。

只有将上述不良阅读习惯加以克服了,考生才能真正提高自己的阅读理解水平,在考试中才能最大限度地将自己掌握的其他方面的英语知识发挥出来。

2.灵活运用阅读技巧

(1)快速阅读

快速阅读是考试中做阅读理解部分题目最实用的阅读方式,所以在备考时掌握一套快速阅读的方法非常必要。快速阅读的精髓是"忽略多余信息,记住重要信息"。具体说来就是:在阅读过程中,读者要利用标题、主题句、关键词语以及章节后面的问题等,迅速有效略过无关信息,筛选有关信息。学习快速阅读的方法还需要掌握略读、寻读和研读等具体技巧。

略读:快速浏览全文和题目,要用最快的速度迅速掌握文章的大概意思、作者大致的阐述过程、问题的题型,不必在文中的某个具体细节上花时间。PETS-2 中的文章都在 200 字左右,一般来说,文章的阅读和浏览文后四到五道题要求在 3 分钟内完成,所以考生应切实掌握略读技巧。

寻读:跳跃式的浏览,找到文中某处具体信息。这种方法一般用在回答细节性的问题时,查找文中与之对应的信息。

研读:仔细的阅读,即精读。

快速阅读其实就是将这三种方式综合使用。我们先用不多于 3 分钟的时间快速浏览全文以及文后问题,在这个过程中,掌握文章中心、作者的阐述过程以及文后问题的题型;然后用寻读法跳跃式浏览,在文中找到与细节性题、词句理解题等问题相应的信息点;此时再对相关细节加以研读,就可以做出答案。把主旨题以及推断题留到最后再做,因为主旨题和推断题在考生对文章的了解越深入时越能得出正确答案。

(2)归类阅读

备考时,大家做的阅读理解一定是非常之多,我们可以按自己的想法制定一个分类标准,然后每做完一篇文章就把它归类,这样积累下来,就可以很系统地掌握不同类型题目的文章特点、出题规律以及专用词汇等很有用的知识和技巧。例如,我们可以按体裁把做过的文章分类成新闻、科普文、人物传记等类型,通过自己的方式找到很有帮助的规律,到考试时使用起来就会得心应手。

(3)计时阅读

计时阅读是我们提倡的一种备考阅读策略。用计时的方式阅读可以提高答题效率:首先,它可以给考生以监督,有时间的限制,考生就会有紧迫感;其次,它可以让考生清楚地认识到自己的英语水平,而并不是单纯的从正确率上去考虑了。具体的做法是先给自己规定一篇文章从开始做直到答题完毕需要的时间,然后开始做题并同时计时。PETS 第 2 级考试中阅读理解的答题时间是 35 分钟,所以五篇文章平均每篇的阅读和答题时间是 7 分钟,练习时考生一般可以把时间定在 7 分钟左右。

三 阅读理解答题技巧

1.细节题

在阅读理解题中,细节性题是出现最多的一类问题,据不完全统计发现,这类问题大约占阅读理解题的 40%。这类问题往往是根据文章中具体的信息,如事件发生的原因、过程、结果,或对事实的描述、例证、论述等方面进行提问。和其他几种类型的题相比较,这类问题要容易些,因为它的答案可以直接在文章中找到。因此,细节题是最容易拿分的题,这类题大家必须掌握。

细节题的设问有两种基本形式:完全式和不完全式,其中绝大多数问题是不完全式。其中完全式如:

According to the text,which of the following . . . ?

What did scientists learn about earthquakes at the area?

What is wrong with the strange man according to the text?

不完全式如:

In the author's opinion,vegetables are good for ____.

If . . . it shows that he ____ you.

The author advises the college student to ____.

解答细节性题的基本步骤是:①仔细阅读问题,找出问题中的关键词或词组;②以此作为线索,返回原文查找该问题的相关句;③用这个相关句来对照备选项,意思一致的就是答案。

显然,解答的步骤并不难掌握。问题是怎样才能迅速在文章中准确地找到答案呢?以下就给大家提供两种比较容易掌握也很实用的技巧:

(1)阅读原文时预测文中重要细节

一篇文章,当你读完开头的几句,就能预知它的体裁。在某一特定体裁的文章中,我们很容易知道问题会涉及到哪些细节。比如说一篇写人们日常生活的记叙文,它的设问往往就会与时间、地点、人物、因果、过程、情景等有关。我们阅读时可以对这些细节作上标记,当遇到问题时,就能很方便快捷地从文中找到相关语句。文章体裁不同,文中交代细节的方式也不同,因此出现了不同的细节结构。了解这些细节结构的特点对于查找特定和具体细节是很有帮助的。我们对不同体裁的文章中的细节进行了分类和总结,最常出现的是以下几种:

释义性细节　　这种类型的细节主要用于解释某一学科、理论或事物等,这些被解释的东西往往是大家不熟悉的,作者常常用例子、比喻、类比等方式进行阐述。出题者常常会针对这种结构设计类似的问题。例如:

Splash is ＿＿＿ .

[A]a certain kind of material used for washing in high quality

[B]something like a machine used to wash clothes

……

选项对应着原文对"Splash"作出的一系列阐释,只要将选项与原文的说法进行对比,找出和原文意思相符的就可以。

描述性细节　　这种类型的细节主要用于描述事物、事件的特点、特征,如对人物的描述(如人物传记)介绍人的身体特征、家庭背景、成长过程、个性爱好、成就贡献等。因此文章中时间、地点、数据等是主要细节,也是解答针对这类细节结构的问题的关键。

论述性细节　　这种类型的细节主要用于分析事物的成因、事件的起因,或者作者先介绍一种观点,这种观点往往被普遍流传,然后对其评论或驳斥,分析其优缺点或危害性,最后再阐明自己的观点等等。

比较性细节　　这种结构主要用于比较两个事物在功能、特点、优缺点或人物在经历、贡献、对同一事实的说法等方面的相同点或不同点,所以要解答一定要先了解清楚比较双方的异同,再选答案。

(2)学会利用文章中的过渡词

所谓过渡词,指连接上下文或表明句与句之间关系的词语。如 however, although 表示转折;in order to, as a result 表示因果;so as to 表示目的;divide into 表示分类等。过渡词在文章中位置往往比较突出、醒目。在阅读中,可以先对它们作出适当的标记,因为绝大多数细节性的问题和它们有密切的联系,如果作了标记,考生在做题时就能够迅速、准确地在原文中把握住细节,获取所需信息。

最后值得考生注意的一点是,出题者常常会在细节题中设置较难的干扰项,这种干扰项的特点是:它往往和原文中某句的说法非常一致,有时甚至套用文章原句,它的错误可能出现在这几点上:①答非所问;②跟原文表述只有些许差别,可这小小差别就使意思面目全非了。而正确答案却比较不明显,它往往将文中说法用另一种方式阐述,稍不小心就会被错过。所以考生在解答这样的题时应小心谨慎。

2.词句理解题

在PETS第2级考试的阅读部分中一般都会出现词句理解题,数量为一道至两道不定。这种题型具体考查考生对题干所示的文中词汇、短语或句子的深层次理解,推测某一单词或短语的意思。这里要说明的是,PETS第2级试题中的词汇基本在大纲要求的范围之内(包括文章和题干、选项等),如有生词将给出注释,所以词句理解题中绝大部分是要求考生分析判断大纲范围内单词的新意或在句中、文中特定情境下的意思,这就要求考生联系上下文推敲词义。对于短语,则是大纲范围内短语的新意、情境义或用大纲范围内单词重组形成的短语意思;对于句子,则可能提取文中某一较长的、语法结构较为复杂的、能够揭示文章线索或中心意思的重点句子来让考生分析。词和句是文章的基本组成部分,只有在对词句意义有了准确和到位的理解的基础上才能进一步对篇章进行理解。因此,对词句的准确理解是考生所必备的阅读技能。词句理解题是PETS第2级考试试题中基本题型,也是传统题型,它能比较有效地考查考生对大纲内词汇的理解和掌握程度,对词义的拓展理解能力,以及对语句意思的准确把握。

此类题目一般有以下几种考查角度:①对文中单词的理解;②对文中短语的理解;③对文中句子的理解。

由这些考查角度可以延伸出千变万化的题目,但万变不离其宗,各种题目之间还是有许多相通之处,由此可以归纳出一些方法和规律,可以帮助考生有效地掌握解答此类题目的技巧。下面我们就来逐一详细地分析说明。

(1)对文中单词的理解

此类问题是词句理解题型中最为常见的,它考查考生对文章中某一单词的意思,出题形式主要有两种:一是在四个选项中写出题干所示单词的意思,供考生进行选择;二是在四个选项中提供四个单词,让考生从中选择一个在文章中可以代替题干所示单词的词,并且将其代入文章中保证文章的意思不被曲解。虽然形式不同,但无论哪种形式都是考查考生的阅读能力。所以总结经验、掌握一定的技巧,此类问题就可以迎刃而解了。下面我们来依据不同的方法来做具体讲解。

①根据构词法知识猜测词义。例如：

The environmental quality is lower than that in the past.

该句中"environmental"一词的含义不得而知，但我们知道"environment"是"环境"的意思，而"-al"后缀通常是将名词转化为形容词，综合这两点可以推测，"environmental"意为"环境的"。再如：

It is impossible that he has made the biggest cake of the world.

推测句中"impossible"的意思。我们知道"possible"是"有可能"的意思，而"im-"前缀是对后面的词语进行否定，生成它的反义词，因此"impossible"的意思是"不可能的"。

②根据句子中的同义、反义、同位等关系推测词义。例如：

Not every car, bus, jeep or other kinds of vehicle can be made in the factory.

句中"other kinds of vehicle"与car, bus, jeep同作主语，是并列关系，所以"vehicle"一词与car, bus, jeep属于同一事物，即"交通工具"。

③通过文中对某一生词的重点描述来猜测此词的含义。例如：

She had a lesion on her arm that would not stop bleeding.

我们对"lesion"一词的含义不大了解。但后面的部分"on her arm that would not stop bleeding"的意思是"她的手臂血流不止"，由此可以推测"lesion"一词的意思是"伤口"。

④根据上下文的联系或文章句子之间的逻辑关系推测词义。有原因才有结果，原因中含有生词的时候可以通过分析结果部分来推断，结果部分意思不明确则可以分析原因部分来推断。例如：

The weather is blazing hot so that people all stay at home to avoid the strong sunshine.

我们不知道"blazing hot"的意思，但后面的结果部分"so that people all stay at home to avoid the strong sunshine"指"人们都待在家里来避免强烈阳光的照射"，可以看出前面一部分在讲天气的炎热，由此可知"blazing hot"意为"酷热"。

(2)对文中短语的理解

此类问题主要有两种形式：一是考查考生对大纲范围内短语在文中特定情境下的引申含义；二是考查考生对大纲范围内单词组成的短语的联系理解（这样的短语就不一定在大纲范围内了）。这要求考生要对大纲所涵盖的短语能够熟练掌握并且运用自如，特别地，还要有良好的语感，以便对新组成的短语意思有正确把握。解答此类题目，主要是通过日常生活中的常识及上下文来推测词义。例如：

> If you want our land to keep *fertile*（肥沃的），you must try to stop soil from being carried away by water or winds. When soil is taken away by flowing water or blowing winds，we call it soil erosion.

我们不知道"soil erosion"的意思。前文"stop soil from being carried away by water or winds"的意思是"阻止泥土被水冲走或被风吹走"，再根据一些常识，可以推测出"soil erosion"的意思是"土壤流失"。

（3）对文中句子的理解

此类题目由于是考查对某一长句的理解，而所选取的长句往往语法结构复杂，包含短语、固定搭配较多，语意较为繁琐，因此难度较大，出题概率不高。但是如果出现此类题型，必是拉开考生档次的，所以值得考生注意。

解答这类问题可以从两种角度进行。其一，由里向外。即侧重理解句中某些构成主干的短语，可以折射出句子语意或作者态度的重点单词，尤其是句中一些重要的连词，由句子内部入手，将句子的各个组成部分有机结合，综合分析其文意。其二，由外向里。即先理解此句的上下文，分析这一段落所要表达的基本意思和感情色彩，或者宏观地把握全文，了解全文的写作背景和感情基调，通过这些外部因素来对所要分析的句子有一个基本的认识，再去深层次理解。这样做的好处是可以较为准确地理解句意，不至于偏离文章的中心意思。当然，在实际解题的过程中，只有针对具体问题，分析其特点，将这两种解题方法科学合理地选择或结合，才能正确地得出答案。

对比较复杂的段落意思要结合句子之间的关系来推测。

由于某些词的意思不明，而造成个别段落的意思也拿捏不准，这是阅读中常遇到的问题。对于一些难懂的句子，如能抓住句子间的逻辑关系，结合上下文反复推敲，同时联系作者的语气语调及所要表明的观点和态度，就可以推测出它的意思。例如：

> I enjoyed the football games，but it was such a wet windy day that I caught cold，so I'm feeling a little under the weather now. I think I have to go to bed early.

句字中间有一个短语"a little under the weather"意思不明，造成对整段话理解的障碍。但通过上下文中的"I caught cold"以及"I think I have to go to bed early."可以看出，"我感冒了"，"我不得不早些去睡觉"，因此"a little under the weather now"的意思是"（感觉）不太好"。

3. 主旨题

任何一篇文章,不管是何种体裁,都有一个主题,文章都是围绕着它而展开。有时主题句可以在文中找到,或在篇首,或居篇尾,或插篇中;有时则不然,它贯穿于文章的始终,要读者自己去领悟去总结。准确把握文章主旨,是阅读理解的重要技能。

主旨题就是考查考生在快速阅读文章后对其主旨的把握能力。典型的主旨题的形式主要有概括段落大意、归纳文章中心思想、给短文起标题这三种。

概括段落或文章大意的题目常用的提问方式有:

Which statement best expresses the main idea?

What is the main topic/idea of the passage?

Which of the following sentences best expresses the main idea?

The passage is primarily concerned with ____.

The topic sentence of the paragraph is ____.

The paragraph/passage informs us that ____.

The best summary of the paragraph/passage is that ____.

给短文起标题类型的问题常用的提问方式有:

The best title for this passage is ____.

What would be the most appropriate title for the passage?

The title that best expresses the main idea is ____.

无论主旨题以哪种形式出现,解答的第一步都是要先抓住文章的中心意思。

要把握整体思想必须先了解各段段意,明确段与段之间的联系;同时还要弄清楚文章的写作背景及作者的写作意图,只有这样才能抓住文章的中心意思。文章的体裁不同,中心意思的具体表达方式也会不同。如记叙文常以人物为中心,以时间、空间等为线索,按事件的发生、发展、高潮、结局来展开故事;议论文则包含论点、论据、论证三大要素,通过讲道理、举例子、引用等来阐述自己的观点。考试的时间是非常有限的,所以考生要根据文章体裁的特点,运用略读、扫读、跳读等阅读技巧,搜寻文章中的关键词和主题句,捕捉时空、人物、情节、观点,并且理清文章脉络,这样才能快速地把握文章大意。另外,抓主题句是快速掌握文章大意的主要方法,对本级别考生来说更是这样。主题句往往对全篇起概括、归纳之作用,所以概括段落大意、归纳中心思想、给短文起标题等类型的题目往往都可直接从主题句中找到答案。

那下面请大家试着找找这段话的主题句:

The panda is a popular animal. Stories about the panda in the Washington Zoo are always front page news and important features on television newscasts. Stuffed pandas are among the most popular toys for children, and panda postcards are always in demand in zoo gift shops.

不难看出，文章围绕着第一句"The panda is a popular animal"展开，所以第一句即是整段的主题句。

在把握了文章中心后，各类型的主旨题便都可以迎刃而解了。

4. 推理判断题

推理判断题是阅读理解中难度较高的一类题。在文章中找不到明确陈述问题答案的句子，考生需要在很好地把握短文主旨大意的基础上，推断出短文中隐含的深层含义，从而准确理解文章寓意或作者的写作意图和观点态度等，得出正确的答案。而领会文章作者隐含意义的能力是一种较高层次的阅读能力，考生要想把握到作者的言外之意，就要根据文章中某些词句所提供的信息，一层层剖析、推导，最后推出合符文章逻辑的结论。所以推理判断题也能反映出考生归纳、概括、推理等较高层次的阅读能力。

从历年的考题来看，推理判断题主要考查考生三个方面的把握能力：①隐含信息；②作者态度；③写作意图。

推理判断题常用的提问方式有以下几种：

What we can conclude from the text?

In your judgment, which of the following might not be true?

In the author's eyes ____.

The author believes/thinks/considers/argues/suggests/deems that ____.

The passage is intended to ____.

What is the main purpose of the passage?

在提问中常用到 conclude, imply, infer, suggest, intend, learn, mean, describe, purpose 等词。另外表示推测的情态动词，如 can, could, might, would 等和其他表示可能性的词，如 probably, most likely 等也常常在提问中被使用。

这种题目的解题思路是：

首先阅读全文，抓住文章的主题和细节，理清文章结构。

然后对暗含于文章中的信息进行推理，这些信息包括：事件的因果关系、人物的行为动机以及作者未言明的倾向、态度、观点、意图等，考生应进行合乎逻辑的判断、分析、推理，进一步增强对文章的理解，从而抓住材料的实质。在推理时要注意联系原文，切不可主观臆断。

　　另外还有一点该注意的是：在推理前，了解所要解答的问题是针对细节还是针对作者的观点态度或写作意图进行推断。若题目是细节的推断，则应先在阅读材料中确定推理依据的位置或范围，再进行推理判断。

　　那么，解答这样的题有哪些技巧呢？

　　(1)抓住某一段话中的关键信息，即某些关键词或短语去分析、推理、判断，利用逆向思维或正面推理，从而推断出这句话所隐含的深层含义。

　　(2)可以根据文章的主旨思想和选材特点来推断作者的观点和态度。比如说议论文中作者表明的是对某件事情的主观看法，或是赞成或是反对，或是表扬或是批评。而科普性文章一般就会坚持实事求是的客观态度，其意图在于介绍新理论、新发现或是提供信息、阐明一个事实。

　　(3)可以根据作者的论述方法、语气、措辞等来推断作者的观点或意图。

　　论述方法是能反映作者的意图或态度的。论述方法指作者论述的详略，对材料的安排等。作者对自己赞同的观点，论述就会比较详细。而对材料的安排，常常是为反映自己的写作意图而设计的。比如说，在论述观点时，作者一般会摆事实、讲道理，来论证自己的观点；在提供建议时，作者一般会使用较多的祈使句，告诉读者方法、做法及分析如此做的好处等等；在介绍事物时，作者一般只介绍和传递信息，而并不发表自己的看法。

　　作者的语气措辞等也是反映作者观点的重要线索。比如说用虚拟语气就可以流露出作者的弦外之音，作者在文中不直接表达自己的态度时，往往会通过一些修饰性的词语来表明自己的态度，或褒或贬，或客观中立。比如说critical(批评的)、approving(赞成的)、disapproving(不赞同的)、neutral(中立的)、argumentative(有争议性的)、doubtful(怀疑的)、positive(肯定的)、negative(否定的)、objective(客观的)、subjective(主观的)、indifferent(冷淡的)、ironic(讽刺的)、factual(事实的)等等。考生在备考过程中要注意积累这方面的词汇。

真 题 剖 析

Example 1　　　　　　　　　　　　　　　　　　　　　(2006.9)

　　阅读下列短文，从短文后所给的四个选项([A]、[B]、[C]和[D])中选出最佳选项，并在答题卡1上将该项涂黑。

　　Robert Fredy was general manager of a large hotel in Ashbury

Park, New Jersey. One cold day two years ago when he stopped his car at a traffic light, Stephen Pearman, an out-of-work taxi and truck driver, walked up to Fredy's car hoping to earn some change by washing his windshield. Like many motorists who try to keep the beggars off, Fredy turned on the wipers to show he wasn't interested.

Pearman put his head close to the window. "Come on, mister. Give me a chance. I need a job." he said. Something in Stephen Pearman's voice moved Robert Fredy. In the seconds before traffic started moving again, Fredy handed Pearman a business card and told him to call if he was serious.

"My friends told me he was just pulling my leg," said Pearman. "But I said, 'No, he's a businessman. I need to give it a shot.'"

Two days later, 29-year-old Pearman appeared in the manager's office of the big hotel. Fredy gave him a job and housing and lent him pocket money while training him.

Today, Pearman works full time setting up the hotel's dining halls for business meetings. In the past two years, he has found a flat, married and repaid Fredy's loans.

"Mr Fredy gave me a second chance," says Pearman, "And I took advantage of it. I could have just come here a while, eaten up and left. But there is no future in washing windshields."

Ordinarily, Fredy keeps away from the street people. "But Pearman seemed so honest and open, asking for a chance rather than just money," Fredy says. "I don't hand my business card to just anybody. But I'm glad I did in this case."

56. When Pearman offered to wash the windshield for Fredy, ____.

　[A]Fredy took him as a beggar

　[B]Pearman was told to do it later

　[C]Fredy gladly agreed to let him do it

　[D]Pearman knew Fredy was a kind man

57. When Fredy told Pearman to call if he was serious, he meant if ____.

　[A]Pearman was really hardworking

　[B]Pearman was really looking for a job

[C]Pearman's conditions were truly serious

[D]Pearman was really interested in washing windshields

58. What did Pearman mean by saying "he's a businessman"(Line 2，Para. 3)?

[A]Fredy knew where he could get a job.

[B]Fredy meant what he had said.

[C]Fredy had enough money to help the poor.

[D]Businessmen always handed others their cards.

59. What has become of Pearman now?

[A]He is in charge of Fredy's loans.

[B]He is still washing car windshields.

[C]He is a full-time employee at the hotel.

[D]He organizes dinner parties for the hotel.

60. What can we learn about Fredy?

[A]He helps those who will work hard themselves.

[B]He likes to give his help to anyone in need.

[C]He always gives help to the unemployed.

[D]He is easily moved by poor people.

> **windshield** *n.* （汽车的）挡风玻璃
> **pull one's leg**：[非正式]开某人的玩笑
> **give sth. a shot**：尝试一下某事
> **loan** *n.* 贷款

答案与分析

56.[A]。细节题。文章第一段最后一句说：Like many motorists ... he wasn't interested(像许多驱赶乞丐的开车者一样，弗雷德打开雨刷，示意他不感兴趣)，表明弗雷德以为皮尔曼是个乞丐，故答案为[A]。

57.[B]。推理判断题。从字面上来看，这句话的意思是"他是严肃认真的"，而由短文最后一段中 asking for a chance rather than just money(想要的是一个机会而不仅仅是钱)可推知，这里弗雷德的意思是如果皮尔曼真的是在找工作而不是为了要钱，故选[B]。

58.[B]。词句理解题。前文说，皮尔曼的朋友认为弗雷德是在开他的玩笑，而后文的叙述则说明弗雷德没有开玩笑，他真的给了皮尔曼一份工作。由此可以看出,皮尔曼在此是指弗雷德说话算数,因此答案是[B]。其他三项都可以根据常识排除。

59.[C]。细节题。答案信息对应于原文第五段第一句:Today,Pearman works full time … for business meetings,选项[C]与此相符。

60.[A]。推理判断题。由文章最后一段弗雷德的话可以看出,他并不是那种向任何人都伸出援助之手的人,他只是看到皮尔曼诚实、坦率,想要的是一个机会而不仅仅是钱才帮助他。由此可以推断,他只帮那些自己能勤奋工作的人,故答案是[A]。

　　罗伯特·弗雷德是新泽西州艾什伯瑞帕克一家大酒店的总经理。两年前很冷的一天,当他在一个交通信号灯处停下车子时,史蒂芬·皮尔曼这个失业了的出租车和卡车司机走向弗雷德的车子,希望为他擦洗挡风玻璃以赚点零钱。像许多驱赶乞丐的开车者一样,弗雷德打开雨刷,以示不感兴趣。

　　皮尔曼向车窗探过头去。"来吧,先生。给我一个机会。我需要一份工作。"他说。史蒂芬·皮尔曼的声音里有种东西打动了罗伯特·弗雷德。在车流重新开动前的几秒钟里,弗雷德递给皮尔曼一张名片并告诉后者,如果皮尔曼是认真的,可以打电话给他。

　　"我的朋友们告诉我,他只是在开玩笑,"皮尔曼说。"但我说:'不,他是个商人,会说话算数的。我要试一试。'"

　　两天后,29岁的皮尔曼出现在那家大酒店的经理办公室里。弗雷德给了他一份工作,为他安排了住处,还在培训期间借给他零花钱。

　　如今,皮尔曼专职为酒店打理商务会议宴会厅。在过去的两年里,他找到了一套公寓,结了婚并且还清了弗雷德借给他的钱。

　　"弗雷德先生给了我第二次机会,"皮尔曼说,"我好好利用了这次机会。我可能会只是来到这里,干不了几天就厌烦了,然后离开。但是,擦洗挡风玻璃是没有前途的。"

　　通常来说,弗雷德会远离那些街边乞丐。"但是皮尔曼看起来这么诚实、坦率,想要的是一个机会而不仅仅是钱,"弗雷德说。"我不会把我的名片随便给人的。但我很高兴这次我给了。"

Example 2   (2006.9)

On Your Children

Friendly Advice: The main cause for boys and girls to start drinking or smoking is whether they have friends who do, a National Institute of Health study suggests. Researchers find that school children are likely to do the same things as their five closest friends do, and girls are more likely than boys to give in to pressure to drink. However, the parents' role makes a difference: children whose moms and dads talk and listen to them regularly are less likely to smoke and drink.

Crying for a Smoke: New moms are often annoyed by the cries of new-born babies, but according to one study, there is something they can do about it: give up smoking. Researchers at a Netherlands organization of scientific research questioned parents of 3 000 babies up to six months old and found that stomachache was three times as likely in small babies whose mothers smoke 15 to 30 cigarettes a day, either before or after their babies were born. No data yet on dad's smoking, but it's a safe suggestion that he should put the cigarettes out, too.

Out of Shape: Even as the number of overweight children increases, many schools are making unhealthy habits worse by cutting back on sports classes. Physical education is meant to provide exercise and encourage lifetime fitness, but a recent study found that only 26% of high schools require at least three years of physical education. It's worse in lower grades: California middle school students get only 25 minutes of physical activity a week.

73. **According to "Friendly Advice", what should parents do to prevent their children from drinking or smoking?**

[A]Do researches on drinking and smoking habits.

[B]Take advice from their children's friends.

[C]Put more pressure on boys than on girls.

[D]Talk with their children like friends.

74. "**Crying for a Smoke**" **suggests there is a cause-and-effect relation between** ____.

[A]the mother's smoking and her baby's stomachache

[B]the mother's annoyance and her baby's cries

[C]research results and the babies' parents

[D]dad's smoking and mom's smoking

75. **What is a common problem in American schools according to** "**Out of Shape**"?

[A]Students spend too little time on physical exercise.

[B]A large number of children are overweight.

[C]Many students have unhealthy habits.

[D]Students' grades are getting lower.

---

pressure *n.* 压力   data *n.* 数据

cut back on sports classes：减少体育课时

physical education：体育，略作 PE 或 P.E.

 答案与分析

73. [D]。细节题。第一段最后一句说：children whose moms and ... to smoke and drink(那些父母定期与之交谈并聆听他们倾诉的孩子吸烟喝酒的可能性要小一些)，也就是说父母可以用定期与孩子交谈、听孩子倾诉来使他们不吸烟喝酒，故答案是[D]。

74. [A]。细节题。第二段第二句说：... stomachache was three times ... after their babies were born(那些母亲每天吸 15～30 支烟的婴儿发生腹痛的可能性是(那些母亲不吸烟的婴儿的)3 倍，不论她们是在婴儿出生前还是出生后吸)，也就是说，母亲吸烟会使婴儿发生腹痛，两者之间有因果关系。至于父亲吸烟，该段最后一句说"No data"表明会引起婴儿腹痛。

75. [A]。推断题。第三段首先指出许多学校将体育课时减少，从而使学生的一些不健康习惯变得更糟糕。然后用数据说明了这一点。因此，综合起来，说明的就是美国孩子在体育锻炼上花的时间太少，这已经是一个很常见的问题了。故答案就是[A]。

关于你的孩子

友情提示：全国健康协会的一份研究表明，男孩和女孩子们开始吸烟或者喝酒的主要原因是看他们是否有吸烟或者喝酒的朋友。研究人员发现，学校里的孩子很有可能会与他们最好的5个朋友做相同的事，而且女孩比男孩更有可能在压力之下开始喝酒。然而，父母的作用可以改变这一点：那些父母定期与之交谈并且听他们倾诉的孩子吸烟和喝酒的可能性会小一些。

因为烟而哭闹：刚做妈妈的人常常会为新生儿的哭闹而心烦，但根据一项研究，有一件事情她们可以做：戒烟。荷兰一个科学研究组织的研究人员调查了3 000名至6个月大的婴儿的父母，发现那些母亲每天吸15～30支烟的婴儿发生腹痛的可能性是那些母亲不吸烟的婴儿的3倍，不论其母亲是在婴儿出生前还是出生后吸烟。然而没有数据表明父亲吸烟会不会引发婴儿腹痛，但为安全起见，父亲也应戒烟。

体形肥胖：尽管过于肥胖的孩子的数量在增加，许多学校减少体育课时的做法却正在使孩子们的一些不健康的习惯变得更糟。体育的目的是提供锻炼和鼓励人们终生保持健康，但最近一项研究却发现只有26％的高中要求至少有3年的体育课时间。在低年级这一状况则更糟：加利弗尼亚的中学生每周只有25分钟的体育活动时间。

📖 *Example 3*　　　　　　　　　　　　　　　　(2006. 3)

阅读下列短文，从短文后所给的四个选项（[A]、[B]、[C]和[D]）中选出最佳选项，并在答题卡1上将该项涂黑。

Like all other mothers who have small children, I, too, have to steal time — from my own children at home and from the children who know me as their teacher — just to put a few words down on paper. Many times I've wanted to write for myself, for other women, for my parents, for my husband, and especially for my children. I would have liked to leave a legacy of words explaining what it has meant to have twins. One reason there is not a great deal written about being a mother of a new baby is that there is seldom a moment to think of anything else but the baby's needs.

With twins, I did not have a spare hand to write with.

Before my twins were born, my days were long and I had nothing to write about. After the twins' birth I did have something to write about, but I found myself facing not a pen and paper but milk bottles.

Some nights, friends would visit. They would leave at 11 p.m., heading for bed, and for us the night was only just beginning. With twins, there is really no night. Each feeding lasts a long time. At 1:00 a.m., each of them would begin crying from hunger. At 4:00 a.m., when I finally put them down, I head for the kitchen and light a cigarette. I haven't smoked in almost a year, but I feel I've never needed it more. I'm so sleepy and so tired that I don't care.

Two years have passed since then and we've managed to live through it all. My days are still very full and even now there isn't one evening when I put the twins down for the night that I don't breathe a sigh of relief. At last a little time for myself.

60. What does the writer mainly write about?
　　[A]Her role as a wife.　　　　[B]Her work as a writer.
　　[C]Her role as a teacher.　　　[D]Her experience as a mother.

61. When did she have time but nothing to write about?
　　[A]Before the birth of her twins.
　　[B]When she faced bottles of milk.
　　[C]After her friends' visit to her home.
　　[D]When she had to think about the babies' needs.

62. When the writer says "I don't care"(Para. 4), she means that she doesn't care about ____.
　　[A]her babies any more
　　[B]the time to go to bed
　　[C]the writing of her book
　　[D]the possible effects of smoking

63. Even when the twins were two years old, the only time the writer could find for herself was ____.
　　[A]when her babies were asleep　　[B]when the feeding was over
　　[C]when her friends left　　　　　[D]when evening began

> legacy *n.* 遗产　　　　　　twins *n.* 双胞胎
> breathe a sigh of relief：松了一口气

 答案与分析

60.[D]。主旨题。文章第一句即指出,作者自己和别的有婴儿的母亲一样得挤时间,然后尽管提到自己是一名教师,但全文都在谈论自己有了双胞胎后抚育工作的繁重与时间的紧张,表达了作者自己的体会。因此,文章的主旨无疑是作者作为一名母亲的体会,答案是[D]。前面三项都是作者的身份之一,但都不是文章说明的主要内容。

61.[A]。细节题。文章第三段第一句指出:Before my twins ... to write about,即在双胞胎出生前,作者是有时间的(my days were long),却无东西可写,故答案是[A]。

62.[D]。词句理解题。本句前两句说,作者已经有近一年没有吸烟了,但她觉得自己现在是最需要香烟的。由常识可知,作者不吸烟肯定是为了自己的孩子,怕对孩子不好。而在这一句说,她又困又乏,以至于"不在乎"了。由此可以推知,她不在乎的就是吸烟(对孩子)的害处,选[D]。其余三项都无法由上下文推知。

63.[A]。推断题。文章最后一句指出,即便是如今(她的孩子两岁后),每天晚上把双胞胎安顿睡好后她都会松一口气,因为终于有一点点属于自己的时间了。原文用的是双重否定,表达的是肯定含意,因此其意即是只有在孩子睡了后她才有时间,答案是[A]。

同步译文

　　像有小孩子的其他所有母亲一样,我也得挤时间——在家里,从我自己的孩子那里挤;在学校,从我的学生们那里挤——只是为了在纸上写点东西。曾经多次,我都想要为自己、为其他女性、为我父母、为我丈夫、尤其是为我的孩子们写点什么。我本来想要留下一份文字遗产,向别人说明有一对双胞胎意味着什么。现在没有写下许多关于做一名新生儿的母亲的文字材料,一个原因就是除了自己孩子的需要,很少有时间去考虑其他的事情。

　　有了双胞胎,我无法腾出手来写东西。

　　在我的双胞胎出生前,我的日子很漫长,但无东西可写。双胞胎出生后,

我确实有东西可写了,却发现自己面对的不再是笔和纸,而是奶瓶。

有些晚上,朋友们会来访。他们会在晚上11点离开,上床睡觉,而对于我们来说,夜晚才刚刚开始。有了双胞胎,就没有了/真正的夜晚。每一次喂食都要很长时间。凌晨1点,他们两个都会因为饿了而开始哭闹。当凌晨4点我终于把他们安抚下来之后,我会走到厨房里点上一支烟。我已经有近一年没有吸烟了,但我觉得没有比现在更需要香烟的时候了。(但现在)我又困又乏,顾不了那么多了。

从那时起两年过去了,我们设法熬过来了。我的日子仍然安排得满满当当,即便是现在,也没有哪天晚上我把双胞胎孩子安抚下来睡觉后,不长松一口气的。终于有一点属于我自己的时间了。

 Example 4 （2006. 3）

Will chips one day be planted
in our bodies for identification?

A US doctor has planted under his skin a computer chip that can send personal information to a scanner, a technology that may someday be widely used as a way to identify people. The chip gives off information which will be scanned by a hand-held reader.

The chip is similar to that planted in more than 1 million dogs, cats and other pets in recent years to track and identify them.

The doctor decided to test the chip himself after the World Trade Center disaster. The dead could have been identified if their names and other important information had been chipped.

Officials of the company said they hope to sell the chips to patients with man-made arms or legs or other body parts. The idea is that the chip will provide immediate and correct medical information when it is needed.

The information can contain name, telephone number and other information. Or it can send out a message that, when connected to a computer, can call up records. The scanner can read it through clothes from over a meter away. The new product also could be used to control prisoners. Workplaces of great importance may want to use the chips for employees, too. Some parents may consider planting chips in young children or elderly relatives who may be unable to say their names, addresses or telephone numbers.

Some medical and technology specialists said the product raises new questions about the relationship between humans and computer technology and could cause problems if it is used against someone's wishes, or if your personal information is read by those who should not see it.

68. **According to the text, computer chips have already been used to ____.**
   [A]catch escaped prisoners   [B]find missing children
   [C]follow lost animals   [D]treat sick people

69. **The doctor decided to test the chips himself because he believed that ____.**
   [A]nobody would dare to try it
   [B]they can be used for identification purposes
   [C]it has been proved successful on animals
   [D]his patients expected him to experience it first

70. **Which of the following statements is best supported by the text?**
   [A]This chip has been proven to be very successful.
   [B]The use of this chip will be favored by everybody.
   [C]There will be a great market for chip planting in humans.
   [D]Doctors will make good money by using chips.

71. **What problem may be caused by planting chips in the human body?**
   [A]People will be controlled by computers.
   [B]Computers could send out wrong information.
   [C]Chips can be the cause of diseases.
   [D]Information may be used improperly.

a computer chip: 电脑芯片.	**scanner** *n.* 扫描仪
identify *v.* 识别	**disaster** *n.* 灾难

答案与分析

68.［C］。推理判断题。文章第二段一句说，这种芯片与近年来植入100多万条狗、猫和其他宠物身上以跟踪和确认它们的芯片一样。由这一句即可推断出，电脑芯片已经应用于动物身上，故答案应选与动物有关的［C］项。其余三项都是第四段和第五段提到的这种芯片可能应用于人身上的展望。

69.［B］。推理判断题。第三段提及了这位医生自己做实验的时间与原因。该段第一句指出，他是在美国世贸中心那场灾难后决定自己做实验的，而第二句用的是虚拟语气，说如果那场灾难中的死者的姓名与其他重要信息储存在植入其体内的芯片上，他们就可以被识别出来。由此可以推断，他做实验的原因就是他相信芯片可以用于识别人的身份。故答案是［B］。其余三项在文中都未提及。

70.［C］。推理判断题。由文章第五段作者所举的例子可以推知这种植入人体的芯片的市场前景很广，故［C］项是对的。文章只指出了已经在动物身上植入这一芯片，而人体植入还处在实验阶段，并且最后一段提出了一些人的担心，并没有说这一技术已经很成功，故［A］不对；同样由最后一段可知这一技术并非人人都赞同，故［B］不对；［D］项文章根本没有提及。

71.［D］。细节题。［D］项即是对文章最后一段一句的概括，故是正确答案。其余三项在文中都未涉及。

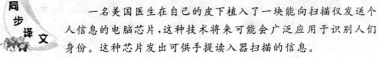

将来有一天芯片会植入我们身体以辨认身份吗？

一名美国医生在自己的皮下植入了一块能向扫描仪发送个人信息的电脑芯片，这种技术将来可能会广泛应用于识别人们身份。这种芯片发出可供手提读入器扫描的信息。

这种芯片与近年来植入100多万条狗、猫和其他宠物身上以跟踪和辨认它们的芯片一样。

这位医生是在世贸中心那次灾难之后决定亲自检验这种芯片的。如果那次灾难中的死者身上植入了存有他们姓名和其他重要信息的芯片，他们本来可以被辨认出来。

该公司的一些官员说，他们希望将这种芯片出售给那些装有人造手臂、腿或者其他人造身体部位的病人。这样，当需要时芯片就能提供及时而准确的医疗信息。

这种信息可以包括姓名、电话号码和其他一些信息。或者，在与电脑连接后,它可以发出一种能调出记录的信息。扫描仪可以在 1 米多的距离透过衣服读取信息。这一新产品也可用来控制囚犯。一些极为重要的工作场所可能也会想要将这种芯片用于雇员身上。一些家长可能会考虑为自己不能说出其姓名、地址或者电话号码的小孩或年老亲属植入这种芯片。

一些医疗和技术专家说,这一产品提出了关于人类与电脑技术之间关系的新问题,而且,如果它的使用违背了某人的意愿,或者个人信息被那些不应该知道这些信息的人读取,都可能引发许多问题。

Example 5　　　　　　　　　　　　　　　　　　　(2005.9)

阅读下列短文,从短文后所给的四个选项([A]、[B]、[C]和[D])中选出最佳选项,并在答题卡 1 上将该项涂黑。

In the United States, the biggest change in spending has been in the amount spent on food, which had decreased from 46% of the total family budget in 1901 to 19% of present day totals. This is due to the fact that people are now able to buy more and better foods at lower prices. As a result of the growth in fast-food restaurants (for example, McDonald's or KFC), more people are also eating out. Thus about 30% of today's food budget goes on meals eaten outside the home while a hundred years ago it was only 3%.

At the beginning of the 20th century, few people owned their homes (only around 19% of working families) and cars (at $1 000 per car, this was well above the average family income of $650 per year), as most people were unable to borrow money. But there was a rapid rise in both home and car ownership during the mid-1900s.

Free time increased considerably following the shortening of the working week, i.e. from six days to five, and from ten hours to eight hours a day. In fact, the working day couldn't be too long, otherwise people wouldn't have the time to spend their money. The amount of a family's budget spent on outside entertainment, such as parties, films and concerts has increased from just under 6% in Ford's day to about 9% today. On the other hand, we spend only a quarter of what our great-grandparents paid for reading materials.

It is difficult to see how our spending patterns may change in the future. We already know that our population is aging and this will have an effect on the amount of money we spend on medical care.

60. What is the subject discussed in the text?

[A]Changing patterns in spending.

[B]Changes in family planning.

[C]Increase in family income.

[D]Decrease in food demand.

61. Why do people spend less on food today than one hundred years ago?

[A]People are eating less.

[B]Foods are less expensive.

[C]Fewer people are eating out.

[D]Eating habits have changed.

62. What is the immediate cause for people to have more time to enjoy life?

[A]The improvement of living conditions.

[B]The development of the fast food industry.

[C]The reduction in working time.

[D]The rapid rise in income.

63. On which of the following did people spend less time and money than before?

[A]Shopping.　　　　　　　　　[B]Reading.

[C]Travelling.　　　　　　　　 [D]Family gatherings.

64. One possible change in the future is that people will ____.

[A]spend less on entertainment

[B]spend more on their health

[C]spend more on books

[D]spend less eating out

amount n. 数目，数量	decrease n. 减少
budget n. 预算	be due to: 由于，因为

答案与分析

60.[A].主旨题。文章一开始就谈论美国人在饮食方面消费支出的减少,然后在第二、三两段扩展到美国人在房、车等方面的消费支出的变化并说明了产生变化的原因,在最后一段指出了这一变化的影响。因此,全文主旨就是美国人消费支出方式的变化,答案是[A]。

61.[B].细节题。第一段第二句指出:This is due to … at lower prices,即是因为如今人们能够以较低的价钱买到更多更好的食品,[B]项与此相符。注意[C]项与该段第三句中的结论不符。

62.[C].细节题。文章第三段第一句指出:Free time increased … eight hours a day,即工作时间的缩短使得人们的空闲时间大大增加,题目只是换了一个说法,故答案是[C]。

63.[B].细节题。由第三段最后一句可知,美国人在阅读材料上花的钱只有他们曾祖父母所花的四分之一。与此相符的只有[B]项。

64.[B].推理判断题。文章最后一句说,人口正在老龄化,这将会对美国人在医疗保健上支出的费用产生影响。联系常识,这一影响当然会是增加在这个方面的支出,故答案是[B]。

同步译文

在美国,支出费用上的最大变化就是饮食上支出费用的变化,从1901年占整个家庭总预算的46%减少到了如今占总预算的19%。这是因为人们如今能以更低的价钱买到更多更好的食品。快餐店(例如麦当劳或者肯德基)数量增加的结果是,更多人还外出就餐。所以如今有30%的饮食预算花在了外出就餐上,而100年前这方面仅占3%。

在20世纪早期,很少有人拥有自己的房子(只有约19%的工人家庭)和汽车(那时平均每辆车要1 000美元,远远高于一般家庭只有650美元的年收入),因为大部分人无法借款。但在20世纪中期,房子和车子的拥有量有了快速增长。

随着工作周的缩短,也就是从每周6天缩短到5天、从每天10小时缩短到8小时,人们的空余时间大大增加了。事实上,工作日不能太长,否则人们没有时间来花他们的钱。家庭在外出娱乐,如晚会、电影、音乐会上的支出预算从福特那时的不足6%增长到了如今的9%。另一方面,我们在阅读材料上花的钱则只有我们曾祖父母所花的四分之一。

我们的支出方式在未来会如何变化还很难预料。我们已经知道人口正在老龄化,而这将会对我们在医疗保健方面的支出产生影响。

Example 6 (2005.3)

阅读下列短文,从短文后所给的四个选项([A]、[B]、[C]和[D])中选出最佳选项,并在答题卡1上将该项涂黑。

Michele Langlois is a young Canadian who works for the police as a handwriting expert. She has helped catch many criminals by using her special skill.

When she was only fourteen, Michele was already so interested in the differences in her school friends' handwriting that she would spend hours studying them. After finishing college she went to France for a special two-year class to learn how to analyze handwriting at the School of Police Science. On her return, she began her work for the Quebec police.

Michele says that it is impossible for people to disguise their handwriting. She can discover most of what she needs to know simply by looking at the writing with her own eyes, but she also has machines that help her analyze different kinds of paper and ink. This knowledge is often of help to the police.

Michele also believes that handwriting is a good sign of the kind of person the writer is. "I wouldn't go out with a fellow if I didn't like his handwriting," she says. But she adds that she fell in love with her future husband, William Smith before she studied his handwriting. It later proved to be all right, however.

60. The best title for the text would be _____.

[A]Police Science [B]Friends of Police

[C]Handwriting Reader [D]Art of Handwriting

61. Where did Michele learn to analyze people's handwriting?

[A]At work. [B]In Quebec Police Station.

[C]In the middle school. [D]In a police school.

62. **Michele usually analyzes handwriting by ____.**

    [A]looking at it   [B]using a machine

    [C]studying the ink used   [D]examining the paper used

63. **Besides helping the police Michele uses her skill to ____.**

    [A]teach her friends

    [B]look for a husband

    [C]decide if a person will do something wrong

    [D]tell what kind of person the writer is from his handwriting

64. **The underlined word "it" in the last sentence refers to ____.**

    [A]Michele's job   [B]William's handwriting

    [C]Michele's analyzing skill [D]William's love for Michele

---

criminal *n.* 罪犯   **analyze** *v.* 分析   **disguise** *v.* 伪装

 答案与分析

60.[C]。主旨题。通读全文可知,文章叙述的是关于笔迹鉴定专家 Michele Langlois 的事迹,因此能概括这一内容的标题应当是[C]。

61.[D]。细节题。文章第二段第二句指出:After finishing ... at the School of Police Science,即她是在警察科学学校学习分析笔迹的,故选[D]。[A]明显不对;[B]是其学成后的工作单位;[C]指的是她对研究笔迹感兴趣的时间。

62.[A]。细节题。答案信息对应于第三段第二句的前半部分:She can discover ... with her own eyes,即她用肉眼观察笔迹就能发现她大部分需要知道的信息。其余三项在文中都有涉及,但都与题目中的 usually 不符。

63.[D]。推理判断题。最后一段第一句说,她认为笔迹是反映书写者为何种类型的人的很好的标志,而在第二句又用直接引语说她不会与一个她不喜欢其笔迹的人出去,这表明她通过笔迹辨别书写者是什么样的人,选[D]。

64.[C]。词句理解题。前文说,Michele Langlois 在爱上未婚夫之前并未研究过他的笔迹,而这里说:“它”后来证明是没有问题的。联系上下文分析,这里应当是指她用笔迹分析人的类型用在自己的未婚夫身上也是正确的,故 it 指代的应当是她的分析技能,选[C]。

同步译文

米切尔·兰格诺伊斯是为加拿大警方工作的一名年轻的笔迹专家。用她独特的技能，她已经协助抓获了许多罪犯。

她还只有 14 岁时，米切尔就已经对她的校友们的笔迹很感兴趣，会花数小时来研究它们。大学毕业后，她去了法国警察科学学校上了两年特殊课程，学会了如何分析笔迹。她回来后就开始为魁北克警方工作。

米切尔说人们不可能伪装自己的笔迹。她只用自己的肉眼观察笔迹就能发现大部分她需要知道的信息，但她也有帮助她分析不同类型纸张和墨水的仪器。这一知识常常对警方很有帮助。

米切尔还认为笔迹是反映书写者是何种类型的人的一个很好的标志。"如果我不喜欢一个人的笔迹，我不会和他出去。"她说。但她补充说，她还没有研究其笔迹之前就爱上了她的未婚夫威廉·史密斯。不过，后来证明这一点也是没有问题的。

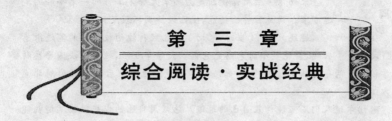

第 三 章
综合阅读·实战经典

第 1 节　完形填空 30 篇

阅读下列短文,从短文后所给各题的四个选项([A]、[B]、[C]和[D])中选出能填入相应空白处的最佳选项,并在答题卡 1 上将该项涂黑。

Exercise 1

　　My sister and I grow up in a little village in England. Our father was a struggling __1__ , but I always knew he was __2__ . He never criticized us, but used __3__ to bring out our best. He'd say, "If you pour water on flowers, they flourish. If you don't give them water, they die." I __4__ as a child I said something __5__ about somebody, and my father said, "__6__ time you say something unpleasant about somebody else, it's a reflection of you." He explained that if I looked for the best __7__ people, I would get the best __8__ . From then on I've always tried to __9__ the principle in my life and later in running my company.

　　Dad's also always been very __10__ . At 15, I started a magazine. It was __11__ a great deal of my time, and the headmaster of my school gave me a __12__ : stay in school or leave to work on my magazine.

　　I decided to leave, and Dad tried to sway me from my decision, __13__ any good father would. When he realized I had made up my mind, he said, "Richard, when I was 23, my dad ___14___ me to go into law. And I've ___15___ regretted it. I wanted to be a biologist, ___16___ I didn't pursue my ___17___ . You know what you want. Go fulfil it."

As ___18___ turned out, my little publication went on to become *Student*, a national ___19___ for young people in the UK. My wife and I have two children, and I'd like to think we are bringing them up in the same way Dad ___20___ me.

1. [A]biologist   [B]manager   [C]lawyer   [D]gardener
2. [A]strict   [B]honest   [C]special   [D]learned
3. [A]praise   [B]courage   [C]power   [D]warmth
4. [A]think   [B]imagine   [C]remember   [D]guess
5. [A]unnecessary [B]unkind   [C]unimportant   [D]unusual
6. [A]Another   [B]Some   [C]Any   [D]Other
7. [A]on   [B]in   [C]at   [D]about
8. [A]in case   [B]by turns   [C]by chance   [D]in return
9. [A]revise   [B]set   [C]review   [D]follow
10. [A]understanding   [B]experienced
    [C]serious   [D]demanding
11. [A]taking up   [B]making up   [C]picking up   [D]keeping up
12. [A]suggestion [B]decision   [C]notice   [D]choice
13. [A]and   [B]as   [C]even if   [D]as if
14. [A]helped   [B]allowed   [C]persuaded   [D]suggested
15. [A]always   [B]never   [C]seldom   [D]almost
16. [A]rather   [B]but   [C]for   [D]therefore
17. [A]promise   [B]task   [C]belief   [D]dream
18. [A]this   [B]he   [C]it   [D]that
19. [A]newspaper   [B]magazine   [C]program   [D]project
20. [A]controlled [B]comforted   [C]reminded   [D]raised

😊 **答案与分析**

1.[C]. 考查名词词义与上下文理解。由第三段中的 go into law 可知作者的父亲是一位律师。biologist 生物学家；manager 经理；gardener 园艺师。

2.[C]。考查形容词词义与上下文理解。由下文描述的父亲的做法可知,作者想要表达的是"父亲与众不同"这一意思,故选 special。其余三项都与文意没有太大关系。

3.[A]。考查上下文理解。由 but 所表达的转折关系可知填入的词应与 criticize(批评)相对,所以选 praise(表扬)。此外,由空格后的 to bring out our best(让我们发挥最好)也可推知。

4.[C]。考查动词词义与上下文理解。由后面的 as a child 可知作者是在回忆过去,所以用 remember(记起)。think 考虑;imagine 想像;guess 猜测。

5.[B]。考查形容词词义。四个形容词都是大纲词汇加否定性前缀 un-构成,而由后面的句意特别是其中的 unpleasant(令人不高兴的)可知应选与之同义的 unkind(不友善的)。unnecessary 不必要的;unimportant 不重要的;unusual 不常见的,异常的。

6.[C]。考查上下文理解。由文意可知,父亲是在强调"任何时候",所以只能用 any。其余三项中,another 用于两者之间,other 一般与 the 连用,而 some 表示"某(一)"。

7.[B]。考查固定搭配。look for sth. in 为固定搭配,指"在…里寻找…",in 后可跟人,此时可译为"在某人身上寻找…"。

8.[D]。考查固定搭配。in case 以防,如果;by turns 轮流;by chance 偶然,碰巧;in return 反过来,作为回报。这里指如果看到别人的优点,自己也会得到最好的回报。

9.[D]。考查动词习惯搭配。与 principle(原则)搭配的动词为 follow,此处指"遵循原则"。

10.[A]。考查上下文理解。由下文所举的例子可以看出,作者的父亲很理解他,所以作为段落主旨句的第一句指的当然也是这个意思。understanding 理解(人)的,宽容的;experienced 有经验的;serious 严肃的,严重的;demanding 要求(很高)的。

11.[A]。考查固定搭配。take up 占用,花费;make up 组成,化妆,补回;pick up 捡起;keep up 保持,跟上。后面的宾语是时间,且表达的是"占用了我许多时间",故选 take up。

12.[D]。考查名词词义与上下文理解。由后面表选择的 or 可知应选 choice(选择),指校长让作者在两者之间进行取舍。

13.[B]。考查连词。根据上下文与常识可知作者表达的是父亲像其他好父亲一样,所以选 as。其余三项:and 表并列;even if 表假设和让步;as if 表达的是一种不真实的情况。

14.[C]。考查动词辨义与用法。help 后一般跟不带 to 的动词不定式；allow 指"允许"；persuade 指"劝说，劝服"；suggest 表"建议"。由句意可以看出，作者的爷爷是说服了作者的父亲学法律，所以作者的父亲才说自己一直后悔，所以应选 persuade。

15.[A]。考查副词与上下文理解。参见上题解析。

16.[B]。考查上下文联系。由后面的 didn't pursue my dream 可知，这里前后两个分句之间是转折关系。

17.[D]。考查上下文理解与习惯搭配。pursue one's dream 指"追求某人的梦想"。promise 诺言，承诺；task 任务，使命；belief 信仰，信念.

18.[C]。考查习惯表达。as it turned out 为习惯表达，指"结果（表明）"，其中 it 不用别的代词代替。

19.[B]。考查上下文理解。文章第二段中明确指出作者办的是一份杂志(magazine)。注意 publication 指"出版（物）"。

20.[D]。考查动词词义与上下文关系。由空格前的 in the same way（以与…一样的方式）可知填入的动词应与前面的 bring up 同义，故选 raise（养育）。control 控制；comfort 安慰；remind 使…记起。

同步译文

　　妹妹和我是在英国的一个小村庄里长大的。父亲是一位很勤奋的律师，但我一直知道他很特别。他从不批评我们，而是用表扬发掘出我们最好的品质。他会说："如果给花浇水，花就会茂盛。如果不给它们浇水，它们就会枯萎。"我记得小时候我说过一个人的坏话，父亲说："任何时候说别人的坏话，都反映出你自己有问题。"他解释说，如果我看到别人的优点，我自己就会得到最好的回报。从那时起，我在生活中和在后来开公司的过程中一起试图遵循这一原则。

　　父亲也很理解我们。我在 15 岁时办了一份杂志。杂志占据了我大量的时间，校长给了我一个选择：要么留在学校里，要么退学去办杂志。

　　我决定退学，父亲与其他任何一个好父亲一样试图动摇我的决心。当他意识到我已经下定了决心后，他说："理查德，我 23 岁时我的父亲说服我学习法律。而我一直对此感到后悔。我想成为一名生物学家，但我没有去追求我的梦想。你明白你想要什么，去实现它吧。"

　　结果，我的小出版物成了一本面向英国年轻人的全国性杂志《学生》。我和妻子有两个孩子，我们将以与我父亲所用的同样的方式养育他们。

Exercise 2

There used to be few people on the earth and natural resources seemed to be unlimited. But today ___1___ are different. The world has become too ___2___ . We are using ___3___ our natural resources too quickly, and at the same time we are polluting our surroundings with dangerous ___4___ . If we continue to do this, ___5___ on earth will not survive(存活).

Everyone realizes today that if too many fish are ___6___ the sea, there will soon be none left. Yet, with modern fishing methods, ___7___ fish are caught. Fish ___8___ at sea so that fishing boats ___9___ return home quickly with their catch, and can fish farther from the coasts. We even use satellites to give us ___10___ about where the fish are.

We know that if too many trees are cut down, forests will ___11___ and nothing will ___12___ on the land. Yet we continue to use bigger and more powerful machines to cut down more and more trees.

We realize that if rivers are ___13___ with waste products from factories, fish will ___14___ . However, in most countries waste products are still put into rivers or into the sea, and there are few laws to ___15___ this.

We know too that if the world population continues to ___16___ at the present rate, in a few years there will not be ___17___ food. Our natural resources will last longer if we learn to ___18___ them. The world population will not rise so quickly if more people come to see the ___19___ of birth control.

Finally, if we educate people to think about the problem, we shall have a better and cleaner ___20___ in the future.

1. [A]situations   [B]things   [C]affairs   [D]matters
2. [A]busy   [B]tiresome   [C]crowded   [D]quiet
3. [A]up   [B]through   [C]away   [D]down
4. [A]medicines   [B]chemicals   [C]products   [D]elements
5. [A]fish   [B]human life   [C]animals   [D]birds

6. [A]driven off　　[B]dying from　　[C]taken from　　[D]brought up

7. [A]a good many　　　　　　　[B]more or less
   [C]more and more　　　　　　[D]a small number of

8. [A]are set free　[B]are freezing　[C]are raised　[D]are frozen

9. [A]haven't to　[B]don't have to　[C]must not　[D]need not

10. [A]notice　　　[B]information　　[C]note　　　　[D]news

11. [A]grow smaller　[B]disappear　[C]get bigger　[D]still increase

12. [A]develop　　[B]produce　　　[C]plant　　　　[D]grow

13. [A]filled　　　[B]polluted　　　[C]stopped　　　[D]blocked

14. [A]smell terrible　　　　　　[B]grow less wide
    [C]become shorter　　　　　[D]die

15. [A]help　　　　[B]do　　　　　[C]manage　　　[D]stop

16. [A]rise　　　　[B]keep to　　　[C]fall down　　[D]be limited

17. [A]valuable　　[B]enough　　　[C]much　　　　[D]good

18. [A]recycling　　　　　　　　[B]recycle
    [C]recycled　　　　　　　　[D]being recycled

19. [A]knowledge　[B]practice　　[C]importance　[D]cost

20. [A]city　　　　[B]country　　　[C]planet　　　　[D]ocean

答案与分析

1.[B]。考查名词词义与用法。由句意可知这里是指"今天的情况不同了"。situations 一般应与 the 连用才能指"情况"；affairs 指"事务"，多用于政治概念；matters 指"事情"，不用于指总体的情况。things 用于泛指"事情、情况"，符合题意。

2.[C]。考查形容词辨义与上下文理解。上文说过去地球上人很少，接着说情况不同了，这里说地球上变得____，无疑填入表示"拥挤"的形容词 crowded 最合逻辑。

3.[A]。考查固定搭配。use up 为固定搭配，指"用光、耗尽"。其余三项都不与 use 连用。

4.[B]。考查名词词义与上下文理解。由空格前的 polluting（污染）与表示手段的介词 with 及常识可知应填入 chemicals（化学品）。medicines（药品）、products（产品）和 elements（元素）都不合逻辑。

5.[C]。考查上下文理解。文章重点论述的是人类破坏环境带来的问题,而根据上下文可知这里应指"人类或者动物不能生存",而不会涉及到具体的鱼类或者鸟类。但 human life 这种用法很不常见,所以选 animals。

6.[C]。考查固定搭配与上下文理解。drive off 赶出,驱出;die from 死于,灭绝;take from 拿出;bring up 养育,提出。由主语 fish 及后一分句的意思可知选 taken from 最恰当,可译为"捕捞"。

7.[C]。考查固定搭配与上下文理解。由句意可看出,这里有与以前的情形进行比较之意,所以用 more and more(越来越多)。a good many 许多,大量;more or less 或多或少;a small number of 少量。

8.[D]。考查上下文理解与动词语态。set free 释放,放生;raise 养殖;这两者都可根据常识加以排除。而此处用的是 fish 作主语,动词 freeze 应用被动语态,所以答案是[D]。

9.[B]。考查情态动词的用法。have to 的否定形式是 don't have to。而 must not 表示的是"禁止",need not 表示"不必",但要用人作主语。

10.[B]。考查名词辨义与上下文理解。notice 通知,布告;information 信息,消息;note 笔记,注意;news 新闻。由空格后的介词结构及常识可知只有 information 能填入文中。

11.[B]。考查上下文理解。由上下文与常识可知,砍伐森林的结果当然是森林消失,选 disappear。而 grow smaller 指在规模、尺寸上的"变小"。

12.[D]。考查动词辨义。develop 发展,成长;produce 出产,生产;plant 种植(植物);grow 生长。由句意及句子主语 nothing 可知应选 grow。

13.[B]。考查上下文理解与动词辨义。由空格后的 with waste products 及常识可知应选 polluted(污染)。fill 注入;stop 停止;block 阻塞。

14.[D]。考查上下文理解。河流受到污染,鱼当然会死,选 die。其他三项:smell terrible 闻起来很臭;grow less wide 变得范围较窄;become shorter 变得更短。它们都不合常识。

15.[D]。考查上下文理解。空格后的 this 指代的是前面一个分句"in most countries ... into the sea"(大部分国家中的废弃物仍在排入河流或者海洋中)这一事实,再根据空格前的主语 laws(法律)与作者要表达的意思可知应选 stop。

16.[A]。考查动词辨义与上下文理解。作者要表达的是"人口按目前的速度继续增长",所以选 rise。而 keep to 指"保持",fall down 指"下降,下落",limit 指"限制"(其后应跟介词 to)。

17.[B]。考查上下文理解。首先可以排除[A]、[D]两项,它们与文意没有联系。而 enough 与 much 都能修饰 food,但 enough 更符合语境与习惯用法。

18.[B]。考查动词形式。由于 learn 后跟动词不定式，所以此处 to 是不定式符号，其后应为动词原形。

19.[C]。考查名词辨义与上下文理解。由句意可知，这里是指人们看到计划生育的重要性，所以选 importance。其他三项填入题中都造成文意不通。

20.[C]。考查上下文理解。由于文章中的 we 是不定指，指的是人类总体，而且对环境的保护不会只局限于一个城市（city）、一个国家（country）或者只是海洋（ocean），所以这里应选 planet（星球），指的就是地球。

　　过去地球上的人口少，自然资源似乎取之不竭。但如今情况不同了。世界变得太拥挤。我们正在过于快速地消耗掉我们的自然资源，同时还在用危险的化学品污染我们的环境。如果我们继续这样干，地球上的动物将无法生存。

　　如今每个人都认识到，如果过度捕捞海洋中的鱼类，海洋中很快就不会再有鱼类生存。然而，由于现代化的捕捞方式，越来越多的鱼被捕捞。人们在海上将鱼冷冻，这样渔船就不用带着捕获的鱼匆匆赶回去，就可以到更远的海洋去捕捞。我们甚至利用卫星来获取鱼群位置的信息。

　　我们知道，如果砍伐过多树木，森林将会消失，地上将没有东西可以生长。但是我们仍在用更强大、更有力的机器砍伐越来越多的树木。

　　我们认识到，如果河流被工厂排出的废弃物污染，鱼类将会死亡。然而，在大多数国家中废弃物仍在排入河流或者海洋中，而现在还几乎没有什么法律制止这种行为。

　　我们也知道，如果世界上的人口仍按照目前的速度增长，用不了多少年将没有充足的食物。如果我们学会循环利用，自然资源将会持续得更久。如果人们认识到计划生育的重要性，世界人口将不会增长得这么快。

　　最后，如果我们教育人们思考这个问题，将来我们就会拥有一个更好的、更清洁的星球。

　　Walking down the street the other day, I happened to notice a small purse. I took the purse to the ___1___ and handed it to the desk sergeant.

　　That evening I went to have dinner with my aunt and uncle. A young woman had also been __2__ so that there could be __3__ people __4__ table. Her face was familiar to __5__ , but I could not __6__ where and how I had seen her. In the course of conversation, however, the young woman __7__ to mention(提及) that she had lost a __8__ with some change and an __9__ photo, and that she had the photo __10__ in her childhood. I at once __11__ where I had seen her. She was the young girl in the photo, __12__ she was now much __13__ . She was very __14__ , of course, when I was able to tell her all about the purse. Then I __15__ that I had __16__ her from the photo I found in the purse. My uncle insisted __17__ going to the police station immediately __18__ the purse. As the police sergeant handed it __19__ , he said that it was all amazing coincidence(惊人的巧合) that I had not only __20__ the purse but also the person who had lost it.

1. [A]home   [B]school   [C]court   [D]police station
2. [A]told   [B]invited   [C]visited   [D]sent
3. [A]two   [B]three   [C]four   [D]five
4. [A]at   [B]by   [C]near   [D]beside
5. [A]me   [B]my uncle   [C]my aunt   [D]us
6. [A]find   [B]think   [C]remember   [D]forget
7. [A]began   [B]started   [C]had   [D]happened
8. [A]bag   [B]bookmark   [C]purse   [D]book
9. [A]old   [B]new   [C]good   [D]beautiful
10. [A]taken   [B]took   [C]taking   [D]take
11. [A]wondered   [B]thought   [C]recognized   [D]realized
12. [A]though   [B]while   [C]as   [D]and
13. [A]younger   [B]older   [C]thinner   [D]more beautiful
14. [A]surprised   [B]shocked   [C]worried   [D]disappointed
15. [A]ordered   [B]explained   [C]apologized   [D]told
16. [A]saw   [B]found   [C]knew   [D]recognized
17. [A]in   [B]on   [C]to   [D]with
18. [A]in search of   [B]for   [C]with   [D]because of
19. [A]in   [B]out   [C]up   [D]over

20. [A]found   [B]found out   [C]noticed   [D]picked up

 **答案与分析**

1.[D]。考查上下文理解。由空格后的 sergeant(警察小队长)及文章倒数第二句中明确出现的 police station 可知应选[D]。

2.[B]。考查动词辨义与上下文理解。tell 告诉;invite 邀请;visit 拜访;send 派遣。由前文中的 have dinner(吃饭)及 was 可知 invite 最合语境。

3.[C]。考查上下文理解。由前文的交代可知,吃饭的有作者、作者的叔叔夫妇及一位青女士,所以总共有 4 个人。

4.[A]。考查固定搭配。at table 为固定搭配,指"(坐在桌边)就餐"。其他三个介词在与 table 连用时都应有定冠词,且都没有"就餐"之意。

5.[A]。考查上下文理解。这里作者谈论的是自己的观察与经历,所以当然是说自己对那位年青女士感到面熟。be familiar to 为固定搭配,指"为…所熟悉"。

6.[C]。考查动词辨义与上下文理解。find 发现,找出;think 认为,考虑;remember 记得,记起;forget 忘记。由上下文文意可知这里是指作者想不起什么地方见过这位女士。

7.[D]。考查动词用法与上下文理解。四个选项都与动词不定式连用,但意思不同。begin/start to do 指"开始做";happen to do 指"碰巧做";have to do 指"不得不做"。由上下文可知,女士是无意中提起自己丢钱包的事。

8.[C]。考查上下文理解。由前文与后文尤其是后文的交代不难选出正确答案。

9.[A]。考查形容词与上下文理解。由空格前的 an 即可知只有 old 能填入题中,指"老照片"。

10.[A]。考查动词语态与习惯表达。have sth. done 是习惯表达,强调 sth. 是 do 的宾语,同时 do 表示的动作不是由主语完成,这里 done 是过去分词。照片是"被拍摄",所以用 taken。

11.[D]。考查动词辨义与上下文理解。wonder 担心,好奇;think 考虑,认为;recognize 认出;realize 意识到。由上下文文意可以看出,选 realize 最合题意。

12.[A]。考查连词与上下文联系。由句子关系进行分析,前后两句间有让步关系,即"尽管她现在年龄大得多了,但她就是照片上的那个年青女孩",故选 though。while 表同时;as 表因果;and 表并列。

13.[B]。考查上下文理解。由前文中的 younger 可知,这里是对女士的年龄进行比较，所以选 older。

14.[A]。考查形容词辨义与上下文理解。由后一分句再结合故事整体及常识可知，女士在听说作者捡了她的钱包后肯定会"惊讶"（surprised）。shocked 虽然也有"惊讶"义，但它指"震惊"，所指的惊讶程度比 surprised 大得多，用在本文这种场合有点太夸张，不合语境。worried 担心，焦急；disappointed 失望的，灰心的。

15.[B]。考查动词辨义与上下文理解。order 命令，订购，点（菜）；explain 解释，说明；apologize 道歉；tell 告诉（后面应跟 sb. 作间接宾语）。这里是指作者向女士解释。

16.[D]。考查动词辨义。由后文中的 from the photo 可知，作者的意思是说他从照片中认出了女士，故选 recognized。其余三项填入都不合逻辑。

17.[B]。考查动词固定搭配。insist（坚持）后跟 that 从句或者用固定搭配 insist on doing sth.。

18.[B]。考查介词。for 表目的，符合文意，即去警察局取回钱包。in search of 搜寻，寻找；because of 由于；with 表示手段或者伴随。

19.[D]。考查固定搭配。hand in 上交，提交；hand out 分发，散发；hand over 移交，交出。这里指警察将钱包移交给失主。hand 一般不与 up 连用。

20.[A]。考查动词辨义与上下文理解。find 找到，发现；find out 找出；notice 注意到；pick up 捡起。由上下文来看，这里指作者发现钱包最合逻辑。

同步译文

那天我在街上走时，偶然注意到了一个钱包。我把钱包送到了警察局，把它交给了值班的小队长。

那天晚上我和我叔叔、婶婶一起吃饭。他们还邀请了一位年青女士，所以一共有4个人吃饭。她的脸我看起来很熟悉，但我却记不起是在哪里和怎样见到她的。在交谈中，那位年青女士偶然说起她丢了一个钱包，里面有一些零钱和一张旧照片，那张照片是她在小时候照的。我立即意识到我是在哪里见到她的了。她就是那张照片上的小姑娘，尽管她现在年龄大多了。当然，我告诉她关于钱包的事后她很惊讶。然后我解释说我是根据在钱包中发现的照片认出了她。我叔叔坚持马上去警察局把钱包取回来。当那位警察小队长把钱包移交给那位女士时，他说我不仅发现了钱包，还找到了钱包的失主，这简直是惊人的巧合。

Exercise 4

Not too long ago, an incident that happened at Walt Disney touched me greatly. A guest __1__ out of our Polynesian Village *resort* (度假胜地) at Walt Disney was asked how she __2__ her visit. She told the front-desk clerk she had had a(n) __3__ vacation, but was heartbroken about __4__ several rolls of Kodak color film she had not yet __5__ . At that moment she was particularly __6__ over the loss of the pictures she had shot at our Polynesian Luau, __7__ this was a memory she especially treasured.

Now, please understand that we have no written service rules __8__ lost photos in the park. __9__ , the clerk at the front-desk __10__ Disney's idea of caring for our __11__ . She asked the woman to leave her a couple rolls of __12__ film, promising she would take care of the rest of our show at Polynesian Luau.

Two weeks later the guest received a __13__ at her home. In it were photos of all the actors of our show, __14__ signed by each performer. There were also __15__ of the public *procession* (游行队伍) and fireworks in the park, taken by the front-desk clerk in her own __16__ after work. I happened to know this __17__ because this guest wrote us a letter. She said that __18__ in her life had she received such good service from any business.

Excellent __19__ does not come from *policy* (政策) handbooks. It comes from people who __20__ — and from a culture that encourages and models that attitude.

1. [A]working　　[B]checking　　[C]trying　　[D]staying
2. [A]expected　　[B]realized　　[C]paid　　[D]enjoyed
3. [A]disappointing　　　　[B]wonderful
　　[C]uncomfortable　　　　[D]important
4. [A]taking　　[B]dropping　　[C]losing　　[D]breaking
5. [A]developed　　[B]taken　　[C]washed　　[D]loaded
6. [A]silly　　[B]nervous　　[C]calm　　[D]sad

7. [A]when [B]where [C]as [D]which
8. [A]covering [B]finding [C]making [D]keeping
9. [A]Excitedly [B]Fortunately [C]Therefore [D]Quietly
10. [A]understood [B]reminded [C]trusted [D]discovered
11. [A]workers [B]guests [C]managers [D]clerks
12. [A]printed [B]shot [C]unused [D]recorded
13. [A]film [B]card [C]camera [D]packet
14. [A]frequently [B]personally [C]alone [D]actually
15. [A]rules [B]pictures [C]handbooks [D]performances
16. [A]case [B]work [C]time [D]position
17. [A]story [B]place [C]photo [D]show
18. [A]only [B]almost [C]never [D]nearly
19. [A]advice [B]experience [C]quality [D]service
20. [A]care [B]serve [C]like [D]know

答案与分析

1.[B]。考查动词固定搭配与上下文理解。check out（of）为固定搭配，意为"（从…）结账离开"。其他三个动词都不合文意。

2.[D]。考查动词辨义与上下文理解。文章指出这位女士是度完假离开前被询问，所以肯定是问及对旅游的感想，故不能用 expect（期待）。而填入 realize（意识到）、pay（付款）在逻辑上也不通。enjoy 指"享受"，符合文意。

3.[B]。考查形容词辨义与上下文理解。由前后两句之间的转折关系可知，女士对自己的假期是肯定的，所以用 wonderful（精彩的，愉快的）。important（重要的）与文意没有联系。

4.[C]。考查上下文理解。由其前的 heartbroken（心碎的）可知女士的胶卷一定是有了不好的结果；再由下文的文意可以看出她是把胶卷丢了，故选 losing（丢失）。

5.[A]。考查动词辨义。develop 除一般用来指"发展"外，还指"冲洗（照片）、显影"。其余三项：take 用于照片时，指"拍摄"；wash 指"洗（衣服）"；load 指"装载"。它们填入题中都不合上下文逻辑。

6.[D]。考查上下文逻辑。此处是递进，表示女士对在 Polynesian Luau 拍摄的照片丢失尤其如何，所以选 sad（沮丧的）。silly 愚蠢的；nervous 紧张的；calm 平静的；它们都不符合女士此时的心情。

7.[C]。考查上下文关系。由逗号前后两分句的意思可知,"这是她特别珍视的记忆"明显是"她尤其对丢失在 Polynesian Luau 拍摄的照片感到沮丧"的原因,因此选引出原因的 as。其余三项表达的关系都不合逻辑。

8.[A]。考查动词辨义。cover 在此指"包括,涵盖",即服务规定中没有为丢失照片服务的内容。其余三项填入空中都不合逻辑。

9.[B]。考查副词辨义。前文说服务规定中没有为丢失照片服务的内容,这里说前台服务人员理解迪斯尼以顾客服务的理念,两者之间有轻微转折,所以选 fortunately(幸运的是)。其余三项:excitedly 兴奋地;therefore 因此;quietly 安静地,平静地。它们都不能用在此处。

10.[A]。考查动词辨义。understand 理解;remind 使记起;trust 信任;discover 发现。后面两项明显不能填入题中,而 remind 一般以物作主语,以人作宾语,也不合题意。

11.[B]。考查上下文理解。由于女士是迪斯尼的游客,所以这里肯定要用与 clerk 及 our 相对的 guests(顾客)。

12.[C]。考查形容词辨义与上下文理解。由下文可以看出,服务员是让女士留下一些空白胶卷,以代她拍摄照片,所以选 unused(没用过的)。printed 打印的;shot 拍摄的;recorded 记录的,录下的。

13.[D]。考查名词辨义与上下文理解。考生容易误选 film(胶片)。指"胶片"时,film 一般用作不可数名词,故肯定不能填入题中。而由下文可以看出,女士收到的是许多照片,所以当然用 packet(小包)。

14.[B]。考查副词辨义。由句意可知这里指照片由演员亲自签名,所以选 personally(亲自)。frequently 频繁地,经常地;alone 独自,单独地;actually 实际上,事实上。

15.[B]。考查上下文理解。由句中的 also 及后文中 taken by ... 结构可知指的仍是照片,故选 pictures。

16.[C]。考查上下文理解。由空格后的 after work(下班后)可知这里强调的是服务员牺牲自己的休息时间为那位女士拍照片,所以用 time。其余三项都与文意没有联系。

17.[A]。考查上下文理解。由空格后表原因的分句可知,作者在此表达的是"知道了这件事"的意思,所以用 story(故事)。

18.[C]。考查表达与上下文理解。由空格后分句用的是倒装(had she received ...)这一点可以看出,应填入一个否定副词,所以只能选 never。

19.[D]。考查上下文理解。作者在叙述时采用的是一人称,表明他/她是迪斯尼中的一员。而由后文的内容来看,他/她是在对自己公司的服务进行评价,所以应填入 service 一词。

　　20.[A]。考查动词用法与上下文理解。四个选项中只有 care 和 know 可用作不及物动词,而 know 用在此处文意不通。care 指"在意"。

　　不久以前,在沃尔特·迪斯尼乐园里发生的一件事极大地触动了我。一位在我们的波利尼西亚度假村结账即将离去的客人被问及她对游览的感觉。她告诉前台服务员说她的假期过得很愉快,但由于丢了几卷尚未冲洗的柯达彩色胶卷而特别失望。那时她对在我们波利尼西亚的鲁阿拍摄的照片丢失了而感到尤为沮丧,因为这是她特别珍视的一段记忆。

　　现在,请理解在我们乐园里没有涉及到照片丢失的书面服务规定。幸运的是,前台的那位服务员理解迪斯尼客户至上的理念。她让那位女士留下一些未用过的胶卷,答应她会留意我们在波利尼西亚的鲁阿的其他演出。

　　两周后那位客人在家里收到了一个包裹。包裹里是我们演出的所有演员亲自签名的照片。还有乐园中的群众游行与焰火表演的照片,都是由那位前台服务员在下班后用自己的时间拍摄的。我碰巧得知了这件事,因为那位客人给我们写了一封信。她说她一生中从未在别的企业受到过如此好的服务。

　　良好的服务并非来自政策性的手册,而是来自那些细心的人,以及鼓励与倡导这种态度的文化。

 Exercise 5

　　You are near the front line of a battle. Around you shells are exploding; people are shooting from a house behind you. What are you doing there? You aren't a soldier. You aren't ___1___ carrying a gun. You're standing in front of a ___2___ and you're telling the TV ___3___ what is happening.

　　It's all in a day's work for a war reporter, and it can be very ___4___. In the first two years of the ___5___ in *former Yugoslavia*(前南斯拉夫), 28 reporters and photographers were killed. Hundreds more were ___6___. What kind of people put themselves in danger to ___7___ pictures to our TV screens and ___8___ to our newspapers? Why do they do it?

"I think it's every young journalist's __9__ to be a foreign reporter," says Michael Nicholson, "that's __10__ you find the excitement. So when the first opportunity comes, you take it __11__ it is a war."

But there are moments of __12__ . Jeremy Bowen says, "Yes, when you're lying on the ground and *bullets*（子弹） are flying __13__ your ears, you think:'What am I doing here? I'm not going to do this again.'But that feeling __14__ after a while and when the next war starts, you'll be __15__ ."

"None of us believes that we're going to __16__ ,"adds Michael. But he always __17__ a lucky *charm*（护身符） with him. It was given to him by his wife for his first war. It's a card which says "Take care of yourself". Does he ever think about dying? "Oh, __18__ , and every time it happens you look to the sky and say to God,'If you get me out of this, I __19__ I'll never do it again.'You can almost hear God __20__ , because you know he doesn't believe you."

1. [A]simply　　[B]really　　[C]merely　　[D]even
2. [A]crowd　　[B]house　　[C]battlefield　　[D]camera
3. [A]producers　　[B]viewers　　[C]directors　　[D]actors
4. [A]dangerous　　[B]exciting　　[C]normal　　[D]disappointing
5. [A]stay　　[B]fight　　[C]war　　[D]life
6. [A]injured　　[B]buried　　[C]defeated　　[D]saved
7. [A]bring　　[B]give　　[C]take　　[D]make
8. [A]scenes　　[B]texts ·　　[C]stories　　[D]contents
9. [A]belief　　[B]dream　　[C]duty　　[D]faith
10. [A]why　　[B]what　　[C]how　　[D]where
11. [A]even so　　[B]ever since　　[C]as if　　[D]even if
12. [A]fear　　[B]surprise　　[C]shame　　[D]sadness
13. [A]into　　[B]around　　[C]past　　[D]through
14. [A]returns　　[B]goes　　[C]continues　　[D]occurs
15. [A]there　　[B]away　　[C]out　　[D]home
16. [A]leave　　[B]escape　　[C]die　　[D]remain
17. [A]hangs　　[B]wears　　[C]holds　　[D]carries
18. [A]never　　[B]many times　　[C]some time　　[D]seldom

19. [A]consider   [B]accept   [C]promise   [D]guess

20. [A]whispering   [B]laughing   [C]screaming   [D]crying

😃 答案与分析

1. [D]。考查上下文联系。空格所在句是完整的,由它与上一句意思之间的关系来看,它们之间应是递进关系,用 even 表否定强调递进,指"甚至"。

2. [D]。考查名词辨义与上下文理解。由后一分句的意思(告诉电视观众所发生的事)可知这里指记者站在摄像机的镜头前,故选 camera。其余三项都不合逻辑:crowd 人群;house 房屋;battlefield 战场。

3. [B]。考查名词辨义与上下文理解。参见上题解析。由后文可知这里描述的是战地记者的工作,所以当然是将战争形势告诉电视观众。producer 生产者,制片人;viewer 观看者,观众;director 指导者,导演;actor 演员。

4. [A]。考查形容词辨义与上下文理解。由下文的内容可以看出,这里是说战地记者的工作很危险(dangerous),而不是说很"令人激动"(exciting)、"正常的"(normal)或者"令人失望的"(disappointing)。

5. [C]。考查上下文理解。由前文的 a war reporter 与后文中的 were killed、全文内容及常识可知这里指前南斯拉夫战争中的伤亡情况,故选 war。stay 与 life 明显不对,fight 指个人之间的"打斗"或者小规模的"战斗"。

6. [A]。考查动词辨义与上下文理解。injure 伤害;bury 埋葬;defeat 打败;save 挽救。由前一句中的 killed 及本句中的 more 可知这里是对前南斯拉夫战争中战地记者的伤、亡两种人数进行比较。

7. [A]。考查动词搭配。bring sth. to 为固定搭配,指"为…带来某物"。give 后一般跟 to sb.;take sth. to 指"将某物带去…",且强调随身携带;make 后不跟介词 to。此处 take 不指"拍摄",否则会让 and 后的搭配不对。

8. [C]。考查名词辨义与上下文理解。由空格前与此并列的成分中 pictures(图片)与 TV screens(电视荧屏)之间的对应关系可知,与 newspaper 相对应的应当是 stories(故事),不可能是"场景"(scenes)、"文本,课文"(texts)或者"目录"(contents)。

9. [B]。考查名词辨义与上下文理解。belief 信念,信仰;dream 梦想;duty 义务,职责;faith 信念,信仰。由下文可知,这里说"成为国外记者"是每个记者的"梦想"最合逻辑。

10. [D]。考查连接词。由句子结构可知,从句主谓完整,所以应填入一个连接副词。而 that 指代的是前面一句话 it's every ... a foreign reporter,所以选 where,意为"那是你找到激情的地方"。

11.[D]。考查固定搭配辨义与句子结构。由句意可以看出,it is a war 与空格前的分句之间为让步关系,所以选 even if(即使)。even so 即便这样(它是副词词组,不引导从句);ever since 从…以后一直;as if 似乎。

12.[A]。考查名词辨义与上下文理解。由下文的描述可知这一段谈及的主要是记者在战场上遇到危险时的"害怕"(fear)心理。

13.[C]。考查介词与上下文理解。past 指"(从旁边)经过",符合文意。into 与 through 都含"在内部"义;around 指"围绕";它们明显都不合此处文意。

14.[B]。考查动词辨义与上下文理解。由 but 所表示的转折关系可知此处应当是指前文中所说的想法消失或者没有了,所以选 goes。其他三项填入都不合逻辑。

15.[A]。考查上下文理解。同样,由 but 可知这里应当是指下一次战争发生时记者仍会去战场才合逻辑,故用 there 代替上文中的 here。其余三项:be away 离去;be out 不在家,出去了;be home 在家。

16.[C]。考查动词辨义与上下文理解。由下一句中提到的护身符及后文中的 think about dying 可知应选 die。

17.[D]。考查固定搭配。能与空格后的介词 with 搭配的是 carry,指"随身携带"。注意不能用表"佩戴,穿戴"的 wear。

18.[B]。考查上下文理解。由下面几句描述说话者心理活动的话可知,说话者肯定不止一次想到过死。这一点也可由常识得知。

19.[C]。考查动词辨义与上下文理解。consider 考虑,认为;accept 接受;promise 保证,承诺;guess 猜测。由于空格所在的这句话是向上帝(God)说的,所以肯定只能用 promise,才能使句意符合逻辑。

20.[B]。考查动词辨义与上下文理解。由后面表示原因的分句的句意可知应选 laughing(笑)。其余三个动词都与后一分句形不成合理的因果关系。

你处在战斗的前沿阵地附近。你的周围炮弹在爆炸;你身后的人躲在房屋后面射击。你在那里干什么?你并非士兵。你甚至没有带枪。你正站在摄像机前,告诉电视观众所发生的事情。

这就是一名战地记者一天的生活,有时会很危险。在前南(斯拉夫)战争的前两年中,有28名记者与摄影师丧生,更有成百上千的记者和摄影师受伤。哪种人会为了把战争的图像带给电视荧屏、把关于战争的故事带给报纸而将他们自己置于危险之中?他们为什么那样做?

"我认为能够到国外去采访是每个年轻记者的梦想,"米切尔·尼古尔逊说,"那是你找到激情的地方。因此当第一次机会降临时,即便是一场战争你也会抓住它。"

但也有害怕的时候。杰瑞米·波文说:"对,当你躺在地上,子弹从你耳边飞过时,你会想:'我在这里干什么?我再也不干这个了。'但一会儿这种想法就消失了,而当下一次战争爆发时,你还会去那里。"

"我们没有人认为自己会死,"米切尔补充说。但他总是随身带着一张护身符。那是他妻子在他第一次战争采访时给他的。那是一张卡片,上面写着:"照顾好自己"。他曾经想过死吗?"噢,想过许多次,每次想到死亡时你都会仰头望天,对上帝说:'如果你让我这次活着挺过来,我保证永远不再干这个了。'你几乎可以听得见上帝在笑,因为你知道上帝不会相信你。"

- -

Exercise 6

When Phillip was on his way to the airport one afternoon, he asked the driver to wait outside the bank while he collected some traveler's checks.

The plane was to __1__ at 5:30. From the bank there was still a __2__ journey to the airport. Phillip __3__ watched the scene along the way. Shortly before arriving, he began __4__ the things he would need for the __5__. Tickets, money, the address of his hotel, traveler's checks ... Just a moment. How about his passport? Phillip went through his pockets. He suddenly __6__ that he must have left his passport __7__.

Whatever could he do? It was now five past four and there would be too little __8__ to return to the bank. This was the __9__ time he was *representing*(代表) his firm for an important __10__ with the manager of a French firm in Paris the following morning. Without a passport he would be __11__ to board the plane. At that moment, the taxi __12__ outside the air terminal. Phillip got out, took his suitcase and

___13___ the driver. He then ___14___ a good deal of *confusion*(混乱) in the building. A ___15___ could be heard over the loudspeaker.

"We very much ___16___ that owing to a twenty-four-hour strike of airport staff, all flights for the rest of today have had to be called off. Passengers are ___17___ to get in touch with their travel agents or with this terminal for ___18___ on tomorrow's flights."

Phillip gave ___19___ . He would let his firm know about this situation and, thank goodness, he would have the opportunity of calling at his bank the following morning to ___20___ his passport.

1. [A]leave   [B]start off   [C]check in   [D]fly
2. [A]pleasant   [B]short   [C]long   [D]rough
3. [A]carefully [B]merely   [C]excitedly   [D]slightly
4. [A]counting   [B]looking over
   [C]thinking about   [D]checking
5. [A]trip   [B]plane   [C]meeting   [D]flight
6. [A]remembered [B]realized   [C]noticed   [D]learned
7. [A]at home   [B]at the office
   [C]at the bank   [D]in the taxi
8. [A]time   [B]chance   [C]possibility   [D]use
9. [A]golden   [B]last   [C]only   [D]first
10. [A]journey   [B]meeting   [C]business   [D]visit
11. [A]sad   [B]unable   [C]impossible   [D]difficult
12. [A]stopped   [B]was driven   [C]reached   [D]was parked
13. [A]left   [B]sent away
    [C]paid   [D]said bye-bye to
14. [A]started   [B]noticed   [C]caught   [D]found
15. [A]voice   [B]noise   [C]call   [D]speech
16. [A]apologize [B]announce   [C]worry   [D]regret
17. [A]advised   [B]forced   [C]told   [D]persuaded
18. [A]ideas   [B]information   [C]plans   [D]time
19. [A]a loud laugh   [B]a deep sigh
    [C]a big smile   [D]a sharp cry
20. [A]return   [B]find   [C]recover   [D]gather

**答案与分析**

1.[A]。考查动词(短语)辨义与上下文理解。由上下文不难看出,这里是指飞机的起飞时间,空格前的 was to 表示将来,所以选 leave(离开)。start off 开始(它一般用人作主语);check in 登记入住;fly 飞行,飞翔,开飞机。

2.[C]。考查上下文理解。由空格前的副词 still(仍然,还有)可知应选 long(远的),否则不合逻辑。

3.[B]。考查副词与上下文理解。carefully 仔细地;merely 仅仅,只是;excitedly 兴奋地,激动地;slightly 稍微,有点。从意思上来说[B]、[C]两项都可,但后者一般放在句首或句末,不放在谓语动词前。

4.[D]。考查动词(短语)辨义与上下文理解。由上下文可知,这里应当指他开始检查或者清点他必须带的东西,所以选 check(检查)。count 点(数),数;look over 浏览;think about 考虑,思索。

5.[A]。考查名词辨义与上下文理解。由后文所列的东西可以看出,他检查的是整个旅行(trip)所需的东西,而不仅仅是会议(meeting)或者这次飞行(flight)所需的东西。

6.[B]。考查动词辨义与上下文理解。remember 记起,记得;realize 意识到;notice 注意到;learn 学会,得知。由空格前的 suddenly 及上下文可知,他"意识到"自己把护照放在了银行最合逻辑。

7.[C]。考查上下文理解。由文章最后一句可知他是把护照落在了银行里。

8.[A]。考查上下文理解。由本句中前一个分句(It was now five past four)可知这里是强调时间紧,他没有时间(time)而不是没有机会(chance)、可能性(possibility)或者用处(use)再回银行去取护照。

9.[D]。考查形容词辨义与上下文理解。由上下文描述的内容可知,这里应当是指他第一次代表公司去参加一个重要会议,所以他才会如此紧张。

10.[B]。考查名词辨义与上下文理解。由空格后面 with 引导的介词结构可知应当选含有两方的 meeting。

11.[B]。考查形容词用法。四个选项中能用人作主语的是 sad 和 unable,但 sad(悲伤的,沮丧的)无疑不能用在此处。

12.[A]。考查动词用法。stop 停下,停止;reach 到达(它是及物动词,后面应跟宾语);而[B]、[D]两项语态都不正确。

13.[C]。考查动词辨义与上下文理解。leave 离开;send away 送走,送往;pay 付(钱)给;say bye-bye to 向…道别。由常识与上下文可知,除了 pay 外其余三项都不恰当。

14.[B]。考查动词辨义与上下文理解。start 开始;notice 注意到;catch 抓住,患上;find 找出,发现。由上下文不难看出,这里指他注意到机场大楼里一片混乱。

15.[A]。考查名词辨义。voice 专用于指人的嗓音,符合题意。noise 指"噪音";call 指"呼叫,电话";speech 指正式的、面对数量较多的观众的"讲话,演讲"。它们肯定不能用来指扬声器里传出的人说话的声音。

16.[D]。考查动词辨义与用法。首先,apologize(道歉)与 announce(宣布)不与 very much 连用。其次,由后文的意思可以看出,罢工已经发生,所以说话者不会是很"担心"(worry),而应是很"抱歉,遗憾"(regret)。

17.[A]。考查动词辨义与上下文理解。advise 建议;force 强迫;tell 告诉;persuade 劝说。由上下文文意与常识来看,机场方面只能是礼貌地"建议"乘客如何做。

18.[B]。考查名词搭配。四个选项中,与介词 on 搭配的是 information (信息),指"关于…的信息"。

19.[B]。考查上下文理解。由上下文可以看出,主人公在得知航班取消后肯定会"松一口气",所以选 a deep sigh。其余三项:a loud laugh 大笑一声;a big smile 咧嘴大笑;a sharp cry 尖叫一声。前面两个虽然看似可以填入题中,但没有 a deep sigh 那样符合上下文语境。

20.[C]。考查动词辨义。return 归还,返回;find 找到,发现;recover 康复,找回;gather 收集,聚集。由上下文可知这里指他去银行找回自己的护照,所以无疑只能用 recover。

同步译文

　　一天下午,菲利浦在去往机场的路上,让司机在银行门外等他,他去领取旅行支票。

　　飞机5:30起飞。从银行到机场还有很远的路。在路上菲利浦只是看着一路的景色。到达机场前不久,他才开始检查自己这次旅行所需的东西。机票,钱,旅馆的地址,旅行支票……等一等。他的护照去哪儿了?菲利浦找遍了自己的口袋。他突然意识到自己一定是把护照落在银行了。

　　他怎么办?现在已经4点过5分了,没有时间再回银行。这是他第一次代表公司去与巴黎的一家法国公司的经理在第二天上午会晤。没有护照他上不了飞机。就在那时，出租车停在了机场候机楼外。菲利浦下了车，拿起自己的手提箱，付了司机钱。然后他看到候机楼里一片混乱。机场广播里能听到一个声音在说：

"很抱歉，由于机场员工的一次24小时罢工，今天剩下的所有航班都只能取消。我们建议旅客们与自己的旅行社或者与本机场联系，以获得明天的航班信息。"

菲利浦长吁了一口气。他会告知公司这一情况，并且——谢天谢地——他能在明天上午去银行找回自己的护照了。

Exercise 7

Gus put his *paws*（爪子）on the window and looked out at the street. His tail began to *wag*（摇摆）when Mr and Mrs Riaz were coming back __1__.

They were __2__ in something new — a __3__. "__4__, this is Anna," said Mrs Riaz. Gus wasn't __5__ if he liked Anna.

Mr and Mrs Riaz spent a lot of time with __6__. Gus watched while they held the baby. He watched them __7__ her and talk to her. "Why __8__ they talk to me like that?" He __9__ to say. Mr Riaz made Gus feel __10__, too. He said: "Gus, you watch the baby __11__ we're in the other room." Gus liked that. He sat __12__ Anna's bed. He watched her __13__ and play. As time went by, Gus became very __14__ of the baby. When visitors came to the house, Gus would __15__ to the baby's bed. He would sit up very __16__ and wag his tail quickly. "See how __17__ I take care of Anna," he seemed to say.

There was one thing about Anna that made Gus __18__. He __19__ like to hear her cry. He always wanted to make her __20__ better.

1. [A]out   [B]home   [C]away   [D]close
2. [A]taking   [B]fetching   [C]bringing   [D]leading
3. [A]god   [B]cat   [C]baby   [D]friend
4. [A]Gus   [B]OK   [C]Hello   [D]Morning

5. [A]sure   [B]true   [C]clear   [D]happy
6. [A]him   [B]her   [C]baby   [D]dog
7. [A]save   [B]beat   [C]feed   [D]help
8. [A]do   [B]don't   [C]will   [D]won't
9. [A]tended   [B]wanted   [C]hoped   [D]seemed
10. [A]important   [B]impossible   [C]easy   [D]difficult
11. [A]before   [B]after   [C]while   [D]as
12. [A]on   [B]by   [C]against   [D]in
13. [A]cry   [B]jump   [C]sleep   [D]run
14. [A]proud   [B]nervous   [C]sad   [D]nice
15. [A]walk   [B]run   [C]climb   [D]lit
16. [A]carefully   [B]angrily   [C]sadly   [D]straight
17. [A]nice   [B]well   [C]important   [D]hard
18. [A]unhappy   [B]happy   [C]glad   [D]pleasant
19. [A]did   [B]didn't   [C]would   [D]wouldn't
20. [A]get   [B]become   [C]sound   [D]feel

答案与分析

1.[B]。考查副词与固定搭配。come back home 是固定搭配，指"回到家里"。其余三项都不与 back 连用。

2.[C]。考查动词辨义。take 将东西从说话处带到别的地方；fetch 指去别的地方把东西拿来或者找来；bring 将东西从别的地方带到说话处来；lead 指"带领，领导"。由于此处的立足点是 Gus，所以应用 bring。

3.[C]。考查上下文理解。由下文可以看出，Riaz 夫妇带回来的是一个婴儿（baby）而不是别的东西。

4.[A]。考查表达。文章是以拟人化手法，从 Gus 的角度进行叙述，这里是 Riaz 夫人告诉 Gus 婴儿的名字，而由下文可知 Gus 是一只狗，所以这里应当直呼 Gus 的名字。

5.[A]。考查形容词与表达。由后面的 if 从句可知应选 sure，即 Gus 不知道自己喜不喜欢那名婴儿。

6.[B]。考查代词与上下文理解。由上下文可知，这里是指 Riaz 夫妇总是与婴儿在一起，而 Anna 是女孩名，所以相应的代词宾格是 her。注意，如果用 baby，则应在其前加定冠词，因为前面已经提到过 baby 这个词，此处应为定指。

7. [C]。考查上下文理解。四个选项中与婴儿有关的动词只有 feed,指给婴儿喂食。

8. [B]。考查上下文理解。这里的 He 指代的是 Gus,表明这是 Gus 的想法。由上下文可以看出,Riaz 夫妇肯定不会像对待婴儿那样对待一条狗,所以 Gus 才会那样问,因此要选否定式助动词。注意这里表示的是一般性情况,不用表将来的 won't。

9. [D]。考查动词辨义与上下文理解。由于主语 He 指代 Gus 这条狗,所以用 seemed,指"似乎",因为狗是不会说话的。其余三项:tend 企图,打算;want 想要;hope 希望。

10. [A]。考查形容词与上下文理解。由空格所在句后面两句的意思特别是 Gus liked that 一句可知 Riaz 给它的是一种正面的、好的感觉,所以选important(重要的)。

11. [C]。考查连词与句子结构。由句子结构可以看出,空格后的部分是一个时间状语从句,而前后两个动作(watch the baby 和 we're in ...)是同时发生的,所以选 while。before 和 after 都不合逻辑;as 作连词时一般用于引出原因状语从句。

12. [B]。考查介词与上下文理解。由常识与后面一句的意思可知这里是指 Gus 坐在婴儿的床边,故用 by。其他三个介词填入都不合逻辑。

13. [C]。考查动词与上下文理解。由后面的 and play 可知应当选 sleep,表示婴儿睡觉和醒着玩两种普通的状态。婴儿肯定不能 jump(跳)或者 run(跑),也不可能老是哭(cry)。

14. [A]。考查固定搭配。be proud of 指"对…感到骄傲"。nervous 后一般用介词 about,而 sad 与 nice 后多用介词 to。

15. [B]。考查动词辨义与上下文理解。walk 一般用于指人;run 和 climb 可用于指动物,但 climb(爬)速度较慢,体现不出 Gus 的心情。lit 是 light(点火)的过去式,明显不对。

16. [D]。考查副词辨义。由于修饰的是动词 sit up(坐起来),所以应用 straight,指"坐得笔直"。其余三项都是用来修饰整个句子的,在意思上都不合逻辑。

17. [B]。考查副词。由句子结构分析,填入的词应当修饰动词 take care of,故应填入一个副词。而选项中除 well 可作副词外,其余三项都是形容词。

18. [A]。考查形容词与上下文理解。由后面两句的意思可以看出,这里是指婴儿给 Gus 的一种不好的感觉,故应选含有否定义的 unhappy。

19.[B]。考查上下文理解。由上一题分析可知,婴儿哭给 Gus 的是一种不好的感觉,那么它肯定是不喜欢听到,故应用助动词的否定式。而 wouldn't 表示将来,不合文章时态。

20.[D]。考查系动词辨义与上下文理解。get/become better 指"好起来,变得更好";sound better 指"听起来更好";feel better 指"觉得好一点,觉得舒服些"。由上下文可知用 feel 最恰当。

同步译文

　　Gus 把爪子趴在窗户上,向街上望去。当瑞亚兹先生和夫人回家时,它的尾巴开始摇动。

　　他们带回了新东西——一个宝宝。"Gus,这是安娜,"瑞亚兹夫人说。Gus 不知道自己喜不喜欢安娜。

　　瑞亚兹先生和夫人总是和宝宝在一起。他们侍弄宝宝时,Gus 就在一旁看着。它看着他给她喂食,和她说话。"他们为什么不那样跟我说话呢?"它似乎在说。瑞亚兹先生也让 Gus 觉得自己很重要。他说:"Gus,我们在别的房间里时你看着宝宝。"Gus 喜欢那样。它坐在安娜的床边,看着她睡觉和玩耍。随着时间流逝,Gus 越来越为宝宝感到骄傲。当有客人来家里时,Gus 会跑到宝宝床边。它会坐得笔直,尾巴摇得飞快。"瞧我把宝宝照顾得多好,"它似乎在说。

　　安娜有一件事让 Gus 觉得不高兴。它不喜欢听到她哭。它总是想让她觉得舒服一点。

Exercise 8

　　Last evening I was watching the evening news on television. The news was about a prize for scientific ___1___. I forgot what it was. The announcer, whose name was Ralph Story, said something that caught my ___2___. "All great discoveries," he said, "are made by people between the ages of twenty-five and thirty." ___3___ a little over thirty myself, I wanted to disagree with him. ___4___ wants to think that he is past the age of making any discovery. The next day I happened to be in the public library and spent several hours looking up the ___5___ of famous people and their discoveries. Ralph was right.

　　First I looked at some of the ___6___ discoveries. One of the earliest discoveries, the famous experiment that proved that bodies of different   7   fall at the same speed, was made by Galileo when he was 26. Madam Curie started her search that   8   to Nobel Prize when she was 28. Einstein was 26 when he published his world-changing theory of relativity. Well,   9   of that. Yet I   10   if those "best years" were true in other   11   .

Then how about the field of   12   ? Surely it needs the wisdom of age to make a good leader. Perhaps it   13   , but look when these people   14   their career. Winston Churchill was elected to the House of Commons at the age of 26. Abraham Lincoln   15   the life of a country lawyer and was elected to the government at what age? Twenty-six.

But why   16   best years come after thirty? After thirty, I   17   , most people do not want to take risks or try   18   ways. Then I thought of people like Shakespeare and Picasso. The former was writing wonderful works at the ripe age of fifty, while the latter was   19   trying new ways of painting when he was ninety!

Perhaps there is still   20   for me.

1. [A]invention   [B]discovery   [C]experiment   [D]progress
2. [A]mind   [B]idea   [C]attention   [D]thought
3. [A]As   [B]Being   [C]However   [D]Beyond
4. [A]Everybody   [B]Somebody   [C]Nobody   [D]Whoever
5. [A]names   [B]ages   [C]addresses   [D]education
6. [A]modern   [B]scientific   [C]last   [D]oldest
7. [A]heights   [B]sizes   [C]weights   [D]things
8. [A]led   [B]meant   [C]stuck   [D]referred
9. [A]plenty   [B]enough   [C]much   [D]none
10. [A]believed   [B]trusted   [C]wondered   [D]asked
11. [A]fields   [B]countries   [C]courses   [D]ages
12. [A]agriculture [B]politics   [C]industry   [D]society
13. [A]is   [B]will   [C]has   [D]does
14. [A]finished   [B]went   [C]started   [D]failed
15. [A]devoted   [B]gave up   [C]began   [D]led

16. [A]don't　　　[B]the　　　　[C]can　　　　[D]not
17. [A]believe　　[B]know　　　[C]guess　　　[D]agree
18. [A]other　　　[B]new　　　　[C]best　　　　[D]their
19. [A]always　　[B]still　　　　[C]seldom　　[D]enjoying
20. [A]discovery　[B]problem　[C]wish　　　[D]hope

答案与分析

1.[B]。考查名词辨义与上下文理解。由后文可以看出,文章谈论的主要是科学家做出科学发现的年龄阶段,所以作为话题引入句,肯定谈及的也是科学发现的问题,且紧跟本句的后一句中出现了 discoveries 一词,故选 discovery。其余三项:invention 发明;experiment 实验;progress 进步。它们都与文章主旨无关。

2.[C]。考查固定搭配。catch one's attention 指"吸引某人的注意力,引起某人注意"。其余三项都不用在 catch 后。

3.[B]。考查句子结构。由句子结构及四个选项可以看出,由于空格所在的部分缺少主语,所以只能是分词独立结构作状语,不能用连接词。

4.[C]。考查代词与上下文理解。由前文中的 disagree(不同意)可知,作者在此要表达的是"没有人会愿意认为自己已经过了做出发现的年龄",所以应选否定的不定代词 nobody。其余三项都含肯定义。

5.[B]。考查上下文理解。由前文的内容可以看出,作者不同意的是科学家做出科学发现的年龄,因此他去查阅以证明自己观点的东西也应当是年龄和发现两个方面之间的对应情况。空格后提到了 discoveries,那么空格处就应是对应的"年龄"(ages),而不会是"名字"(names)、"地址"(addresses)或者"教育程度"(education)。

6.[B]。考查形容词与上下文理解。由此处的 First 及下面一段第一句中的 Then 可知作者谈及的是两个方面;而由本段的内容可以看出,这一段说的应是科学发现,故选 scientific。其余三项都是从发现距今的时间方面来说的,与段落主旨无关。

7.[C]。考查上下文理解。由上下文及常识可知这里说明的是伽利略的自由落体理论这一发现。该理论是说不同重量的物体下落的速度一样,所以用 weight。其余三项填入都不合逻辑。

8.[A]。考查固定搭配辨义。lead to 导致,通向;mean to(do)意味着,打算(做);stick to 坚持;refer to 参考,指的是。这里指居里夫人的研究获得了诺贝尔奖，故用 lead。

9.[B]。考查上下文理解与表达。这里是省略句。由作者使用的语气词 well 可知，作者认为有这几个例子就可以了，不用列出更多的例子，故选 e-nough。而[A]、[C]两项都指"许多"，尽管意思上可能合乎逻辑，但用法不对。plenty 前应有 a，而 much 用于指不可数名词。

10.[C]。由 yet 表达的转折关系及空格后的 if 从句可知作者的意思是对在其他领域里的科学发现是否有最好的年龄段提出疑问，故选 wonder(想知道，好奇)。

11.[A]。考查上下文理解。参见上题解析。countries(国家)、courses (课程)及 ages(年代，年龄)都与上下文构不成合乎逻辑的顺承关系，且下一段第一句就明确提到了 field 一词。fields 在此指"领域"。

12.[B]。考查上下文理解。由这一段下面的内容可以看出，论述的是一些政治家的情况，所以这里要选 politics(政治)。agriculture 农业；industry 工业；society 社会。

13.[D]。考查助动词。关键是理解此处助动词代替的是上文中的 needs 一词，所以用 does。其他几个动词填入都不合逻辑。

14.[C]。考查动词与上下文理解。由前文中的 make a good leader(成为一名好的领导者)及后文所举的两个例子可以看出，作者要表达的是这些人开始政治生涯的时间，所以用 start，而不是 finish(结束)或者 fail(失败)。

15.[B]。考查动词辨义与上下文理解。由这一句中 and 后的分句可以看出，林肯从政后肯定不能再做乡村律师，所以应选 give up(放弃)。其他三项都不合文意：devote(奉献)后应跟介词 to；begin 指"开始"，与句意矛盾；lead (领导，引领)后也应跟 to。

16.[A]。考查表达。疑问句中谓语动词用的是原形，那么缺少的是一个助动词或者情态动词。而由文意可知，文章的观点是 30 岁以后不是科学发现的最好年龄，所以应用否定形式。符合这两个方面的只有[A]。

17.[C]。考查表达与上下文理解。空格所在句是一个插入语，而由文意来看，对于 30 岁后的人为何做不出重要的科学发现只是作者的一种猜测，所以选 guess(猜想)最恰当。

18.[B]。考查上下文理解。由文意特别是后文中出现的 trying new ways 可知这里也应选 new，指"尝试新的方法"。other 指"其他的"，best 指"最好的"，但这里并没有对一些方式进行比较或者分别说明；their 则明显不合句意。

19.[B]。考查上下文理解。seldom 和 enjoying 明显不合文意，可以排除。而 still 指"仍然",含有与通常情况不一样之意;always 指"总是、一直",含有说话者不赞成的否定义,且与后面的时间状语不符。所以应选[B]。

20.[D]。考查一致性与上下文理解。由谓语 is 及空格前无不定冠词可知应填入一个不可数名词。而前面三个选项都是可数名词,只有 hope 为不可数名词,所以答案就是它,指"我还有(做出发现的)希望"。

昨天晚上我在看电视上的新闻节目。那是关于一项科学发现奖的新闻。我不记得名字叫什么了。那位名叫拉尔夫·斯托瑞的主持人说了些吸引了我的注意力的话。"所有伟大的发现,"他说,"都是人们在 25 岁至 30 岁之间时做出的。"我自己已经 30 岁多一点了,想对他的观点表示点不同意见。没有人愿意认为自己已经过了做出发现的年龄。第二天我碰巧去公立图书馆,就花了好几个小时查阅那些名人的年龄与他们做出的发现。拉尔夫是对的。

首先我看了一些科学发现。最早的发现之一,那个证明不同重量的物体下落速度相同的著名实验,是由伽利略在他 26 岁时做出的。居里夫人在 28 岁时开始进行那项让她获得诺贝尔奖的研究。爱因斯坦发表他那改变世界的相对论时是 26 岁。好,这些例子已经足够了。然而我想知道在其他领域里那些"最佳年龄"是否也是这样。

那么,政治学领域里是什么样子呢?成为一名好的领导者肯定需要岁月积淀下来的智慧。也许的确需要,但是看看这些人是什么时候开始他们的政治生涯的。温斯顿·丘吉尔在 26 岁时被选入下议院。亚伯拉罕·林肯放弃自己的乡村律师职业、被选入政府是在什么年龄? 26 岁。

但是为什么最佳年龄不是出现在 30 岁以后呢?我猜想,30 岁以后大多数人都不想冒险或者尝试新的方法。然后我想起了莎士比亚和毕加索这样的人。前者在 50 岁这种成熟的年龄时还在写精彩的著作,而后者在 90 岁时还在尝试新的画法!

也许我还有希望。

Exercise 9

On May 27, 1995, our life was suddenly changed. It happened a few minutes past three, __1__ my husband, Chris, fell from his horse as it __2__ over a fence. Chris was *paralyzed*(瘫痪) from the chest down， __3__ to breathe normally. As he was thrown from his horse，we entered into a life of __4__ with lots of unexpected challenges. We went from the "haves" to the "have-nots". Or so we thought.

__5__ what we discovered later were all the gifts that came out of __6__ difficulties. We came to learn that something __7__ could happen in a disaster. All over the world people __8__ Chris so much that letters and postcards poured in every day. By the end of the third week in a __9__ center in Virginia，about 35 000 pieces of __10__ had been received and sorted.

As __11__ ，we opened letter after letter. They gave us __12__ and became a source of strength for us. We used them to __13__ ourselves. I would go to the pile of letters marked with "Funny" if we needed a __14__ ，or to the "Disabled" box to find advice from people in wheelchairs or __15__ in bed living happily and __16__ .

These letters，we realized，had to be shared. And so __17__ we offer one of them to you.

Dear Chris，

My husband and I were so sorry to hear of your __18__ accident last week. No doubt your family and your friends are giving you the strength to face this __19__ challenge. People everywhere are also giving you best wishes every day and we are among those who are keeping you __20__ ...

1. [A]how   [B]which   [C]when   [D]that
2. [A]walked   [B]climbed   [C]pulled   [D]jumped
3. [A]able   [B]unable   [C]suitable   [D]unsuitable
4. [A]disability   [B]possibility   [C]knowledge   [D]experience
5. [A]So   [B]For   [C]Or   [D]Yet
6. [A]sharing   [B]separating   [C]fearing   [D]exploiting
7. [A]terrible   [B]similar   [C]wonderful   [D]practical
8. [A]wrote for   [B]cared for   [C]hoped for   [D]sent for
9. [A]medical   [B]postal   [C]experimental   [D]mental
10. [A]news   [B]paper   [C]equipment   [D]mail
11. [A]patients   [B]a family   [C]nurses   [D]a group

12. [A]effect   [B]effort   [C]comfort   [D]explanation

13. [A]encourage   [B]express   [C]control   [D]treat

14. [A]cry   [B]laugh   [C]chat   [D]sigh

15. [A]much   [B]never   [C]even   [D]seldom

16. [A]bitterly   [B]fairly   [C]weakly   [D]successfully

17. [A]here   [B]there   [C]therefore   [D]forward

18. [A]driving   [B]flying   [C]running   [D]riding

19. [A]technical   [B]different   [C]difficult   [D]valuable

20. [A]nearby   [B]close   [C]busy   [D]alive

答案与分析

1.[C]。考查句子结构与上下文联系。由空格前后两个句子的意思可以看出，空格后是一个时间定语从句，修饰 a few minutes past three，所以选表时间的连接词 when。注意不是时间状语从句。

2.[D]。考查动词搭配与上下文理解。由 horse(马)与 fence(篱笆，障碍)的关系可知应填入 jump(跳)。walk(走)不与 over 连用；climb over 爬过；pull over (车辆等)停在路边。

3.[B]。考查形容词与上下文理解。由前一句的意思可知这里应当是指"呼吸困难"，所以应填入表否定的形容词。而 unsuitable 指"不适合于"，明显不合文意。

4.[D]。考查名词辨义。disability 残疾，伤残；possibility 可能性；knowledge 知识，学问。由文意可知，这三个都不能填入题中。experience 经历。此处指作者一家进入了一种经历许多意想不到的挑战的生活。

5.[D]。考查上下文联系。由于前面一段谈论的是事故给作者一家带来的不利影响，而这一段谈及的则是作者一家从事故中得到的益处，两者之间有明显的转折关系，所以选 yet。

6.[A]。考查动词辨义与上下文理解。由下文可知这里指作者一家及其他人分担困难。

7.[C]。考查形容词辨义与上下文理解。由下文叙述的是事故后作者一家收到了许多人的来信和卡片，所以用"灾难中令人高兴的事情"来说明这一点最恰当。

8.[B]。考查固定搭配辨义。write 一般不单独与介词 for 连用；care for 关心，照顾；hope for 希望，想要；send for 派人去请。由句意可知只能选 care for,指许多人关心作者的丈夫。

9.[A]。考查上下文理解。Chris 受伤后肯定是住在医疗中心,故选 medical。其余三项:postal 邮政的;experimental 实验的;mental 精神的。

10.[D]。考查上下文理解。前面说明他们收到的是信件(letters)和卡片(cards),所以这里应用 mail(邮件)来概括它们。

11.[B]。考查上下文理解。由后面的 we 可知这里是指全家人一起拆信。[A]、[C]两项明显不对;而[D]中的 group 仅指"群体"。

12.[C]。考查名词辨义与上下文理解。effect 效果,作用;effort 努力;comfort 安慰;explanation 解释,阐述。由后文及全文语境可知,人们给予他们一家的是"安慰"。

13.[A]。考查动词辨义与上下文理解。由前文出现的 strength(力量)可知作者对别人的安慰持肯定态度,因此安慰的作用也会是积极的,故选含褒义的 encourage(鼓舞,鼓励)。express 表达;control 控制;treat 对待,处理。

14.[B]。考查上下文理解。由前面的 Funny(有趣)一词可知这里应选与之对应的 laugh(笑)。

15.[C]。考查上下文联系。even 表示的是递进关系,表示"甚至",因为躺在床上的比坐在轮椅上的人病情更严重。其余三项都不能表达这一关系。

16.[D]。考查上下文理解。空格前的 and 表示并列,且作者对这些人是持肯定态度的,所以选与 happily 一样含褒义的 successfully(成功地)。

17.[A]。考查上下文理解。短文后面是附的一封信,所以要填入表"这里"的 here。

18.[D]。考查上下文理解。前文交代作者的丈夫是骑马摔伤的,所以这里应用 riding 修饰 accident。

19.[C]。考查形容词辨义与用法。与 challenge(挑战)一词常搭配的是 difficult(困难的)。technical 技术(上)的;different 不同的;valuable 宝贵的。它们虽然都可修饰 challenge,但都不合上下文逻辑。

20.[D]。考查搭配与上下文理解。keep sb. 后跟形容词作宾补,意为使某人处于某种状态。而由上下文来看,这里只能选 alive,意为使作者的丈夫活下去。nearby 附近;close 紧密的,临近的;busy 忙碌的。

同步译文

1995 年 5 月 27 日,我们的生活突然全变了。事故是在 3 点过几分发生的,我的丈夫克里斯在他的马跃过障碍时从马背上摔了下来。克里斯的胸部往下都瘫痪了,让他难以正常呼吸。随着他从马背上摔下,我们进入了一种经历着许多意想不到的挑战的生活。我们从富有家庭变成了贫困家庭。或者是我们这么想。

　　然而,我们后来发现的都是分担困难所带来的礼物。我们开始理解灾难中也会有令人愉快的事情。全世界的人都如此关心克里斯,我们每天都收到大量的信件和明信片。在弗吉尼亚一个医疗中心住院的第三周周末时,我们就收到和整理了大约 35 000 封邮件。

　　我们一家人拆信件拆了一封又一封。它们给了我们安慰,成了我们的力量之源。我们用它们来鼓励自己。如果我们需要笑一笑,我就会去标有"有趣"字样的信件堆里寻找,或者去标有"残疾人"字样的信件盒中寻求来自那些坐在轮椅上甚至躺在床上却活得很快乐、很成功的人的建议。

　　我们认识到,这些信件应当与人分享。因此在这里我们为你提供其中的一封。

　　亲爱的克里斯:

　　我和我丈夫上周听到你骑马摔伤的事故后都很难过。无疑你的家人和朋友都正在给予你力量来面对这一艰苦挑战。每天各地的人们都在把最好的祝福送给你,而我们也是这些让你活下去的人们当中的成员……

✎ Exercise 10

　　On the shore of Lake Sawyer, there is a mountain. I ___1___ it Treasure Mountain. When I was a young man, I used to ___2___ there alone. One day in June while I was taking a walk, it began to ___3___. A terrific storm moved in very quickly, and I was quite ___4___. It was ___5___ like mad, trees were ___6___ over, and lightning was ___7___ all around me. After wandering ___8___ for several hours, I found a cave in the side of the mountain. The cave was about five feet ___9___ and 100 yards in depth. It was good ___10___ from the storm. I was cold, wet, and sad so I went far into the back of the ___11___ and lighted a match. To my surprise, I saw a large wooden ___12___ with a strong iron lock. The lock was too thick for me to ___13___, and the chest was too ___14___ for me to carry. I ___15___ what might be in the chest. Could there be jewels or golden coins inside? I was so ___16___ that I couldn't sleep. In the morning, I left and found my way home. I ___17___ myself to return with tools to open the chest and get the ___18___.

I have tried to keep that promise. Every summer for 20 years I have gone back alone to Treasure Mountain. However，I have ___19___ to find the cave. Sometimes life is too ___20___ to believe!

1. [A]name   [B]call   [C]describe   [D]say

2. [A]walk   [B]enter   [C]climb   [D]run

3. [A]rain   [B]wind   [C]storm   [D]lightening

4. [A]sad   [B]excited   [C]worried   [D]happy

5. [A]shouting   [B]raining   [C]pouring   [D]blowing

6. [A]blowing   [B]bending   [C]pulling   [D]coming

7. [A]crashing   [B]dashing   [C]washing   [D]throwing

8. [A]slowly   [B]carefully   [C]quickly   [D]aimlessly

9. [A]long   [B]deep   [C]high   [D]narrow

10. [A]time   [B]place   [C]thing   [D]protection

11. [A]cave   [B]trees   [C]mountain   [D]storm

12. [A]suitcase   [B]box   [C]chest   [D]tool

13. [A]break   [B]carry   [C]take   [D]keep

14. [A]big   [B]old   [C]thick   [D]heavy

15. [A]found out   [B]thought about
    [C]drew up   [D]wrote about

16. [A]worried   [B]disappointed   [C]excited   [D]happy

17. [A]forced   [B]told   [C]asked   [D]promised

18. [A]money   [B]jewels   [C]golden coins   [D]treasure

19. [A]managed   [B]failed   [C]continued   [D]decided

20. [A]cruel   [B]exciting   [C]wonderful   [D]changeable

答案与分析

1.[B]。考查动词用法与上下文理解。name 与 call 后都可跟复合宾语，但 name 一般指较为正式的"命名"，含有命名之后不再更改的意思，而 call 则指通常的"称作、叫"。此处指作者个人把山称作珍宝山，当然用 call 更恰当。describe 描述，描绘；say 说。

2.[A]。考查动词用法。walk（散步）为不及物动词，后面直接跟副词 there，且后面一句中紧跟着出现了 taking a walk，因此是正确答案。enter 指

"进入，参加"；climb 指"爬"；run 指"跑"。

3．[A]。考查上下文联系。由后文中的 storm(暴风雨)及 cold、wet 等词可知这里要用动词 rain。其余三项都是名词。

4．[C]。考查形容词与上下文理解。由后文对作者寻找避雨处的描写，再结合常识可知应选 worried(焦急的)。sad(悲哀的，沮丧的)、excited(兴奋的，激动的)及 happy(快乐的)用在此处都不合逻辑。

5．[D]。考查动词辨义与上下文理解。由于本句主语 it 指代的是前一句中的 storm，所以应用与之对应的动词 blowing(吹)。shout 一般用于人；rain 单指下雨；pour 也用于指雨，形容雨下得大。

6．[B]。考查固定搭配与上下文理解。由句意不难看出这里是指树被吹得倒伏，故用 bend，与 over 构成固定搭配，指"弯曲，俯身"。blow over 刮倒，吹倒，停止(它在此处语态不对，应用被动语态)；pull over (车辆等)停靠在路边；come over 来到，过来，突然袭向。

7．[A]。考查动词辨义与上下文理解。由于主语是 lightning(闪电)，所以应用 crashing，指"突然发出喀嚓巨响"。dash 指"猛冲"；wash 指"冲洗"；throw 指"投掷"。它们都不用于指闪电。

8．[D]。考查副词与上下文理解。由空格前的动词 wander(游荡)、下文及常识可以看出，作者在山中遇雨，肯定是漫无目的地寻找避雨处，所以选 aimlessly。而 slowly 指"缓慢地"，carefully 指"仔细地"，quickly 指"迅速地"，它们都与语境不符。

9．[C]。考查表达与上下文理解。由下文的 100 yards in depth 可知这里是在描述山洞的大小，既然后面说"深 100 码"，那么前面应当是说洞高多少，所以选 high。而 long 与 deep 填入都与后面的 in depth 重复和矛盾。

10．[D]。考查名词用法与句子结构。由空格前谓语用的是第三人称单数形式(was)及空格前无不定冠词可知应填入一个不可数名词；同时主语 it 指代的是山洞，故表语不能用 time(时间)。

11．[A]。考查上下文理解。由上下文不难看出这里是指作者走进山洞的里面。

12．[C]。考查上下文理解。由后文中多次出现的 chest 可知作者发现的就是它。注意 chest 指"大箱子"，它还可指"胸部"。

13．[A]。考查动词辨义与上下文理解。由上下文及常识不难看出，作者是想要打开锁，但锁太大，打不开，所以用动词 break(打开)。carry 与 take 都指"带"，而 keep 则指"保存"，它们都不合语境。

14．[D]。考查形容词辨义与上下文理解。由空格后的 to carry(搬运)可知最合逻辑的是 heavy(重的)。big 仅指体积大,它与搬不搬得动没有逻辑上的关系。

15.[B]。考查固定搭配辨义。find out 发现,查明(它与后面从句的语气矛盾);think about 考虑,琢磨;draw up 起草,停下;write about 描述,写的是。

16.[C]。考查上下文理解。由空格前的问句的意思及常识可以看出作者的兴奋心理。

17.[D]。考查动词辨义与上下文理解。force 强迫;tell 告诉;ask 询问。它们都不合语境。promise 承诺,保证,此处指作者决定带工具来打开箱子。

18.[D]。考查名词辨义与上下文理解。treasure 是前文提到过的 jewels(珠宝)和 golden coins(金币)的总称,且与文章第二句作者给山起名相呼应,因此最合文意。

19.[B]。考查动词辨义与上下文理解。由 however 所表达的转折关系可知作者没有找到那个山洞,故用 fail(失败,没能)。其余三项都含肯定义。

20.[A]。考查形容词辨义与上下文理解。作者遇雨躲进一个山洞,发现有个箱子,但打不开,又无法带走,所以决定回去后再来,可回去后却再也找不到山洞了。理解了全文内容后可知,这里作者表达的是命运的“无情”最合文意。exciting(令人兴奋的)、wonderful(令人惊奇的,精彩的)和 changeable(可变的,多变的)都不能表达出作者的失望心情。

同步译文

在 Sawyer 湖边有一座山。我把它叫做珍宝山。我年轻时常去山上散步。有一年六月的一天,我正在散步时,天开始下雨。一场可怕的暴风雨很快接踵而至,我很着急。狂风乱吹,树木被刮得倒伏,闪电在我周围喀嚓作响。漫无目的地走了好几个小时后,我在山中发现了一个山洞。山洞大约有 5 英尺高,100 码深。这是个躲避暴风雨的好去处。我又冷又湿,还很沮丧,就向山洞深处走去,点着了一根火柴。让我惊讶的是,我看到了一个上了一把坚固的铁锁的大箱子。锁太大,我打不开,而箱子太沉,我搬不动。我想着箱子里面会有些什么东西。里面会有珠宝或者金币吗?我兴奋得无法入睡。第二天早上,我离开了山洞,找到了回家的路。我向自己承诺说一定带上工具回来,打开箱子取出珍宝。

我一直试图信守这个承诺。20 年来,每年夏天我都独自回到珍宝山。然而,我没有再找到那个山洞。有时生活无情得令人难以置信!

Exercise 11

It often appears that we have more to gain by speaking than by listening. One big advantage of speaking is that it gives you a chance to control others' thoughts and actions.   1   your goal — to have a boss   2   you, to   3   others to vote for the person of your   4   , or to describe the   5   you want your hair cut — the key   6   success seems to be the   7   to speak well.

  8   obvious advantage of speaking is the chance it provides to   9   the admiration, respect, or liking of others.   10   jokes, and everyone will think you're really a wise man.   11   advice, and they'll be thankful for help. Tell them all you know, and they'll be   12   by your wisdom.   13   keep quiet and it seems as if you'll look like a   14   nobody.

Finally, talking gives you the   15   to release energy in a way that listening can't. When you're   16   , the chance to talk about your problems can often help you feel   17   . In the same way, you can often   18   your anger by letting it out orally. It is also helpful to   19   your excitement with others by talking about it, for keeping it inside often   20   you feeling as if you might burst.

1. [A]What   [B]That   [C]Which   [D]Whatever
2. [A]to hire   [B]hired   [C]hire   [D]hiring
3. [A]persist   [B]advise   [C]persuade   [D]suggest
4. [A]friend   [B]relation   [C]choice   [D]leader
5. [A]method   [B]way   [C]means   [D]plan
6. [A]of   [B]with   [C]on   [D]to
7. [A]efficiency   [B]energy   [C]mentality   [D]ability
8. [A]Another   [B]The other   [C]A second   [D]Secondly
9. [A]gain   [B]grasp   [C]receive   [D]seize
10. [A]Say   [B]Speak   [C]Talk   [D]Tell
11. [A]Accept   [B]Follow   [C]Offer   [D]Obtain
12. [A]affected   [B]impressed   [C]influence   [D]moved

13. [A]And 　　　　[B]But 　　　　[C]When 　　　　[D]While

14. [A]fruitless 　　[B]priceless 　　[C]worthless 　　[D]senseless

15. [A]pleasure 　　[B]course 　　　[C]duty 　　　　[D]chance

16. [A]in trouble 　[B]in danger 　　[C]in debt 　　　[D]in silence

17. [A]well 　　　　[B]good 　　　　[C]better 　　　　[D]best

18. [A]lessen 　　　[B]brighten 　　[C]darken 　　　[D]deepen

19. [A]control 　　　[B]share 　　　　[C]enjoy 　　　　[D]remove

20. [A]makes 　　　[B]causes 　　　[C]leaves 　　　[D]enables

☺ 答案与分析

　　1.[D]。考查句子结构与代词。本句两个破折号之间的成分是插入语，所以由句子结构分析这里是一个省略句，相当于____ your goal is，并且可看出作者强调的是无论什么目标，应选 whatever。

　　2.[C]。考查习惯表达。have sb. do sth. 是习惯表达，意为"让某人做某事"，have 后的动词用不带 to 的不定式，强调 do 的动作由 sb. 发出。

　　3.[C]。考查动词辨义与用法。persist 坚持（其后跟 in 或者 in doing sth.，不跟不定式）；advise 建议；persuade 劝说，说服；suggest 建议。由上下文与用法来看，persuade 含有成功义，故最恰当。

　　4.[C]。考查上下文理解。由常识可知，你投票支持的人不一定是你的朋友（friend）、亲戚（relation）或者领导（leader），但一定是你选定的人（choice）。

　　5.[B]。考查名词辨义。method 和 means 都指做某事的"方法"，但都较为正式和系统；way 指做某事的"方式"；plan 指做某事的"计划"。由空格后的内容来看选常用的 way 最恰当。

　　6.[D]。考查介词固定搭配。名词 key 后的介词用 to。

　　7.[D]。考查名词辨义与用法。efficiency 效率，效能；energy 能量；mentality 心态。这三个在意义上都不合文意，且其后一般不跟不定式。ability 能力。

　　8.[A]。考查代词。another 特指两者中的"另一个"，符合文意。the other 强调的是三者或三者以上的"其他的"，后面应跟复数名词；second 应与定冠词连用，而 secondly 是副词。

　　9.[A]。考查动词辨义。gain 指"获得（好的东西）"，由空格后的几个并列的褒义宾语可知用 gain 恰当。grasp 抓住，握住；receive 收到；seize 抓住，攫取。

　　10.[D]。考查动词辨义。四个选项都含"说"义，但 say 多作不及物动词，如作及物动词，其后应跟从句；speak 只用语言作宾语；talk 一般作不及物词,其后跟 about 等介词。只有 tell 后可直接跟宾语。

11.[C]。考查动词辨义与上下文理解。由上下文文意不难看出,这里指向别人提出建议,所以用 offer(提供)。accept 接受;follow 跟随,按照;obtain 获得。

12.[B]。考查动词辨义。affect 影响,感动;impress 使钦佩,给…留下深刻印象;influence 影响;move 感动,移动。由上下文可知,别人只会对你的知识感到钦佩,所以应选[B]。[C]项语态错误。

13.[B]。考查上下文联系。由上下文句意可以看出,两者之间是明显的转折关系(前文说说话的好处,而后文说不说话的坏处),所以选 but。

14.[C]。考查形容词辨义。fruitless 无成果的,无结果的;priceless 无价的,昂贵的;worthless 无价值的,无用的;senseless 无意义的。因为修饰的是 nobody,所以选含贬义的[C]。

15.[D]。考查名词辨义。这里指使人有机会释放能量,所以选 chance。说有"愉快"(pleasure)、"课程"(course)或者"职责"(duty)释放能量都不合逻辑。

16.[A]。考查固定搭配与上下文理解。由这一句后面的 problems(问题)可推知应选 in trouble(有麻烦)。in danger 处于危险之中;in debt 欠债,负债;in silence 静默,不出声。

17.[C]。考查形容词比较级与上下文理解。由于这里含有与不诉说自己的问题相比较的意思,所以应选比较级 better,指"觉得好一点"。

18.[A]。考查动词辨义。lessen 减少,降低;brighten 使变亮;darken 使变黑;deepen 加深。由空格后的 letting it out(释放)可知应选 lessen。

19.[B]。考查动词辨义与搭配。由于空格后有 with others,所以用 share(分享),构成固定搭配 share with sb.,指"与某人分享"。

20.[C]。考查动词搭配。make 后应跟不带 to 的不定式即动词原形;cause 与 enable 后都应跟带 to 的动词不定式。只有 leave 后可跟动名词。

同步译文

　　我们通过"说"得到的东西常常似乎要比通过"听"得到的东西多。说的一大好处就是让你有机会去控制别人的思想和行为。不管你的目的是什么——为了让老板雇用你,为了说服别人给你选择的候选人投票,或者是为了描述你想要理的发型——成功的关键似乎都是良好的说话能力。

　　说话的另一个明显好处是它提供了获得别人钦佩、尊敬或者喜欢的机会。

会讲笑话，大家就会认为你是个机智的人。提出建议，他们会感激你的帮助。把你所知道的都告诉他们，他们会为你的智慧所折服。但是如果保持沉默，你看起来似乎就像是一个毫无用处的人。

最后，说话让你有机会通过"听"所不能提供的方式释放自己的能量。如果你有麻烦，谈论自己的问题常常会让你觉得好一点。同样地，你常常可以通过用言语释放来降低你的怒气。通过交谈与别人分享自己的兴奋感也很有好处，因为把兴奋感强抑在心里常常会让你感到自己似乎会爆炸。

Exercise 12

Our country has many opportunities for adults who want to make their lives better. There are public schools you can   1   . In the schools, you can take things   2   English, arithmetic and history. You can find classes in almost any subject you want to study. You may want to   3   to type, sew, paint or fix TV sets. You may want to learn   4   about the trade you are already in. You may want to get a high school *diploma*(文凭). You may   5   want to go to college. All it   6   is time and effort.

In many cities, there are adult classes in the public schools. You can attend many of these without   7   to pay money. In some schools you may have to pay a small fee. There are   8   many kinds of private schools for adults, where you may have to pay more money.

Many job opportunities are   9   to those who wish to work. It helps if you know   10   than one language. There are good jobs for interpreters and typists who know English.

There are many good jobs in government. In most cases, you   11   be a citizen of this country, and you must   12   a civil service examination. These examinations are   13   to everyone, regardless of race, religion or color.

For many civil service jobs you   14   a high school diploma. The person who does not have a high school diploma can get one. There are several ways. You can study high school   15   at home and then take special tests.   16   you pass the tests, you can get a diploma.

__17__ you can go to night school. There are classes that __18__ you to take special tests to get a diploma.

　　Be as well trained as you can. Get as much training as you can. __19__ knocks at every door. Be sure that when it knocks at your door you are __20__ .

1. 〔A〕go　　　　〔B〕study　　　　〔C〕learn　　　　〔D〕attend
2. 〔A〕like　　　　〔B〕in　　　　　〔C〕of　　　　　〔D〕as
3. 〔A〕know　　　〔B〕study　　　　〔C〕learn　　　　〔D〕begin
4. 〔A〕what　　　〔B〕more　　　　〔C〕again　　　　〔D〕others
5. 〔A〕perhaps　　〔B〕never　　　　〔C〕very　　　　　〔D〕even
6. 〔A〕takes　　　〔B〕makes　　　　〔C〕gives　　　　〔D〕uses
7. 〔A〕regretting　〔B〕agreeing　　　〔C〕having　　　　〔D〕beginning
8. 〔A〕still　　　　〔B〕also　　　　　〔C〕almost　　　　〔D〕such
9. 〔A〕chosen　　　〔B〕allowed　　　〔C〕promised　　　〔D〕offered
10. 〔A〕better　　　〔B〕more　　　　〔C〕fewer　　　　〔D〕less
11. 〔A〕can　　　　〔B〕may　　　　　〔C〕must　　　　〔D〕need
12. 〔A〕take　　　　〔B〕join　　　　　〔C〕hold　　　　〔D〕give
13. 〔A〕possible　　〔B〕open　　　　　〔C〕limited　　　〔D〕permitted
14. 〔A〕want　　　　〔B〕get　　　　　〔C〕demand　　　〔D〕need
15. 〔A〕subjects　　〔B〕classes　　　〔C〕tests　　　　〔D〕English
16. 〔A〕Until　　　　〔B〕First　　　　〔C〕If　　　　　〔D〕Though
17. 〔A〕Or　　　　　〔B〕And　　　　　〔C〕But　　　　〔D〕So
18. 〔A〕make　　　　〔B〕permit　　　　〔C〕lead　　　　〔D〕prepare
19. 〔A〕Text　　　　〔B〕Job　　　　　〔C〕Diploma　　　〔D〕Opportunity
20. 〔A〕prepare　　〔B〕ready　　　　〔C〕studying　　　〔D〕waiting

😊 **答案与分析**

　　1.〔D〕。考查动词辨义与搭配。you can ____是 school 的定语从句,而 school 应在从句中作宾语,所以填入的词能直接跟 school 作宾语。除 attend 外,其余三项都应跟上相应的介词才能再跟 school。

　　2.〔A〕。考查介词用法。由空格后的并列学科名词可知这里是表列举,所以只能填入 like(如)。注意 as 在表示"如"时是连词,连接句子。

3.[C]。考查动词辨义与用法。begin 明显不对；know 后跟不定式时，不定式前应当跟疑问词 what/how 等；study 指"学习"时后面跟名词，不跟不定式。只有 learn 后可跟不定式，指"学习"。

4.[B]。考查上下文理解。由空格后 trade 的定语从句的意思可知，这种人对自己的工作领域本来就有一定的知识，他们是来学习更多知识的，故当然应选 more。其余三项填入都不合逻辑。

5.[D]。考查副词辨义与上下文理解。由常识可首先排除 never(从不)。而由文意联系来看，go to college(上大学)与前面几句(学习打字等技术、学习工作领域的更多知识、得一张高中文凭)之间是层层递进的关系，所以这里应用能表递进的副词 even(甚至)。perhaps(也许)与谓语动词 may 意思重复；very 不用于动词前修饰动词。

6.[A]。考查动词用法。由空格后的表语 time and effort 可知，这里填入的词应表"花费"，只有 take 有此意。use 指"使用，利用"。

7.[C]。考查动词搭配与上下文理解。由后面两句中出现的 have to pay 可知这里也应用这一搭配。但此处用在介词后，故用动名词形式。without having to pay 指"不要付钱"。

8.[B]。考查副词与上下文联系。由句子结构可知应填入一个副词；而由这一句与前两句的句意可知它们是递进关系，所以选 also，表示"还"。still 指"仍然"，用于修饰动词；almost 表示"几乎"，表程度，不表递进；such 不是副词。

9.[D]。考查动词辨义。这里用被动语态，所以实际上 job opportunities 应当是填入的动词的宾语。choose 选择；allow 允许；promise 承诺，保证；offer 提供。而由空格后的 to those ... 可知，只能选用 offer。

10.[B]。考查固定搭配。more than (one)是固定搭配，指"多于(一个)，不止(一个)"。

11.[C]。考查情态动词与上下文理解。can 表示"能够"；may 表示"可能"；must 表示"必须"；need 表示一种"需要"。由上下文与常识可知，公务员首先必须是公民，且紧跟的一句中出现了 must 这个词，所以应选 must。

12.[A]。考查习惯搭配。take an examination 是习惯搭配，指"参加考试"。其余三个动词中，join 不与 examination 连用，而 hold/give an examination 指的是"举行考试"。

13.[B]。考查形容词辨义与上下文理解。由本句中后半部分(regardless of ...)可知这里要表达的意思是每个人都可参加考试，故用 open(公开的)，be open to sb. 指"对某人开放，某人可以参加"。possible 可能的；limited 限制的;permitted 允许的,许可的。

14.[D]。考查上下文理解。由前后两部分的意思可以看出,这里表达的是"需要有高中文凭"这一含意,所以选 need。而 want 指"想要",get 指"得到",demand 指"要求(有)",它们填入都不合逻辑。

15.[A]。考查名词辨义与上下文理解。English 明显不合题意。subject 科目,课程;class 班级,上课时间;test 测验。由于谓语是 study(学习),所以只能选 subjects。

16.[C]。考查句子关系。由常识可知,通过考试(pass the tests)是获得文凭(get a diploma)的条件,所以应填入引导条件状语从句的连词 if。

17.[A]。考查上下文联系。去上夜校与前文说的在家里学习是两种不同的获取文凭的方式,两者之间是任选关系,所以填入表选择的 Or。

18.[D]。考查动词辨义与用法。make 后跟不带 to 的不定式,明显不合题目要求。permit sb. to do 指"允许某人做",lead sb. to(do)指"带领某人(做)",prepare sb. to do 指"使某人准备好做"。这些课程或者班级当然是为了使学习者通过考试而设置的,所以用 prepare。

19.[D]。考查名词辨义与习惯表达。text 课文,文本;job 工作;diploma 文凭,毕业证;opportunity 机会,运气。Opportunity knocks at every door 是一句习语,指"机会人人都有"。

20.[B]。考查句子结构与上下文理解。由上下文可知,作者在这里要表达的是"做好了准备",而由空格前的 are 可知应填入一个形容词或者分词。prepare(准备)是动词原形;studying 指"学习";waiting 指"等待"。只有 ready 是形容词且意思符合上下文逻辑。

同步译文

    我国对那些想改善自己生活水平的成人来说有很多机会。有许多公立学校可以就读。在学校里,可以学习如英语、数学和历史之类的课程。可以找到开设了几乎任何你想学习的课程的班级。你也许想学习打字、缝纫、画画或者修理电视机。你也许想学习你已经从事的领域里的更多知识。你也许想获得一张高中文凭。你也许甚至想要上大学。所有要付出的只是时间和努力。

    许多城市的公立学校里有成人班级。你不用交钱就可以到许多这样的班级学习。在一些学校里可能会要交一小笔学费。还有多种成人私立学校,在这些学校里你可能得多交学费。

    有许多就业机会提供给那些愿意工作的人。如果懂两种以上的语言会很有好处。对于翻译和那些懂英语的打字员来说有许多好工作。

在政府机关里有许多好职位。大部分情况下，你必须是我国公民，并且必须参加公务员考试。不论种族、宗教信仰或者肤色，每一个人都可以参加这些考试。

对于许多公务员职位来说，需要有一张高中文凭。没有高中文凭的人可以获得一张文凭。有多种获得文凭的途径。你可以在家里自学高中课程，然后参加特殊的考试。如果通过了考试，就可以获得文凭。你也可以去读夜校。夜校开设有课程，使你做好准备，参加那种特殊考试以获得文凭。

尽量使自己训练有素。尽量多参加培训。机会人人都有。确保当机会来临时你作好了准备。

Exercise 13

Memory, they say, is a matter of practice and exercise. If you have the __1__, and if you really make a conscious effort, you can quite __2__ improve your __3__ to remember things. But even if you are successful, there are times when your memory seems to __4__ tricks on you. Sometimes you remember things that __5__ did not happen. One __6__ last week, for example, I got up and found out that I had __7__ the front door unlocked all night, yet I clearly remembered __8__ it carefully the night before. And another time, a few nights ago, I put on my overcoat to go out some place and found a __9__ I had written folded up in one of the __10__. I had obviously not mailed it, and yet I remembered quite clearly that I __11__. I even remembered the exact *circumstances*(情形).

Memory "tricks" __12__ the other way as well. __13__ in a while you remember not doing something, and then find out that you did. One day last month, I was __14__ in a barber's shop waiting for my __15__ to get a haircut, and __16__ I realized that I had gotten a haircut two days __17__ at the barber's shop across the street from my office.

We always seem to find __18__ in incidents involving people's forgetfulness or absent-mindedness. __19__, however, absent-mindedness is not always laughable. There are times when "tricks" of our memory can __20__ us great embarrassment and inconvenience.

1. [A]desire [B]way [C]need [D]idea
2. [A]simply [B]quickly [C]easily [D]slowly
3. [A]strength [B]force [C]means [D]power
4. [A]make [B]play [C]give [D]do
5. [A]exactly [B]really [C]clearly [D]merely
6. [A]morning [B]afternoon [C]night [D]evening
7. [A]held [B]opened [C]left [D]let
8. [A]to lock [B]to close [C]locking [D]closing
9. [A]newspaper [B]paper [C]notice [D]letter
10. [A]coats [B]pockets [C]trousers [D]shirts
11. [A]had [B]did [C]mailed [D]do
12. [A]work [B]affect [C]effect [D]do
13. [A]Just [B]Only [C]Once [D]Ever
14. [A]standing [B]lying [C]living [D]sitting
15. [A]time [B]turn [C]chance [D]order
16. [A]suddenly [B]clearly [C]gradually [D]greatly
17. [A]ago [B]later [C]before [D]on
18. [A]pleasure [B]joke [C]humor [D]laugh
19. [A]Unsuspectingly [B]Uncomfortably
    [C]Unnaturally [D]Unfortunately
20. [A]make [B]cause [C]lead [D]let

答案与分析

1.[A]。考查名词辨义与搭配。have the desire 有（做某事的）愿望。have the way 有（做某事的）方法或途径；have the need 有（做某事的）需要；have the idea 有（…的）想法。由后面与这一句并列的 If you really... 可知这里指主动地希望提高记忆力，所以应选[A]。

2.[C]。考查副词辨义与上下文理解。simply 简单地；quickly 迅速地；easily 轻松地，轻易地；slowly 缓慢地。由句意特别是空格前的 quite（相当）可知，这里强调的是难易而不是速度，所以选 easily。

3.[D]。考查名词辨义。由文意不难看出此处指的是记住事物的"能力",所以只能选 power(力量,能力)。strength 和 force 都用于指"力度,力量",但都不含"能力"义;means 指"方式"。

4.[B]。考查固定搭配。play a trick on sb. 是固定搭配,指"与某人开玩笑,捉弄某人"。

5.[B]。考查上下文理解。由空格前后两部分的意思可以看出,这里指"记得事实上并未发生过的事",所以应选 really(实际上,真正地)。exactly 正是,准确地;clearly 清晰地,明了地;merely 仅仅,只。

6.[A]。考查上下文理解。由后文中的 got up(起床)、all night 及 the night before 三处可以推知这里是指早上。

7.[C]。考查动词搭配。由空格后的部分可知这里是用分词作宾语补语,而后面能这样用的动词只有 leave,指"让宾语处于某种状态"。此处 leave the front door unlocked 指"没锁前门"。

8.[C]。考查动词用法。remember 后可跟不定式或者动名词,前者(to do)指事情还没有做,后者(doing)指事情已经做过。由于这里是说自己记得锁上了门即已经做过,所以用动名词形式。

9.[D]。考查名词辨义与上下文理解。由后文中的两个动词 written(写)与 mailed(邮寄)不难推知这里选 letter(信)。newspaper 报纸;paper(报)纸,纸张;notice 通知,布告。

10.[B]。考查名词辨义与上下文理解。coats、trousers 和 shirts 都指衣服,pockets 指衣服上的口袋。由上下文与常识可知,信只能在口袋里。

11.[A]。考查动词的替代。由于前面一个分句中用的是过去完成时态(had ... mailed it),后面在省略时助动词要用 had,不能用其他形式。

12.[A]。考查动词用法。此处需要一个不及物动词,因为 the other way 是副词短语,指"另一个方面"。四个选项中只有 work 和 do 可作不及物动词,work 指"起作用",符合文意,而 do 没有此义。

13.[C]。考查固定搭配。once in a while 是固定搭配,指"偶尔,间或"。

14.[D]。考查动词辨义与上下文理解。stand 站立;lie 躺,位于;live 生活;sit 坐。由文意与常识可知应是在理发店里坐着等候。

15.[B]。考查名词辨义。由上下文文意可知这里指等着轮到自己理发,所以选 turn(轮流),构成 wait for one's turn to do sth. 这一习惯表达。

16.[A]。考查副词与上下文理解。suddenly 强调的是在前一个动作发生的过程中"突然"发生另一事,符合这里的语境,指作者在等待理发的过程中突然意识到自己已经理过发了。其余三项填入都不合上下文逻辑。

17.[C]。考查副词用法。ago 指的是现在某个时间"以前"，而 before 表示的是过去某个时间"以前"。由于这里叙述的是过去发生的事，那么在说"以前"时当然要用 before。later 表示的是"以后"，on 不能用于时间后。

18.[C]。考查名词辨义与上下文理解。由后面一句中的 laughable(可笑的)可知此处应是指健忘与心不在焉让人觉得好笑，所以选 humor(幽默，风趣)。pleasure 愉快；joke 玩笑；laugh 笑(声)。它们填入题中都造成逻辑不通。

19.[D]。考查副词辨义与上下文理解。由上下文可以看出，这一句与前面的内容之间是转折关系，所以用 unfortunately(不幸的是)。

20.[B]。考查动词用法。空格后是双宾语，而四个选项中只有 cause(使，引起)后可跟双宾语，所以是正确答案。

他们说记忆就是训练和练习。如果你有提高记忆的愿望，并且如果你真是做出了努力，你就能轻松提高自己记住事情的能力。但是即便你成功地提高了，还是会有记忆似乎在捉弄你的时候。

有时你会记得事实上并没有发生过的事情。比如说，上周的一天早上，我起来后发现前门整个晚上都没锁，但我清楚地记得前一天晚上我仔细锁好了门。另一次是几天前的一个晚上，我穿上外套去一个地方，发现其中一个口袋里有我写好并封好了的一封信。很明显，我并没有把信寄出去，但我很清楚地记得自己把信发了。我甚至还记得当时的准确情形。

记忆开的"玩笑"在别的方面也一样有。你偶尔会记起没有做过什么，然后却发现自己做过。上个月的一天，我坐在理发店等着轮到我理发，但突然意识到两天前我在办公室街对面的理发店里已经理过了。

我们似乎总能从别人因健忘和心不在焉而发生的事情中发现幽默。然而，不幸的是心不在焉并非总是可笑的。我们记忆开的"玩笑"有时可以给我们带来极大的尴尬和不便。

Exercise 14

　　Mr Harkness, a clever salesman, arrived at the bus station. He was ready for some ___1___ business in town.

　　"Goodness," he cried, taking a quick look in a ___2___. "My hair looks ___3___ . It would be reasonable to get a good ___4___ ___5___ I start selling my goods to these people."

Mr Harkness looked in both ___6___ on Main Street for the position of a ___7___ barbershop(理发店). He saw ___8___ .

"Now the question is which barbershop is ___9___ ." he said.

One shop was in the ___10___ part of town. Mr Harkness stared in the ___11___ ."An excellent, successful-looking shop." he said.

"The ___12___ has a wonderful haircut, just the ___13___ I want."

___14___ was a basement shop that looked as ___15___ as possible. It would not win any ___16___ for cleanness or neatness. The barber was half ___17___ . His hair was long and ___18___ cut. ___19___ for a moment at the entrance, Mr Harkness ___20___ and had his hair cut.

1. [A]funny   [B]certain   [C]perfect   [D]serious
2. [A]mirror   [B]shop   [C]hurry   [D]face
3. [A]fair   [B]thick   [C]poor   [D]terrible
4. [A]cleaning   [B]look   [C]haircut   [D]way
5. [A]before   [B]while   [C]if   [D]which
6. [A]mirrors   [B]streets   [C]sides   [D]directions
7. [A]modern   [B]suitable   [C]necessary   [D]empty
8. [A]one   [B]two   [C]three   [D]none
9. [A]good   [B]better   [C]bad   [D]worse
10. [A]good   [B]better   [C]bad   [D]worst
11. [A]direction   [B]seat   [C]barber   [D]window
12. [A]skill   [B]people   [C]barber   [D]barbershop
13. [A]kind   [B]place   [C]thing   [D]hair
14. [A]Another   [B]The other   [C]The one   [D]Another one
15. [A]unpleasant [B]pleasant   [C]cheap   [D]expensive
16. [A]prizes   [B]criticism   [C]regret   [D]games
17. [A]smiling   [B]asleep   [C]hearted   [D]frozen
18. [A]well   [B]badly   [C]freely   [D]loosely
19. [A]Staring   [B]Feeling   [C]Thinking   [D]Asking
20. [A]marched in [B]went out   [C]stepped out   [D]left for

 **答案与分析**

1. [D]。考查形容词辨义与上下文理解。由于修饰的是 business(生意)，所以 funny(滑稽的)肯定不对。而由下文所述的主人公要理发、注意自己的仪表等内容来看，这次生意应当是比较重要和严肃的，所以选 serious(重大的)。certain 指"某一(个)"；perfect 指"优秀的、完美的"。

2. [A]。考查上下文理解。由空格后一句的直接引语中的 looks 可以看出，这里指他在镜中看到自己的头发，所以当然要选 mirror(镜子)。其余三项都不合逻辑。

3. [D]。考查形容词辨义与上下文理解。由前文的语气词 Goodness 及后面一句说明要理发可知他的头发应当是难看的，故选 terrible(糟糕的)。

4. [C]。考查上下文理解。由下文内容可知，Harkness 先生是想理发，所以应选 haircut。注意 get a good cleaning 指"好好清理或打扫一下"。

5. [A]。考查连词。由上下文与常识不难看出，理发应当在与客户做生意之前，故选 before。

6. [C]。考查名词辨义与上下文理解。由空格后表目的的 for the position ... 可知，他是在街上找理发店。由空格前的 both 可知应选 sides，指街的两边。其余三项填入都不合逻辑。

7. [B]。考查形容词辨义。modern 现代(化)的；suitable 合适的，适宜的；necessary 必要的，必需的；empty 空的。由句意来看，说他在找一家合适的理发店最合逻辑。

8. [B]。考查上下文理解。由后文的描述及对比可以看出有两家理发店。

9. [B]。考查形容词比较级与上下文理解。对两家进行比较应用比较级。而由上下文及常识来看，一般是为了比较哪个更好而不是更差，所以选 better。

10. [B]。考查形容词比较级与上下文理解。这里仍含有对两家理发店的位置进行比较之意，故仍用比较级。而由后文的 excellent 可知应用 better。

11. [D]。考查习惯表达。look/stare in the window 为习惯表达，指"从窗户往里看"。其余三项都不合上下文逻辑。

12. [C]。考查上下文理解。由空格后的 has a wonderful haircut 可知主语应当是人，而 people 为泛指，在此不合语境。

13. [A]。考查上下文理解。由于空格所在句为省略句，其主语应当是前一句中的 haircut(发型),所以用来指代它只能用 kind(种类)。

14.[B]。考查代词用法。the other 单用时用于特指两者中的另一个,这里与前面的 One shop is ... 构成 One ... the other ... 这种表达。

15.[A]。考查形容词辨义与上下文理解。由后文的描述可知第二家理发店让人感觉不舒服,所以选否定的 unpleasant(令人不快的)。cheap 和 expensive 都指价钱或价格。

16.[A]。考查名词辨义与上下文理解。由上下文文意及空格前的动词 win(赢得)可知选 prizes(奖项),此处可译为人们的"称赞"或者"好评"。

17.[B]。考查上下文理解与搭配。be half asleep 指"半睡半醒,打瞌睡",符合上下文逻辑。其余三项都不能表达"令人不快"这一否定义。

18.[B]。考查上下文理解。由前文可知 Harkness 先生对第二家理发店是持否定态度的,所以这里也要用含否定义的 badly。

19.[C]。考查动词辨义与上下文理解。stare 瞪,盯,凝视;feel 感觉;think 思考,思索;ask 询问。由空格后的 for a moment 可知选择 think 最恰当,因为他选择不好的一家理发店理发,肯定要考虑一阵。

20.[A]。考查固定搭配辨义与上下文理解。由空格后的内容可知他理发了,说明他是进了理发店。march in 走进去;go out 出去;step out 走出来;leave for 动身前往。

同步译文

　　　　哈克尼斯先生是位精明的销售员,他到达了公共汽车站。他在市里有一些重要的生意要做。

　　　　"天哪!"他往镜子里很快看了一眼后惊呼道,"我的头发看起来糟糕得很。我应当在把东西卖给这些人之前把我的头发好好理一理。"

哈克尼斯先生向大街两边看,寻找合适的理发店。他看到了两家。

"现在的问题是看哪一家更好一点。"他说。

一家理发店位于该市位置较好的地段。哈克尼斯先生透过窗户向里看去。"这是一家不错的、看起来很成功的理发店。"他说。

"理发师的发型很好,正是我想要的那种。"

另一家是位于地下室的理发店,看起来令人极不愉快。从清洁与整洁方面来说它得不到人们的任何好评。理发师在打瞌睡。他的头发又长,理得又不好。在门口考虑了一会儿,哈克尼斯先生走了进去,理了发。

Exercise 15

Several days ago, I met a stranger in the street who stopped and asked me directions. I __1__ to show him the way to the destination, but to my __2__ , he coldly refused my offer. I asked him why. Finally he told me that he was __3__ I would ask him for money if I __4__ him in this way.

Money! I __5__ deep into thought. Is it money that comes between us? Money has no __6__ ; it cannot be __7__ with good or bad. The problem __8__ what attitude we have towards it.

At present, we have a more __9__ material life than ever before, but we're becoming more and more __10__ . Why? In my opinion, the __11__ is the change in people's personal __12__ . They wrongly believe that __13__ money should be their only aim in life, so they __14__ all sorts of ways they can to __15__ this aim. They are afraid of being __16__ and fooled. If everyone acts like this, what will our __17__ be like?

Needless to say, money is becoming more and more important in our society, __18__ it shouldn't be the "be-all and end-all" of life. If a person only *concentrates*(全神贯注) on __19__ , he will be lonely and *void*(空虚), and even *go astray*(犯错误).

It is up to us to make our lives happy, not money. We should try our best to help others __20__ and freely. If everyone does so, our society will be better and better.

1. [A]advised   [B]offered   [C]asked   [D]wished
2. [A]joy   [B]fear   [C]excitement   [D]surprise
3. [A]anxious   [B]glad   [C]sorry   [D]afraid
4. [A]stopped   [B]told   [C]asked   [D]helped
5. [A]fell   [B]felt   [C]kept   [D]caught
6. [A]problem   [B]price   [C]life   [D]use
7. [A]joined   [B]judged   [C]connected   [D]seemed
8. [A]takes in   [B]depends on

　　[C]leads to　　　　　　　　　　[D]smoothes away

9. [A]powerful　　[B]beautiful　　[C]plentiful　　[D]healthy

10. [A]cold-hearted　　　　　　　[B]warm-hearted

　　[C]good-looking　　　　　　　[D]humorous

11. [A]key　　　[B]money　　　[C]man　　　[D]creature

12. [A]worth　　[B]habits　　　[C]fame　　[D]values

13. [A]taking　　[B]costing　　[C]spending　　[D]making

14. [A]think up　　[B]pick up　　[C]give off　　[D]break out

15. [A]realize　　[B]recognize　　[C]take　　[D]shoot

16. [A]found　　[B]discovered　　[C]cheated　　[D]followed

17. [A]life　　　[B]society　　[C]belief　　[D]money

18. [A]or　　　[B]but　　　[C]if　　　[D]since

19. [A]life　　　[B]nature　　[C]society　　[D]money

20. [A]separately　　　　　　　[B]obviously

　　[C]mainly　　　　　　　　[D]whole-heartedly

答案与分析

　　1. [B]。考查动词辨义与上下文理解。advise 建议;offer 提供,提出;ask 询问;wish 希望。由后面一句中复现的名词形式 offer 可知这里用其动词过去式 offered,含有"主动提出"之意。

　　2. [D]。考查搭配义与上下文理解。四个选项中的名词都可用在 to one's 后构成常见搭配,意思分别是"令人高兴的是"、"令人害怕的是"、"令人兴奋的是"和"令人惊讶的是",都用作插入语。由空格后一句的意思可知陌生人拒绝了作者的好意,当然会让作者感到惊讶,即应选[D]。

　　3. [D]。考查上下文理解。由空格后的从句句意可知,陌生人是担心作者问他要钱,所以选 afraid。

　　4. [D]。考查动词辨义与上下文理解。作者给陌生人带路当然是"帮助"(help)他,而不是"阻止"(stop)、"告诉"(tell)、"询问"(ask)他。

　　5. [A]。考查固定搭配。fall into 为固定搭配,指"掉入,陷入",fall deep into thought 指"陷入沉思"。其他三个动词一般都不与介词 into 连用。

　　6. [A]。考查上下文理解。由后一句的意思可知作者的意思是责任不在于钱本身,所以选 problem(问题)。其余三项填入都不合逻辑。

　　7. [C]。考查固定搭配。能与介词 with 搭配的是 join(加入,连接)与

connect(联系,连接)两个动词。但由句意可知好坏是与钱"联系"在一起的,故选connected。

8.[B]。考查固定搭配。take in 吸入,吸收;depend on 依赖,取决于;lead to 导致;smooth away 抹掉。由主语(problem)与宾语(attitude 态度)之间的关系可知只能用depend on。

9.[C]。考查形容词辨义与上下文理解。powerful 有力的,强大的;beautiful 美丽的;plentiful 大量的,丰富的;healthy 健康的。由于修饰的是material life(物质生活),所以只能选[C]、[D]两项。但文章没有提及健康问题,故选[C]。

10.[A]。考查上下文理解。由but表示的转折关系及上文提到例子可以看出,作者在这里表达的是一种贬义,故选cold-hearted(冷漠的,冷酷的)。warm-hearted 与此相反,指"好心的";good-looking 指"漂亮的,好看的";humorous 指"幽默的"。

11.[A]。考查名词辨义与上下文理解。key 关键,钥匙;money 钱;man 人(类);creature 生物。由上下文及常识不难看出作者在此是分析问题的症结所在,故应选key,指"关键是…",其余三项都不合逻辑。

12.[D]。考查名词辨义。worth (物的)价值;habits 习惯;fame 名声;values 价值观。全文论述的是钱与人们之间关系,与这两方面都联系起来的是价值观,故选values。

13.[D]。考查固定搭配与上下文理解。由句意可知,这里指"赚钱"才合逻辑,所以用固定搭配make money(赚钱)。其余三项都可指"花费",但都不用money直接作宾语,且不合句意逻辑。

14.[A]。考查固定搭配。think up 想出;pick up 捡起,学到;give off 发出;break out 爆发。由于宾语是抽象名词ways(方法),所以应选think up。

15.[A]。考查动词搭配。由宾语aim(目标)可知应选realize(实现)。其他几项填入句中都不合逻辑。

16.[C]。考查动词辨义与上下文理解。由空格后表并列的连词and可知填入的词应与fooled同义,故选cheated(欺骗),指人们害怕上当受骗。find 发现;discover 发现;follow 跟随。

17.[B]。考查上下文理解。由空格前的everyone及上下文可知,作者是站在整个社会这一立场上来论述的,且下一段第一句中明确出现了society一词,因此这里也用society。

18.[B]。考查上下文联系。作者在空格前肯定说钱越来越重要,而在空格后说不能把钱当作生活的惟一目标,很明显两者之间是转折关系,故选 but。

19.[D]。考查上下文理解。作者本句是用条件句假设一种与前一句相反的情况,所以仍是针对人们对钱的态度而说的,即一个人醉心于金钱,故选money 才符合语篇的一致性。

20.[D]。考查副词辨义与上下文理解。由空格后表并列的 and 可知,填入的词与 freely(不遗余力地,自由地)一样应当含褒义,故选 whole-heartedly (全心全意地)。separately 分别地;obviously 明显地;mainly 主要地,大部分。

同步译文

几天前,我在街上遇到一位拦住我问路的陌生人。我主动提出带着他去他的目的地,但让我惊讶的是他冷冷地拒绝了我的提议。我问他为什么拒绝。最后他告诉我说,他担心如果我这样帮助他,我会向他要钱。

钱!我陷入了沉思。横在我们中间的是金钱么?问题不在金钱上,金钱与好坏无关。问题取决于我们对待金钱的态度。

如今我们的物质生活比以往任何时候都要丰富,但我们却变得越来越冷漠。为什么?我认为,关键在于人们的个人价值观发生了改变。他们错误地认为赚钱是他们生活中的惟一目标,因此尽可能地想出各种手段来实现这一目标。他们害怕上当受骗。如果人人都这样行事,我们的社会将会是个什么样子?

毋庸置疑,钱在我们的社会中正在变得越来越重要,但金钱不能成为生活中无所不能的一切。如果一个人只醉心于金钱,他就会变得孤独和空虚,甚至会误入歧途。

该由我们而不是金钱来使生活幸福。我们应当尽力全心全意地、不遗余力地帮助别人。如果人人都这样,我们的社会就会变得越来越好。

Exercise 16

Mike Wilson worked as a low rank official in the war office during the Second World War. Though he did not __1__ an important position, he got along very well with __2__ everybody, and was __3__ by most of his leaders.

Every day, Wilson arrived at the office in an expensive car. __4__ as his salary was, he __5__ to have got a lot of money to spend. He

bought an expensive house and gave   6   one after another. At one
of the parties he   7   a beautiful woman and   8   in love with her.
When he was   9   by his girlfriend one evening how he got so much
money to spend, Wilson   10   that he had a very rich uncle who lived
abroad and   11   him money nearly each month. But this story could
not cheat a policeman who had been sent to   12   him closely, because the police had noticed   13   he had often stayed behind in the
  14   and was usually the last person to   15   the war office.

His "girlfriend" and three other policemen entered his house when
he was   16   and discovered copies of government   17   papers
and a *radio transmitter*(无线电发报机)   18   inside a piano. After
Mike Wilson was caught, it was learned that his real name was Jack
Brown, and that he had been   19   as a spy   20   the Germans.

1. [A]attend [B]make [C]hold [D]stand
2. [A]mostly [B]hardly [C]even [D]almost
3. [A]hated [B]trusted [C]respected [D]admired
4. [A]Small [B]Large [C]Much [D]Rich
5. [A]decided [B]hoped [C]expected [D]appeared
6. [A]money [B]parties [C]pleasure [D]others
7. [A]watched [B]searched [C]met [D]caught
8. [A]dropped [B]took [C]turned [D]fell
9. [A]appreciated [B]required [C]asked [D]loved
10. [A]explained [B]excused [C]answered [D]refused
11. [A]saved [B]spared [C]left [D]posted
12. [A]glare [B]search [C]star [D]watch
13. [A]when [B]that [C]what [D]why
14. [A]houses [B]streets [C]evenings [D]mornings
15. [A]get [B]reach [C]arrive [D]leave
16. [A]asleep [B]out [C]in [D]on
17. [A]valuable [B]useful [C]secret [D]well-known
18. [A]lied [B]laying [C]made [D]hidden
19. [A]caught [B]hired [C]fired [D]regarded
20. [A]in [B]to [C]for [D]like

😊 **答案与分析**

1.[C]。考查动词搭配。hold a...position 为固定搭配,指"占据…的位置或职位"。其他三项都不与 position 搭配。

2.[D]。考查副词辨义。mostly 主要地,大部分;hardly 几乎不;even 甚至;almost 几乎。由于修饰的是 everyone,所以只能用 almost。

3.[B]。考查动词辨义与上下文理解。hate 憎恨,讨厌;trust 相信,信任;respect 尊敬;admire 钦佩,崇拜。由于空格后面指出动作的发出者是 leaders(领导),所以选 trust。

4.[A]。考查上下文理解。由句子前后的意思可知表达的是他的工资不高,但很有钱,所以只能用 small。

5.[D]。考查动词用法。decide(决定)、hope(希望)、expect(期望)三个动词一般都不跟不定式的完成式。appear 看起来(似乎)。

6.[B]。考查上下文理解。由下一句中的 among one of the parties 和语篇的一致性、前后连贯性可知此处应填入 parties(晚会)。

7.[C]。考查动词辨义。watch 看,观察;search 搜寻;meet 遇见;catch 抓住,赶上。由上下文句意不难推知这里指他遇到了一位女士。

8.[D]。考查固定搭配。fall in love with sb. 为固定搭配,指"爱上某人"。其余动词都不用在这一搭配中。

9.[C]。考查上下文理解。由下文 Wilson 对自己的钱的来路进行解释可知这里是指他女友询问了这个问题,故选 asked。而 appreciate 指"欣赏";require 指"要求";love 指"爱"。

10.[A]。考查动词辨义与上下文理解。参见上题解析。由空格后的内容可知他是在对自己的钱的来路进行解释,故用 explain(解释,说明)。其余三项:excuse 抱歉,原谅;answer 回答;refuse 拒绝。

11.[D]。考查动词辨义与上下文理解。由空格前的 lived abroad(住在国外)及句意可知这里应选 posted(邮寄)。其余三项都与文意无关。

12.[D]。考查动词辨义。watch 除指"观看(电影等)"外,还可指"监视",符合文意。glare 仅指长时间地"盯,注视";search 指"搜寻";stare 指目不转睛地"瞪"。它们无疑都不能用来指警察对嫌疑人的监视。

13.[B]。考查句子结构。由空格后的句子可知,这是警方注意到的内容,应当是动词 notice 的宾语,所以应填入引导宾语从句的连接词 that。

14.[C]。考查上下文理解。由后文中的 the last person(最后的人)可知这里是指他在办公室里待到很晚，所以用表时间的 evenings。

15.[D]。考查上下文理解。由 the last person 及上题的解析可知这里应是指他最后一个离开办公室才会被警方怀疑，才合乎逻辑。所以填入 leave（离开）。其余三个都指"到达"。

16.[B]。考查上下文逻辑。根据常识，警方应当会在嫌疑人不在家时才会秘密搜查，所以选 out。

17.[C]。考查形容词辨义与上下文理解。后文说 Wilson 被捕后发现他是一名间谍，由此可以推知在他家发现的文件应当属于机密（secret）文件。valuable 珍贵的；useful 有用的；well-known 众所周知的，著名的。

18.[D]。考查动词的非谓语形式与上下文理解。由句意可知在钢琴里发现了发报机，因此其意就是发报机藏在钢琴里。hidden 是动词 hide（藏匿）的过去分词，在这里用作宾语补足语。

19.[B]。考查动词辨义与上下文理解。catch 抓住，赶上；hire 雇用；fire 解雇，开火；regard 看作，认为。由上下文逻辑可知，这里指他受雇当间谍。

20.[C]。考查介词用法与固定搭配。四个选项中只有 for 可表目的和对象，be hired for 指"受雇为…工作或干活"。

同步译文

迈克·威尔逊是二战期间战争办公室里的一名下级官员。尽管他的职位不是很重要，但他与几乎每一个人的关系都处得很好，深受大多数领导的信任。

威尔逊每天开着一辆昂贵的汽车来办公室上班。尽管他的工资不高，但他似乎很有钱。他购买了一栋昂贵的房子，并且不断地举办晚会。在一次晚会上，他遇见了一位美丽的女士，并且爱上了她。一天晚上他的女友问他为何有这么多钱，威尔逊解释说他在国外有一个很有钱的叔叔，几乎每个月都给他寄钱。但他的这一说法骗不了一名被派来密切监视他的警察，因为警方已经注意到他经常在办公室里待到晚上，并且总是最后一个离开办公室。

他的"女友"和另外3名警察在他外出时进入了他家，发现了一些政府的机密文件和藏在一架钢琴里的无线电发报机。威尔逊被捕后，人们才得知他的真名叫杰克·布朗，是受雇于德国人的一名间谍。

Exercise 17

It is commonly believed that school is where people go to get education. __1__ , it has been __2__ that today children interrupt their education to go to school. The __3__ between schooling and education suggested by this is important.

Education is __4__ , compared with schooling. Education __5__ no edges. It can take place __6__ , whether in the shower or on the job, whether in a kitchen or on a tractor. It includes both the __7__ learning that takes place in schools and the whole universe of learning out of class. __8__ the experience of schooling can be known __9__ advance, education quite often produces surprises. A chance talk with a __10__ may lead to a person to discover how __11__ he knows of another country. People obtain education from __12__ on. Education, __13__ , is a very __14__ and unlimited term. Schooling, on the other hand, is a __15__ experience, whose style changes __16__ from one way to the next. Throughout a country, children arrive at school at the same time, take __17__ seats, use __18__ textbooks, do homework, and __19__ , and so on. Schooling has usually been __20__ by the edges of the subjects being taught.

1. [A]Then   [B]However   [C]This   [D]Therefore
2. [A]understood   [B]told   [C]argued   [D]say
3. [A]difference   [B]importance   [C]use   [D]problem
4. [A]unexpected   [B]endless   [C]countless   [D]simple
5. [A]have   [B]are   [C]knows   [D]is
6. [A]anywhere   [B]whichever   [C]somewhere   [D]whatever
7. [A]standard   [B]public   [C]part-time   [D]strict
8. [A]If   [B]Because   [C]So   [D]Though
9. [A]on   [B]in   [C]at   [D]with
10. [A]neighbor   [B]friend   [C]foreigner   [D]teacher
11. [A]wonderfully   [B]quickly   [C]greatly   [D]little
12. [A]babies   [B]grown-ups   [C]women   [D]men

13. [A]still　　　[B]next　　　[C]then　　　[D]yet

14. [A]long　　　[B]wide　　　[C]narrow　　　[D]short

15. [A]basic　　　[B]strict　　　[C]final　　　[D]irregular

16. [A]unusually　[B]differently　[C]little　　　[D]frequently

17. [A]large　　　[B]new　　　[C]fixed　　　[D]small

18. [A]different　[B]difficult　[C]likely　　　[D]similar

19. [A]take exams　[B]hold exams　[C]mark papers　[D]read papers

20. [A]changed　　[B]limited　　[C]chosen　　　[D]controlled

 答案与分析

1.[B]。考查上下文逻辑联系。文章第一句指出的是一种普遍的观点，而这一句则提及了另一种观点，由句意可知这种观点与上一种观点是相反的，所以两句间应是转折关系，选 However。then 表达的是时间与顺承关系；thus 与 therefore 表达的都是因果关系。

2.[C]。考查习惯表达。say 说；understand 理解；tell 告诉；argue 争论。It is argued 为常用表达，指"有人认为"，提出不同意见。say 也能这样用，指"据说"，但此处语态不对。

3.[A]。考查名词辨义与上下文理解。由空格后的 between ... and ... 可知应填入一个表示"关系"或者"不同"的名词，所以选 difference(差异、区别)。而后文论述的也是教育与上学之间的不同，由这一点也可确定答案。importance 重要(性)；use 利用；problem 问题。它们后面都不跟 between。

4.[B]。考查形容词辨义与上下文理解。由下面一句：Education knows no edges(教育没有止境)及文章第一段第二句对教育与上学的比较可以看出，作者认为教育是无止境的，故选 endless。unexpected 出人意料的；countless 无数的；simple 简单的。

5.[C]。考查主谓一致与固定搭配。首先，主语 education 是抽象名词，谓语动词要用单数。而系词表示的是主语与表语是同一事物，在此肯定不对，故选 knows。事实上，know no edges/bound 是固定搭配，指"无止境，无限"。

6.[A]。考查副词与上下文理解。由句子结构可知缺少的是一个副词，所以[B]、[D]两项明显不对。而由空格后两个排比句的意思可知这里强调的是"任何地方"，所以选 anywhere。

7.[A]。考查上下文理解。由句子结构可知本句包括两个并列的宾语(both ... and ...)，所以此处填入的词的词性应与 and 后的 whole 相对，故选

standard(标准的)。这里指学校的标准化教育和无所不在的更广阔领域的教育,所以其他三项均不合语境。

8.[D]。考查上下文联系。由句子结构可知,这里是一个让步状语从句,所以选 though。

9.[B]。考查固定搭配。in advance 是固定搭配,意为"提前,预先",与后文中的 surprises(惊讶)形成对比。

10.[C]。考查上下文理解。由这一句最后的 knows of another country (了解别的国家)可知这里应指与外国人(foreigner)交谈,否则就不合逻辑了。neighbour 邻居;friend 朋友;teacher 老师。

11.[D]。考查上下文理解。首先填入的词应做从句谓语 knows 的宾语,所以不能用副词;其次,这里的意思是与外国人交谈可以让人认识到自己对外国的了解多么少,所以选 little。

12.[A]。考查上下文理解。由上下文与常识可知我们应当是从小就接受各种各样的教育,所以选 babies,而不应是从某一个特定时候才开始受教育的。from ... on 为固定搭配,指"从…起"。

13.[C]。考查上下文联系。由上下文文意可以看出,这里是作者由前面的论述得出一个结论,所以应选表示顺承的 then。

14.[A]。考查形容词辨义与上下文联系。由空格后表并列的 and 可知填入的词应与 unlimited(无限的)同义;而修饰的又是 term,故应填入 long(长久的)。

15.[A]。考查形容词辨义与上下文理解。basic 基本的,基础的;strict 严格的;final 最后的;irregular 不规律的。由于文章并没有提及学校教育的方式,所以 strict 与 irregular 都不对。而从常识来看,学校教育当然是一种基本的教育,故答案是[A]。

16.[C]。考查上下文理解。由下文的说明可知这里强调的是学校教育方式都差不多,所以应选含否定义的 little。unusually 非常,异常;differently 不同地;frequently 经常,频繁地。

17.[C]。考查形容词辨义与上下文理解。由上下文与常识可知在学校里学生的座位一般都是固定的(fixed)。其余三项都与文意无联系。

18.[D]。考查形容词辨义与上下文理解。同样,学生的课本也是相同的(similar)。注意 likely 指"可能的"。

19.[A]。考查习惯表达。take exams 指"(学生)参加考试";hold exams 指"(老师等)举行考试";mark papers 指"阅卷";read papers 指"看报"。

20.[B]。考查动词辨义与上下文理解。由前文的论述可知作者认为学校教育是有限的,故此处选表示"限制,局限"的 limited。change 改变;choose 选择;control 控制。

同步译文

　　人们一般认为学校就是人们接受教育的地方。然而,有人认为如今的孩子们去上学是中断了他们的教育。这表明上学与教育之间的区别是很重要的。

　　与上学相比,教育是无止境的。教育没有任何条条框框。任何地方都可以接受教育,不管是在洗淋浴还是在上班,也不管是在厨房里还是在拖拉机上。它包括在上学时学到的知识和在课外学习到的更为广阔的知识。上学的经验能够提前预知,但教育却常常让人出乎意料。与一名外国人谈话可以让一个人发现自己对另一个国家的了解有多么少。人们从小就开始接受教育。因此,教育是一个长期而无限的过程。另一方面,上学则是一种基本的教育,它的方式很少变化。一个国家中孩子们都在同一时间到校,坐在固定的座位上,使用相同的教材,做家庭作业,参加考试,如此等等。上学通常止于所教的课程结束之时。

Exercise 18

Have you ever thought of the possibility that the earth will be *invaded*(侵入) by the people from other planets?

The evening of October 30th, was just like any other ___1___ Sunday night to most of the people of America. Many families were at home ___2___ the papers or listening to the radio. There were two programmes that night which ___3___ large audiences. One was a comedy and the other was a play ___4___ by the actor-writer Orson Wells.

The listeners ___5___ themselves for an hour of comfortable excitement but, after the opening announcement, the play did not start. ___6___ there was dance music. Then just as people were beginning to wonder if something had gone wrong, an announcer ___7___ with a *dramatic*(戏剧性的) "news-flash". In an ___8___ voice, he said that a professor in an observatory had just noticed "some gas explosions on the planet of *Mars*(火星)". This news was ___9___ by a set of rapid on-the-spot broadcasts. These told the uneasy listeners the news that Martians had come to __10__ war on the earth.

Such reporting made nearly everyone believe the "invasion" was really taking place. At nine o'clock that evening, people in the United States had a __11__ feeling of fear. In New York City hundreds of families ran away in great fear from their houses and ran for __12__ to the parks. In San Francisco on the West Coast, citizens ran into the streets and __13__ the sky for the invaders. Some people, thinking they were under gas attack, even __14__ wet towels and handkerchiefs round their heads.

As the play went on that night Orson Wells was __15__ to see the studio control room full of police. They were warned about the *panic* (恐慌) which was __16__ traffic and filled the hospitals with screaming women. They ordered that announcements __17__ be made pointing out that it was only a radio play, not an __18__ news broadcast. The message was given four times __19__ the programme ended, but it was not enough to __20__ nationwide fear. Further announcements were made as late as midnight.

1. [A]exciting   [B]dull   [C]quiet   [D]free
2. [A]reading   [B]discussing   [C]correcting   [D]checking
3. [A]attracted   [B]won   [C]cheated   [D]disappointed
4. [A]bought   [B]produced   [C]read   [D]acted
5. [A]helped   [B]prepared   [C]expected   [D]enjoyed
6. [A]Even   [B]Besides   [C]Though   [D]Instead
7. [A]broke in   [B]broke off   [C]broke out   [D]broke down
8. [A]excited   [B]sweet   [C]angry   [D]strange
9. [A]included   [B]followed   [C]stopped   [D]ended
10. [A]fight   [B]stop   [C]make   [D]save
11. [A]strong   [B]little   [C]unknown   [D]normal
12. [A]safety   [B]enjoyment   [C]fun   [D]protection
13. [A]looked   [B]studied   [C]stared   [D]searched
14. [A]tied   [B]wrapped   [C]fastened   [D]wound
15. [A]frightened   [B]astonished   [C]excited   [D]pleased
16. [A]stopping   [B]controlling   [C]disturbing   [D]blocking

17. [A]should　　　[B]would　　　[C]will　　　[D]shall

18. [A]practical　　[B]right　　　[C]actual　　[D]dangerous

19. [A]after　　　　[B]since　　　[C]by　　　　[D]before

20. [A]calm　　　　[B]break　　　[C]reduce　　[D]beat

答案与分析

1.[C]。考查形容词辨义与上下文理解。exciting 兴奋的，激动的；dull 沉闷的；quiet 宁静的，平静的；free 自由的，免费的。由于下文描述的是一种恐慌，所以这里选与"恐慌"对立的 quiet 最恰当。

2.[A]。考查动词搭配。paper 用作可数名词时，指"报纸"，与之搭配的动词是 read。

3.[A]。考查动词辨义与上下文理解。attract 吸引；win 赢得（奖品等）；cheat 欺骗；disappoint 使失望。由下文可知，这两档节目有大批听众，否则就不会有那么多人听到那则外星人人侵的消息了，所以选 attract。

4.[B]。考查动词辨义。produce 在此指"制片，出品"，专用于影视、戏剧等。[A]、[C]两项明显不对，而 act 指"表演"，与动作发出者的身份不符。

5.[B]。考查固定搭配与上下文理解。prepare sb. for 是固定搭配，指"使某人准备好（做某事）"。在这里根据上下文的意思可知是说观众们作好了准备享受一个小时的兴奋，但结果却并非如此。其余三个动词都不用于这一搭配。

6.[D]。考查上下文理解。由句意不难看出，这里指喜剧没有开始，播放的却是舞曲，所以选表替代的 instead（相反，而是）。其余三项填入都不合逻辑。

7.[A]。考查固定搭配和上下文理解。break in 打断，插话；break off 中止，中断；break out 爆发，打破；break down 出故障，失败，分解。由文意可知，这里指播音员打断正常的播放，所以用 break in。

8.[A]。考查形容词辨义与上下文理解。excited 兴奋的，激动的；sweet 甜甜的；angry 愤怒的，生气的；strange 奇怪的，陌生的。由上文特别是前面一句中的 dramatic 及后文的描述可知，播音员的声音肯定是激动的。

9.[B]。考查动词辨义。include 包括；follow 跟随；stop 中止；end 结束。由上下文可知，这里指新闻之后紧接着是一系列现场报道，故选[B]。

10.[C]。考查固定搭配。make war on 为固定搭配，指"向…发动战争"。其余三项都不用在这一搭配中。

11.[A]。考查形容词辨义与上下文理解。由前面一句的交代可以看出，美国人对"入侵"信以为真，所以充满了强烈的恐惧感。little 含否定义，与前后文文意明显不符；unknown(未知的)与 normal(正常的)都不合逻辑。

12.[A]。考查名词辨义与上下文理解。首先，由上文中说美国人充满恐惧，可知他们去公园肯定不是为了娱乐(enjoyment)和找乐子(fun)，而由常识可知，公园是提供不了"保护"(protection)，所以只能选 safety，指人们跑到公园里是为了寻求安全感。

13.[D]。考查动词辨义。look 看(为不及物动词，不能直接跟宾语)；study 学习，研究；stare 瞪，凝视(也为不及物动词)；search 搜索，搜寻。

14.[A]。考查动词辨义。tie 系，拴；wrap 包，裹；fasten 系紧，系牢；wind 蜿蜒，缠绕。从战争常识看人们是用湿毛巾捂住口鼻以防毒气，一般用 tie。而 wrap 是用一层覆盖物包裹，不合题意。

15.[B]。考查形容词辨义与上下文理解。由上下文及常识可知，制片人没有想到节目会让那么多人恐慌，看到播音室里这么多警察肯定是"震惊"(astonished)，而不应该是"害怕"(frightened)、"兴奋"(excited)甚至"高兴"(pleased)。

16.[D]。考查动词辨义与上下文理解。与 traffic(交通)连用的动词一般是 block(堵塞)。其余三项都不合题意。

17.[A]。考查虚拟语气。动词 order 指"命令"且后跟宾语从句时，从句用虚拟语气，谓语动词用"should＋动词原形"，其中 should 可省略。

18.[C]。考查形容词与上下文理解。由空格前的 an 即可确定应选 actual(实际的，真实的)。practical 实用的；right 正确的；dangerous 危险的。

19.[D]。考查连词与上下文理解。由上下文可以看出，声明应当是在节目结束前播放，所以选 before 才合乎逻辑。

20.[A]。考查动词辨义。calm 平息，使平静；break 打破；reduce 减少，削减；beat 打击。由于宾语是 fear(恐惧感)，所以用 calm 最恰当。

你曾经想过地球被外星人侵略的这种可能性吗？

那个 10 月 30 日的晚上，对于大部分美国人来说就像是其他任何一个平静的周日晚上一样。许多家庭都在家里看报纸或者听收音机。那天晚上有两个有着大批听众的节目。其中一个是喜剧，另一个则是由演员兼作家奥森·韦尔斯制作的戏剧。

听众们都已经做好准备，打算享受舒适而令人兴奋的一个小时，但是在宣布开幕后，戏剧却并没有开始，而是播放舞曲。然后，就在人们开始猜测是不是哪儿出了问题时，一名播音员戏剧性地插播了一则"新闻简讯"。播音员用激动的声音说一位教授在一次观测中刚刚注意到"火星上发生了几次气体爆炸"。这则新闻之后是一系列快速的现场报道。这些报道告诉那些神经紧张的听众一个消息，火星人已经向地球开战了。

这样的报道让几乎每一个人都相信"入侵"真的发生了。那天晚上9点钟时，美国人心里充满了强烈的恐惧感。在纽约市，成百上千的家庭极为恐惧地从家里跑出来，跑到公园里寻求安全之所。在西海岸的旧金山，市民们跑上街头，搜寻天空中的入侵者。一些人认为他们受到了毒气攻击，甚至在头上裹上了湿毛巾和湿手帕。

那天晚上戏剧继续播放时，奥森·韦尔斯看到播音控制室里满是警察时大为震惊。他们得到警告说恐慌造成了交通堵塞，使医院里住满了尖叫不止的妇女。他们命令播放声明，指出这只是一个广播剧，不是实际的新闻报道。声明在节目结束前播放了4次，但不足以平息全国性的恐慌。进一步的声明直到午夜还在播放。

🔊 Exercise 19

　　From Monday until Friday most people are busy working or studying, but in the evenings and at weekends they are free and can enjoy themselves. Some watch TV or go to the *movies*（电影院）; others ___1___ sports. It depends on *individual*（个人的） ___2___ . There are many different ways to spend our ___3___ time.

　　Almost everyone has ___4___ kind of *hobby*（业余爱好）. It may be ___5___ from collecting stamps to making model airplanes. Some hobbies are very ___6___ ; others don't ___7___ at all. Some collections are ___8___ a lot of money; others are valuable only ___9___ their owners.

　　I know a man who has a coin collection worth several thousand dollars. A short time ago he bought a *rare*（稀有的） fifty-cent piece ___10___ $ 250!

　　He was very happy about his collection and thought the price was ___11___ . ___12___ , my youngest brother ___13___ match boxes. He has almost 600 of them but I doubt if they are worth any money. However,

___14___ my brother they are *extremely*(尤其) ___15___ . Nothing makes him ___16___ than to find a new match box for his collection. That's ___17___ a bobby means，I think. It is something we like to do in our spare time simply for the ___18___ of it. The value in dollars is not important，___19___ the pleasure it gives us ___20___ .

1. [A]like　　　　 [B]attend　　　　 [C]tend　　　　 [D]take part in
2. [A]time　　　　 [B]energy　　　　 [C]interests　　　 [D]fun
3. [A]spare　　　　[B]working　　　　[C]own　　　　　[D]day
4. [A]some　　　　 [B]any　　　　　 [C]certain　　　　[D]every
5. [A]OK　　　　　[B]all right　　　　[C]anything　　　 [D]something
6. [A]expensive　 [B]interesting　　 [C]exciting　　　　[D]cheap
7. [A]spend anything　　　　　　　 [B]cost anything
   [C]pay nothing　　　　　　　　　[D]need something
8. [A]worth　　　　[B]worthy　　　　 [C]valued　　　　 [D]paid
9. [A]for　　　　　[B]to　　　　　　 [C]with　　　　　 [D]of
10. [A]worth　　　 [B]spent　　　　　[C]worthy　　　　 [D]used
11. [A]a little too higher　　　　　　[B]too expensive
    [C]cheap　　　　　　　　　　　 [D]reasonable
12. [A]At the same time　　　　　　 [B]On the other hand
    [C]On the contrary　　　　　　　[D]As a matter of fact
13. [A]collects　　 [B]buys　　　　　[C]chooses　　　　[D]selects
14. [A]for　　　　　[B]to　　　　　　[C]in　　　　　　 [D]with
15. [A]dear　　　　[B]expensive　　　[C]valuable　　　 [D]costly
16. [A]so happy　　[B]that happy　　 [C]more happily　[D]happier
17. [A]what　　　　[B]how　　　　　 [C]how much　　　[D]where
18. [A]price　　　　[B]value　　　　　[C]interest　　　　[D]fun
19. [A]though　　　[B]and　　　　　 [C]but　　　　　　[D]when
20. [A]is　　　　　 [B]does　　　　　[C]will　　　　　　[D]has

😊 **答案与分析**

1．[D]。考查动词辨义与上下文理解。like 喜欢；attend 出席；tend 照料；take part in 参加。由上下文可知这里指"参加体育活动"，故选[D]。

2.[C]。考查名词辨义与上下文理解。time 时间；energy 能量，精力；interest 兴趣；fun 乐趣。由上下文及常识可知，业余活动取决于个人的兴趣，所以选[C]最恰当。

3.[A]。考查固定短语。spare time 为固定短语，指"业余时间"。

4.[A]。考查形容词辨义。some 可用于指"某种"，后面接单数名词。certain 虽然也指"某种"，但它应与不定冠词连用。其余两个都明显不对。

5.[C]。考查表达与上下文理解。由空格后的 from ... to ... 结构的内容可以看出，作者的意思是业余爱好可能是其中的任何一种，故应选含"任一"义的代词 anything。something 不含"任一"义，OK 和 all right 都指"没问题"，其后不跟其他成分。

6.[A]。考查形容词辨义与上下文理解。由下文可以看出，这里指有的爱好很费钱，有的却不需要任何花费，故此处选 expensive(昂贵的)。interesting 指"有趣的"，exciting 指"令人兴奋的"，它们与文意都没有关系。

7.[B]。考查动词搭配与上下文理解。参见上题解析。spend 应用人作主语；pay 要用人作宾语；只有 cost 可用物作主语。而 need something 填入题中不合逻辑。

8.[A]。考查搭配。be worth sth. 相当于 be worthy of sth.，指"值(多少钱)"。[C]、[D]两项时态都不对。

9.[A]。考查固定搭配。be valuable for sb. 为固定搭配，指"对某人而言很珍贵"，其中介词 for 表对象。

10.[A]。考查搭配。本题考点与第8题相同，参见该题解析。spent 和 used 都为动词的过去分词，但都不能表"值多少钱"。

11.[D]。考查形容词辨义与上下文理解。由空格前的 happy 可知这位收藏者并不认为价钱高，故选 reasonable(公道的，合理的)。注意 cheap 指"便宜"，但这里并不是说收藏者认为价钱便宜，且它不能用来修饰 price。

12.[C]。考查固定搭配与上下文联系。空格前面部分是举例说明费钱的爱好，而后面是举例说明不费钱的爱好，两者之间是对立的关系，故选 on the contrary(相反)。at the same time 同时；on the other hand 另一方面；as a matter of fact 事实上。

13.[A]。考查上下文理解。文章谈论的是爱好，这里所举的两个例子都是"收藏"，所以可根据上下文中出现多次的 collection(收集)确定选用 collects。buy 指"买"；choose 和 select 都指"选择，挑选"。

14.[A]。考查介词辨异。for 引出对象或者目的；to 表示方向；with 引出方式；of 表示所属关系。这里指"对…来说"，故应用 for。

15.[C]。考查形容词辨义。dear 钟爱的；expensive 价钱昂贵的；valuable 珍贵的；costly 代价高的，奢华的。这里并不是指邮票的价格，而是指收藏者心目中的价值，所以选 valuable。

16.[D]。考查形容词比较级。由空格后的 than 可知应用比较级，而填入的词应作 makes 的宾语补语，只能是形容词，故答案是[D]。

17.[A]。考查句子结构与连接词。由句子结构分析，空格后的部分是一个表语从句，而填入的连接词又应作从句中谓语动词 means 的宾语。四个选项中能引导表语从句且在从句中充当宾语的只有 what。

18.[D]。考查名词辨义与上下文理解。由前文的论述可知作者的意思是爱好不在于其价值，而在于它给我们带来的快乐，所以此处应选 fun（乐趣）。interest 在词义上说得通，但在这里搭配不正确，其后应用介词 in。

19.[C]。考查上下文联系。由上下文可看出，空格前的句意与空格后是转折关系，故选 but。其余三项表达的关系都不合上下文逻辑。

20.[A]。考查表达。这里是一个 not ... but ... 结构的省略句，其完整的形式应该是 the pleasure it gives us is important，前后两句的句子结构应当相同，所以省略谓语要用 is。

同步译文

　　从周一到周五，大多数人都在忙于工作或者学习，但在晚上和周末他们都有空闲，能好好娱乐。一些人看电视或者去看电影，另一些人则参加体育活动。这取决于个人的兴趣。我们有许多度过业余时间的方式。

　　几乎每个人都有某种业余爱好。它可以是从集邮到制作飞机模型中的任何一种。有些业余爱好很贵钱，其他的则根本不用花钱。有些藏品值很多钱，其他的则只对收藏者本身有价值。

　　我认识一个人，他收藏了价值几千美元的硬币。不久前他买了一枚稀有的 50 美分的硬币，花了 250 美元！

　　他对他的藏品感到很高兴，认为这物有所值。相反，我最小的弟弟收集的是火柴盒。他收集了近 600 个了，但我不知道它们是否值钱。然而，对于我弟弟来说它们却特别珍贵。没有什么比发现一种新火柴盒并加以收藏能让他更高兴的了。我想，那就是业余爱好的意义所在。它是一种我们喜欢在业余时间里做的事情，我们做它只是为了其中的乐趣。它值多少美元并不重要，重要的是它给我们带来的快乐。

Exercise 20

Animals and insects can communicate with others of __1__ kind through signals or sounds. Bees, for example, use signals to communicate information to other bees. When a bee __2__ food, it goes towards its hive. It " __3__ " in the air to tell the other bees about its __4__ . The __5__ of the dance give information about the place where the food is, and about the __6__ between that place to the *hive*(蜂巢).

Some animals make __7__ to communicate their feelings, or to pass information to each other. For example, a dog barks when it is angry, or excited. Birds make different kinds of sounds to signal, for example, danger or __8__ . __9__ , however, have something that no animal has. Human beings have the ability to express their action, feelings and ideas through __10__ . They can also write words down, in order to communicate past events and to __11__ message to people far away.

Even though some birds have learned to __12__ words, they do not understand the __13__ of the words, and therefore they cannot __14__ them to communicate ideas.

How did man first learn to __15__ ? Perhaps we shall never know. However, we do know __16__ as man's knowledge increased he __17__ use more sounds in order to express a greater number of feelings and ideas. It became necessary for him to communicate about a greater number of things. He began to make __18__ different sounds, and gradually he put these sounds together to form first words __19__ groups of words, and then __20__ . In different parts of the world, people developed their own systems of sounds and words. Today we call these systems "languages".

1. [A]different　　[B]the different　　[C]same　　[D]the same
2. [A]has found　　[B]had found　　[C]has looked　　[D]finds
3. [A]walks　　[B]steps　　[C]dances　　[D]shouts
4. [A]enemy　　[B]discovery　　[C]discover　　[D]friend

5. [A]movements　　[B]dresses　　　[C]meanings　　[D]languages

6. [A]way　　　　　[B]road　　　　[C]distance　　　[D]path

7. [A]sounds　　　[B]voice　　　　[C]sound　　　　[D]noise

8. [A]friend　　　[B]friendship　　[C]friends　　　[D]friendly

9. [A]Human beings　　　　　　　　[B]People

   [C]Persons　　　　　　　　　　[D]Beasts

10. [A]words　　　[B]world　　　　[C]warms　　　　[D]work

11. [A]set　　　　[B]sad　　　　　[C]send　　　　　[D]sent

12. [A]sing　　　[B]repeat　　　　[C]cry　　　　　[D]call

13. [A]spelling　[B]meaning　　　[C]function　　　[D]part of speech

14. [A]use　　　　[B]do　　　　　[C]force　　　　　[D]make

15. [A]tell　　　[B]talk　　　　[C]say　　　　　　[D]speak

16. [A]that　　　[B]which　　　　[C]if　　　　　　[D]where

17. [A]needs　　[B]needs to　　[C]needed to　　[D]needed

18. [A]less and less　　　　　　　[B]much and much

    [C]more and more　　　　　　　[D]little and little

19. [A]at last　　[B]finally　　　[C]in the end　　[D]then

20. [A]paragraphs　[B]languages　[C]letters　　　[D]sentences

答案与分析

1.[D]。考查上下文理解。由上下文及常识可知,一般是同类的动物之间才能交流,而这里是特指,same 前应有定冠词 the,所以选[D]。

2.[D]。考查时态。这里描述的是一般情况,且全文用的都是一般现在时,所以此处也应用一般现在时态。[C]明显不对,look 为不及物动词。

3.[C]。考查上下文理解。由引号及空格所在句中的下一句中的 dance 可知此处应用其动词第三人称单数形式。

4.[B]。考查名词辨义与上下文理解。前文说蜜蜂发现了食物,这里说它将自己的　　告诉别的蜜蜂,当然就是指"发现"了,故选 discovery。enemy 敌人;friend 朋友。discover 是动词。

5.[A]。考查名词辨义与上下文理解。movement 运动;dress 服装;meaning 意义;language 语言。这里只是强调蜜蜂"跳舞"的动作,并没有涉及其他方面,故选[A]。

6.[C]。考查名词辨义与上下文理解。由空格后的 between . . . and . . .

结构可知这里指两地的距离,故选 distance。其余三项都指"路(径)",不指远近。

　　7.[A]。考查名词辨义与上下文理解。下文所举的例子都是动物用叫声交流信息,且后面直接出现了 sound 一词。而主语是复数形式,动物的叫声也多种多样,应用复数形式 sounds。而 voice 专用于指人的嗓音,noise 指噪音。

　　8.[B]。考查上下文理解。由空格前表选择的连词 or 可知,填入的词在词义上应与 danger(危险)相对,而词性应与之相同。danger 是抽象名词,所以应填入抽象名词 friendship(友谊)。

　　9.[A]。考查上下文理解。由本句中表转折的 however 及下一句中的 human beings 可知,这里是将话题从动物转移到人类了,所以选[A]。

　　10.[A]。考查名词辨义与上下文理解。words 指"话语",world 指"世界",warms 形式不对,work 指"工作"。文章谈论的是人类的语言,且由常识可知人类是通过话语交流思想感情的。

　　11.[C]。考查动词搭配。与 message(信息)连用的动词是 send(递送)。

　　12.[B]。考查动词辨义与上下文理解。四个选项中能以 words 直接做宾语的是 repeat(重复,复述)。sing 的宾语只能是 song,cry 只作不及物动词,shout 指"喊叫"。这里指鸟类能学会说话。

　　13.[B]。考查名词辨义与上下文理解。spelling 拼写;meaning 意义;function 功能;speech 讲话。由空格前的 understand(理解)可知,这里是指鸟类尽管能学会说话,但并不理解话的意思。

　　14.[A]。考查动词辨义。use 利用,使用。do 做;force 强迫;make 使,制作。空格后的 them 指代的是前文的 words,故只能选[A]。

　　15.[D]。考查动词辨义。tell 为及物动词,指"告诉";talk 指"谈话";say 指"说",表示的是具体动作;speak 指"说话"。这里当然是问人类何时学会说话,故选[D]。

　　16.[A]。考查句子结构。由句子结构分析,空格后的部分都是动词 know 的宾语,而连接词在从句中并不充当句子成分,所以应填入 that。注意不能被宾语从句中的状语从句 as . . . 迷惑。

　　17.[C]。考查 need 的用法。need 作情态动词时跟动词原形,其本身没有人称和数的变化;作普通动词时,本身有词形变化,其后应跟动词不定式。结合这两个方面可知只有[C]对。

　　18.[C]。考查上下文理解。由上下文文意可知,既然需要交流的事情多了,那么声音的种类也应当越来越多,故选 more and more。[B]与[D]两种形式是错误的。

19.[D]。考查固定搭配与上下文理解。at last,finally 及 in the end 三个为近义词,都指"最后,最终",then 指"然后"。由空格前的 first(首先)及后文中的 and then 可知这里应选 then,而不能是其他三项。

20.[D]。考查名词辨义与上下文理解。paragraph 段落;language 语言;letter 字母;sentence 句子。由前文所说明的发展顺序(words → groups of words)可知,由 groups of words 发展下去应是 sentence 了,再发展才会是 paragraph 和 language。至于 letter 明显不对。

同步译文

动物与昆虫能通过信号或者声音与其同类交流。比如,蜜蜂能用信号与其他蜜蜂交流信息。一只蜜蜂发现食物后,就向蜂巢飞去,在空中"跳舞"把自己的发现告诉其他蜜蜂。舞蹈的不同动作可以给出食物的地点、食物距蜂巢的大致远近等信息。

一些动物通过发出声音来交流感情或者在彼此之间传递信息。比如,狗在生气或者兴奋时会吠。鸟类发出不同的声音来示意,比如说危险或者友好行为。然而,人类具有其他动物都没有的本事。人类有用话语表达自己动作、情感和想法的能力。他们还能把话语写下来,以交流过去发生的事情及向远处的人递送信息。

尽管有一些鸟类已经学会说单词,但它们并不理解这些单词的意思,因此无法用这些单词来交流想法。

人类是如何首先学会说话的?也许我们永远都无法知道。然而,我们确实知道随着人类知识的增加,他需要用更多的声音来表达更多的情感和想法。因此就更多的事情进行交流变得很必要。他开始发出越来越多的不同声音,并逐渐把这些声音组合起来,首先形成单词,然后形成词组,然后再形成句子。世界上不同地区的人们形成了各自的声音与词汇系统。今天我们把这些系统称为"语言"。

Exercise 21

If you travel in some areas in India, you will be lucky enough to be waited on by special guide-monkeys. __1__ in *waistcoat*(马甲), these monkeys are always __2__ to be of service to you. Hungry, you only have to point to your own __3__ and they will lead you to the __4__ .

___5___ the service is done, they're just ___6___ for a little money as a tip. After that, they ___7___ their hands as if they were saying good-bye to you.

___8___ it or not, the monkeys are from the School for Monkeys in India, ___9___ they were trained for one year to ___10___ their *diplomas* (文凭). They're not the only monkey students in the world. Some are now being trained ___11___ nurses in an American ___12___ college.

A ___13___ monkey named Helen has learned to ___14___ on and off the light, use a recorder and open doors and windows when she is ___15___ to. In the *tropical*(热带的) Malaysia where *coconut trees*(椰子树) ___16___ high up to the sky, monkeys would jump to the top and ___17___ off the coconuts for people. ___18___ the job is done, they would rush to their master, ___19___ to get some wild ___20___ as re-wards(奖赏).

1. [A]Acted   [B]Dressed   [C]Offered   [D]Put
2. [A]afraid   [B]against   [C]busy   [D]ready
3. [A]body   [B]food   [C]head   [D]stomach
4. [A]hotel   [B]bar   [C]restaurant   [D]motel
5. [A]After   [B]Before   [C]Since   [D]Till
6. [A]asking   [B]caring   [C]looking   [D]waiting
7. [A]close   [B]show   [C]spread   [D]wave
8. [A]Believe   [B]Guess   [C]Suppose   [D]Think
9. [A]when   [B]where   [C]which   [D]who
10. [A]accept   [B]buy   [C]get   [D]win
11. [A]as   [B]for   [C]like   [D]with
12. [A]technical   [B]medical   [C]science   [D]chemical
13. [A]three-year-old   [B]three years-old
    [C]three-years-old   [D]three-years old
14. [A]close   [B]make   [C]open   [D]turn
15. [A]allowed   [B]forced   [C]praised   [D]told
16. [A]arrive   [B]measure   [C]reach   [D]stand
17. [A]give   [B]pick   [C]take   [D]turn
18. [A]Although   [B]Because   [C]Once   [D]Since

19. [A]hope   [B]hoping   [C]to hope   [D]hoped
20. [A]animals   [B]birds   [C]fruits   [D]plants

☺ **答案与分析**

1.[B]。考查搭配与句子结构。(be) dressed in 为固定搭配,指"穿着…",这里作句子的状语。

2.[D]。考查形容词与上下文理解。afraid 害怕的,担心的;against 是介词;busy 忙碌的;ready 准备好的。由句意可知这里指猴子们随时准备为游客服务,所以选 ready。

3.[D]。考查名词辨义与上下文理解。由上下文与常识可知,饿了当然是指指自己的肚子(stomach)。

4.[C]。考查名词辨义与上下文理解。restaurant 是指就餐的"饭店"。hotel 旅馆;bar 酒吧;motel 汽车旅馆。这里指猴子会把游客带到吃饭的地方。

5.[A]。考查介词与上下文理解。由上下文与常识可知。要小费当然会是在服务结束之后,故选 after。

6.[A]。考查固定搭配与上下文理解。ask for 为固定搭配,指"要求"。care for 喜欢;look for 寻找;wait for 等待。它们都不合上下文文意。

7.[D]。考查搭配与上下文理解。由后面的 say good-bye(道别)可知这里指猴子挥手,而"挥手"用 wave one's hand。

8.[A]。考查习惯表达。believe it or not 是习惯表达,指"信不信由你",用作插入语。

9.[B]。考查定语从句。由句子结构可以看出,从句指的是地点,修饰前面的 the School for Monkeys,且填入的词在从句中做状语,故应用 where。

10.[C]。考查动词辨义。accept 接受;buy 购买;get 获得,得到;win 赢得。在学校里是通过培训获得文凭,故用 get。

11.[A]。考查介词。as 指"作为,当";for 表示"对于,向";like 指"像";with 表示"和,以"。这里指把猴子培训作护士,故用 as。

12.[B]。考查形容词辨义与上下文理解。由前面的 nurse(护士)可知培训它们的是医疗机构,故选 medical(医疗的)。technical 技术的;science 科学的,理工的;chemical 化学的。

13.[A]。考查表达。在作定语时,表年龄的数量词应组成复合词,其中名词不用复数形式,即 three-year-old。

14.[D]。考查固定搭配。turn on/off 为固定搭配,指"打开/关上(电器)"。

15.[D]。考查动词辨义与上下文理解。由上下文与常识可知,猴子应当在听到指令时才会做某些特定的事情,所以此处要用 tell(吩咐,告诉)的过去分词。allow 允许;force 强迫;praise 表扬。

16.[C]。考查动词搭配。reach 表示"伸(手)向",与介词 to 连用,此处指树高耸入云。arrive(到达)后用介词 at/in;measure 指"衡量,丈量";stand 指"站立,忍受"。

17.[B]。考查动词搭配。pick off 为固定搭配,指"摘下"。其余三项虽可与 off 构成固定搭配,但都不合句意。

18.[C]。考查连词与上下文理解。although 表让步,"尽管";because 表因果,"由于";once 表条件,"一旦",相当于 as soon as;since 表时间或者因果,"自从,由于"。由上下文来看,这里指猴子工作完了之后就跑到主人那里去讨赏,故选 once。

19.[B]。考查动词形式与句子结构。由句子结构可知,这里应用动词的非谓语形式作句子的状语。而由于 hope(希望)这一动作由句子主语(they 即猴子)发出,故用其-ing 形式而不用过去分词或不定式。

20.[C]。考查名词辨义与常识。由常识可知,猴子是吃水果的,故应选 fruits。animal 动物;bird 鸟;plant 植物。

同步译文

　　　如果在印度的一些地方旅游,够幸运的话你就会受到一些特殊的"猴导游"的服务。这些猴子穿着马甲,总是随时准备为你服务。饿了,你只要指指自己的肚子,它们就会带你到饭店去。

　　服务完之后,它们会问你要一点点钱作为小费。然后,它们就会挥挥手,似乎在跟你说再见。

　　信不信由你,这些猴子都是从印度的猴子学校出来的,在那里它们接受了一年的培训,拿到了它们的文凭。它们并不是世界上惟一的猴子学生。在美国一所医学院,一些猴子正在接受培训当护士。

　　一只名叫海伦的3岁的猴子已经学会按照指令开灯、关灯、使用录音机及打开门和窗户。在椰子树高耸入云的热带国家马来西亚,猴子们会爬到树梢为人们摘下椰子。一完成工作,它们就会跑向自己的主人,希望得到一些野果作为奖赏。

Exercise 22

My First Job

I was six when I joined my father and two elder brothers at sunrise in the fields of Eufaula, Okla. __1__ the time I was eight I was helping Dad fix up old furniture. He gave me a cent for every nail I __2__ out of old boards.

I got my first __3__ job, at JM's Restaurant in town, when I was 12. My main *responsibilities*（职责） were __4__ tables and washing dishes, __5__ sometimes I helped cook.

Every day after school I would __6__ to JM's and work until ten. Even on Saturdays I __7__ from two until eleven. At that age it was difficult going to work and __8__ my friends run off to swim or play. I didn't necessarily like work, but I loved what working __9__ me to have. Because of my __10__ I was always the one buying when my friends and I went to the local Tastee Freez. This made me __11__ .

Word that I was *trustworthy*（值得信赖的） and hard-working __12__ around town. A local clothing store offered me *credit*（赊账） __13__ I was only in seventh grade. I immediately __14__ a ＄68 sports coat and a ＄22 pair of shoes. I was __15__ only 65 cents an hour, and I already owed the storekeeper ＄90! So I learned __16__ the danger of easy credit. I paid it __17__ as soon as I could.

My first job taught me self-control, responsibility and brought me a __18__ of personal satisfaction few of my friends had experienced. As my father, __19__ worked three jobs, once told me, "If you __20__ sacrifice（奉献） and responsibility, there are not many things in life you can't have." How right he was.

1. [A]Before 　　[B]Within 　　[C]From 　　[D]By
2. [A]pulled 　　[B]put 　　[C]picked 　　[D]pressed
3. [A]usual 　　[B]real 　　[C]main 　　[D]particular
4. [A]sweeping 　　[B]packing 　　[C]clearing 　　[D]emptying
5. [A]or 　　[B]so 　　[C]but 　　[D]even

6. [A]head   [B]turn   [C]change   [D]move

7. [A]studied   [B]worked   [C]played   [D]slept

8. [A]helping   [B]having   [C]watching   [D]letting

9. [A]asked   [B]told   [C]promised   [D]allowed

10. [A]study   [B]power   [C]age   [D]job

11. [A]proud   [B]friendly   [C]lucky   [D]hopeful

12. [A]ran   [B]got   [C]flew   [D]carried

13. [A]although   [B]while   [C]if   [D]since

14. [A]sold   [B]borrowed   [C]charged   [D]wore

15. [A]keeping   [B]making   [C]paying   [D]taking

16. [A]gradually   [B]greatly   [C]hardly   [D]early

17. [A]out   [B]over   [C]away   [D]off

18. [A]point   [B]level   [C]part   [D]sign

19. [A]he   [B]that   [C]who   [D]whoever

20. [A]understand   [B]demand   [C]offer   [D]fear

答案与分析

1.[D]。考查介词用法。by the time 指"到…时"。before、within、from 用于这一搭配中时句子一般要用完成时态。

2.[A]。考查固定搭配。pull out 指"取出";put out 指"镇压,平息";pick out 指"挑出";press out 指"榨出,挤出"。由于这里指从旧木板上取钉子,所以[A]最恰当。

3.[B]。考查形容词辨义与上下文理解。usual 通常的,平常的;real 真正的;main 主要的;particular 特别的。由上下文可以看出,作者是将这一工作与前面所述的替父亲干活进行比较,意思是这一份工作才算得上是真正的工作,并没有强调工作的性质,所以选 real。

4.[C]。由于宾语是 tables(桌子),所以用 clearing(清理、收拾)。sweep 打扫,清扫(地面);pack 装箱,打包;empty 清空。

5.[C]。考查上下文联系。空格前说主要的工作是收拾桌子和刷盘子,空格后说有时也帮着做饭,两者之间应是转折关系,故选 but。or 表选择,so 表因果,even 表递进。

6.[A]。考查固定搭配。head to 朝…前进,径直去…;turn to 转向…;change to 变为…;move to 搬到…。这里是指作者去店里工作,只能用 head。

7.[B]。考查上下文理解。由句首的 even 可知这里是进一步说明自己的工作情况,故仍用 worked。

8.[C]。考查动词辨义与上下文理解。由空格后的内容可以看出,作者的朋友们都在玩,他却在工作,当然只能说是"看着朋友们跑去游泳或者玩",选 watching。其余三个动词填入都不合逻辑。

9.[D]。考查动词辨义与上下文理解。ask 询问,要求;tell 告诉;promise 承诺,保证;allow 允许。除了 allow 外,其余三项填入题中都不合上下文逻辑。

10.[D]。考查上下文理解。文章谈论的就是作者工作的情况,而正是工作让他可以替朋友们付钱。

11.[A]。考查形容词辨义与上下文理解。由上下文及本句中的 made (使)可知是在说明作者的心情,故选 proud(自豪的)。friendly 友好的;lucky 幸运的;hopeful 充满希望的。

12.[B]。考查固定搭配。get around 指"传遍",符合文意。

13.[A]。考查上下文联系。空格前说"服装店让我赊账",后面说"我还只上七年级",两者之间应当是让步关系,故选 although(尽管),表示了这一做法的不同寻常。

14.[C]。考查动词辨义与上下文理解。sell 卖;borrow 借;charge 付款(购买);wear 穿。前文说商店让作者赊账,那么紧跟着应当是说作者赊账买东西。除 charge 外其余三项都与此无关。

15.[B]。考查动词辨义。make 可用于指"赚(钱)",其余三项都不能这样用。

16.[D]。考查副词辨义与上下文理解。由作者前文的描述可知,他七年级时就可赊账,然后他买东西欠下了许多钱,而他挣的却不多,因此这里得出结论说他很早就(通过自己的经历)了解到了赊账太容易的危险性。

17.[D]。考查固定搭配。pay out 付出大笔款项;pay over 为…正式付款;pay 一般不与 away 连用;pay off 付清,还清(债务)。由上下文可知这里用 pay off 最恰当。

18.[B]。考查名词辨义。point 点;level 水平,程度;part 部分;sign 标志。除 level 外,其余三项填入句中都造成无法理解。

19.[C]。考查连接代词。由句子结构可知这里是一个定语从句,填入的代词做从句主语,故用 who。whoever 为不定指,意为"任何人",明显不对。

20.[A]。考查动词辨义与上下文理解。understand 理解,明白;demand 要求;offer 提供,提出;fear 害怕。[B]、[D]两项明显不对;offer 后应当跟 sb.。

我的第一份工作

我6岁时就开始和我的父亲、两个哥哥在天亮后去奥克拉何马州尤法拉的地里干活了。到我8岁时,我就在协助父亲修理旧家具了。我每从旧木板上拔出一颗钉子,他就给我1美分。

我12岁时在市里的JM饭店找到了第一份真正的工作。我的主要职责是收拾桌子和洗盘子,但有时也帮着做饭。

每天放学后我都径直去JM饭店,工作到10点。就算是周六我也从2点工作到11点。在那个年龄,看着我的朋友们跑去游泳或者玩,而我要去工作是一件很难受的事情。我不一定喜欢工作,但我喜欢工作给我带来的东西。由于我有工作,当我和朋友们一起去本地的Tastee Frezee时总是我买单。这样我很自豪。

我值得信任、工作勤奋的话语开始传遍了市里。一家本地的服装店在我还在上七年级时就让我赊账。我立即买了一件68美元的运动服和一双22美元的鞋子。那时我每小时只挣65美分,而我欠服装店老板就有90美元!因此我很早就了解到了轻易赊账的危险性。我尽快偿清了债务。

我的第一份工作教给了我自制、责任,并给我带来了我的朋友们很少经历的个人满足感。就像我那干过三种工作的父亲曾经告诉我的那样:"如果理解了奉献和责任感,生活中没有太多你无法得到的东西。"他的话多么正确啊。

Exercise 23

Humans and *orangutans*(猩猩) are 97 percent exactly alike according to DNA. Orangutans are as skilled in learning ___1___ language as the other great *apes*(类人猿) — and their attention ___2___ is longer. They can unlock a cage's lock ___3___ a piece of wire. They can even be ___4___ to make *flint*(火石) knives, the ___5___ our *ancestors*(祖先) ___6___ two million years ago. But the trees are ___7___ and orangutans — whose name means man of the forest in Malay — are disappearing ___8___ them. Once ___9___ across Southeast Asia, orangutans are now found only on the islands of Bomeo and Sumatra. ___10___ the past twenty years, due to ___11___ cut down in great number and plantation agriculture, the rain forests ___12___ they live have been ___13___ by 80 percent. ___14___ 1987 the wild orangutan population has fallen rapidly from 180 000 to 27 000.

_____15_____ the orangutans have a determined friend. She has spent 27 years __16__ __17__ orangutans while having to face all possible kinds of __18__ in the tropical forests. She has __19__ and *rehabilita-ted*(安置) scores of __20__ orangutans and for their *survival*(生存) she traveled around the world to get help.

1. [A]spoken　　[B]sign　　　　[C]body　　　　[D]written
2. [A]thing　　　[B]advantage　　[C]nature　　　[D]period
3. [A]upon　　　[B]on　　　　　[C]without　　　[D]with
4. [A]seen　　　[B]taught　　　[C]asked　　　　[D]forced
5. [A]figure　　[B]system　　　[C]kind　　　　[D]one
6. [A]thought of　[B]found　　　[C]made　　　　[D]imitated
7. [A]disappearing[B]growing　　[C]existing　　[D]dying
8. [A]with　　　[B]for　　　　[C]because of　[D]around
9. [A]general　　[B]strong　　　[C]common　　　[D]usual
10. [A]Around　　[B]Over　　　　[C]In　　　　　[D]About
11. [A]being　　[B]be　　　　　[C]been　　　　[D]be being
12. [A]which　　[B]that　　　　[C]of　　　　　[D]where
13. [A]reduced　[B]broken　　　[C]destroyed　[D]saved
14. [A]In　　　[B]After　　　[C]Since　　　[D]When
15. [A]Often　　[B]Actually　　[C]Meanwhile　[D]Fortunately
16. [A]on　　　[B]in　　　　　[C]at　　　　　[D]to
17. [A]learning　[B]catching　　[C]searching　[D]studying
18. [A]danger　　[B]weather　　[C]disasters　[D]sicknesses
19. [A]saved　　[B]cured　　　[C]raised　　　[D]liberated
20. [A]major　　[B]homeless　　[C]rare　　　　[D]lovely

答案与分析

1.[B]。考查习惯搭配与上下文理解。spoken language 口语；sign language 手语；body language 肢体语言；written language 书面语。由上下文与常识可知，猩猩最可能学会的就是手语，故选[B]。

2.[D]。考查名词辨义与上下文理解。thing 事情，东西；advantage 好处，优点;nature 自然,性质;period 时期,时间。由于受 attention(注意力)修饰,且表语为 longer(更长),所以此处选 period,指注意力可持续的时间。

3.[D]。考查介词用法。由于空格后是工具,所以应选表"用,以"的 with。而 upon 和 on 一般表方位,without 明确不合文意。

4.[B]。考查动词辨义与上下文理解。see 看到;teach 教;ask 询问;force 强迫。由上下文与常识可知这里应指猩猩被教会制作石刀。说它们能被"看到"、"询问"或者"强迫"制作石刀都不合逻辑。

5.[C]。考查上下文理解。由句子结构可知,空格所在分句为 flint knives 的同位语,意思是它们制作的石刀与我们的祖先制作的一样,所以选 kind(种类)。其余三项都不合逻辑:figure 数字,人物;system 系统;one 为代词单数,与前面用复数形式及逻辑上都矛盾。

6.[C]。考查上下文理解。在同位语中含有一个定语从句,the kind 作从句谓语动词的宾语,而由上题解析可知 the kind 指的就是 flint knives,故承前而来,应用动词 made。

7.[A]。考查动词辨义。disappear 消失;grow 生长;exist 存在;die 死亡 (dying 则表示"临死的")。由下文句意及其中的 disappearing 可知应选[A]。

8.[A]。考查介词用法。空格后的 them 指代前文中的 trees,所以这里是指猩猩与树木一起消失,故选表示"和,与"的介词 with。for 表目的、对象,即 "为";because of 表示原因,即"由于";around 表示"周围,大约"。

9.[C]。考查形容词辨义与上下文理解。由逗号后的句子意思可以看出,这里指猩猩在东南亚曾经很多,故选表示"常见"的 common。general 普通的,总体的;strong 强壮的,强大的;usual 通常的。它们都不用于指因数量多而"常见"。

10.[B]。考查介词用法。[A]、[D]两项明显不对。in 表示在一段时间之内或者之后,但它多用于一段相对较短的时间。而 over 除指"…之上"外,还可指"经过"一段较长的时间,符合文意。

11.[B]。考查介词搭配。thanks to(由于)是介词,故其后应跟动名词形式。

12.[D]。考查定语从句的连接词。由于此处需要填入的连接词在从句中作地点状语,故应用表地点的连接词 where。

13.[A]。考查搭配。"reduce by + 百分比数词"指"减少了百分之多少"。其余三个动词都不用于这种搭配。

14.[C]。考查连词用法。由句子使用的是现在完成时态可知应选 since (自从)。"in+年份"一般与过去时态或者将来时态连用;after 一般与过去时态连用；when 表示的是时间点，不用于年份前。

15.[D]。考查副词与上下文理解。often 常常（表示频率）；actually 实际上（用于修正前文）；meanwhile 同时（表示同步）；fortunately 幸运的是，幸运地。由后文的描述可知一位女士一直为保护猩猩而努力，所以这里要选含褒义的[D]项。

16.[B]。考查固定搭配。spend 的常用搭配有两种：spend ... on sth. / sb. 和 spend ... （in）doing sth.。由后面一空中的选项可知是一个动词，所以用后一种搭配，介词用 in。

17.[D]。考查动词辨义。learn 学会，学习；catch 抓住，捕捉；search 搜索，搜寻；study 学习，研究。由后文的描述可推断出这位女士从事的应当是对猩猩进行研究的工作，故选[D]。

18.[A]。考查名词辨义与上下文理解。danger 危险；weather 天气；disaster 灾难；sickness 疾病。由常识可知她要面对的是热带雨林中的种种危险，其他三项都只可能是某一次具体的危险。

19.[A]。考查动词辨义与上下文理解。save 挽救；cure 治愈；raise 养育；liberate 解放。由空格后的 rehabilitated 及最后一句中的 survival 与常识可知选 save 最恰当。

20.[B]。考查形容词辨义与上下文理解。由 rehabilitated 一词及前文中提到的森林被砍伐两点即可确定这里要选 homeless（无家可归的），即为无家可归的猩猩找到安置之所。

同步译文

人类和猩猩的基因有97％完全相同。猩猩学习手语与其他高级类人猿一样熟练，而它们的注意力持续时间更长。它们可以用一根铁丝打开笼子上的锁。甚至能教会它们制作石刀，与我们的祖先在两百万年前制作的那一种一样。但是森林正在消失，猩猩这种其名字在马来语中指"森林里的人"的动物也正随着它们消失。曾经在东南亚分布广泛的猩猩，如今只在 Bomeo 和 Sumatra 两个岛上发现有。在过去的20年里，由于大量砍伐和农耕，它们居住的热带雨林已经减少了80％。从1987年以来野生猩猩的数量从180 000只锐减到了27 000只。

幸运的是，猩猩们有一位坚毅的朋友。她已经对猩猩进行了27年的研究，同时必须面对热带雨林中的一切危险。她已经挽救和安置了大批无家可归的猩猩，并且为了猩猩们的生存她游走于世界各地以寻求帮助。

Exercise 24

　　We have known for a long time that flowers of different plants open and close at __1__ time of day. This is so familiar that there seems to be no need to ask the __2__ for it. Yet no one really understands why __3__ open and close like this at particular time. The process is not as simple as we might think, as recent __4__ have shown. In one, flowers were kept in constant darkness. We might expect that the flowers, without any information about the time of day, did not open as they __5__ do. In fact, they __6__ to open at their usual time. This suggests that they have some *mysterious*（神秘的）ways of knowing the __7__ . Their sense of time does not depend on information from the outside world; it is, so to speak, __8__ them, a kind of "inner clock".

　　This discovery may not seem to be very important. __9__ , it was __10__ found that not just plants but animals — including man — have this "inner clock", which __11__ the working of their bodies and *influences*（影响）their activities. Human beings, then, are also influenced by this __12__ power. __13__ we wish it or not, it affects such things in our life as our need for sleep, our need for food, and our __14__ to *concentrate*（集中）.

　　In the past, this did not matter very much because people lived in natural __15__ . In the __16__ world, things are __17__ ; now there are spacemen, airplane pilots and, in ordinary life, a lot of people who have to work at night. It would be very __18__ , then, to know more about the "inner clock". Such ordinary things as __19__ might help us to understand more about __20__ .

1. [A]same　　　[B]different　　　[C]some　　　[D]all
2. [A]shape　　　[B]beauty　　　[C]reason　　　[D]kind
3. [A]plants　　　[B]leaves　　　[C]seeds　　　[D]flowers
4. [A]experiments　[B]books　　　[C]programmes　[D]flowers
5. [A]seldom　　　[B]normally　　[C]hardly　　　[D]unusually
6. [A]stopped　　　[B]continued　　[C]kept　　　[D]happened

7. [A]time　　　[B]place　　　[C]kind　　　[D]duty

8. [A]outside　　[B]inside　　[C]out of　　[D]from

9. [A]But　　　　[B]Although　[C]However　[D]Still

10. [A]later　　　[B]earlier　　[C]soon　　　[D]latest

11. [A]connects　[B]controls　[C]deals with　[D]knows

12. [A]common　[B]mysterious　[C]little　　　[D]known

13. [A]If　　　　[B]Why　　　[C]Whether　[D]That

14. [A]ability　　[B]realization　[C]motivation　[D]activity

15. [A]land　　　[B]society　　[C]conditions　[D]air

16. [A]ancient　[B]same　　　[C]modern　　[D]different

17. [A]same　　[B]usual　　　[C]different　[D]ordinary

18. [A]harmful　[B]useful　　[C]impossible　[D]useless

19. [A]time　　　[B]flowers　　[C]ourselves　[D]work

20. [A]life　　　[B]flowers　　[C]plants　　[D]ourselves

 答案与分析

　　1.[B]。考查上下文理解。由空格前的 open(开放)和 close(闭合)及常识可知这两个时间是不同的,故选 different。

　　2.[C]。考查搭配与上下文理解。由空格后的 for 及下文的 why 可知应选 reason(原因)。其余三个词都不与 for 连用。

　　3.[D]。考查上下文理解。文章第一句就说的是 flowers(花)的开放与闭合,且植物(plants)、树叶(leaves)和种子(seeds)都不用 open 与 close 作谓语。

　　4.[A]。考查名词辨义与上下文理解。由空格后的谓语动词 show(表明)可知应选 experiments(实验)才符合逻辑。books(书)、programmes(节目)与 flowers 无疑都不用 show 作谓语。

　　5.[B]。考查副词辨义与上下文理解。这里是指我们希望花不像它们在正常情况下那样开放或者闭合。除 normally(正常地)外,其余三个副词都是否定副词,填入句中都成了双重否定表达肯定含意,都不合上下文逻辑。

　　6.[B]。考查动词辨义与搭配。stop to do 指"停下来去做(另一事)";keep 后应当跟动名词;happen to do 指"碰巧做"。因此它们都不合题意。continue to do 指"继续做"。

　　7.[A]。考查上下文理解。前文中说的都是花开和花合的时间,所以这里也是指它们知道时间,才能在确定的时间分别开花和闭合。

8.[B]。考查上下文理解。由句子结构可知,空格所在分句是对前一分句的解释;前一分句中用否定句式 not ... outside,那么这一分句中用肯定形式就应当是 inside。由本句中的 inner(内部的)也可推知答案。

9.[C]。考查上下文联系。由上下文不难看出本句与前一句之间是转折关系。但 but 不用于句首,故应用 however。although 表示的是让步关系,still 表示的是"仍然"。

10.[A]。考查副词辨义与上下文理解。later 后来;earlier 早前,更早时(它是比较级);soon 不久,很快(它与所用过去时态不符);latest 最后(它是最高级)。这里指"后来发现…"最合逻辑。

11.[B]。考查动词辨义。connect 联系(其后应跟介词 with);control 控制;deal with 处理,对付;know 知道,了解。由后面与之并列的动词 influence 及常识可知选 control。

12.[B]。考查形容词辨义与上下文理解。文章第一段指出植物内部的"时钟"能控制花的开放和闭合时间,这是一种神秘的方式,而人体内也有这种力量,但由于人们并不知道原因,所以它应当是"神秘的"。其余三个形容词在词义上都不合文意。

13.[C]。考查固定搭配。只有 whether 能与 or not 连用。

14.[A]。考查名词辨义与搭配。ability 能力;realization 实现;motivation 动机;activity 活动。除 ability 后跟不定式作后置定语,其余三项都不能这样用,且意思上也不合逻辑。

15.[C]。考查名词辨义。land 土地;society 社会;conditions 状态;air 气氛,氛围,空气。由修饰词 natural(自然的)可知应选[C]。

16.[C]。考查上下文理解。由后文中的 now(如今)可知,这里是对现代社会里的情况进行说明,与前一句形成对比,故选 modern。

17.[C]。考查上下文理解。参见上题解析。现代社会的情况肯定与过去不同,应选 different。

18.[B]。考查形容词辨义与上下文理解。由前文分析的原因与上下文不难看出作者对"更多地了解'体内时钟'"是持肯定态度的,所以选 useful(有用的)。其余三项都否定义。

19.[B]。考查上下文理解。这一句是对全文进行总结。文章论述了由花的开放和闭合时间引起人们对自身"体内时钟"的研究,所以由下文(有助于我们了解自己)可知这里所说的"普通事物"指的就是花。

20.[D]。考查上下文理解。参见上题解析。这里是将文章涉及的两个方面(人类自己与花之类的普通事物)之间的关系联系起来。

同步
译文

我们很早就知道,不同植物的花朵每天在不同的时间开放和闭合。这一现象如此普遍,似乎没有必要去问它们为何这样。然而没有人真正明白为什么花朵会这样在特定的时间开放和闭合。近来的实验表明,这一过程不像我们想像的那样简单。在一个实验中,花朵被一直放在黑暗中。我们也许认为,那些花在没有白天的时间信息的情况下,不会像在正常情况下那样开放和闭合。事实上,它们却继续在平常的时间开放。这表明它们有一些知道时间的神秘方法。它们的时间感并不取决于来自外部世界的信息;这么说吧,在它们内部有一种"体内时钟"。

这一发现也许看起来不是很重要。然而,后来发现不仅是植物有,而且动物,包括人类,也有这种"体内时钟"在控制着他们的身体机能、影响着他们的活动。因此人类也受到这一神秘力量的影响。不管我们希望与否,它都影响到我们生活中诸如我们的睡眠需要、我们的食物需要和我们集中注意力的能力之类的事情。

过去由于人们生活在自然状态下,所以这一点并不很重要。在现代世界,情况就不同了;如今有宇航员、飞行员,在日常生活中还有许多要上夜班的人。那么多了解一些关于"体内时钟"的知识就会很有用处。像花这样的普通事物也许会有助于我们更多地了解我们自己。

Exercise 25

As late as 1800, women's only place was in the home. The idea of women in the business world was unthinkable. No "nice" women would ___1___ of entering what was strictly a "man's" world. Men believed that ___2___ woman could handle a job outside her home. This was such a ___3___ accepted idea that when the famous Brontë sisters began writing books in 1846, they *disguised*(伪装) themselves by ___4___ their books with men's names.

Teaching was the first profession ___5___ to women soon after 1800. But even that was not an easy profession for women to enter because ___6___ high schools and colleges were open only to men. Oberlin College in Ohio was the first college in America to ___7___ women.

Hospital ___8___ became acceptable work for women only ___9___ Florence Nightingale became famous. Because she was a ___10___ and educated woman, as well as a nurse, people began to believe __11__ was possible for women to nurse the __12__ and still be "ladies". Miss Nightingale opened England's first training school for nurses in 1860.

The __13__ of the typewriter in 1867 helped to bring women out of the home and into the business world. Because women had *slender*（纤细）, quick __14__ , they learned to __15__ typewriters quickly and well. Businessmen found that they had to __16__ women for this new kind of work.

__17__ 1900, thousands of women were working at real __18__ in schools, hospitals and offices in both England and America. Some women even __19__ to become doctors or lawyers. The idea __20__ "nice" women could work in the business world had been accepted.

1. [A]think　　[B]dream　　[C]be afraid　　[D]be proud
2. [A]every　　[B]each　　[C]no　　[D]any
3. [A]widely　　[B]highly　　[C]wide　　[D]generally
4. [A]naming　　[B]giving　　[C]signing　　[D]writing
5. [A]offered　　[B]given　　[C]closed　　[D]open
6. [A]no　　[B]all　　[C]many　　[D]most
7. [A]take　　[B]accept　　[C]receive　　[D]use
8. [A]nurses　　[B]nursing　　[C]doctors　　[D]nursery
9. [A]after　　[B]since　　[C]until　　[D]before
10. [A]healthy　　[B]lovely　　[C]wealthy　　[D]lively
11. [A]it　　[B]she　　[C]that　　[D]what
12. [A]ill　　[B]poor　　[C]rich　　[D]sick
13. [A]discovery　　[B]invention　　[C]foundation　　[D]invitation
14. [A]eyes　　[B]fingers　　[C]minds　　[D]hands
15. [A]operate　　[B]make　　[C]clean　　[D]repair
16. [A]fire　　[B]ask　　[C]employ　　[D]thank
17. [A]By　　[B]To　　[C]From　　[D]In
18. [A]works　　[B]offices　　[C]jobs　　[D]names
19. [A]succeeded　　[B]learned　　[C]tried　　[D]managed
20. [A]that　　[B]if　　[C]whether　　[D]why

答案与分析

1.[B]。考查动词搭配与上下文理解。think of 考虑；dream of 梦想；be afraid of 害怕；be proud of 自豪。文章第一、二句即指出，过去女性只能待在家里，女性进入商业世界不可想像。因此，女人进入男性世界肯定只能是一个梦想。用 dream 比用 think 更形象化。

2.[C]。考查形容词与上下文理解。参见上题分析。前面几句都是否定女性进入外部世界的，而本句用的是肯定句式，所以形容词就要用否定的 no。

3.[A]。考查副词辨义与用法。wide 是形容词，widely 是副词，指"广泛地"。highly 高度地；generally 通常。由于修饰的是 accepted（接受的），所以用表范围的[A]。

4.[C]。考查动词辨义。name 命名；give 给；sign 签名；write 写。由于这里指在书上署名，所以要用 sign。

5.[D]。考查搭配与上下文理解。由后一句中相同的结构 were open only to men 可知此处要用 open。be open to 指"对…开放"，即可以参加、从事等，其后多跟 sb.。

6.[D]。考查上下文理解。由空格前的结果可以看出原因是大多数高中和大学都只对男性开放，选 most。[B]项 all 太绝对，因为女性已经能教学了，说明肯定有一些学校对女性是开放的，否则女性就达不到与教师这一职业相应的文化水平。

7.[B]。考查动词辨义。accept 与 receive 的区别在于前者指"（愿意）接受"，而后者仅指"收到"这一动作。美国的这个大学让女性去上学，说明是愿意接受的，故选 accept 最恰当。而 take 与 use 都不能指"接收"。

8.[B]。考查名词辨义与上下文理解。nurse 指具体的"护士"；nursing 指"护理（学）"；nursery 指"托儿所"。由句子的表语 work 可知主语应当是抽象的 nursing。

9.[A]。考查介词与上下文理解。由上下文文意与常识可知，是在南丁格尔的影响下人们才接受女性做护理工作这一现象，故选 after。

10.[C]。考查形容词辨义与上下文理解。由空格后表并列的 and 可知填入的词应与 educated（受过教育的）内涵相同，故选 wealthy（富有的）。healthy 指"健康的"；lovely 指"可爱的"；lively 指"生动的，活泼的"；它们都与 educated 不形成并列关系。

11.[A]。考查习惯表达。在 believe 后的宾语从句中多用 it 作形式主

语，而把真正主语(to nurse ...)后置。

12.[D]。考查习惯表达。由动词 nurse 可知其宾语应当是指"病人"，而"病人"的习惯表达是 the sick，这是"the＋形容词"表一类人的用法。

13.[B]。考查名词辨义。discovery 指"发现"本已存在的事物；invention 指"发明"本不存在的事物；foundation 指"基础，地基"；invitation 指"邀请"。由文意可知这里指打字机的发明。

14.[B]。考查上下文理解。由常识与上下文可知，女性的手指纤长，更适合于打字。其余三项都不是女性善于打字的原因。

15.[A]。考查动词辨义与上下文理解。由于这里指的是女性从事打字工作，所以应选 operate(操作)。make 制造；clean 打扫，清理；repair 修理。它们都与女性手指长度和速度没有关系，所以不合文意。

16.[C]。考查动词辨义与上下文理解。由上下文不难推知这里指男性不得不聘请女性打字，所以选 employ(雇用)。fire 指"解雇"；ask 指"询问"(ask for 指"要求")；thank 指"感谢"。

17.[A]。考查介词用法。"by＋年份"表示的是"到哪一年时"，符合文章对女性工作情况发展过程的描述。

18.[C]。考查名词辨义与用法。works 指"著作"，work 指"工作"时为不可数名词；offices 指"办公室"，其前的介词用 in；names 指"名字"。只有 jobs(工作)可用在介词 at 后，意思上也符合文意。

19.[D]。考查动词辨义。succeed 指"成功"，其后一般不跟不定式而跟 in (doing) sth.；learn 指"学会"，说"学会成为…"不合逻辑；try 指"尝试"，含有结果未知或者不成功之意；manage 指"设法(做成)"，符合语法与文意。

20.[A]。考查句子结构。由句子结构分析，空格后的部分是 idea 的同位语从句，而选项中只有 that 能引导同位语从句。

　　直到 1800 年，妇女都还只能待在家里。妇女进入商业世界的想法令人不可想像。没有一名"正派的"女性会梦想进入一个严格属于"男性"的世界。男性认为没有女性能处理家庭以外的工作。这一观点被广泛接受，以至于著名的勃朗特姐妹在 1846 年开始写书时，还要在她们的书上署上男性名字来伪装自己。

　　1800 年后教师很快成了向女性开放的第一门职业。但是甚至教师对女性来说也不是一个容易进入的职业，因为大多数高中和大学都只对男性开放。俄亥俄州的奥伯林学院是美国第一所接纳女性的学院。

在弗罗伦斯•南丁格尔出名后,医院护理才变成了一种可以接受的女性工作。因为她是一位富有且受过教育的女性,也是一名护士,人们开始认为女性可以在护理病人的同时仍保持"女士"身份。南丁格尔小姐在 1860 年开办了英国的第一所护士培训学校。

1867 年打字机的发明对让女性走出家门进入商业世界起了很大作用。由于女性拥有纤长、敏捷的手指,她们学会操作打字机速度很快,打得也很好。商人们发现他们不得不雇用女性来从事这一类新工作。

到 1900 年时,英国和美国都有成千上万的女性在学校、医院和办公室里真正的工作岗位上工作。一些女性甚至设法成为了医生或者律师。"正派的"女性能在商业世界里工作的观点已被广为接受。

Exercise 26

Historically，London is one of Britain's great ___1___ port. So today there are many sights along the ___2___ Thames which remind the visitors of ___3___ Britain's *maritime*（海上的）history. One of the most interesting places is Greenwich in the South East of London，___4___ you can go round the famous Cutty Sark.

The Cutty Sark is a type of sailing ship. They got her ___5___ in 1869，and wanted her to be the fastest ship in the China tea trade. For that is what the ship ___6___ — tea, from the Far East. In those days there was a lot of competition ___7___ the shipowners to ___8___ home tea from China as ___9___ as possible. In 1954，many years later，the Cutty Sark stopped at Greenwich so that ___10___ can now admire her.

When you look ___11___ the ship，you see lots of things which tell the story of the sailors who ___12___ months on board the ship. When they built the Suez Canal，steamers took over the sea trade and Cutty Sark started to carry wool ___13___ Australia.

The sailors' ___14___ place is ___15___ of a visit to it. The sailors slept in bare wooden bed with *straw mattresses*（草垫）. Conditions for the officers were ___16___ ，but still very bad by modern standard.

In ___17___ part of the ship you can see the kitchen and the workshop. The living and working areas are very small and were very

_____18_____ for the sailors on a long _____19_____. It is hard to _____20_____ what their life was like. They worked at least twenty hours a day，seven days a week，often in cold，wet and dangerous conditions. And the men only earned a few pounds a month.

A visit to the Cutty Sark reminds us that the history of the sailing ship were not as *romantic*（浪漫的）as they seem to us now！

1. [A]buying　　　[B]trading　　　[C]showing　　　[D]selling
2. [A]river　　　　[B]sea　　　　　[C]ocean　　　　[D]brook
3. [A]before　　　[B]passed　　　[C]past　　　　　[D]ago
4. [A]which　　　[B]what　　　　[C]where　　　　[D]while
5. [A]started　　[B]start　　　　[C]begun　　　　[D]begin
6. [A]took　　　　[B]carried　　　[C]held　　　　　[D]put
7. [A]with　　　　[B]between　　[C]among　　　　[D]from
8. [A]get　　　　[B]load　　　　　[C]burden　　　　[D]bring
9. [A]fast　　　　[B]quickly　　　[C]rapidly　　　　[D]soon
10. [A]visitors　　[B]soldiers　　[C]officials　　　[D]citizens
11. [A]down　　　[B]up　　　　　[C]at　　　　　　[D]round
12. [A]made　　　[B]spent　　　　[C]took　　　　　[D]had
13. [A]at　　　　　[B]off　　　　　[C]from　　　　　[D]to
14. [A]sleeping　[B]eating　　　[C]drilling　　　　[D]shooting
15. [A]worthy　　[B]worth　　　[C]necessary　　[D]cost
16. [A]well　　　　[B]bad　　　　[C]worse　　　　[D]better
17. [A]the front　[B]before　　　[C]front　　　　　[D]ahead
18. [A]enjoyable　　　　　　　　[B]good
　　　[C]uncomfortable　　　　[D]pleasant
19. [A]journey　　[B]voyage　　[C]trip　　　　　　[D]travel
20. [A]imagine　　[B]enjoy　　　[C]believe　　　　[D]follow

😊 **答案与分析**

1.[B]。考查动词辨义与上下文理解。buy 买；trade 贸易；show 出示，展示；sell 卖。由上下文及常识可知，一个港口的功能不可能只是卖或者买，或者展示，而应当是一个"贸易港"。

2.[A]。考查上下文理解与常识。Thames 是一条河名,作填入词的同位语,故选 river。brook 指"小溪"。

3.[C]。考查形近词辨异。由句子结构可知这里应填入一个形容词,选项中只有[B]、[C]两项能作形容词。passed 是动词 pass 的过去分词,指"通过的";past 指"过去的"。由前面的 remind(使记起)及后面的 history(历史)可知只能选 past。

4.[C]。考查连接词。由句子结构不难看出这里是一个定语从句,连接词在从句中作地点状语,故选 where。

5.[A]。考查动词辨义与语态。由上下文可知 her 指代的是船,而船的"发动"用 start。但由于船只能是"被发动",故应用过去分词形式。

6.[B]。考查动词辨义。take 拿、携带;carry 运载、携带;hold 握、持有、保持;put 放置。茶叶由船"运载",所以选[B]。

7.[C]。考查介词用法。between 用于指两者之间,among 用于三者或三者以上之间。由于船肯定不止两个,所以用 among。with 和 from 都不合逻辑。

8.[D]。考查动词辨义。get 到达;load 装载;burden 负担;bring 携带。由于宾语是 tea,所以用 bring,指将茶叶带回家。不要被副词 home 干扰。

9.[A]。考查副词辨义。四个选项都是副词,都含"快"的意思。但 fast 强调的是机器、交通工具等运动的速度快,而 quickly 和 soon 强调的是人的动作、采取行动的速度快,rapidly 指"迅速地",强调用时短。由上下文来看,这里强调船速,故用 fast 最恰当。

10.[A]。考查上下文理解。第一段最后一句即指出,游客可以参观 Cutty Sark 这条著名的船,这里说可以瞻仰这条船,当然指的仍是游客可以参观了,故选 visitors。

11.[D]。考查固定搭配。look down 朝下看,小瞧;look up 向上看,查阅;look at 看;look round 环顾。由后一分句指出的能看到的东西之多可知选 round 最恰当。

12.[B]。考查动词搭配。四个选项中只有 spend 一词后可跟 on,指"花时间…"。

13.[C]。考查搭配与上下文理解。这里指从澳大利亚运羊毛到英国,选 from。上文已经出现过 bring ... from ... 这一搭配,可以据此确定答案。

14.[A]。考查上下文理解。由下文中介绍的 slept(睡觉)、bed(床)、mattresses(草垫)等可知这里指的是水手们睡觉的地方。

15.[A]。考查固定搭配。be worthy of 相当于 be worth,指"值得…"。

16.[D]。考查形容词比较级与上下文理解。由上下文可以看出,这里是将军官们住的条件与水手们住的条件进行比较，所以用比较级。而由常识可知军官们的条件肯定要好一点，选 better。

17.[A]。考查冠词用法与固定搭配。由于这里特指这条船的前部，所以要用定冠词。in the front of 指"在…的前部"，所指位置仍在船上；in front of 指"在…的前面"，所指位置已不在船上。厨房等肯定在船上，故应用前者。

18.[C]。考查上下文理解。由空格前 small 一词即可知含肯定义的[A]、[B]、[C]三项都不对。

19.[B]。考查名词辨义。journey 指长途旅行；voyage 特指海上的旅程；trip 指往返旅程；travel 多指为了娱乐而进行的旅行。由于这里指的是水手们的旅程，所以 voyage 最恰当。

20.[A]。考查动词辨义与上下文理解。imagine 想像；enjoy 欣赏；believe 相信；follow 跟随。由宾语从句中的 like(像)可知 imagine 最恰当。

同步译文

　　伦敦在历史上曾是英国伟大的贸易港口之一。因此，如今沿泰晤士河有许多景点，让旅客们记起英国的海上历史。其中最有意思的地方之一是伦敦东南的格林尼治，在那里你可以参观 Cutty Sark 这条著名的船。

　　Cutty Sark 是一艘帆船。他们在 1869 年建造了这条船，想让她成为在与中国进行的茶叶贸易中速度最快的一条船。船上载运的是从远东过来的茶叶。那时船主都想尽快把从中国的茶叶运回英国，因此船主们之间的竞争很激烈。许多年以后的 1954 年，Cutty Sark 停在了格林尼治，因此如今游客们可以瞻仰她。

　　如果环顾船上，你会看到许多东西，它们会将水手们好几个月在船上生活的故事告诉你。苏伊士运河修好后，蒸汽船控制了海上贸易，Cutty Sark 开始从澳大利亚运羊毛。

　　水手们住的地方值得参观一下。水手们睡在只铺有草垫的木床上。军官们的条件要好一点，但按现代的标准来说仍然很差。

　　在船的前部可以看到厨房和工作间。生活和工作区域都很小，对于远航的水手来说很不舒适。很难想像他们的生活是个什么样子。他们至少每天工作 20 个小时，每周工作 7 天，且常常处于又冷又湿而且危险的条件下。而那些水手每月只挣几英镑。

　　参观 Cutty Sark 提醒我们，航船的历史并不像我们现在看起来那样浪漫！

Exercise 27

Mary's parents are different from the average. While she was __1__ up they required her to __2__ . First of all she had to work around their home. Later on Mary worked for other people.

When Mary was 14 years old, her mother and father told her that they were no __3__ going to buy her clothes. Sure, they would continue to buy shoes for her and also the special clothes __4__ suits, but __5__ else was her *responsibility*(责任). Some people thought that they were __6__ . But they wanted to teach Mary some __7__ lessons. One thing she learned was that nothing is cheap or __8__ . She learned how to deal with her money __9__ . Another thing she learned was how to keep from __10__ out her clothes too fast.

Also, even __11__ Mary went to school she was __12__ to work. All through her high school and __13__ years she worked as well as studied. Mary's parents had plenty of __14__ but they felt she would __15__ her education more if she had to __16__ it. And strange __17__ it may seem, they had heard that students who worked part-time generally got __18__ grades than students who did no work.

Now Mary is a mother herself. She requires her __19__ to do the same __20__ she did, especially working part-time as they go to school.

1. [A]standing   [B]bringing   [C]growing   [D]getting
2. [A]study   [B]play   [C]learn   [D]work
3. [A]longer   [B]money   [C]more   [D]hope
4. [A]and   [B]or   [C]as   [D]like
5. [A]what   [B]anything   [C]nothing   [D]everything
6. [A]responsible   [B]lazy   [C]poor   [D]careless
7. [A]difficult   [B]daily   [C]valuable   [D]useless
8. [A]free   [B]expensive   [C]useful   [D]proper
9. [A]quickly   [B]slowly   [C]carefully   [D]suddenly
10. [A]working   [B]wearing   [C]giving   [D]taking
11. [A]when   [B]as   [C]until   [D]since

12. [A]permitted 　　[B]required 　　[C]going 　　[D]forced
13. [A]hard 　　　　 [B]work 　　　[C]other 　　[D]college
14. [A]time 　　　　 [B]children 　[C]money 　[D]work
15. [A]value 　　　　[B]have 　　[C]use 　　[D]receive
16. [A]enjoy 　　　　[B]pay 　　[C]pay for 　[D]work for
17. [A]thing 　　　　[B]as 　　　[C]when 　[D]although
18. [A]worse 　　　　[B]better 　[C]more 　[D]less
19. [A]husband 　　　[B]mother 　[C]parents 　[D]children
20. [A]as 　　　　　　[B]what 　　[C]which 　[D]like

答案与分析

1.[C]。考查动词辨义与上下文理解。stand up 站起来；bring up 养大；grow up 长大，成长；get up 起床。[D]明显不合常识；[A]一般不用于进行时态；[B]在此语态不对。

2.[D]。考查上下文理解。由紧接着的两句中的 work 即可确定此处也应用 work 才合上下文逻辑。

3.[A]。考查句子结构与固定搭配。由句子结构可知这里应填入一个词与 no 构成副词词组作句子的状语。no longer 为固定搭配，指"不再"，符合语法与逻辑。由上下文文意可知 Mary 父母并不是没有钱给她买衣服，故 money 不对；no more 虽可指"不再"，但它属于非常文学化的用法，它的一般用法是与 than 连用；hope 指"希望"，用在此处不知所云。

4.[D]。考查介词与上下文理解。关键是理解空格前后两个名词的关系。special clothes 指"特殊服装"，而 suits 则指特定的一套衣服。因此，后者肯定是用于说明前者的例子，故用表示例举的 like。

5.[D]。考查代词与上下文理解。由于此处是并列的两个分句而不是从句，也不是疑问句，故首先排除 what。而 anything 一般用于否定和疑问句、nothing 与上文意思相反，故只能选 everything，指其余的一切。

6.[C]。考查形容词辨义与上下文理解。父母不给孩子买衣服只能是给人以"穷"（poor）的感觉。responsible 负责的；lazy 懒惰的；careless 粗心的。

7.[C]。考查上下文理解。由文意可知，对于 Mary 的父母来说，让孩子自己挣钱的出发点肯定是正面的，故选含褒义的 valuable（宝贵的）。其余三项都与文意不符。

8.[A]。考查形容词辨义与上下文理解。由常识可知东西价有贵贱，故填入 expensive 肯定不合逻辑；useful(有用的)与 proper(正常的)与空格前的 cheap(便宜的)不属于同一范畴。free 指"免费的"，这里指"没有东西是便宜或者免费的"。

9.[C]。考查副词辨义与上下文理解。由前一句及常识可推知她学到的是花钱谨慎，故选 carefully(小心地，仔细地)。quickly 迅速地；slowly 缓慢地；suddenly 突然。

10.[B]。考查固定搭配。wear out 是固定搭配，指"穿破，磨破"。其余三项都不对。

11.[A]。考查连接词。由句子结构分析，不难看出此句中"___ Mary went to school"是从句，而其后的部分为主句。由于它表示的是时间，所以应选引导时间状语从句的连接副词 when。

12.[B]。考查动词辨义与上下文理解。由前文可知是父母要求 Mary 工作，故此处也应用表"要求"的 required。其余三项：permit 允许；force 强迫，迫使；going 用在此处构成 be going to do 句式，表示的是"打算"，不合文意。

13.[D]。考查上下文理解。高中以后就是大学，故选 college，指从高中到大学的几年中。

14.[C]。考查上下文理解。由空格后的内容可知这里说的是她父母有钱，但让她自己付学费，故选 money。其余三项都与文意无关。

15.[A]。考查动词辨义与上下文理解。由于宾语是 education(教育)，故其余三项都不能填入题中。value 指"珍惜"。

16.[C]。考查动词用法。pay 作及物动词时，宾语一般是人或者金额；要指"付款以得到某物"，要用 pay for。此处指她自己付钱来上学，所以用 pay for。

17.[B]。考查表达与句子结构。由句子结构可知，空格所在的部分应当是一个让步状语从句，并且用的是倒装句式，故只能用 as。其余三项填入句中都造成无法理解与语法错误。

18.[B]。考查上下文理解。由上下文与常识可知这里是指由于听说兼职的学生的成绩通常比不工作的学生要好，所以他们让 Mary 也做兼职工作。注意有些考生误选了 more，语法上看似正确，但 grade(成绩)一般不用多少而是用好坏来衡量的。

19.[D]。考查上下文理解。由前后两句话不难推知这里指 Mary 也这样要求自己的孩子，故选 children。

20.[A]。考查固定搭配。the same (...) as 为固定搭配，指"和…一样，与…相同"。

玛丽的父母与一般的父母不同。她还在成长时他们就要求她去工作。一开始她得在家里干活。后来玛丽开始替别人工作。

玛丽14岁时，她的父母告诉她说，他们不会再给她买衣服。当然，他们会继续给她买鞋子和特殊衣服如套装，但其余的都由她自己负责。一些人认为她父母很穷。但他们是想教给玛丽一些宝贵的经验教训。她学到的一件事是没有什么便宜或者免费的东西。她学会了如何谨慎花钱。她学到的另一件事情是如何让自己的衣服不会很快穿破。

甚至玛丽上学后他们也要求她工作。从高中到大学的那些年中玛丽边工作边学习。玛丽的父母很有钱，但他们觉得如果她得自己付学费的话，她会更加珍惜自己的学业。尽管似乎很奇怪，但他们听说做兼职工作的学生通常学习成绩比那些不做兼职工作的学生要好。

如今玛丽是一位母亲了。她要求自己的孩子像她曾经做过的那样，尤其是他们上学后要做兼职工作。

Exercise 28

Since my family were not going to be helpful, I decided I would look for one all by myself and not tell them about it until I'd got one.

I had seen an *agency*(中介) advertised in a local newspaper. I rushed out of the __1__ in search of it. I was wildly excited, and as __2__ as if I were going on the stage. Finding the __3__ quite easily, I ran breathlessly through a door which said "Enter without knocking, if you please".

The simple atmosphere of the office __4__ me. The woman looked carefully at me __5__ through her glasses, and then __6__ me in a low voice. I answered softly. All of a sudden I started to feel rather __7__. She wondered why I was looking for this sort of __8__. I felt even more helpless when she told me that it would be __9__ to get a job without __10__. I wondered whether I ought to leave, __11__ the telephone on her desk rang. I heard her say:

"__12__, I've got someone in the __13__ at this very moment who might __14__." She wrote down a __15__, and held it out to me, saying: "Ring up this lady. She wants a ___16___ immediately. In fact, you would have to start tomorrow by cooking dinner for ten people."

"Oh, yes," said I — ___17___ having cooked for more than four in my life. I ___18___ her again and again, and rushed out to the ___19___ telephone box. I collected my thoughts, took a deep breath, and rang the number. I said confidently that I was just what she was looking for.

I spent the next few hours ___20___ cook books.

1. [A]bed [B]house [C]agency [D]office
2. [A]proud [B]pleased [C]nervous [D]worried
3. [A]family [B]door [C]place [D]stage
4. [A]calmed [B]excited [C]frightened [D]disturbed
5. [A]as usual [B]for a while [C]in a minute [D]once again
6. [A]advised [B]examined [C]informed [D]questioned
7. [A]encouraged [B]dissatisfied [C]helpless [D]pleased
8. [A]place [B]job [C]advice [D]help
9. [A]difficult [B]helpless [C]possible [D]unusual
10. [A]ability [B]experience [C]knowledge [D]study
11. [A]after [B]since [C]until [D]when
12. [A]Above all [B]As a matter of fact
    [C]As a result [D]In spite of that
13. [A]family [B]house [C]office [D]restaurant
14. [A]hire [B]accept [C]suit [D]offer
15. [A]letter [B]name [C]note [D]number
16. [A]cook [B]help [C]teacher [D]secretary
17. [A]almost [B]never [C]nearly [D]really
18. [A]answered [B]promised [C]thanked [D]told
19. [A]outside [B]local [C]closest [D]nearest
20. [A]borrowing [B]buying [C]reading [D]writing

答案与分析

1.[B]。考查名词辨义与上下文理解。由上下文可知,这里应当是指作者冲出家门去找那个中介公司,故选 house(房子)。bed 床;agency 中介机构;

office 办公室。这三项填入都不合逻辑。

2.[C]。考查形容词辨义与上下文理解。由前面的 excited(激动的)和后文的 going on the stage(走上舞台表演)可知应选 nervous(紧张的)。proud 自豪的；pleased 高兴的；worried 焦急的，担心的。

3.[C]。考查上下文理解。由上下文可知作者是轻松地找到了中介公司所在，故只能填入 place(地方)。其余三项都与文意无关。

4.[A]。考查动词辨义与上下文理解。前文说作者很兴奋很紧张，这里说"办公室里的简单氛围"肯定是说让作者"平静"了下来，故选 calmed。excite 使兴奋；frighten 吓唬,使害怕；disturb 打扰。它们填入句中都不合逻辑。

5.[B]。考查固定搭配辨义与上下文理解。as usual 照常；for a while 一会儿；in a minute 马上；once again 一再。由后文中的 then 及常识可知这里应指那位女士看了作者一会儿。

6.[D]。考查动词辨义与上下文理解。advise 建议；examine 检查；inform 通知；question 询问。由常识与上下文可知,见到求职者,中介公司的人肯定会询问求职者的相关情况。

7.[C]。考查上下文理解。由下文中的 more helpless 可知此处应选 helpless(无助的)。

8.[B]。考查上下文理解。文章说的是作者找工作的事,而这里中介公司的人询问作者为什么要找这一类的___,当然应填入 job。

9.[A]。考查形容词辨义与上下文理解。由下文的叙述可知,作者没有任何工作经验,所以这里中介公司的人当然是说没有经验要找工作会很"困难",因此作者才感到无助。

10.[B]。考查名词辨义与上下文理解。参见上题解析。由后面的叙述可知作者无工作经验。

11.[D]。考查连接词。空格后指的是动作发生的时间,所以选 when,引导一个时间状语从句。

12.[B]。考查固定搭配。above all 尤其是,最重要的是；as a matter of fact 事实上；as a result 结果是；in spite of that 不管,尽管。

13.[C]。考查上下文理解。由下文可知那位女士所指的人就是作者,他们此时就在中介公司的办公室里而不是在别处。

14.[C]。考查动词辨义与上下文理解。除 suit(适合)可作不及物动词外,其余三项都是及物动词,都要跟宾语；hire 雇用；accept 接受；offer 提供。它们在意思上也不合上下文文意。

15.[D]。考查名词辨义与上下文理解。由后一句可知女士写下的只是一个电话号码,故选 number(号码)。note 指"便条"。

16.[A]。考查名词辨义与上下文理解。由后文提及的替 10 个人做饭、作者找厨艺书等可知那人找的是厨师(cook)。

17.[B]。考查上下文理解。由上文所说的作者没有工作经验和下文作者找厨艺书等内容可以推知这里指作者从来没有做过供 4 个以上的人吃的饭菜,故选 never。

18.[C]。考查动词辨义与上下文理解。由上下文与常识可知,中介公司的人帮作者找到了工作,作者肯定得感谢她。answer 回答;promise 承诺,保证;tell 告诉。它们都不合文章逻辑。

19.[D]。考查形容词辨义与上下文理解。由上文的描述可知作者找到工作的心情迫切,因此这里要用 nearest(最近的)才能表达出他的这种心情。outside 外面的;local 本地的;closest 最亲密的。

20.[C]。考查动词辨义与上下文理解。作者没有做 10 个人的饭的经验,所以这里肯定指他"临时抱佛脚",找相关的书来看(reading)。borrow 借;buy 买;write 写。最后一个明显不对;而不管是借还是买,作者的最终目的都是拿来看,故[C]最恰当。

同步译文

由于我的家人不准备帮我,我决心自己去找一份工作,在找到之前不告诉他们。

我在本地的一份报纸上看到了一家中介机构的广告,就冲出家门去找那里。我极为兴奋,也很紧张,就像是走上舞台去表演一样。我很容易就找到了那个地方,然后气喘吁吁地跑进一扇门,门上写着:"请进,无需敲门"。

办公室里的气氛显得很平易近人,这让我平静下来了。那位女士透过眼镜仔细看了我一会儿,然后低声询问我。我轻轻地回答她。突然,我开始觉得很无助起来。她想知道我为什么会找这种工作。当她告诉我说我没有经验很难找到一份工作时我觉得更无助了。我不知道自己是否应该离开,就在这时她桌上的电话响了。我听到她说:

"事实上,此刻我的办公室里就有一位,可能合适。"她写下了一个号码,递给我,说:"给这位女士打电话。她想马上要一位厨师。事实上,你得从明天就开始工作,为 10 个人做饭。"

"噢,好的,"我说——我一生中从未做过供超过 4 个人吃的饭菜。我一再感谢她,然后冲出去到了最近的电话亭。我定了定神,深呼吸了一下,拨通了那个电话号码。我充满信心地说我就是她要找的人。

我把接下来的几个小时都用来看厨艺书籍。

✒ *Exercise 29*

Many thousands of years ago, there were no houses such as people live in today. In those *ancient*（古代的） __1__ , men sometimes __2__ their homes in trees, using the leaves to keep __3__ rain and sun. Their object in building their houses in trees is to be __4__ from their enemies and from wild beasts. __5__ people in those old times were more *civilized*（文明的）, they would have had stronger building __6__ than the leaves and branches. In colder countries, the people of long ago __7__ to live in caves. It was too __8__ and stormy to live in trees. Sometimes, across the opening of the cave they made a __9__ of stones, in order to __10__ out wild animals.

As years went on and the human race __11__ , men learned more about living in comfort and safety. They became more civilized and __12__ trees and caves. They built houses of different materials such as mud, __13__ or stones.

During the __14__ hundred years, many new building methods have been __15__ . One of the most recent discoveries is to __16__ steel as building material. Nowadays, when it is necessary to make a very tall building, *the frame*（框架） of it first is built of steel, and then the building is __17__ in *concrete*（混凝土）. But __18__ building it may be it should be __19__ , airy, and comfortable. For a human being cannot keep __20__ without sunlight and fresh, clean air to breathe.

1. ［A］places　　　［B］years　　　［C］times　　　［D］countries
2. ［A］moved　　　［B］made　　　［C］settled　　　［D］kept
3. ［A］up　　　　　［B］off　　　　［C］from　　　　［D］on
4. ［A］safe　　　　［B］separated　　［C］prevented　　［D］far
5. ［A］If　　　　　［B］Though　　　［C］As　　　　　［D］Then
6. ［A］materials　　［B］models　　　［C］places　　　［D］methods

7. [A]were   [B]wanted   [C]began   [D]used
8. [A]cool   [B]windy   [C]cold   [D]warm
9. [A]wall   [B]ceiling   [C]room   [D]door
10. [A]drive   [B]send   [C]keep   [D]find
11. [A]improved   [B]changed   [C]moved   [D]progressed
12. [A]liked   [B]left   [C]broke   [D]kept
13. [A]steel   [B]wood   [C]glass   [D]iron
14. [A]first   [B]following   [C]next   [D]last
15. [A]discovered [B]founded   [C]done   [D]formed
16. [A]use   [B]make   [C]get   [D]find
17. [A]completed [B]built   [C]ended   [D]painted
18. [A]whatever   [B]wherever   [C]whichever   [D]whenever
19. [A]straight   [B]light   [C]heavy   [D]beautiful
20. [A]working   [B]right   [C]healthy   [D]on

 答案与分析

1.[C]。考查词汇意义。places 指"地方"，years 指"那些年"，countries 指"国家"。根据前文所指的时间和本句前的修饰词 ancient(古代的)可以看出，这里要表达"在远古时代"，所以选 times。事实上，后文中又出现了 in those old times 这个时间短语，可以提示考生选择。

2.[B]。考查动词词义与上下文理解。分析此句意思应为"人们有时把房屋建在树上"，只有 make 可表示"建造"。move 指"迁移"，settle 指"安排定居"，keep 指"保持"。

3.[B]。考查动词固定搭配。keep up 表示"维持"，keep off 表示"避开"，keep on 表示"保持"，keep 与 from 连用只能用在 keep sb. from sth. 这一结构中。本句要表达的是"避雨"，所以 keep off 最合适。

4.[A]。考查固定搭配和上下文理解。从上下文意思可以看出，人们在树上建房的目的是为了安全，可以不受敌人和野兽的攻击，所以这里选 safe，构成固定搭配 be safe from，表示"安全，不受…侵害"。

5.[A]。考查句子结构和上下文理解。由主句的谓语形式可以看出，它用的是虚拟语气。与虚拟语气连用的一般是 if 引导的条件状语从句。其余三项填入题中都造成上下文文意不通。

6.[A]。考查词义和上下文理解。materials 表示"材料"，models 表示"模

型",places 表示"地方",methods 表示"方法"。所选词应与后面作比较的 leaves and branches(树叶和树枝)属于同一类型,而后者都是建造房屋的材料,所以 materials 最合适。

7.[D]。考查词的搭配。used to 表示"过去常常",它是过去时态。其余三项用在题中都造成上下文文意不通。这里指"很久以前人们常常居住在山洞里"。

8.[C]。考查词汇意义。cold 指"寒冷的",与后面的 stormy 连用表示"寒冷且风吹雨打的",用在 too ... to ... 这一结构中。

9.[A]。考查上下文理解。本句说人们住在山洞里,要用石头堵在洞口,起的自然是墙的作用,所以用 wall。

10.[C]。考查动词搭配。这里要表达"防御野兽",用 keep out 表示"将野兽挡在洞口外"最为符合。drive out 表示"赶出",send out 表示"送出",find out 表示"查出",均不符合文意。

11.[D]。考查词汇意义。improve 指"改进",change 指"改变",move 指"移动",progress 指"发展"。这里要表达的是"随着时间的推移,人类在发展",除了 progress 外,其余三项都不能正确表达此意。

12.[B]。考查上下文理解。上文一直在写人们住在树上或山洞里,而后文写的是人们使用土石建房,可见人们是脱离了树和山洞,所以用 left。

13.[B]。考查词汇意义及上下文联系。文中的 mud 和 stones 分别指"泥土"和"石块",都是建房的材料。选项中的 grass 指"草",iron 指"铁",在文中都未提及过,所以明显不符。steel 指"钢",它出现在文章第三段所描述的时期,而不是这一段所写的时期。wood 指"木材",符合题意。

14.[D]。考查词汇意义及上下文理解。first 指"最初的",following 和 next 都指"下一个",last 指"最近的"。下文说明的是钢等新型建筑材料的发现,通过常识可以知道,用钢材和混凝土建造房屋是近一个世纪才出现的,所以选 last。

15.[A]。考查词汇意义。found 指"建立",form 指"形成",do 指"做",均不符合文意。discover 表示"发现",而且后文有 most recent discoveries 与之呼应,故为正确答案。

16.[A]。考查词汇意义。use 在这里与 as 连用,表示"使用…作为…"。其余三项填入题中都会造成上下文文意不通。

17.[A]。考查词汇意义。complete 表示"完成",其后跟介词 in,表示"用混凝土来完成"。build 表示"建造"(前面已经出现,后跟介词 of 引出材料);end 表示"结束",一般用于抽象的会议、讨论等;paint 表示"刷漆",均不符合。

18.[A]。考查词汇意义。whatever指"任何",wherever指"无论哪里",whichever指"无论哪一个",whenever指"无论何时"。分析句子可知,这里填入的词应修饰名词building,只有whatever有形容词性质,指"无论它是什么样的建筑"。

19.[B]。考查词汇意义及上下文理解。straight指"直的",light指"光亮的",heavy指"重的",beautiful指"漂亮的"。而本句airy和comfortable分别指"透气的"和"舒适的",都是修饰房屋居住质量的,因此只有light可以形容房子的这个性质,而且后文又有sunlight与之对应。

20.[C]。考查词义与上下文理解。本句意思是"如果没有阳光和新鲜干净的空气,人就不能保持健康",所以用healthy。

同步译文

　　几千年前,还没有像今天人们那样居住的房子。在那些远古时代,人们有时把家安在树上,用树叶遮挡日晒雨淋。他们把房子建在树上的目的是为了躲避敌人和野兽。如果那些远古时代的人们文明程度更高一些的话,他们会用比树叶和树枝更牢固的建筑材料。在一些气候较冷的国家,很久以前的人们常常住在洞穴里。住在树林里太冷,又多暴风雪。有时他们为了把野兽挡在外面,会在洞口筑一堵石墙。

　　随着一年年过去和人类的进步,人们学会了更多有关舒适和安全居住的知识。他们变得更加文明,离开了树林和洞穴。他们建起了用不同材料如泥土、木头或者石块筑成的房屋。

　　在过去的一百年中,发现了许多新的建筑方法。最近的发现之一是用钢材作建筑材料。如今如果要建一座很高的建筑,首先用钢材打好其框架,然后再用混凝土完成整个建筑。但是不管什么样的建筑,都应当明亮、通风和舒适,因为一个人如果没有阳光、呼吸不到新鲜清洁的空气,就无法保持健康。

✎ Exercise 30

　　When I joined a private football league a few years ago, the sport meant everything to me. My *coach*(教练) said that I had lots of *potential*(潜力), and I became captain of my __1__. That was before all the fun was taken out of __2__.

　　At first, everyone on the team got __3__ playing time. Then the team moved up to the top division after winning all its games, and the __4__ started. Some parents, who had paid the coach extra so their daughters could have __5__ one-on-one training, got angry when she didn't give them more playing time in our __6__ . The coach was replaced.

The new coach, however, took all the fun out of the game: all we did during practice was __7__ . I always wished to God that it would rain so we would not have the __8__ . Of course, all teams run drills; they are __9__ . But we ran much that, afterwards, we had trouble __10__ . Younger people shouldn't be doing exercises __11__ for 18-year-old.

I was very thin __12__ I started football, but as a member of this team I wouldn't eat much, because I was afraid of being too __13__ to run. I feared making mistakes, and the added pressure caused me to make more than my usual __14__ .

Is all this pressure necessary? I __15__ up leaving the football team. Four other girls did the same, and two of them stopped playing football completely. That's __16__ , because they had so much potential. They were just burned out with all the pressure they __17__ from the coach or their parents.

I continued playing football at school and __18__ my love for it. I joined a private team coached by my school coach. When I started playing __19__ him, he told me I needed to relax because I looked nervous. After I __20__ down, I played better. When you enjoy something, it's a lot easier to do it well.

1. [A]class   [B]club   [C]team   [D]board
2. [A]playing   [B]living   [C]learning   [D]working
3. [A]great   [B]equal   [C]right   [D]extra
4. [A]business   [B]struggle   [C]attempt   [D]pressure
5. [A]free   [B]private   [C]good   [D]basic
6. [A]matches   [B]courses   [C]lessons   [D]programs
7. [A]jump   [B]play   [C]run   [D]school
8. [A]duty   [B]meeting   [C]operation   [D]training

9. [A]necessary   [B]boring   [C]scientific   [D]practical

10. [A]speaking   [B]moving   [C]sleeping   [D]breathing

11. [A]used   [B]intended   [C]made   [D]described

12. [A]till   [B]since   [C]before   [D]because

13. [A]full   [B]tired   [C]lazy   [D]excited

14. [A]size   [B]share   [C]space   [D]state

15. [A]gave   [B]kept   [C]ended   [D]picked

16. [A]sad   [B]shameful   [C]silly   [D]serious

17. [A]received   [B]suffered   [C]brought   [D]felt

18. [A]reconsidered [B]rediscovered [C]reformed   [D]replaced

19. [A]at   [B]by   [C]for   [D]around

20. [A]fell   [B]stepped   [C]slowed   [D]calmed

 **答案与分析**

1. [C]。考查名词辨义与上下文理解。由上下文可知这里指作者成为橄榄球队的队长。team 队；class 班；club 俱乐部；board 董事会。

2. [A]。考查上下文理解。文章的主要内容就是打橄榄球，即 play，所以此处也要用 playing。其余各项：living 生活；learning 学习；working 工作。它们都与文意无关。后文中又出现了 took all the fun out of the game 一句，据此也可以确定正确答案。

3. [B]。考查形容词辨义与上下文理解。后文叙述的是一些队员的家长多付钱给教练以多得指导时间，所以此处应是指一开始时大家的训练时间都相等，故选 equal（相等的）。great 巨大的，伟大的；right 正确的；extra 额外的。

4. [D]。考查名词辨义与上下文理解。由上下文文意可知，作者所在的队升入最高级别后，肯定会增加许多压力，此外后文第四段中明确提到压力使作者出错，故此处选 pressure（压力）最合文意。

5. [B]。考查形容词辨义与上下文理解。一些家长给教练多付钱，就是为了让自己的孩子多得到教练的一对一的私下训练，故由空格后的 one-on-one 可知应选 private（私人的）。其余各项在文中都没有体现。

6. [A]。考查上下文理解与名词辨义。空格前的 playing time 指的是比赛时的上场时间，所以此处选 matches（比赛）。其余三项：course 课程，过程；lesson 课，教训；program 节目，程序。由于文章谈论的是体育训练，所以与这三者都没有联系。

7.[C]。考查上下文理解。下文中出现了 we ran so much that … 一句，由此可知新教练的练习就是让作者她们跑。

8.[D]。考查名词辨义与上下文理解。由上下文可知这里指作者希望下雨，这样就不用训练了，故选 training。其余三项：duty 义务；meeting 会议，集会；operation 操作，手术。

9.[A]。考查形容词辨义与上下文理解。由空格前一句 all teams run drills(所有队都进行跑步训练)可知作者对跑步训练是持肯定态度的，只是她们自己的队跑得太多，故选 necessary(必要的)。其余三项都不合文意。

10.[D]。考查动词辨义与上下文理解。由上下文与常识可知，跑步太多导致的是"呼吸(breathe)困难"。speak 说话；move 移动；sleep 睡觉。这三项都有可能出现，但不如[D]合文意。

11.[B]。考查固定搭配与上下文理解。由句意可知这里指给小孩进行18 岁的人才能进行的训练。(be) intended for 指"为…而设计或者制作等"，符合句意。(be) used for 为了…而使用；(be) made for 为…而制作；(be) described for 为…而描述。

12.[C]。考查连词与上下文理解。由上下文可知，作者在加入球队前就很瘦，但在球队里不敢多吃，因为担心吃得太多而跑不动，故用 before。用 till(直到)、since(自从，因为)及 because(因为)都造成逻辑混乱。

13.[A]。考查上下文理解。四个选项中只有 full(饱的)与前文中说的"多吃"有关。这里指吃得太饱，跑不动。

14.[B]。考查名词辨义与上下文理解。size 尺寸，体积；share 份额；space 空间；state 状态。容易混淆的是[B]、[D]两项。在球队中一个队员的"出错"只是一部分，故应选 share。而 state 如果填入此处，就变成了 mistakes 与它进行比较，显然不对。如果题目是 in my usual ____，那么答案就是[D]了。

15.[C]。考查固定搭配。give up 放弃；keep up 保持；pick up 捡起，学会。这三个都与后面的 leaving the football team 矛盾。只有 end up 指"以…结束"，符合上下文文意。

16.[A]。考查形容词辨义与上下文理解。由后面表原因的分句可知作者对她们放弃打橄榄球是很惋惜的，所以选 sad(令人难过的)。shameful 可耻的，丢脸的；silly 愚蠢的；serious 严肃的，严重的。它们都与后文构不成合乎逻辑的因果关系。

17.[D]。考查动词辨义。压力(pressure)只能说是"感受到"(feel)，而不能说是"收到"(receive)、"遭受到"(suffer)或者从教练和父母那里"带来"

(bring)的。

18.[B]。考查动词辨义。reconsider 重新考虑；rediscover 重新发现；re-
form 改革；replace 取代。由上下文可知，作者是重新发现自己对橄榄球的喜
爱才继续在学校打橄榄球的。

19.[C]。考查介词与上下文理解。play at 为固定搭配，指"敷衍，假扮"；
by 表示方式，一般不与 play 连用；for 表示目的与对象；play around 指"玩弄"。
因此，除了[C]外其余三项都不能填入文中。这里指"为教练打橄榄球"，即为
教练效力。

20.[D]。考查固定搭配。fall down 摔倒；slow down 慢下来，放慢；step
down 走下来；calm down 平静下来。由前面的 nervous(紧张的)可知应选与
之相对的[D]。

同步译文

几年前我加入一个私人橄榄球联合会时，这一体育运动对
我来说就是一切。我的教练说我有很大的潜力，我成了我们队
的队长。那是在玩球被剥夺了一切乐趣之前。

开始时，队里每个人都有同等的出场时间。然而我们队每
次比赛都赢，升入了最高级别后，就开始有压力了。一些付了钱给教练以使他
们的孩子能得到一对一的私下训练的家长，因为教练在我们比赛时没有给那
些孩子更多的出场时间而生气了。那位教练被换掉了。

然而，新教练把这一运动中的所有乐趣都剥夺了：在训练中我们所做的就
是跑步。我总是希望下雨，这样就不用训练了。当然，所有队都进行跑步训
练，它们是必要的。但我们跑得太多了，以至于后来我们呼吸都有困难了。小
孩子们不应当进行为 18 岁的人设计的训练。

我开始打橄榄球前很瘦，但作为这个队的一员，我不敢多吃，因为怕吃得
太饱跑不了步。我害怕出错，而增加的压力让我出的错比平常更多。

这种压力有必要吗？我最后离开了球队。另外有 4 个女孩也离开了，其
中有 2 个彻底不再打橄榄球。那是很令人难过的，因为她们都有很大的潜力。
她们只是不堪教练或者家长给予她们的压力。

上学时我继续打橄榄球，重新发现了我对这项运动的喜爱。我加入了一
个由我们学校的教练执教的私人球队。我开始为他打球时，他告诉我说我需
要放松，因为我看起来很紧张。我平静下来之后就打得好一些了。当你喜欢
一件事情时，你把它做好要容易得多。

第 2 节　阅读理解 40 篇

阅读下列短文，从短文后所给的四个选项（[A]、[B]、[C]和[D]）中选出最佳选项，并在答题卡 1 上将该项涂黑。

Exercise 1

　　H5N1 avian influenza, known commonly as bird flu, has killed at least 15 people across Asia and was confirmed in China on January 27. No human cases have been found in the mainland, but 13 of the country's 31 provinces, *autonomous regions, and municipalities*（自治区和直辖市）have reported the disease in <u>poultry</u>.

　　The Chinese government has taken measures to prevent and control the disease. Poultry within 3 km of infected farms is to be killed and those within 5 km *vaccinated*（注射疫苗）. Meanwhile, there will be constant monitoring and daily reports on the disease across the country, and increased production of bird flu vaccines.

　　Among the Asian countries and regions affected by bird flu in animals, only Vietnam and Thailand have reported human cases. The people infected were reported to have caught the disease from poultry. While the World Health Organization（WHO）said there is "no proof of human-to-human *transmission*（传播）" of bird flu.

　　The big fear is that the disease could combine with a human influenza *virus*（病毒）to create a deadly new disease that will kill millions of people across the globe. Many Asian farmers live closely with their animals and sell live chickens in the market. This greatly increases the possibility of human beings infected with bird flu.

　　A spokesman of the WHO said that Asian countries affected by bird flu should introduce a more healthy way of raising and selling chickens. And the people there have to completely change their lifestyle and attitude towards animals. Here are some safety measures for people to stay healthy:

⊙ Keep fit and well through regular exercise.

⊙ Avoid infected poultry and infected people.

⊙ Avoid eating raw or under-done poultry and eggs.

⊙ Make sure there is always fresh air in your home.

⊙ Cover your mouth and nose when coughing or sneezing.

⊙ Wash your hands frequently.

1. What does the underlined word "poultry"（Para. 1）mean?

　[A]Wild birds.　　　　　　　　[B]Wild animals.

　[C]Home-raised birds.　　　　　[D]Home-raised animals.

2. From the passage，we can learn that ＿＿．

　[A]infected poultry within 3 km was killed in China

　[B]bird flu case was confirmed in China on Jan. 27

　[C]human infected cases were found in 13 Asian countries

　[D]over two thirds of China have been effected by the bird flu

3. What fears people most?

　[A]Poultry will infect many people.

　[B]The disease can spread quickly among people.

　[C]There will be human-to-human transmission.

　[D]A new disease combining bird and a human flu will break out.

4. One of the right ways for us to avoid bird flu is ＿＿．

　[A]to kill all the poultry　　　　[B]to eat no more chickens

　[C]to form a healthy habit　　　 [D]to keep separated from others

5. Which must be wrong for the Asians to change their lifestyle?

　[A]Farmers should live more closely with their poultry.

　[B]Farmers should vaccinate their poultry regularly.

　[C]Farmers should avoid selling live poultry in the market.

　[D]People should avoid buying live poultry in the market.

😊 **答案与分析**

1.[C]。词句理解题。首先由第一句中的 bird flu 可知这种病是鸟禽的一种病；其次，由第二段中的 Poultry with 3 km of infected farms 及第四、五两段中出现的 chickens 一词即可推知 poultry 指的是人们养殖的家禽。注意

[D]项范围太大,在文中 poultry 与 animals(家畜)是分开、并列说明的。

2.[B]。细节题。[A]对应于第二段第二句,但少了限定范围的 of infected farms,原文意思是受感染农场附近 3 公里内的家禽被宰杀;[B]与文章第
一句话的内容相符;[C]与第三段第一句不符,该句说亚洲只有越南和泰国出
现了人感染禽流感;[D]与第一段第二句中两个数字之间的比例不符。

3.[D]。细节题。第四段第一句指出,最大的担心就是禽流感病毒与人
类流感病毒结合形成一种新的致命性病毒,即[D]项的意思。

4.[C]。推断题。将四个选项与文章最后指出的六种方法进行对照,可
知只有[C]全面地概括了这些方法的内容,而其他三项在文中都没有体现,根
据常识也可将它们排除。

5.[A]。推断题。由第四段后半部分及第五段的内容可知,亚洲人与家
禽生活得很近、买卖活家禽,这增加了感染禽流感的可能性,所以世界卫生组
织建议他们改变养殖和买卖家禽的方式,也就是说,要与家禽拉开距离、不要
买卖活家禽。由此可知,四个选项中只有[A]不正确。

同步译文

　　　　H5N1 型流感,即人们常说的禽流感,已经在亚洲使至少
15 人丧生,且 1 月 27 日被证实已在中国出现。目前大陆尚没
有人类感染的病例报道,但全国 31 个省中有 13 个省、自治区和
直辖市已报告在家禽中发现这一疾病。

中国政府已经采取措施阻止和控制这一疾病的传播。受感染农场 3 公里
范围内的家禽都将被宰杀,5 公里以内的将接种疫苗。同时,将在全国范围内
对疫情进行不间断的监控和日报告,并增加禽流感疫苗的生产。

在亚洲受动物禽流感影响的国家和地区中,只有越南和泰国有人类感染
的病例报告。据报告称,受感染的人是从家禽感染此病的。同时,世界卫生组
织说没有证据表明禽流感能在人类之间传播。

最令人担忧的是这一疾病可能会与人类流感病毒结合而产生一种新的致
命性疾病,它能在全球范围内杀死数百万人。许多亚洲农民与他们的牲畜相
邻而居,并在市场上买卖活禽。这极大地增加了人类感染禽流感的可能性。

世界卫生组织的一位发言人说亚洲受禽流感影响的国家应该采取更加健
康的饲养和买卖家禽的方法。这些国家的人们必须完全改变他们的生活方式
和对待动物的态度。下面是一些保持健康的安全措施:

⊙定时锻炼,保持身体健康。

⊙避免与受感染的家禽和人员接触。

⊙避免吃生的或未煮熟的禽和蛋。

⊙确保室内空气新鲜。

⊙咳嗽或打喷嚏时，要掩住口鼻。

⊙经常洗手。

Exercise 2

Not very long ago, the computer was a strange machine. Not many people understand it. Not many people said yes to it. Today, much of that is changing. The first computer system was introduced for use in business in the mid-1950s. Since then, the number of computer systems used in business, governments, and industries has grown rapidly. In September, 2000, about 30 000 000 systems were in use in the United States. This figure is growing by tens of thousands every year.

The electric computer is an important part in our lives. Each year we use computer more and more to help us to collect *data*（数据）and to provide us with information. At one time, people thought computers were only useful for banks, department stores and governments, but today the rapidly increasing number of computers are used for many other purposes.

Have you ever stopped to think how you are affected by a digital computer? The clothes you wear probably made with the help of a digital computer.

Computers today are playing important roles in education, transportation and medicine. They are used to *predict*（预报）the weather, to examine the river or ocean and to develop defence systems. They are being used by business, governments and industries. There is no reason to think that their uses will decrease. Computers will become a greater part of our lives. The effect of the computer is very great.

The list of its uses could go on and on. Although the first computer was only introduced in the mid-1950s, computers now affect millions of people in countless ways every day.

1. From the text we can know before 1950s the computer was ____.

[A] widely used

[B] no use at all

[C] liked by people

[D] not understood by many people

2. Every year the number of computers being used has ____.

[A] reduced　　　　　　　　　[B] increased fast

[C] not changed　　　　　　　[D] increased slowly

3. The writer thinks our lives are affected, but we ____.

[A] don't quite hate it　　　　[B] have not known it clearly

[C] don't want to know about it　[D] don't like it

4. The last sentence of the passage means ____.

[A] the writer did not like computers

[B] the writer liked computers

[C] the writer thought computers have developed quickly

[D] the writer thought we couldn't live without computers

答案与分析

1. [D]。推断题。由文章第一段的前三句中的 strange，Not ... understand，Not ... said yes to it 等可以推知，那时人们对计算机不是很了解。

2. [B]。细节题。答案信息对应于第一段第六句：Since then ... has grown rapidly 及第二段最后一句中的 ... but today the rapidly increasing number of ... 。

3. [B]。推断题。由第二段最后一句：At one time，people ... for many other purposes 及第三段中的问句与语气可以推知作者认为人们对计算机如何影响他们的生活不甚了解。

4. [C]。词句理解题。这句话的意思是："尽管第一台计算机在 20 世纪 50 年代中期才出现，但如今计算机每天都以不可胜数的方式影响着千百万人的生活。"由于前文中作者一直在强调计算机的发展迅速及它对人们生活影响的巨大，所以这里当然也是这个意思，即作者认为计算机的发展速度非常快。

不久以前,计算机还是一种人们陌生的机器。没有多少人理解这种机器,也没有多少人接受它。如今这一切都正在改变。第一台计算机系统是在 20 世纪 50 年代中期出现的,用于商业。从那以后,用于商业、政府和工业企业的计算机系统数量迅速增长。到了 2000 年 9 月,全美国使用的计算机系统有约 3 千万台。这一数字每年正以万计地在增长。

　　电子计算机是我们生活中的一个重要的组成部分。每年我们都用越来越多的计算机来帮助我们收集数据和提供信息。曾几何时,人们认为计算机只对银行、百货商店和政府有用,但如今越来越多的计算机正被用于其他许多目的。

　　你曾经静下心来好好思考过数字计算机是如何影响你的吗?你穿的衣服很有可能就是在数字计算机的协助下制作出来的。

　　如今计算机在教育、交通和医疗上起着重要作用。它们被用于天气预报、检测河海和发展国防。它们正用于商业、政府和工业企业。没有理由认为会减少使用它们。计算机将会成为我们生活中更加重要的一个部分。计算机的影响是巨大的。

　　计算机的用途将会越来越广泛。尽管在 20 世纪 50 年代中期才有了第一台计算机,但如今计算机每天正以不可胜数的方式影响着千百万人。

🎧 *Exercise 3*

　　Pearl Carlson was shaken awake at 3:30 a.m. by a forceful pull. King, the family dog, was trying to pull her out of bed. Then she smelled smoke and heard the sound of fire from her parents' room. Pearl's screams awaked her mother, Fern, and father Howard, who had recently been in hospital for lung disease. Helping Howard to a first-floor window, Fern told him to climb out, then ran to her daughter.

　　Still inside, King appeared at Pearl's window, making squeaking sound. When running toward Pearl's bedroom, Fern realized her husband hadn't yet escaped. She made her way back through the smoke and flames, following King's sound to where Howard lay *semiconscious*(半昏迷的) on the floor. Fern helped him get outside. King came out only after both were safe.

As day dawned, the Carlsons saw that King's *paws*(爪子) were badly burned and his entire body was burned too. His chain collar had gotten so hot that it burned his throat, making it impossible for him to bark normally. Only after the seven-year-old dog refused food did they find pieces of wood in his mouth and realized that King, who slept outside, had bitten through a wood door to warn his family.

1. According to the story, who was the first to get out of the house?
　[A]Howard.　　[B]Fern.　　[C]King.　　[D]Pearl.

2. When the room caught fire, King ____.
　[A]was sleeping in Pearl's room
　[B]broke into the house to wake up Pearl
　[C]was barking outside the room
　[D]jumped out of the fire

3. Which of the following is TRUE about King according to the story?
　[A]King died soon after the fire.
　[B]King was the first to run away.
　[C]King was burned so much that he couldn't eat.
　[D]King made a big hole in the door.

4. Who was Pearl in this story?
　[A]The husband.　　　　　[B]The daughter.
　[C]The father.　　　　　[D]The mother.

☺ **答案与分析**

1.[A]。推断题。首先，在文章第一段最后一句指出，妻子 Fern 第一个把丈夫挪到一楼的窗户边，让他自己爬出去；其次，第二段第二句以后的部分讲述的是 Fern 在去救女儿的过程中意识到丈夫没有爬出去，又返回去救丈夫。由这两个方面可知，尽管有波折，但还是丈夫 Howard 最先逃出房子。

2.[B]。推断题。由第一段知狗是先叫醒了女儿 Pearl，而由文章最后一句可知，狗是咬破房门进去的。所以答案是[B]。

3.[D]。细节题。[D]与文章最后一句话的意思相符。由最后一段可知狗并没有死，而它不能吃东西并不是由于烧伤，而是嘴巴里有碎木头，故[A]、

[B]不对；由第二段最后一句可知狗是最后出来的，所以[C]也不对。

4.[B]。推断题。由第一段第三句中的 her parent's room 及该段最后一句中的 her daughter 可以推知 Pearl 是 Howard 和 Fern 的女儿。

同步译文

凌晨3：30分，帕尔·卡尔森被一阵有力的拉扯拽醒了。家里的狗"国王"正试图把她拉下床。然后她闻到了烟味，听到从她父母房间里传来了起火的声音。帕尔的尖叫惊醒了她母亲菲恩和由于肺病最近刚住过院的父亲霍华德。菲恩帮助霍华德来到一楼的窗户旁，告诉他自己爬出去，然后跑去救她女儿。

"国王"仍在帕尔的窗户旁狂吠，没有出去。在向帕尔的卧室跑去时，菲恩意识到丈夫还没有脱离危险。她在浓烟和火舌中摸索着，跟着"国王"的叫声找到丈夫所在的位置，发现他躺在地板上，已经半昏迷了。菲恩帮助他逃了出来。"国王"在等到父女俩都安全后才出来。

天亮后，卡尔森一家看到"国王"的爪子烧伤很严重，它的全身也都被烧伤了。它的项圈因为过热而烫伤了它的喉咙，使它没法正常叫唤了。直到这只7岁大的狗不肯吃东西后，他们才发现它的嘴巴里有碎木头，这才意识到睡在屋外的"国王"是在一扇木门上咬开了一个大洞进屋唤醒他们一家的。

Exercise 4

My husband is a born *shopper*（购物者）. He loves to look at things and to touch them. He likes to compare prices between the same *items*（产品） in different shops. He would never think of buying anything without looking around in several different shops. On the other hand, I'm not a shopper. I think shopping is boring and unpleasant. If I like something and I have enough money to take it, I buy it at once. I never look around for a good price or a better deal. Of course my husband and I never go shopping together. Doing shopping together would be too painful to both of us. When it comes to shopping, we go our different ways.

Sometimes I ask my son Jimmy to buy some food in the shop not far from our home. But he is always absent-minded. This was his story.

One day I said to him, "I hope you won't forget what I have told

you to buy." "No," said Jimmy, "I won't forget. You want three oran-
,ges, six eggs and a pound of meat."

He went running down the street to the shop. As he ran, he said
to himself over and over again, "Three oranges, six eggs and a pound
of meat."

In the beginning he remembered everything but he stopped several
times. Once he saw two men fighting outside a clothes shop until a policeman stopped them. One of them was badly hurt. Then he stopped
to give ten cents to a beggar. Then he met some of his friends and he
played with them for a while. When he reached the shop, he had forgotten everything except six eggs.

As he walked home, his face became sadder and sadder. When
he saw me he said, "I'm sorry, Mum. I have forgotten to buy oranges
and the meat. I only remembered to buy six eggs, but I've dropped
three of them."

1. **The husband loves shopping because ____.**
   [A]he has much money
   [B]he likes the shops
   [C]he likes to compare the prices between the same items
   [D]he has nothing to do but shopping

2. **The wife doesn't like shopping because ____.**
   [A]she has no money
   [B]she has no time
   [C]she doesn't love her husband
   [D]she feels it boring to go shopping

3. **They never go shopping together because ____.**
   [A]their ways of shopping are quite different
   [B]they hate each other
   [C]they needn't buy anything for the family
   [D]they don't have time for it

4. **Jimmy cannot do the shopping well because ____.**
   [A]he is young   [B]he is absent-minded
   [C]he often loses his money   [D]he doesn't like shopping

5. Jimmy didn't buy what his mother wanted because ____.

[A]the shop was closed that day

[B]the policeman stopped him

[C]he forgot some of them

[D]he gave all the money to the beggar

 答案与分析

1.[C]。细节题。文章第一段指出作者的丈夫是个天生的购物者,然后用三个排比句指出了其喜欢购物的表现。尽管没有明确说明,但可看出这些表现也就是他喜欢购物的原因。对照选项与原文,发现只有[C]与原文相符。其余三项在文中都没有体现。

2.[D]。细节题。第一段在说明丈夫喜欢购物后作者指出自己不喜欢购物。在第六句中作者说:I think shopping is boring and unpleasant,即[D]项的意思。

3.[A]。推断题。第一段最后三句说,作者和丈夫从不一起购物,因为一起购物对他们俩来说都让人痛苦,在购物时他们有自己各自不同的方式。由此可以推知,他们不一起购物的原因就是他们的购物方式不同,彼此无法忍受对方的方式。

4.[B]。细节题。文章第二段第二句明确指出:But he is always absent-minded。后文所描述的故事就是为了说明这一点而所举的例子。

5.[C]。细节题。在第五段最后一句和文章最后一句中作者都明确指出Jimmy没有买回作者所需的东西的原因,由 had forgotten 和 have forgotten 两处即可知应选[C]。

同步译文

　　我丈夫是个天生的购物者。他喜欢看东西、摸那些商品。他喜欢比较同一产品在不同的商店中的价格。如果没有货比三家,他是不会考虑买东西的。另一方面,我则不是个会买东西的人。我认为购物又累又烦人。如果我喜欢某件商品而我又带够了钱,我会立即买下来。我从不到处看,去找个好价格或找笔更划算的买卖。当然我丈夫和我从不一起去购物。一起购物对我们俩来说都会是种折磨。对于购物,我们有着不同的方式。

　　有时我让儿子吉米去附近的商店买食品。但他总是心不在焉。下面是一个关于他的故事。

一天我对他说:"我希望你别忘记我要你买的东西。""不会的,"吉米说,"我不会忘记。您想要3个橙子、6个鸡蛋和1磅肉。"

他顺着街道向商店跑去。他边跑边不停地对自己说:"3个橙子,6个鸡蛋,1磅肉。"

一开始他什么都记得,但他中途停了好几次。一次他看到两个人在一家服装店门口打架,直到一个警察来制止了他们。其中有一个人受伤严重。后来他停下来给了一个乞丐10美分。然后他碰到了几个朋友,跟他们玩了一会儿。等他到了商店,除了6个鸡蛋,他什么都不记得了。

他走回家时,他的脸色变得越来越沮丧。等他见到我时,他说:"对不起,妈妈。我忘了要买橙子和肉,只记得要6个鸡蛋,但打碎了3个。"

Exercise 5

Most of the talk these days is about global warming. But in fact the opposite could happen: it would only take the tiniest change in the Earth's orbit around the Sun to bring another Ice Age. A change of as little as 5 degrees centigrade would have a huge effect on life on Earth.

Climate Shift

The main effect would be to shift climate about 1 500 kilometers towards the Equator, so that Spain, say, would have a climate much the same as England's is now, and Buenos Aires could look forward to the kind of weather now found around Cape Horn.

Food

The same would be true of crops: wheat would grow in Spain, but no longer in Britain; it would be impossible to grow rice in most of China; and grapes would be much happier growing in Africa than in France.

Turning the Desert Green

On the brighter side, a number of *inhospitable*(条件恶劣的) places would become more pleasant to live in. Cave paintings in the Sahara Desert show that it was once full of people and animals. A drop in temperature together with increased rainfall might begin to turn the desert green again.

1. **If another Ice Age came，all the following would happen EXCEPT that ____.**

   [A]it would be better to grow grapes in Africa than in France

   [B]people would be able to live in Sahara Desert

   [C]Spain would have a climate much different from now

   [D]rice in China would be the best

2. **____ may turn desert into a more pleasant place to live in.**

   [A]Increased rainfall   [B]A drop in temperature

   [C]More plants   [D]All the above

3. **The writer of the passage is worrying about ____.**

   [A]global warming   [B]climate shift

   [C]coming of another Ice Age   [D]food shortage

4. **According to the text，which of the following is TRUE?**

   [A]Climate shift might occur along with the tiniest change in the Earth's orbit.

   [B]A change as little as 5 degrees centigrade would have a little effect on life on Earth.

   [C]The tiniest change in the Earth's orbit around the Sun would cause global warming.

   [D]Countries could keep growing the same crops in spite of the tiniest change in the Earth's orbit.

😊 **答案与分析**

1.[D]。细节题。[A]对应于"Food"部分最后一个分句：... grapes would be much happier growing in Africa than in France，即非洲将比法国更适宜于种葡萄；[B]与"Turning the Desert Green"（把沙漠变成绿洲）的意思相符；[C]与"Climate Shift"中"Spain ... would have a climate much ..."的意思相同，即西班牙的气候将与现在大不一样。只有[D]项，与"Food"部分 it would be impossible to grow rice in China 一句不符。

2.[D]。细节题。答案是文章最后一句。注意 plants 在这一句中并未提及，但既然是把沙漠变绿，那么肯定是有植物了，所以植物多也是沙漠变绿的一个条件。

3.[C]。主旨题。文章以 bring another Ice Age 入手，全文都在说明这样一种气候变化给地球带来的影响,所以作者关注的也就是这个问题。

    4.[A]。细节题。[A]与第一段第二句的意思相符;[B]中的 little 与该段最后一句中的 huge 不符;[C]与该段第二句的内容不符,该句说 bring another Ice Age,而选项中则说 cause global warming;[D]与"Food"部分所说的变化不符。

    如今人们都在谈论全球变暖。但事实上相反的情况也可能发生:只要地球绕太阳运行的轨道改变极小的一点点,就足以带来另一个冰川期。气温只要改变小小的 5 摄氏度,就会给地球上的生命带来巨大的影响。

气候变化

    主要的影响将是气候向赤道方向 1 500 公里产生变化,比如说西班牙的气候将会和现在的英国一样,而布宜诺斯艾利斯的气候将有望和现在合恩角附近的气候一样。

食物

    粮食作物也会一样变化:西班牙将会种小麦,但英国将不能;中国的大部分地区将不适合种水稻;葡萄将在非洲比在法国长得更好。

沙漠变绿洲

    而乐观一点的一个方面是,许多条件恶劣的地方将会成为适合人类居住的地方。撒哈拉沙漠的岩画表明,那里曾有许多人口居住和动物安家。气温的下降和雨量的增加可能将会使沙漠重新变绿。

Exercise 6

Buy a Joint Ticket and Visit the
Historic Royal Palaces, the Tower of London

Royal(皇家的) palace and *fortress*(要塞) for over 900 years, scenes of mystery, murder and home to the Crown Jewels.

Kensington Palace

Birthplace of Queen Victoria, this royal retreat is home to magnificent State Apartments and the stunning Royal Ceremonial Dress Collection, which includes dresses worn by Queen Elizabeth II and Diana, Princess of Wales.

Historic Royal Palaces

Hampton Court Palace is part of Historic Royal Palaces, a registered *charity*(慈善机构)(NO:1068852) that receives on public *funding*(资金). We rely on the income from admission tickets to the palaces to pay for vital protection work, necessary for the *preservation*(保护) of these national monuments and collections for future generations. Please ask at the ticket office for more information or visit www. hrp. org. uk.

Carriage Rides

Take a trip around Home Park in a horse-drawn carriage. Rides begin and end in Home Park at the entrance by the East Front Gardens. Available all day. 20 minutes duration. £10.00 per carriage. Subject to weather and ground conditions.

Enquiries

For details of admission charges, group rates, the friends of Hampton Court Palace and *facilities*(设施) for disabled visitors, call 0870-752-7777 or visit www. Hampton-Court-palace. org. uk.

Restaurants & Shops

Choose from the Tiltyard Tearooms or the privy Kitchen Coffee Shop. There are also a number of icecream kiosks open in the summer. The palace shops offer a wide range of gifts and *souvenirs*(纪念品).

Audio(音频的) Guides

Audio guides are included in the palace ticket and are available in English, French, German, Italian, Spanish and Japanese.

1. **If you want to take a look at the dresses worn by some royal members, you go to ____.**

   [A]Kensington Palace   [B]the Tower of London

   [C]Hampton Court Palace   [D]Historic Royal Palaces

2. **You have to pay extra money if you want to ____.**

   [A]have an audio guide   [B]visit the royal palace and fortress

   [C]take a horse-drawn carriage   [D]visit Hampton Court Palace

3. **Which of the following information is NOT given in the passage?**

   [A]The protection of the national monuments.

[B]Admission charges for group visitors.

[C]Free gifts and souvenirs.

[D]Conditions in which to take a horse-drawn carriage.

4. If you want to take your disabled sister for a visit, you can ＿＿＿.

[A]get a free ticket for her

[B]get help from Hampton Court Palace

[C]log on www. Hampton-Court-Palace. org. uk for information

[D]visit www. hrp. org. uk

😊 答案与分析

1.[A]。细节题。文章在"Kensington Palace"一段中介绍说,这里举行皇家大典礼服展览(Royal Ceremonial Dress Collection)。

2.[C]。细节题。文章在一开篇就说买张套票可以参观皇家宫殿,然后在文章中只有在"Carriage Rides"一段中提到了钱(£10. 00 per carriage),表明乘坐马车游玩 Home Park 还需要另外付钱。

3.[C]。细节题。文章在"Historic Royal Palaces"中提到了保护国家的纪念物(the preservation of these national monuments)([A]项);在"Enquiries"一段中提到了团体票率(group rates)([B]项);在"Carriage Rides"中提到了坐马车的天气和地面条件(Subject to weather and ground conditions)([D]项)。只有在"Restaurant & Shops"中提到宫廷商店有很多礼物和纪念品(a wide range of gifts and souvenirs),但并没有说是免费的(free)。

4.[C]。推断题。在"Enquiries"中指出,了解残疾人使用设施可以打电话,也可以登录网址,即 www. Hampton-Court-Palace. org. uk,所以选[C]。

购买套票,参观历史性皇家宫殿群和伦敦塔

同步译文

　　皇家宫殿和要塞有着900多年的历史,有着悬案和谋杀场景,也是皇室珠宝的归宿。

金斯顿宫

　　这一皇家静园是维多利亚女王的出生地,也是壮观的国家部门建筑、极具吸引力的皇家大典礼服展览之所,礼服展览包括伊丽莎白二世和威尔士亲王王妃戴安娜穿过的服装。

历史性皇家宫殿群

　　汉普顿皇宫是"历史性皇家宫殿群"的一个部分。"历史性皇家宫殿"是一

个注册慈善机构(注册号:1068852),接受公众捐资。我们依靠宫殿门票收入来支付重大保护工作的费用,这些工作对为后代保护这些国家纪念场所和收藏品是必需的。更多信息请向售票处咨询或者登录网站 www.hrp.org.uk。

乘坐马车

乘坐马车游览御花园。乘坐起点和终点都在御花园位于东前花园的入口处。整天都能坐。20分钟一次。每次10英镑。根据天气和地面情况进行调整。

咨询

想要知道门票、团体票价、汉普顿皇宫的友人及为残疾游客提供的设施,请致电 0870 – 752 – 7777 或者访问网站 www. Hampton-Court-Palace. org. uk。

餐馆和商店

可以选择 Tiltyard 茶餐厅或者内部的 Kitchen 咖啡店。夏天还有许多冰淇淋摊。宫殿里的商店出售多种多样的礼品与纪念品。

语音导游

语音导游的费用包括在宫殿票价当中,可提供英、法、德、意、西班牙和日语服务。

〽️ Exercise 7

When you enter a supermarket, you see shelves full of food. You walk between the shelves. You carry a shopping basket and put your food in it.

You probably hear soft, slow music as you walk between the shelves. If you hear fast music, you walk quickly. The supermarket plays slow music. You walk slowly and have more time to buy things.

Maybe you go to the meat department first. There is some meat on sale, and you want to find it. The manager of the supermarket knows where the customers enter the meat department. The cheap meat is at the other end of the meat department, away from where the customers enter. You have to walk by all the expensive meat before you find the cheaper meat. Maybe you will buy some of the expensive meat instead of the meat on sale.

The department selling milk and milk products such as butter and milk powder is called the dairy department. Many customers like milk that has only a little *butterfat*（油脂）in it. One store has three different jars of low fat milk. One says "1 percent fat" on the jar. The second says "99 percent fat free". The third says "LOW FAT" in big letters and "1%" in small letters. As you can see, the milk is all the same. However, in this store the three jars of milk cost three different amount of money. Maybe the customers will buy the milk that costs him most.

Most of the food in supermarket is very pleasing. It all says "Buy me!" to the customers. The expensive meat says "Buy me!" as you walk by. The expensive milk jar says "Buy me! I have less fat."

1. The best title of the passage may be ____.
　[A]Buy Me　　　　　　　[B]Food on Sale
　[C]Supermarket　　　　　[D]Low Fat Milk

2. Three different jars of low fat milk ____.
　[A]have the same amount of fat
　[B]have the same weight
　[C]cost the same amount of money
　[D]have the same taste

3. When you enter the meat department, you will see ____ first.
　[A]milk powder　　　　　[B]cheap meat
　[C]butter　　　　　　　　[D]expensive meat

4. Which of the following is TRUE?
　[A]Customers will choose cheap food.
　[B]Customers always prefer expensive food.
　[C]Most food in the supermarket is attractive to customers.
　[D]The more expensive the food is, the more attractive it is.

答案与分析

1.[A]。主旨题。文章从超市为留住顾客、让顾客购买较贵的商品而采取的几种手段，如播放舒缓的背景音乐、在商品的外包装上做文章等方面入手，并在最后用拟人的手法，用商品的口吻，突出了"买我"的这一目的。因此，用"买我"做文章的标题不仅能很好地概括全文主旨,还很生动形象。其余三项:"甩卖食品"([B]项)、"超市"([C]项)和"低脂牛奶"([D]项)都明显无法概括上述主旨。

2.[A]。细节题。第四段倒数第三句说:the milk is all the same,结合前文对三种奶中脂肪的数字说明可知[A]对。

3.[D]。推断题。文章第二段指出,超市总是将贵的商品摆放在超市入口,而将便宜的放在远离入口的另一端,这样顾客在找到便宜的商品前得经过所有贵的商品,那样他们就有可能买贵的商品而不去买便宜的。由此可以推知,去超市买肉时,顾客肯定会先看到价钱贵的肉。

4.[C]。细节题。[C]与最后一段第一句的内容相符;[A]、[B]两项根据常识即可排除;[D]项在文中并未提及,因为文章没有就价钱与商品的吸引力之间的关系进行阐述。

同步译文

当你进入超市时,你会看到超市货架上食品堆放得满满当当。你在这些货架之间穿行。你提着购物筐,把要买的食品放在里面。

在货架之间穿行时,你可能会听到柔和、舒缓的音乐。如果听到快节奏的音乐,你就会走得很快。超市里放的都是舒缓的音乐。这样你会慢慢地走,从而有更多的时间买东西。

也许你会先来到肉食部。有一些肉降价出售,你想找这种肉。超市经理知道顾客从什么地方进入超市。便宜的肉会放在肉食部的另一端,远离顾客进入的地方。在找到更便宜的肉之前,你得经过所有贵的肉。也许你会买了贵的而不会买降价销售的肉。

出售牛奶与奶制品比如黄油、奶粉的部门叫乳品部。许多顾客喜欢只含有少量脂肪的牛奶。有一家商店里有三种不同的低脂罐装奶。一种在罐上标有"含1%的脂肪",第二种标着"99%不含脂肪",第三种用大字标明"低脂肪",而用小字标着"1%"。可以看出,牛奶都是一样的。然而,在这家商店里,这三种罐装牛奶的价格却大不一样。也许顾客会买最贵的那一种。

超市里的大部分食品都很诱人。它们都在向顾客说"买我!"在你经过时,那种贵的肉在说:"买我!"而那种贵的牛奶在说:"买我!我含的脂肪少一些。"

Exercise 8

When 15-year-old Michael Thomas left home for school last May, he couldn't have been prouder. On his feet, thanks to his mother's hard work, were a pair of new Air Jordans — $ 100 worth of leather, rubber and status that to today's youth are the Mercedes-Benz of *athletic* (运动员的) footwear.

The next day it was James David Martin, 17, who was walking down the street in Thomas' new sneakers, while Thomas lay dead in a field not far from his school. Martin was *arrested* (逮捕) for murder.

For the Baltimore school system, Thomas' death was the last straw. He was the third youngster to have been killed over his clothes in five years. Dozens of others had been robbed of name brand sneakers, designer jogging suits, leather jackets and jewelry.

This fall, the school board announced a dress code preventing leather skirts and jackets, jogging suits, gold chains and other expensive items.

Clothes, said board president Joseph Smith, had just gotten out of hand.

Across the nation, parents, school officials, psychologists and even some children agree.

They say that today's youngsters, throughout the nation, have become clothes *fixated* (专注的). They worry about them, compete over them, *neglect* (忽视) school for them and sometimes even rob and kill for them.

In many cases, students are so concerned about what they and their classmates are wearing, they forget what they come to school for, educators said.

In response, many public schools, mainly in Eastern cities, have adopted school uniforms to cut down on competition. Educators say, in the current fashion climate, dressing students alike allows them more freedom to be individuals.

1. Why was Michael so proud of himself?

[A]His hard-working mother earned a lot of money.

[B]He wore expensive clothes worth $100.

[C]He was in a pair of name brand shoes.

[D]He was good at playing basketball.

2. Martin was arrested for ____.

[A]killing Thomas

[B]robbing several students

[C]stealing expensive things

[D]murdering three people for their clothes

3. When the board president said "Clothes had just gotten out of hand", he meant clothes were gotten ____.

[A]by force   [B]too easily

[C]out of control   [D]through hard work

4. According to the text, adopting school uniforms means to ____.

[A]have students wear ordinary clothes

[B]make students less competitive

[C]keep students more disciplined

[D]dress students all alike

答案与分析

1.[C]。细节题。文章第一句说 15 岁的迈克尔·托马斯上学时心里非常骄傲,然后在第二句说明了他感到骄傲的原因:他母亲给他买了一双新的"飞人乔丹"牌的运动鞋,并且说明这双鞋在如今年轻人心目中的分量——运动鞋中的奔驰。[C]项很好地概括了这一句的内容。

2.[A]。推断题。首先,第二段一句的最后指出马丁是因谋杀(murder)而被捕的;其次,由前面描述的他穿着托马斯的新运动鞋、而托马斯死在离学校不远的一块地里的内容可以推知,他杀死了托马斯并抢了后者的运动鞋。

3.[C]。词句理解题。"(be) out of hand"的意思是"失控,脱手",所以校董事会主席的意思就是在校青少年因服装上的攀比而变得难以控制,出现各种各样的问题。

4.[D]。细节题。文章最后一句对于采用校服的作用进行了说明,即"dressing students alike"。注意,在该段第一句中有"to cut down on competition"，但这是一句话的目的状语，而题中的 means 表示解释"school uniform"的含义，故选[D]。

去年5月当15岁的迈克尔·托马斯离家上学时，他的心里无比骄傲。在他的脚上，穿着由他母亲辛勤工作换来的一双新的"飞人乔丹"牌运动鞋——价值100美元、用皮革、橡胶制作、其地位在如今的年轻人眼中是梅塞迪斯-奔驰级的运动鞋。

但第二天却是17岁的詹姆斯·戴维·马丁穿着托马斯的新运动鞋在街上走，而托马斯死在了离学校不远的一块地里。马丁因为谋杀罪而被捕了。

对于巴尔的摩的教育系统来说，托马斯的死使人们再也无法容忍这样的事情了。他是5年内因其服装而被杀的第三个青少年。还有其他许多人被抢走了名牌运动鞋、由著名设计师设计的慢跑服、皮夹克和珠宝。

今年秋季，该校董事会宣布了一项着装规定，不准穿戴皮革裙装、皮夹克、慢跑服、金项链和其他贵重东西。

校董事会主席约瑟夫·史密斯说，学生的服装已经变得失控了。

在全国，学生家长、教育官员、心理学家、甚至一些孩子都同意这一点。

他们说，如今全国的年轻人都变得专注于自己的服装。他们担心自己的服装，在服装上攀比，因为服装而忽视学习，有时甚至因为服装而抢劫、杀人。

在许多情况下，学生们太过关注自己和同学们的穿着而忘记了自己上学的目的，教育家们说。

作为应对，许多公立学校——主要是东部城市里——已经采用校服制度，以减少学生之间的攀比。教育家们说，在如今这种时尚的社会氛围下，让学生们着装相同可以给孩子们的个性以更大的自由空间。

 Exercise 9

　　Our village *carpenter*（木匠），John Hill，came one day and made a dining table for my wife. He made it just the right size to fill the space between the two windows. When I got home that evening，John was drinking a cup of tea and writing out his bill for the job.

　　My wife said to me quietly，"It's his ninth cup of tea today."But she said in a loud voice，"It's a beautiful table，dear，isn't it?"

　　"I'll decide about that when I see the bill，"I read：

　　One dining table，10 November，1989.

Cost of wood: $ 17.00

Paint: $ 1.50

Work: 8 hours ($ 1 an hour), $ 8.00

Total: $ 36.50

When I was looking at the bill, John said, "It's been a fine day, hasn't it? Quite sunny." "Yes," I said, "I'm glad it's only the 10th of November."

"Me, too," said John. "You wait. It'll be a lot colder by the end of the month."

"Yes, colder ..., and more expensive! Dining tables will be $ 20 more expensive on November 30th, won't they, John?"

John looked hard at me for half a minute. Was there a little smile in his two blue eyes? I gave his bill back to him.

"If it isn't too much trouble, John," I said, "please add it up again and you can forget the date."

I paid him $ 26.50 and he was happy to get it.

1. Why did John talk about the weather when the writer was looking at the bill?

[A]Because he didn't want the writer to go through the bill carefully.

[B]Because it was really a fine day.

[C]Because he wanted the writer to check the bill carefully.

[D]Because he wanted to tell the writer what the weather was like.

2. Why did the writer say that dining table would be $ 20 more expensive on November 30th?

[A]Because it was difficult to make dining tables in cold weather.

[B]Because paint would be more expensive.

[C]Because the cost of wood would be more expensive.

[D]Because he thought John would certainly add the date to the cost of the dining table.

3. The writer thought John would ask for ＿＿ if he made a dining table on the last day of November.

[A] $ 56.50　　[B] $ 46.50　　[C] $ 26.50　　[D] $ 20.00

4. From the story we know that ＿＿.

[A]John made a mistake in the bill

[B]John tried to fool the writer in order to get more money for his work

[C]John had written out the bill before the writer got home

[D]John still wanted to get ＄36.50 for his work in the end

答案与分析

1.[A]。推断题。文章记叙了一位木匠为作者家做完餐桌后结账时,故意把工作的日期和工资、材料费用等加在一起,企图蒙骗作者多赚钱的故事。通读全文及作者的语气可以看出,木匠在作者核查账单时谈论天气是有意的,目的是分散作者的注意力,不让作者看出其中的奥妙,所以答案为[A]。

2.[D]。推断题。作者在核查后发现木匠把日期加到了费用里,所以作者故意这么说,一是揭穿木匠的用意,二是揶揄木匠。11 月 30 日比 11 月 10 日多 20 天,所以根据木匠的做法,在 11 月 30 日做餐桌时,费用就会比 11 月 10 日时做多 20 美元。

3.[A]。细节题。参见上题解析。根据木匠的做法,11 月 10 日的费用是 36.5 美元,那么 11 月底(30 日)的费用就会是 36.5＋20＝56.5 美元。

4.[B]。推断题。参见第 1 题解析。根据文意,作者查看账单时木匠谈论天气,作者发现问题后木匠盯着作者、眼睛里似乎有一丝笑意,由这两方面即可推断木匠是故意弄错以蒙骗作者。

同步译文

有一天,我们村里的木匠约翰·希尔来为我妻子做了一张餐桌。他把餐桌做成正好放在两个窗户之间的尺寸。那天晚上我回到家里时,约翰正在边喝茶边填写他的工作账单。

我妻子悄悄对我说:"这是他今天喝的第 9 杯茶了。"然后用很大的声音说:"亲爱的,桌子做得很漂亮,不是吗?"

"我看完账单再来评判。"我说。然后我看账单:

1989 年 11 月 10 日,一张餐桌。

木料费用:17 美元。

油漆:1.5 美元。

工作:8 小时(每小时 1 美元),8 美元。

总计:36.5 美元。

我看账单时,约翰说:"今天天气真不错,不是吗? 很晴朗。""对,"我说,"我很高兴现在才 11 月 10 日。"

"我也是，"约翰说。"你等着吧。到了月底就会冷得多了。"

"对，冷得多……而且也贵得多！餐桌在 11 月 30 日会贵 20 美元，对吗，约翰？"

约翰盯了我一会儿。他的两只蓝眼睛里有一点笑意吗？我把账单还给他。

"如果不是太麻烦的话，约翰，"我说，"请重新加一遍，你就会把日期忘了的。"

我付了他 26.5 美元，他很高兴地拿着了。

Exercise 10

Most people's experience of flying is limited to the inside of an airplane. Several more forms of flying, however, have developed into increasingly popular leisure *pastimes*（休闲娱乐）. Flying sports are divided into various kinds in terms of length of time in the air, necessary training, cost, technical equipment and knowledge required.

Ballooning（气球运动）was man's first experience of flight over 200 years ago. However, it was not until the late 1960s that hot-air ballooning really developed in Britain. It is a very unusual experience to stand and look at the countryside disappearing in front of you as you rise higher and higher. If you wish to learn to fly a balloon yourself and can afford it（they cost several thousand pounds）, it is possible to buy your own. Some producers provide instruction or you can learn on an hourly basis at a club.

Hang gliding（滑翔）is to realize man's dream of stepping off a hill or mountain and flying like a bird. It has made flying a possibility for almost everyone since it is relatively inexpensive and involves very little equipment. It is done from a hill facing into the wind and by the end of the course you should be able to make flights from the hilltop, turn left and right, land *accurately*（准确地）at the bottom of the hill. A five-day course is normally needed to reach this standard. You should wear warm and waterproof clothing and a special cap to protect your head. You are not allowed to do it if you are under 17. Once you have com-

pleted a course you can join the club. The telephone number is（0234）
751688.

1. Which of the following statements is TRUE according to the article?

　[A]People cannot fly without airplanes.

　[B]People need special training to fly.

　[C]You can't fly a balloon by yourself.

　[D]Ballooning is a new kind of sport.

2. Hang gliding has become part of people's leisure pastime because they ____.

　[A]have a dream of flying like a bird

　[B]want to look at the country from the above

　[C]are rich enough to afford a balloon

　[D]have made hot-air balloons

3. Almost everyone can learn hang gliding because ____.

　[A]it's like a real bird flying　　[B]you don't have to be skillful

　[C]it needs less equipment　　[D]you can turn left and right

4. One thing to remember when you take hang gliding is to ____.

　[A]become a club member　　[B]keep yourself warm

　[C]call the gliding club first　　[D]be good at mountain climbing

答案与分析

1.[B]。细节题。文章第一句指出许多人的飞行经历限于坐飞机,但后面介绍了其他几种飞行运动,因此[A]不对;[B]与第一段最后一句中的 necessary training 表达的意思相符;第二段倒数第二句中的 If you wish to learn to fly a balloon yourself 表明可以自己一个人驾驶气球,故[C]不对;由第二段第一、二句可知气球的历史很久了,并不是一种新兴运动,故[D]也不对。

2.[A]。细节题。文章第三段第一句用 to realize man's dream of ... like a bird 一句表明了人们喜欢滑翔的原因:实现人类像鸟一样飞翔的梦想。

3.[C]。细节题。第三段第二句用 since it is relatively inexpensive and involves very little equipment 一句说明了原因,与[C]一致。

4.[B]。细节题。第三段倒数第四句说明了滑翔时要注意的问题:穿暖和、防水的衣服,戴特殊头盔。对照四个选项可知只有[B]对。

大多数人的飞行经历都局限于坐在飞机内部飞行。然而，有几种其他的飞行方式已经发展成了日渐大众化的休闲娱乐活动。根据在空中飞行的时间长短、必要的训练、费用、技术装备和需要掌握的知识，飞行运动分成了不同的类型。

　　气球是人类在200多年前的首次飞行经历。然而，直到20世纪60年代，热气球运动才真正在英国得到发展。随着气球越升越高，站在气球上看着乡村在眼前逐渐消失，这是一种极不寻常的经历。如果想学会自己一个人驾驶气球并且买得起气球（它们要几千英镑），自己可以买一个。一些气球制造商提供驾驶指导，你也可以在以小时计费的俱乐部里学会驾驶。

　　滑翔是为了实现人类在山峰上跳下并像鸟儿一样飞翔的梦想。由于滑翔相对来说不贵，必要的装备也少，所以它让几乎每个人都可以飞翔。滑翔在一个向风的山顶上进行，在课程的最后你应能从山顶上起飞，左右转向，并准确地在山脚下着陆。通常要达到这个标准，需要学习5天的课程。你应当穿上暖和、防水的衣服，戴特殊的头盔以保护头部。不满17岁的人不允许进行滑翔。一旦完成课程，就可以加入俱乐部。俱乐部的电话号码是(0234)751688。

Exercise 11

President Abraham Lincoln often visited hospitals to talk with wounded soldiers during the Civil War. Once, doctors pointed out a young soldier who was near death and Lincoln went over to his bedside.

"Is there anything I can do for you?"asked the President.

The soldier obviously didn't recognize Lincoln, and with some effort he was able to whisper. "Would you please write a letter to my mother?"

A pen and paper were provided and the President carefully began writing down what the young man was able to say:

"My dearest mother, I was badly hurt while doing my duty. I'm afraid I'm not going to recover. Don't *grieve*(悲伤) too much for me, please. Kiss Mary and John for me. May God bless you and father."

The soldier was too weak to continue, so Lincoln signed the letter for him and added,"written for your son by Abraham Lincoln."

The young man asked to see the note and was astonished when he discovered who had written it. "Are you really the President?" he asked.

"Yes, I am," Lincoln replied quietly. Then he asked if there was anything else he could do.

"Would you please hold my hand?" the soldier asked. "It will help to see me through to the end."

In the quiet room, the President took the boy's hand in his and spoke warm words of encouragement until death came.

1. The young soldier ____.

[A] wrote a letter to his mother himself

[B] was in hospital for a long time

[C] couldn't say any words when he saw the president

[D] was badly hurt in the Civil War

2. What kind of man do you think Abraham Lincoln was?

[A] He was a kind and warm-hearted man.

[B] He was the greatest president in the United States.

[C] He was always ready to help his soldiers.

[D] He was not only a president but also a doctor.

3. When he discovered who had written the letter to his mother for him, the soldier ____.

[A] was filled with great surprise

[B] recognized Lincoln at once

[C] asked Lincoln who he was

[D] asked Lincoln to write another letter

4. Why did Lincoln added in the letter "written for your son by Abraham Lincoln"? Because he wanted ____.

[A] to let the mother remember him

[B] people to know he was the president

[C] to show his thanks and kindness to the mother

[D] to encourage the young soldier

 答案与分析

1.[D]。细节题。文章第一句即指出,林肯经常去医院 to talk with wounded soldiers during the Civil War(在内战期间同受伤的战士交谈),紧接着描述他和一位临死的年轻战士交谈的情况,所以这位战士当然是内战中受的伤。[A]、[C]两项与后文描述的事实不符;[B]在文中没有提及。

2.[A]。推断题。由文章对林肯的描述(与受伤的战士交谈,替临死的战士写信,陪伴临死的战士走完生命的最后一刻)等不难推知作者想表现的是林肯的善良。其余三项在文中都没有体现。

3.[A]。细节题。文章指出,那名年轻战士 ... was astonished when he discovered who had written it,其中的 astonished(震惊)就是[A]中的 filled with great surprise。

4.[C]。推断题。本题应当根据常识来进行推断。由第 2 题的分析可知,作者讲述这个故事就是为了表现林肯的善良,而且因为信是给战士母亲的,这名战士又快死了,肯定不是为了鼓励战士,所以答案只能是[C]。

同步译文

　　　　　在美国内战期间,亚伯拉罕·林肯总统经常到医院和受伤战士交谈。有一次,医生指出了一位临死的年轻战士,林肯走到他的床前。

　　　　　"我能帮你做点什么吗?"总统问。

　　那位士兵很明显没有认出林肯,他费了好大劲才用微弱的声音说:"请您给我妈妈写封信好吗?"

　　笔和纸拿来后,总统开始仔细写下那个年轻人说的话:

　　"我最亲爱的妈妈,我在执行任务时受了很重的伤。我恐怕再也不能康复了。请不要为我太过悲伤。替我亲亲玛丽和约翰。愿上帝赐福给您和父亲。"

　　那位战士太虚弱了,不能继续说下去,所以林肯在信上为他署上名并附加了"由亚伯拉罕·林肯代您的儿子书写"。

　　年轻人要求看这封信,当发现是谁替他写的之后非常震惊。"您真是的总统?"他问道。

　　"是的,我是。"林肯轻轻回答说。然后他问还有没有其他事需要他做。

　　"您能握着我的手吗?"战士问道,"这会帮助我走到生命的终点。"

　　在那间安静的房间里,总统握着男孩的手,说着鼓励的温暖话语,直到死亡降临。

Exercise 12

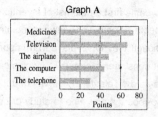

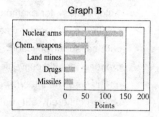

The above graphs are based on the results of a *survey*（调查）that asked 102 Japanese people from various fields what things made human life better and what things made it worse. In this survey, *interviewees*（被采访者）were asked to choose the top three 20th century inventions and products in each of three following classes: those that brought the most happiness (Graph A); those that brought the most misfortune (Graph B); and those that brought both happiness and misfortune to humans (no graph is shown here). Answers from each of the 102 interviewees were graded. Three points were given for those selected first in each class, two points for those selected second and one point for those chose third.

Graph A shows that *antibiotic medicines*（抗生素类药物）, such as penicillin, came out on top in the survey as making the most important contribution to the improvement of the quality of life with 73 points. Many interviewees thought of such medicines in a purely positive light, with the opinion that they help humans realize a common hope — freedom from disease and longer life. Television was ranked second by a small gap. Many interviewees appreciated television's function in bringing information from all over the world into people's living rooms.

On the other hand, according to Graph B, nuclear arms, including atomic bombs, were repeatedly mentioned by interviewees as the invention that made people extremely unhappy. Many interviewees answered that the atomic bomb was the worst invention of the century. Other weapons created to kill humans in an *indiscriminate*（不加选择的）manner, like the *landmine*（地雷）, were also ranked high.

Asked about what kinds of inventions or discoveries brought us both happiness and misfortune, interviewees said that automobiles, television and nuclear energy have their good points and bad points. Automobiles, for example, came first on the list of inventions with both positive and negative aspects. Some interviewees pointed out that cars cause air pollution, though they have played an important role in creating today's convenient consumer society. Television came second on this list. An interviewee said, "Television is a wonderful tool for educating children, but it also robs them of time to study or communicate with family members."

1. The purpose of this survey is to find out ____.

[A] what inventions and products will bring humans happiness or misfortune in the future

[B] what inventions and products made humans happy or unhappy in the 20th century

[C] what inventions and products made Japanese people happy in the 20th century

[D] what inventions and products were bought by famous people around the world

2. Graph A shows that ____.

[A] the points given to television were more than twice the points given to the telephone

[B] the points given to medicines were less than half the points given to the computer

[C] the points given to the airplane were almost the same as the points given to the telephone

[D] the points given to the computer were more than those given to the airplane

3. As for the result of negative inventions, ____.

[A] nuclear arms were mentioned most because the interviewees thought chemical weapons were the worst inventions

[B] missiles were mentioned least because the interviewees thought the airplane had good and bad points

[C]nuclear arms were mentioned most because the interviewees thought the atomic bomb was the worst invention

[D]missiles were mentioned least because the interviewees thought the airplane played an important role in the war

4. According to the article，many interviewees thought that ＿＿＿.

[A] cars were one of the inventions that brought us both happiness and misfortune

[B]medicines were the best invention because they played an important role during the war

[C]the airplane had bad points because it sometimes caused air pollution

[D]nuclear energy was one of the most dangerous things

答案与分析

1.[B]。细节题。由文章第一段第二句可知应选[B]。其余三项：[A]中的 in the future 与原文中的 20th century 不符；[C]中的 Japanese 只是被调查对象；[D]文章没有提及。

2.[A]。细节题。由第二段的内容与图表可以看出[A]对。其余三项中的比较关系都与原文及图表内容相反。

3.[C]细节题。答案对应于第三段第一、二两句。

4.[A]。细节题。最后一段第二句指出，汽车位于具有正反两方面影响的列表之首。

同步译文

上述图表是基于一项对来自不同领域的 102 名日本人进行的、询问使人类生活更好或更坏的事物的调查作出的。在这项调查中，被采访者被要求从下面三个方面选择出 20 世纪中的三大发明和产品：带来最多幸福的发明和产品（图表 A）；带来最多不幸的发明和产品（图表 B）；那些给人类既带来幸福、又带来不幸的发明和产品（此处无图表）。102 位被访者中每个人的答案都被打分。在每个方面选择第一位的给 3 分，选择第二的给 2 分，那些选择第三的给 1 分。

图表 A 表明抗生素类药物，如盘尼西林，以 73 分位居调查中对于改进人类生活质量的最重要的贡献这一问题之首。许多被访者对这些药品持纯粹的赞成态度，认为它们帮助人类实现了一个普遍的希望——不受疾病困扰和长寿。电视以微弱之差位居第二。许多被访者欣赏电视将信息从世界各地带到人们起居室里的这一作用。

另一方面,根据图表B可以看出,被访者一遍遍地重复提到核武器(包括原子弹)是使人们极为不幸的发明。许多被访者回答说原子弹是这个世纪最差的发明。其他一些以不加选择的方式杀害人类的武器如地雷,在图表中所处的位置也很高。

在问及哪些发明或者发现给我们同时带来幸福和不幸时,被访者们说汽车、电视和核能有好的方面,也有坏的方面。比如说汽车,位于同时具有正反两面的发明列表之首。一些被访者指出,汽车造成空气污染,尽管它们在形成如今这种便利的消费社会过程中起了重要作用。在这一列表上,电视位居第二。一位被访者说:"电视是一种教育孩子的很好的工具,但它们也剥夺了他们学习及与家人交流的时间。"

Exercise 13

How much rain has fallen on the earth in the past? Man has not always kept weather records. Because scientists need a way to learn about past rainfall, they study rings. A tree's *trunk*(树干) grows bigger each year. Beneath its *bark*(树皮), a tree adds a layer of new wood each year it lives. If you look at a tree *stump*(桩), you can see the layers. They are called *annual*(每年的) rings. On some trees all of the rings are of the same width. But the Ponderosa *pines*(松树) that grow in American southwest have rings of different width. The soil in the southwest is dry. The pines depend on rainfall. In a wet year, they form wide rings. In a dry year, they form narrow ones. Scientists do not have to cut down a pine to see its rings. With a special tool, they can remove a narrow piece of wood from the trunk without harming the tree, then they look at the width of each ring to see how much rain fell in the year it formed. Some pines are hundreds of years old and so have hundreds of rings. These rings form an annual record of past rainfall in the southwest.

1. **What is the main topic of the passage?**

[A]The Ponderosa pines in American southwest.

[B]Trees that lived hundreds of years ago.

[C]What makes tree trunks grow bigger.

[D]Why scientists study tree rings.

2. We can infer from the text that ____ .

[A]a tree grows faster when it has a lot of water

[B]the Ponderosa pine grows in American southwest

[C]pine trees form wide rings each year

[D]scientists cut down trees to study tree rings

3. Why do scientists study the width of the tree rings?

[A]They want to move the pine trees.

[B]They want to know how big the trees can grow.

[C]The rings can tell how much rain has fallen.

[D]The trees depend on rainfall for water.

4. Which of the following is TRUE according to the text?

[A]Young trees have fewer annual rings.

[B]The soil in the southwest is fit for the growth of trees.

[C]The trunk of a tree never changes in size.

[D]The more it rains，the more rings a tree has.

 答案与分析

1.[D]。主旨题。文章以一问句入手，提问过去有多少雨水降到地球上。然后介绍了科学家们研究松树年轮的方法、目的与原理，就是要回答这一问题。因此，文章的主旨无疑就是科学家们研究树的年轮的原因或者目的：研究过去地球上有多少降水。因此答案是[D]。其余三项都只是描述科学家们研究过程中的一个方面，不能概括全文。

2.[A]。推断题。题目要求推断文中未明示的结论。由 They depend on rainfall. In a wet year，they form wide rings 两句可知雨水多时形成的年轮宽，而由 Beneath its bark ... it lives 可知，年轮越宽说明树长得越快，所以[A]是正确的。[B]是文章中已经明示出来的信息；[C]与 In a dry year，they form narrow ones 一句不符；[D]与原文倒数第四句话相反。

3.[C]。细节题。答案对应于第三句及最后一句话。

4.[A]。推断题。由文章第四句至第七句对年轮的解释可以推知[A]对。年轮每年一个，那么小树的年轮肯定也要少。至于其他三项，都与文意不符。

过去地球上降了多少雨？人类并没有一直记录气候情况。由于科学家们需要一条了解过去降雨量的途径，所以他们研究年轮。一棵树的树干每年都长粗。在树皮下，每一年树都会增加一层新的木质。如果观察一个树桩，就可以看到这些层。它们被称作年轮。一些树的所有年轮都一样宽。但生长在美国西南部的Ponderosa松却有着宽度不同的年轮。西南部的土壤很干旱，这些松树靠雨水存活。它们的年轮很宽。在干旱年份，它们则形成窄年轮。科学家们不用把松树砍倒来观察它的年轮。用一种特殊的工具，他们能从树干上取下一窄片木头而不伤及松树，然后他们观察每个年轮的宽度，来了解年轮形成的那一年的降雨量。一些松树有几百岁了，因此有几百个年轮。这些年轮记录了西南部地区过去每一年的降雨量。

Exercise 14

Everyone gets headaches. Some people get them very often. Other people are lucky — they only get them once in a while.

There are some ways to prevent headaches. They don't work 100% of the time but they can reduce the number of the headaches you get.

⊙ Eat regular meals. Don't skip meals.

⊙ Get enough sleep.

⊙ Get fresh air and exercise.

⊙ Avoid drinking a lot of coffee or alcohol.

⊙ Try to avoid stress.

What should you do when you get a headache? How can you treat it? There are many different ways. There are some suggestions that may help.

⊙ Massage(按摩) in a circular motion(循环运动) behind your ear and across the back of your neck while relaxing in a warm bath.

⊙ Massage your scalp(头皮) (as if you are washing your hair). Gently pull the hair all around your head.

⊙ While sitting, breathe in and bend your head back gently, looking up at the ceiling. Don't bend too far back. Breathe out and bring your head down so that your chin rests on your chest. Repeat two times.

⊙ Breathe out and turn your head to look over your right shoulder. Don't bend your chin to your shoulder. Keep your chin level. Breathe in as you turn your head back，looking straight ahead. Do the same thing over your left shoulder. Repeat two times on each side.

⊙ Take medicine，such as aspirin.

Why don't you try one of these the next time you get a headache? See what works for you.

1. This text mainly discusses ____.

[A]causes of headaches

[B]symptoms of headaches

[C]prevention and treatments of headaches

[D]effects of headaches

2. ____ does NOT help to prevent headaches.

[A]Doing Exercises　　　　[B]Drinking a lot of coffee

[C]Eating regularly　　　　[D]Having enough sleep

3. Which of the following can be a good suggestion to treat headaches?

[A]Have a cold shower.

[B]Bend your head far back.

[C]Take aspirin.

[D]Bend your chin to your shoulder.

 答案与分析

1.[C]。主旨题。通读全文,不难发现文章由两个部分组成:一是如何预防头疼,二是如何减轻头疼。因此答案无疑是[C]。

2.[B]。细节题。文章第二段以后分条列举了预防头疼的方法。将四个选项与之逐一对照可知只有[B]与文章提及的相反。

3.[C]。细节题。答题方法与上一题相同。逐一对照选项与原文,发现只有[C]与原文中最后一条的内容相符。

每个人都会头疼。一些人经常头疼。其他人则幸运一些——他们只是偶尔会头疼。

　　有一些预防头疼的方法。它们并不是任何时候都100%有效,但它们能减少你患头疼的次数。

⊙饮食规律。不要饱一顿饥一顿。

⊙睡眠充足。

⊙呼吸新鲜空气,锻炼身体。

⊙避免喝过多咖啡和酒。

⊙避免紧张。

　　头疼时怎么办?怎样治疗头疼?有许多不同的方法。这里有一些可能会有用的建议。

⊙在洗热水澡放松时,从耳后绕过后颈循环按摩。

⊙按摩头皮(就像洗头一样)。轻拉头上的所有头发。

⊙如果坐着,吸气并把头轻轻后仰,向上看天花板。不能太向后仰。呼气并把头低下,使下巴触到胸部。重复两次。

⊙呼气并把头转向右肩上。不要将下巴曲向肩膀。保持下巴水平。把头转回来时吸气,双眼向前平视。转向左肩进行同样的步骤。每一边重复两遍。

⊙吃药,如阿司匹林。

　　下次头疼时何不试试其中的一种方法?看哪种方法对你有效。

Exercise 15

　　Every country had its heroes. The heroes are the people the nation and especially the young people admire. If you get a list of the heroes of a nation, it will tell you the *potential*(潜力) of that nation.

　　Today in America, if you ask the high school students to list their heroes, their choices would probably fall into three groups. The first group of heroes would be the rock stars — the people connected with rock music. There is no doubt that such people do have *talent*(天才) but one wonders if one should hold up rock stars as a model. The rock stars too often are mixed with drugs and their personal life is not all that good. The rock stars are rich and wear the latest fashion styles.

However, one should seek more in a hero than such things as money and good clothes.

A second type of hero for the American youth is the sports stars. Again you have a person who has a great ability in one area — sports. However, too often, the personal life of the sports stars is a bit of a disorder. Too frequently drugs and drinking are a part of life of the sports stars.

A third type of hero is the TV or movie stars. These persons may have lots of acting talent and are quite handsome. However, the personal life of too many actors is quite sad and they should not be held up as a model of young people.

Today, the rock star, the athlete, and the actor all have become the models of the youth in America. Really, do you hear a young person say that his hero is a doctor, a teacher, or a scientist? These people are not rich and do not wear fashionable clothes. However, they are talented people who work hard to make the world a better place for everyone.

What is really sad is that the young try to *imitate*(模仿) their heroes. They like to wear the same clothes and follow their styles. If the heroes of today for the American young people are limited only to rock stars, athletes and actors, the future does not look too bright.

1. **From the passage, we know that the heroes the American youth admire are those _____.**
   [A]who are not bright but are good-looking
   [B]who are rich but are strict with themselves
   [C]who are talented in some area but lead an improper life
   [D]who are perfect in all areas

2. **It can be inferred that the American young people will not admire _____.**
   [A]a university professor　　　　[B]a popular singer
   [C]a football player　　　　　　[D]a film actress

3. **According to the writer, people should admire those _____.**
   [A]who are rich and wear the latest fashionable clothes
   [B]who can express people's feelings

[C]whose personal life is good

[D]who work in the interests of the people

4. What is the writer's *attitude*(态度) towards American youth's admiration?

[A]He understands it.   [B]He criticizes it.

[C]He is angry about it.   [D]He is uninterested in it.

答案与分析

1.[C]。推断题。根据文章第二、三、四、五段的分析可得出结论:这些受崇拜的偶像虽然有某方面的才能,但是他们的生活都是 improper(不正常的),故选[C]。

2.[A]。推断题。根据文章第五段可推导出来:美国的年轻人不会把老师作为他们崇拜的偶像。

3.[D]。推断题。根据文中第五段:However,they are talented people who work hard to make the world a better place for everyone 及文章的最后一句可知作者的意图是劝说人们应该把像医生、老师、科学家这样为人民利益而工作的人作为崇拜偶像,故选[D]。

4.[B]。主旨题。根据文章中各段的意思特别是最后一段可知:作者对美国年轻人的偶像崇拜持否定态度,故选[B]。

同步译文

每个国家都有自己的英雄。这些英雄是国人特别是年轻人崇拜的偶像。如果把一个国家的英雄列出来,这张列表可以告诉你这个国家的潜力。

如今在美国,如果让高中生列出他们的英雄,他们的选择很可能分成三类。第一类英雄会是摇滚歌星——那些与摇滚乐有关的人。无疑这些人确实有天才,但人们会怀疑是否应当把摇滚歌星当作榜样。摇滚歌星们经常与毒品有染,他们的个人生活也不那么好。摇滚歌星们都很有钱,穿的都是最新款式的服装。然而,一个人应当从英雄那里寻求更多的东西,而不是金钱和华丽这样的东西。

美国年轻人的第二类英雄是体育明星。同样,这种人在某一个领域——体育内很有才能。然而,体育明星们的个人生活经常有点糟糕。毒品、酗酒经常是这些体育明星们生活的一部分。

第三类英雄是影视明星。这些人可能很有表演才能,长得也很漂亮。然而,太多演员的个人生活相当糟,他们不应当被作为年轻人的榜样。

　　如今，摇滚歌星、运动员和演员都成了美国年轻人的榜样。确实，你听说过一位年轻人说他的英雄是医生、教师或者科学家吗？这些人并不富有，也不穿时髦的服装。然而，他们都是努力工作、让世界对每个人来说都变得更好的天才人物。

　　真正让人觉得悲哀的是年轻人试图模仿他们的"英雄"。他们喜欢穿与"英雄"们相同的服装，跟随"英雄"们的生活方式。如果对于美国的年轻人来说，如今的英雄仅限于摇滚歌星、运动员和演员，那么其未来看起来并不会太美好。

Exercise 16

　　On the way back from Mexico to Cleveland an *amusing*(有趣的) thing happened. During the trip to the *border*(边境), several American whites on the train mistook me for a Mexican, and some of them even spoke to me in Spanish, since I am of a copper-brown *complexion*(肤色), with black hair that can be made quite slick and shiny if it has enough *pomade*(润发油) on it in the Mexican fashion. But I made no pretence of passing for a Mexican, or anything else, since there was no need for it — except in changing trains at San Antonio in Texas, where colored people had to use *Jim Crow*(黑人) waiting room, and could not purchase a Pullman *berth*(卧铺). There, I simply went in the main waiting room, as any Mexican would do, and made my sleeping-car reservations in Spanish.

　　But that evening, crossing Texas, I was sitting alone at a small table in the diner, when a white man came in and took the seat just across the table from mine. Shortly, I noticed him staring at me, as if trying to figure out something. He stared at me a long time. Then, suddenly, with a loud cry, the white man jumped up and shouted: "You're a nigger, ain't you?" and rushed out of the car as if *pursued by a plague*(受到瘟疫追逐).

　　I couldn't help smiling to myself. I had heard before that white Southerners never sat down to table with a *Negro*(黑人), but I didn't know until then that we frightened them that badly.

Something rather less amusing happened at St. Louis. The train pulled into the station on a blazing-hot September afternoon, after a sticky, dusty trip, for there were no air-cooled *coaches*(车厢) in those days. I had a short wait between trains. In the center of the station platform there was a *newsstand*(报刊亭) and soda fountain where cool drinks were being served. I went up to the counter and asked for an ice cream soda.

The clerk said:"Are you a Mexican or a Negro?"

I said:"Why?"

"Because if you're a Mexican, I'll serve you,"he said. "If you're colored, I won't."

"I'm colored," I replied. The clerk turned to wait on someone else. I knew I was home in the USA.

1. **What seemed amusing to the writer when he crossed the border into Texas?**

[A]Most people had to speak Spanish to each other.

[B]Mexicans were treated like black Americans.

[C]There were a lot of Mexicans on the train.

[D]Most people thought he was a Mexican.

2. **In Texas at that time, American blacks ____.**

[A]did not ride in the same coach as the Whites

[B]spoke Spanish to pretend they were Mexicans

[C]were thought to carry diseases feared by whites

[D]liked to frighten people with their strange actions

3. **It can be inferred from the story that ____.**

[A]the writer didn't take the whites' reaction to him seriously at first

[B]the writer was good at dealing with people unfriendly to blacks

[C]passenger cars for blacks were not air-conditioned

[D]blacks were not served drinks or food on trains

4. **What made the writer begin to feel uncomfortable about the way blacks were treated in the South?**

[A]That he couldn't make a sleeping-car reservation.

[B]That he couldn't get served a drink he needed.

[C]That a white man wouldn't share a table with him.

[D]That people asked him whether he was a Negro.

5. It can also be inferred that the writer worked and lived in a place where
racial discrimination（种族歧视）**was ____.**

[A]unheard of　　　　　　　[B]less serious

[C]more common　　　　　　[D]much talked about

 答案与分析

1.[D]。细节题。文章第一段第二句指出：... several American whites on the train mistook me for a Mexican ...，即一些美国白人误以为他是墨西哥人，并在后面详细解释了自己被误认的外貌特征。

2.[A]。推断题。第一段倒数第二句说：... could not purchase a Pull-man berth，即在得克萨斯州黑人得到专门的候车室，不能买卧铺；而在后面几段中又专门描述白人对黑人的态度，因此可以推知不让黑人买卧铺就是为了不让他们与白人同处一节车厢。

3.[A]。推断题。文章第三段指出，一位白人认出作者是黑人后惟恐避之不及的态度并没有让作者生气，作者只是 smiling to myself，由此可以看出他对白人的态度并不是太在意。而在后面一段中作者开始用 rather less a-musing（不那么好笑）来描述自己的心情，也可以看出开始他只是觉得白人的反应和态度好笑而已。

4.[B]。推断题。参见上题解析。文章最后几段描述了作者在圣路易斯承认自己是黑人后被拒绝服务、买不到饮料的经过。作者用 rather less amus-ing 表达了自己的反感。其余三项中，[A]与第一段最后一句不符，[C]与第二段不符，[D]在文中没有提及。

5.[B]。推断题。由作者起初并不是很在意白人对待自己的态度，及后来询问侍者"Why"等事实可以推知，作者生活的地方种族歧视应当没那么严重。因为如果也是这么严重的话，作为黑人的作者的反应就不会那么轻松，也就不会去询问侍者说话的意图了。

 从墨西哥返回克里夫兰的路上，发生了一件有趣的事情。在去边境的途中，列车上的一些美国白人把我误认为是墨西哥人，他们中的一些人甚至用西班牙语和我说话，因为我有着古铜色的皮肤、如果有足够多的润发油就可以按照墨西哥的时尚弄得又光又滑的黑头发。但我一点也没有去假装自己是墨西哥人或者其他人种,因为没有必要——除了在得克萨斯州的圣安东尼奥换乘时,那里有色人种必须用黑人候车室、不能买卧铺。在那里,我只是像墨西哥人一样直接走到主候车室,用西班牙语办理了卧铺预订。

但是那天晚上横跨得克萨斯州时,我正独自坐在餐车里的一张小桌旁,一个白人走过来坐在我正对面的桌子旁。不久我就注意到他在盯着我看,似乎想弄明白什么。他盯了我很久。然后,那个白人突然大叫一声,跳起来嚷嚷道:"你是个黑鬼,对不对?"就跑出了餐车,似乎被瘟疫追赶一样。

我禁不住微笑了一下。我以前听说过南方的白人从不与黑人同桌吃饭,但直到这时我才知道我们让他们如此害怕。

在圣路易斯发生的事就不是那么有趣了。这是九月一个炎热的下午,那时车厢里没有冷气,在一段黏黏糊糊、满是灰尘的旅程后,列车驶入了车站。我要换乘列车,得等一会儿。在车站月台中央有一个报刊亭和苏打饮水器,出售冷饮。我走到柜台前,要一杯冰淇淋苏打。

侍者问:"您是墨西哥人还是黑人?"

我说:"你问这干什么?"

"因为如果您是墨西哥人,我就卖给您,"他说。"如果您是黑人,我就不卖。"

"我是黑人,"我回答说。侍者转过身去,招呼别人去了。我知道我回到美国了。

Exercise 17

London Business School's *Master*(硕士学位) in *Finance*(金融) is a specialist program designed for people pursuing a successful career in finance. It can be completed in nine months of full-time study or in two years of part-time attendance at the school.

The Master in Finance is practical and *career-oriented*(面向就业的) and is taught by the school's internationally famous finance teachers. To find out more, come to one of the information sessions below:

Milan — Monday, 16 February at 7:00 p.m.

Melbourne — Monday, 16 February at 6:15 p.m.

Sydney — Wednesday, 18 February at 9:00 a.m.

London — Monday, 9 March at 8:00 a.m.

Hong Kong — Tuesday, 17 March at 7:00 p.m.

Singapore — Friday, 21 March at 1:30 p.m.

⊙ For further information contact:

Telephone: 1717066840　　Fax: 1717231788

⊙ For information about our MBA and Master in Management contact:

Telephone: 1717165483　　Fax: 1717684256

1. **If you live in England, you can attend the class on ____.**

　　[A]Tuesday, 17 March at 7:00 p.m.

　　[B]Friday, 21 March at 1:30 p.m.

　　[C]Monday, 9 March at 8:00 a.m.

　　[D]Monday, 16 February at 6:15 p.m.

2. **Who is most likely to take this course?**

　　[A]A policeman.　　　　　　[B]A doctor.

　　[C]An artist.　　　　　　　[D]A bank clerk.

3. **If you want to enquire about the course of Management, please call ____.**

　　[A]1717231788　　　　　　[B]1717165483

　　[C]1717684256　　　　　　[D]1717066840

4. **This passage may be a ____.**

　　[A]job advertisement　　　　[B]film poster

　　[C]term paper　　　　　　　[D]school notice

答案与分析

1. [C]。细节题。题目给出的地点是英国,而短文中与英国相关的就是 London(伦敦),不难确定答案。

2. [D]。推断题。短文第一句即指出,伦敦商业学院的金融硕士学位课程是为那些想在金融领域内求得职业成功的人士专门设计的。四个选项中属于金融领域的职业当然是银行职员了。

3. [B]。细节题。文章最后部分特别说明了工商管理硕士及管理学硕士学位的咨询电话与传真等信息。注意题目中用的是 call,所以应选[B]。[C]是传真号码。

4.[D]。推断题。文章交代的是一门课程的相关情况及相应的咨询电话、传真等信息,所以最有可能的应当是学校的一则通知。

同步译文

伦敦商业学院的金融硕士学位课程是为那些想在金融领域内求得职业成功的人士设计的专业课程。这一课程可以在 9 个月的脱产学习或者 2 年的业余学习期间完成。

金融硕士学位课程实用并面向就业,由学院里具有国际知名度的金融学教师授课。如想了解更多信息,请在下述信息咨询期间咨询:

米兰——周一,2 月 16 日,下午 7:00。

墨尔本——周一,2 月 16 日,下午 6:15。

悉尼——周三,2 月 18 日,上午 9:00。

伦敦——周一,3 月 9 日,上午 8:00。

香港——周二,3 月 17 日,下午 7:00。

新加坡——周五,3 月 21 日,下午 1:30。

⊙更多信息请联系:

电话:1717066840　　传真:1717231788

⊙咨询 MBA 与管理学硕士学位信息请联系:

电话:1717165483　　传真:1717684256

Exercise 18

Visit Iceland and you'll enter a whole new region of experience. You'll discover original nature as you've never seen it before, and the equally original people for whom timeless nature, ancient *heritage*(遗产) and modern lifestyle coexist in harmony. The freedom to wander in the city or the wilds as you please is the key to the Iceland experience.

Reykjavik, the capital of Iceland, is just a part of the Icelandic experience with its midnight sun or the magical landscapes mixed with ice and fire. Reykjavik has a population of around 170 000 and offers an interesting mix of *cosmopolitan*(世界各地的) culture and local village roots.

Old accounts say the ancient gods themselves guided Iceland's first settler to make his home in Reykjavik. He named the place Rey-kjavik（Steamy Bay）after the *geothermal*（地热的）steam he saw, which today heats homes and outdoor swimming pools throughout the city, a pollution-free energy source that leaves the air outstandingly fresh, clean and clear.

A beautiful river runs through the city limits and so do fine parks and even wild outdoor areas. In the outskirts are places for horse trek-king and golf. But against this backcloth of nature, Reykjavik has a packed program of familiar city joys too: art museums, several thea-ters, an opera house, a symphony orchestra and concerts meeting the needs of the whole spectrum of age and taste.

One must for all visitors is dining out on Icelandic specialties, in-cluding delicious seafood, ocean-fresh from the morning's catch, high-land lamb and unusual varieties of game. Its purely natural food imagi-natively served to delight the most *discerning*（内行的）of diners. Rey-kjavik is also famous as one of Europe's hottest nightspots, where the action on the friendly pub and nightlife scene lasts right through the night. In the evening, the downtown area filled with activity, reaching its peak on Friday or Saturday. The number of pubs, cafes, discos, and other nightspots in the downtown area is astonishing. There is a rich variety of places to go: European-style cafes, nightclubs with live entertainment, dance halls for seniors, sports-theme pubs with big TV screens, cafes that offer over 100 types of beer, an Irish pub, a Span-ish cafe, a French wine bar.

Walking distances are short downtown, and everything worth see-ing outside the city center can be quickly and conveniently reached by bus. With its long, easy-going main street and large shopping mall, Iceland's capital is a great place to shop too — with a bonus of tax-free shopping for visitors! Be careful not just for *souvenirs*（纪念品）（especially woolens and handicrafts）but also for stylish consumer goods and designer labels at competitive prices.

A full range of *accommodations*（住宿）is available in Reykjavik, from international-standard hotels with good conference facilities, through smaller hotels and comfortable guesthouses, to a campsite in the city's biggest park.

1. It can be learned from the passage Reykjavik ____ .

[A]was named by the ancient gods

[B]got its name from the visitors

[C]was named by Iceland's first settler

[D]was named after Iceland's first settler

2. While visiting Iceland, the most enjoyable thing is ____ .

[A]to taste its purely natural food

[B]to wander freely in the city or the wilds as you please

[C]to visit the nightspots there

[D]to do tax-free shopping

3. Which of the following subjects are mentioned in the fifth paragraph?

[A]Shopping and accommodations.

[B]Dining and nightspots.

[C]City joys and backcloth of nature.

[D]Transportation and landscapes.

4. It can be inferred from the passage that ____ .

[A]all visitors must dine out while visiting Iceland

[B]hotel accommodation is so scarce that visitors usually camp in the city's biggest parks

[C]people living in Reykjavik seldom get heat from coal

[D]you have to walk a short distance if you want to go sightseeing outside the city

答案与分析

1.[C]。细节题。本题问的是冰岛首都雷克雅未克这个名称的由来。在第三段提到了这一点,该段第一句说:He named the place Reykjavik ... ,注意其中的 he 指代的是前面一句中的 first settler(第一个定居者)。

2.[B]。细节题。第一段最后一句话与选项[B]的意思一致,其中的 the key(关键,最重要的事)与题目中的 the most enjoyable 对应。其余三项都只是文章提到的部分内容,但都不是最值得享受的经历。

3.[B]。主旨题。[A]"购物与住宿"是最后两段提到的内容;[C]"城市乐趣与自然背景"是第四段提及的内容；[D]"交通与风景"见于第六段。只有第五段讲述的是饮食和夜景。

4.[C]。推断题。第三段中指出，冰岛全城用地热取暖，使得这里的空气清新、干净而明朗，由此可以推知这里的人很少或者不用煤来供热。[A]误解了第五段第一句话的意思，这一句中的 must 是名词，意为"非常值得做的事情"，而不是作情态动词指"必须"；[B]与最后一段的第一个分句的意思相反；[D]与第六段第一句中的 conveniently reached by bus 不符。

同步译文

    游览冰岛会让你体验到一种全新的经历。你会发现那种你从未领略过的原生态自然，发现与无尽的自然、古老的遗产及现代的生活方式和谐共存的同样原生态的人们。自由自在地徜徉在市区里或者荒野上是在冰岛最重要的经历。

    冰岛首都雷克雅未克以其午夜的阳光和那魔术般的、融合了冰与火的风景而成为经历冰岛的一个组成部分。雷克雅未克约有 17 万人口，有趣地融合了世界各地文化与本地乡土渊源。

    古老传说讲，古时候众神引导冰岛的第一个定居者在雷克雅未克安下了家。看到地热冒出的蒸汽后，他把这个地方命名为雷克雅未克（"蒸汽港湾"）。如今冰岛全城的家庭与室外游泳池都是用地热这种无污染能源供热，使得空气尤为清新、干净而明朗。

    一条美丽的河流经市区，到处都是精致的公园与户外的荒野。市郊是纵马驰骋与打高尔夫的地方。但在自然背景之下，雷克雅未克还有着丰富而熟悉的城市乐趣：艺术博物馆，几家影剧院，一个歌剧院，一个管弦乐团，以及音乐厅，以满足不同年龄、不同品味的人的需要。

    所有游客都值得一做的事是出去吃冰岛的特色饮食，包括美味的海产品，当天早上捕捞的海鲜，高原羊羔和各种各样的奇珍野味。可以想像，纯粹自然的食物是为了取悦最挑剔的美食家。雷克雅未克还以有欧洲最火热的夜景著称，那里友好的酒馆里的表演与夜生活场景夜夜不断。晚上，市中心的活动丰富多彩，在周五或者周六达到高峰。市中心的酒馆、咖啡屋、迪厅及其他夜生活场所的数量惊人。有各种各样的地方可以去：欧洲风格的咖啡馆，有现场娱乐表演的夜总会，老年舞厅，有着巨大电视屏幕的体育主题酒吧，提供 100 多种啤酒的咖啡店，一家爱尔兰酒吧，一家西班牙咖啡店，一家法国酒吧。

    市中心步行的距离不远，而市中心以外所有值得一看的地方都可以很便捷地乘坐公共汽车到达。由于有着长而易行的大街与规模巨大的购物中心，冰岛的首都也是购物的好去处——游客购物还可以免税！注意不要只顾买纪念品（尤其是羊毛制品和手工艺品），还能以不错的价格买到时尚消费品与名牌产品。

雷克雅未克提供各种条件的住宿，从不错的会议设施的国际标准的酒店，从较小的旅店和舒适的客房，到在该市最大公园里露营都可提供。

Exercise 19

I attend Boston University. One-third of the students who attend this school are international students. They come from all over the world, many of them from Latin America. There is a large, comfortable dining hall on campus. I go there every day during school with my friends. Many of them are from Latin America and Spain. For the most part, the American students eat lunch in the dining hall between noon and two o'clock. I rarely see any of them stay for more than an hour. They get their food and eat as quickly as they can. When they leave, the dining hall is still full of *Latinos*(拉丁美洲人). The Latinos stay for several hours talking, laughing, smoking, and drinking soda and coffee. Sometimes their lunch goes until four o'clock. They stay as long as their friends stay. They don't leave because they have to do something else. I think that there are also a lot of *Arab*(阿拉伯的) students there. They seem to take more time to eat and talk as well.

I think the Latinos stay longer for three reasons. First, they are used to eating their breakfast, lunch, and dinner later in the day than Americans eat theirs. Second, they are used to taking more time at each meal, eating slowly and leisurely. They don't eat more food; they just take more time. Third, I think that family and friends are more important to Spanish speakers than school or work. They would rather relax and talk to their friends during a meal than rush off to study or work. Maybe this is not true everywhere, but I think it is true here at Boston University.

1. From the passage, we may guess that the writer comes from ____.

[A]the United States [B]South America

[C]Arab [D]Not mentioned in the passage

2. The Latinos spend most of their lunchtime ＿＿.

[A]eating delicious food [B]talking about their studies

[C]waiting for their orders [D]chatting with friends

3. When the American students end their meal，they usually ＿＿.

[A]leave in a hurry [B]look worried

[C]have some drinks [D]stay a little longer

4. Which of the following statements is TRUE?

[A]The dining hall usually closes at 4 o'clock.

[B]Americans are not friendly with people.

[C]Arab students take longer lunchtime.

[D]Latinos are not busier than Americans.

5. One of the reasons that Latinos have longer lunchtime is that ＿＿.

[A]they get up late in the morning

[B]lunch is the major meal of the day

[C]talking is more important than eating

[D]they consider meals as a time to rest

答案与分析

1.[D]。推断题。文章并没有直接说明作者自己是什么地方的人，但从叙述时使用的人称及角度，特别是第一段第六句中的 the American students 可以看出，他肯定不是美国人。该段倒数第二句表明他也不是阿拉伯人。而从第一段第四、五两句可以看出，他也不是拉丁美洲人和西班牙人。因此，从文章内容无法推断出作者到底是哪儿的人，选[D]。

2.[D]。细节题。第一段倒数第六句说：The Latinos stay for hours talking ... and coffee，即拉丁美洲人吃饭时主要是在交谈。而第二段最后几句也表明他们吃饭时主要是在和朋友聊天。

3.[A]。细节题。第一段第八、九两句在谈到美国人吃午饭的情况时说，作者很少看到他们在食堂里待到超过 1 个小时，他们买了饭菜后很快吃完离开了。

4.[C]。细节题。文章没有交代食堂关门的时间，"4 点"是指拉丁美洲人有时在食堂里待到这个时候（第一段倒数第五句），所以[A]不对；文章也没有提及美国学生对待朋友的态度,也无法推知,故[B]不对;而第一段最后两句提到阿拉伯学生与拉丁美洲学生一样,吃饭时间也很长,所以[C]是对的;第一段倒数第三句说,拉丁美洲学生不离开食堂是另有事情要做,而在第二段分析原因时也说明他们并不是没有美国学生忙,故[D]也不对。

5.[D]。推断题。第二段说明了拉丁美洲学生吃饭时间长的原因:一是他们习惯于晚点吃饭;二是他们习惯于慢慢吃,边吃边聊,把吃饭时间当成休闲时间;三是家人和朋友对他们更重要,他们喜欢在吃饭时与朋友们聊天。对照四个选项,可知应选[D]。

　　　　　　　我在波士顿大学上学。在这个学校就读的学生中有三分之一是外国学生。他们来自世界各地,其中有许多学生来自拉丁美洲。校园里有一个宽大、舒适的食堂。我每天在课间与我的朋友们去那里吃饭。朋友中有许多人来自拉丁美洲和西班牙。大部分情况下,美国学生正午和 2:00 在食堂吃午饭。我很少看到他们中有人在食堂里待到超过 1 个小时。他们买了饭菜就尽快吃完。他们走了后,食堂里仍坐满了拉丁美洲学生。拉丁美洲学生通常在食堂待上几个小时,交谈着、笑着、抽着烟、喝着苏打水和咖啡。有时他们的午饭要吃到 4 点。他们和朋友们待得一样久。他们不离开食堂是因为他们有别的事做。我想那里也有许多阿拉伯学生。他们似乎在吃和交谈上花的时间更多。

我认为拉丁美洲学生待的时间长的原因有三。首先,他们比美国学生更习惯于晚一点吃早、中、晚饭。第二,他们习惯于用更多时间、细嚼慢咽而且很放松地来吃每顿饭。他们吃的并不多,只是用餐时间更长而已。第三,我认为家人与朋友对说西班牙语的学生来说比学习或者工作更重要。他们宁愿放松下来,边吃边与朋友们聊天,而不愿匆匆忙忙地去学习或者工作。也许并非每个地方都这样,但我认为在波士顿大学就是这样。

Exercise 20

　　　Mr White lived in Florida and owned a company there. Some computers were made in his company. He was nice to his *employees*(雇员) and often had a joke with them. They liked him very much and worked hard. So he paid them a lot.

　　　The man had lots of work to do and often went to bed late at night. His friends advised him to do some exercise. He thought he was strong and didn't agree with them. But one day he *fell in a faint*(暈倒) while he was working in his office. He was sent to a hospital at once and the doctors examined him carefully. They found something was wrong with his heart and he had to be in hospital. Several months later he returned home and asked his son to manage the company.

Once his daughter wanted to travel in Australia. The old man decided to go there with her. As he went to the country for the first time, he was interested in all. He played well, had a good sleep and visited some places of interest. And one day they visited a farm. It was big and beautiful. Cows and sheep could be seen everywhere.

Pointing to a cow, Mr White asked, "What's this?"

"Haven't you seen a cow?"the guide asked surprisedly.

"Cow?"Mr White said with a smile. "A cow in our country is five times as big as it!"

Having heard this, all the visitors began to laugh. After a while he saw a *kangaroo*(袋鼠) and asked again, "What's that?"

"It's a *flea*(跳蚤), sir. "answered the guide.

1. **The employees worked hard because _____.**

　　[A]Mr White was kind to them

　　[B]Mr White had a company

　　[C]Mr White often had a joke with them

　　[D]they liked to use computers

2. **Mr White fell in a faint because _____.**

　　[A]he was very busy

　　[B]he went to bed late

　　[C]he didn't get up on time in the morning

　　[D]he had got a heart disease

3. **Mr White was interested in all because _____.**

　　[A]he hadn't been in Australia before

　　[B]he had never left his hometown before

　　[C]he had to be a traveler

　　[D]he hoped to live in the country

4. Which of the following is true?

［A］There weren't any cows in Florida.

［B］Mr White had a joke with the guide.

［C］Mr White hadn't seen any cows before.

［D］The cows in Florida were much bigger than those in Australia.

答案与分析

1.［A］。细节题。文章第一段第三、四句指出,怀特先生对雇员们很好,经常与他们开玩笑,员工们都喜欢他,工作都很努力。由此可知,雇员们工作努力的原因就是因为怀特先生对他们好。

2.［D］。细节题。第二段倒数第二句指出,医生们发现怀特先生得了心脏病,得住院。因此,他晕倒的直接原因就是患了心脏病。有些考生误选［A］或者［B］,但它们只是文章交代的两个事实,并不会必然导致怀特先生晕倒。

3.［A］。细节题。文章第三段第三句明确指出了原因:As he went to the country for the first time, he was interested in all(由于他是第一次去澳大利亚,所以他对什么都很感兴趣)。

4.［B］。推断题。文章一开始就交代说怀特先生喜欢开玩笑,这也是文章的主旨,后面的例子是用来说明这一主旨的。再由怀特先生与导游的对话及其他游客的反应可以看出,他是和导游开了一个玩笑,因此［B］是正确的。其余三项都可根据文意与常识加以排除。

同步译文

怀特先生住在佛罗里达,并拥有一家公司。他的公司生产电脑。他对雇员们很好,常和雇员们开玩笑。雇员们都很喜欢他,工作都很努力,因此他付给他们很多工钱。

怀特先生工作繁重,每天常常很晚才睡。朋友们都建议他锻炼身体。但他认为自己很健壮,就没有听从他们的意见。但是有一天他在办公室工作时晕倒了。他马上被送往医院,医生详细地给他做了检查。医生们发现他得了心脏病,必须住院治疗。几个月后他回到家中,让他的儿子为他管理公司。

一次他女儿想去澳大利亚旅行。老人决定与她一起去。因为他是第一次去澳大利亚,所以他对一切都很感兴趣。他玩得很愉快,睡眠也很好,还参观了许多名胜。有一天他们参观了一个农场。那里辽阔美丽,牛羊随处可见。

指着一头牛,怀特先生问道:"这是什么?"

“难道您从来没有见过牛么?”导游很惊讶地问。

“牛?”怀特先生笑着说,“我们国家的牛有它5倍大哩!”

听了这个,所有游客都笑了。过了一会儿他看见了一只袋鼠,又问道:“那是什么?”

“是一只跳蚤,先生。”导游回答道。

Exercise 21

My first *performance*(表演) in front of an audience was coming up soon.

I tried as hard as I could to remain calm, but my heart was racing, I stared down at my sweat-covered, shaking hands.

I looked up again at the audience, realizing that these were real people. They were not just my mum and dad, who would say “Good job!” even if I messed up the entire piece.

What if I had the wrong music? What if I played the wrong notes?

As it turned out, I was never able to answer these questions because the *spotlight*(聚光灯) was waiting for me. I grasped my hands tightly together, drying off the sweat.

Slowly I walked to the mud-brown piano in the center of the room. It contained 88 demanding keys, which were waiting impatiently to be played. Slowly, I opened the music. Next, I rested my still shaking hands on the *ivory*(象牙色的) keys.

As my fingers played across the keys, I was becoming more unsure of my preparation for this moment. But the memory of my years of training came flooding back. I knew that I had practiced this piece so many times that I could play it backwards if requested.

Although at one point I accidentally played two keys instead of the intended one, I continued to move my fingers *automatically*(自动地).

My eyes burned holes into (were fixed on) the pages in front of me.

There was no way that I was going to lose my concentration. To keep this to myself, I leaned forward and focused carefully on the music.

When I came to the end of the page, a warning went off inside my head: DON'T MAKE A MISTAKE WHEN YOU TURN THE PAGE!

Needless to say, I obeyed myself with all my heart and mind. And, proud of my page-turning *feat*（技艺）, I finished the rest of the piece without making a single mistake. After the final note died away, a celebration went into action inside my head. I had finished. I had mastered the impossible.

1. **The author was nervous before the performance because ____.**

[A]his/her mother and father weren't present

[B]he/she hadn't mastered the entire piece

[C]the strong spotlight was shinning onto the stage

[D]he/she had never performed in public before

2. **The expression "mess up" in paragraph 3 probably means "____".**

[A]put into disorder 　　　　　[B]forget about

[C]stop halfway 　　　　　　　[D]do well in

3. **The author ____.**

[A]didn't make any mistake in the performance

[B]felt better at the beginning of the performance

[C]paid all attention to nothing but his/her performance

[D]lost his/her concentration sometimes during the performance

4. **What did the author feel about his/her performance?**

[A]He/She thought it was comfortable and successful.

[B]He/She thought it was very difficult but successful.

[C]He/She thought he/she had never played so beautifully before.

[D]He/She thought he/she played through the piece carefully but light-heartedly.

5. **There was sweat in the author's hands because ____.**

[A]of the spotlight

[B]it was very hot that day

[C]there were too many people in the room

[D]he/she felt very nervous

答案与分析

1.[D]。推断题。从文章第一句话：My first performance in front of an audience was coming up soon 及常识可推知这是作者第一次在公共场合表演，故感到很紧张。而在后文中作者又用大量文字描述了自己的心理活动，也可知[A]、[B]、[C]项不是作者感到紧张的原因。

2.[A]。词句理解题。该短语见于第三段第二句：They were not just my mum and dad, ... the entire piece(他们不是我的父母，父母即使在我做得一团糟的时候也会说"做得好")。由句意特别是 Good job 与 mess up 之间的关系及 if 所表达的假设可以推知 mess up 指"弄糟"。

3.[C]。推断题。从文章后面几段的描述、作者的心理活动、特别是倒数第三段 There was no way that ... on the music 一句可知作者想方设法把注意力集中在演奏上，故[C]对。其余三项都与原文不符。

4.[B]。推断题。从最后一段中 After the final note died away, ... mastered the impossible 三句可推知作者认为虽然艰难，但他/她还是成功地完成了演奏，故[B]项正确。其余三项都与原文表达的意思有出入。

5.[D]。推断题。参见第1题解析。作者之所以手心有汗，那是因为他第一次在公共场合表演，没有经验，感到很紧张，因此手心出汗，而不是因为天气太热([B]项)、屋里人太多([C]项)、或者是聚光灯的原因([A]项)。本题也可根据常识进行排除。

同步译文

我第一次在观众面前的表演很快就要到了。

我尽力保持镇静，但我的心跳在加速。我往下看了看我那满是汗水并且发抖的双手。

我重新抬起头看着观众，意识到这些是真正的人。他们不是我那即使我搞得一团糟也会说"干得好！"的父母。

如果我弹错曲目了怎么办？如果我弹错音符了怎么办？

结果是，我永远无法回答这些问题，因为聚光灯在等着我。我把双手紧握在一起，攥干了汗水。

我慢慢地走向房间中央那台泥棕色的钢琴。它有88个琴键，正在急不可耐地等待有人去弹奏。我慢慢地打开乐谱，然后把仍在颤抖的双手放到了象牙色的琴键上。

当我的手指滑过琴键时，我对自己为这一刻所做的准备变得越来越没有把握。但我多年来训练所形成的记忆如潮水般涌回。我知道自己练习这支曲子已经许多遍了,如果需要我甚至可以倒着演奏。

尽管有时我偶尔在本来只应弹一个键的地方弹了两个键,但我仍自动地移动着我的手指。

我的双眼紧盯着面前的乐谱。

无论如何我都不能分散注意力。为做到这一点,我身体向前倾,小心地把注意力全都放在音乐上。

当弹到一页末尾时,我脑海中出现了警告:翻页时别出错!

不用说,我全心全意地服从了自己的提醒。而且,由于我值得骄傲的翻页技巧,我毫无失误地演奏完了乐曲余下的部分。最后一个音符的声音消失后,我心里一阵狂喜。我演奏完了。我掌握了不可能掌握的东西。

Exercise 22

Alaska became the forty-ninth state of the United States in 1958. Ninety years earlier Secretary of State Seward had with great difficulty persuaded the *Congress*(国会) to buy it from Russia for $ 15 000 000. For many years people who failed to recognize the wisdom of this action called Alaska "Seward's Folly" — a foolish act.

Alaska is the largest of the states in area, but the smallest in population. It has *magnificent*(壮观的) scenery with high mountains, including the highest peak in North America, and vast *glaciers*(冰川). Where the Alaskan *Peninsula*(半岛) begins, there is the Valley of Ten Thousand Smokes, where steaming volcanic *vapors*(蒸汽) rise all year round. There are also interesting animals on land and in the sea, including polar bears, reindeer, wolves, seals, and whales.

It is a land of great contrasts. In the treeless, snow-covered north, the Eskimos live by hunting seals and polar bears and keep up the customs and skills handed down from generation to generation. But farther south there are modern cities with tall buildings and comfortable homes equipped with all the modern *conveniences*(便利). People and goods come and go by airline, railroad, and automobiles. There is a fine education system, including universities and two-year colleges.

Alaska also has great contrasts in its weather conditions. While the northern part, within the Arctic Circle, is bitter cold, the south, near Canada, is quite warm and damp. Even in the central part there are some places warm enough for raising cows and growing vegetables.

The population of Alaska was only 200 000 at the time it was bought, but it grew very fast, especially after gold was discovered in the Yukon Valley in 1897. After the end of that gold rush many Americans continued to move to Alaska, in search of opportunities on the new frontier of the United States.

1. **People called Alaska "Seward's Folly" because ____.**
   [A]they did not recognize Seward's wisdom in buying Alaska
   [B]even the US Congress objected to Seward's action
   [C]Secretary of State Seward was known to be rather foolish
   [D]the land in Alaska was not properly developed at that time

2. **The writer of the text tries to tell us that Alaska ____.**
   [A]has the largest number of rare animals
   [B]is the most thinly populated in the world
   [C]is the largest country in North America
   [D]has beautiful and unusual scenery

3. **What does the underlined word "contrast"(Paragraph 3) mean?**
   [A]Great change.   [B]Vast difference.
   [C]Striking similarity.   [D]Rapid development.

4. **What event marked the beginning of population increase in Alaska?**
   [A]The discovery of gold.
   [B]The setting up of universities.
   [C]The drawing of the Arctic Circle.
   [D]The industrialization of the Yukon Valley

☺ 答案与分析

1.[A]。细节题。第一段最后一句指出,许多年中那些没有认识到此举的英明的人把阿拉斯加称作"西沃德的蠢事"。选项[A]只是与这一句的表达不同而已。

　　2.[D]。推断题。文章的主体部分主要描述的是阿拉斯加的自然风貌与气候特点等内容,尤其是第二段,描述了那里美丽奇异的景色。对照四个选项,可知应选[D]。该段最后一句提到了 animals,但并没有说那里的珍稀野生动物最多,故[A]不对;该段第一句提到了人口,但这只是说它在美国是人口最少的州,并非世界上人口密度最小的地方,故[B]不对;[C]项根据阿拉斯加与美国的关系就可判定为错误。

　　3.[B]。词句理解题。该词所在句为该段的主旨句,该段后面的内容实际上就是阐述了这个词的意思。其中第二句与第三、四、五句相互对比,突出了该地南北之间的不同,所以可以推断 contrast 指"不同,差异"。

　　4.[A]。细节题。最后一段第一句中后一分句明确指出阿拉斯加的人口是在发现金矿之后才快速增加的。

　　1958 年阿拉斯加成为了美国的 49 个州。90 年前国务卿西沃德费了很大的劲才说服国会同意以 1 千 500 万美元从俄国手中买下了它。许多年中那些没有认识到此举的英明的人把阿拉斯加称作"西沃德的蠢事"——一次愚蠢的行动。

　　阿拉斯加是面积最大的一个州,但人口最少。这里有崇山峻岭(包括北美最高峰)和广袤冰川的壮观景色。在阿拉斯加半岛开始的地方是万烟谷,那里火山喷发出来的蒸汽终年不断。陆地和海洋中还有许多有趣的动物,包括北极熊、驯鹿、狼、海豹和鲸鱼。

　　这是一块有着巨大差异的土地。在没有树木、冰雪覆盖的北方,爱斯基摩人以猎取海豹、北极熊为生,他们的风俗和技艺代代相传。但在遥远的南方,却是现代化的城市,是高楼、有着各种现代化便利设施的舒适的房屋。人员和货物通过飞机、铁路、汽车往来运送。那里有良好的教育系统,有多所大学和 2 年制专科学校。

　　阿拉斯加在气候方面也有着巨大的差异。北部位于北极圈以内的地区极为寒冷,而南部靠近加拿大的地区则相当温暖、湿润。即使在阿拉斯加中部地区,有些地方气候也很温暖,可以养牛、种蔬菜。

　　在购买时,阿拉斯加的人口只有 20 万,但人口增长很快,尤其是 1897 年在 Yukon 峡谷发现金矿之后。那次淘金热过去之后,许多美国人仍然继续迁往阿拉斯加,在美国这个新的疆土上寻找自己的机会。

Exercise 23

Surfing is an exciting and dangerous activity in which a person tries to control himself on a board and rides the surface of a big, high-rising ocean wave. *Channel*（频道）surfing is a bit different. A person sits in a comfortable armchair and pushes the button of a television *remote-control*（遥控）board many times a minute to check and recheck all the channels. In the United States, channel surfing is by far the more popular sport.

When television first replaced radio, in the 1950s, channel surfing was unknown. Back then, there were only a few stations. People who loved TV had their favorite shows and watched them whole-heartedly all the way through. In fact, studies showed that when a family sat down to watch a favorite program at 7:00 p.m., they stayed with the same channel the rest of the evening.

With the coming of *cable*（有线）television, dozens of channels now offer a great variety of films, news, weather, talk shows, science shows, and so on. Faced with so many choices, people often become restless and feel a need to check out all the other stations.

Men in an ordinary US family usually want to hold the remote control and surf the channels; women usually like to choose one program and watch it through.

Interestingly, many experts say that channel surfing may be seen as a skill for dealing with the modern world. More and more people are called upon to change their attention among many things in their work, which usually involves sitting in front of a computer and playing with it. The person with a limited time of attention is also someone who can live in a world where business is done on-line.

1. **This article is mainly about ____.**

   [A] the ways people watch television

   [B] the popularity of a television program

   [C] the role of television in modern society

[D]the history of television

2. Many people like changing channels while watching TV because ____.

[A]they are too young to stay on one channel

[B]they have little time to watch everything

[C]the quality of the program is terrible

[D]there are many choices of programs

3. An important idea of the article is that channel surfing is probably ____.

[A]a bad way to watch television

[B]a hard habit to break

[C]natural because of the fast changing technology

[D]showing men's powerful position at home

4. According to the article, women usually ____.

[A]like to channel-surf　　　　[B]stick to one program

[C]do not like television　　　　[D]watch TV for a long time

5. Before the time of cable TV, people ____.

[A]could only listen to the radio　[B]didn't have film programs

[C]spent evenings out a lot　　　[D]had no idea of TV surfing

☺ 答案与分析

1.[A]。主旨题。文章以"冲浪"这一体育运动入手,转入"电视频道冲浪"这一现象,然后主要分析了过去和现在人们看电视的方式及专家们对"电视频道冲浪"这一现象的解读。因此,文章的主旨实际上就是分析人们看电视的不同方式。

2.[D]。细节题。答案对应于第三段最后一句:Faced with so many choices....即由于可选择的频道与节目太多,使人们想要看所有的台。

3.[C]。推断题。文章最后一段提到了专家对"电视频道冲浪"这一现象的解读。文章指出,频道冲浪可以看成是一个人对待现代世界的一种技巧,并指出现在人们要注意的事情很多,使得人们对一件事物注意的时间有限。这也就是说,是快速变化的世界让人们自然而然地形成了频道冲浪的习惯,故答案为[C]。[B]、[D]两项在文章中都没有体现;[A]也不对,作者并没有表现出反对频道冲浪的态度。

4.[B]。细节题。第四段后一分句明确指出女性喜欢选择一个频道并从头看到尾。

5.[D]。细节题。第二段第一句说,20世纪50年代电视取代收音机时,频道冲浪还不为人所知。

冲浪是种令人兴奋而又危险的活动,在这一运动中,冲浪者试图将自己控制在冲浪板上,在巨大而高高掀起的海浪表面驰骋。频道冲浪有点不同。它是指一个人坐在舒适的躺椅上,手拿电视遥控板快速按着上面的按键,不停地搜索和回看所有的电视频道。在美国,如今频道冲浪是一种要流行得多的运动。

20世纪50年代电视首次取代收音机时,频道冲浪还不为人知。那时只有少数几个电视台。爱看电视的人有自己偏爱的节目,并且全心全意地一直收看这些节目。事实上,研究表明,那时一家人在晚上7:00坐下来看喜欢的节目后,他们那天晚上会一直收看同一个频道。

随着有线电视的出现,如今有许许多多的频道提供大量不同的电影、新闻、天气、脱口秀、科技等等节目。面对如此之多的选择,人们常常会倾向于求变,想要看到其他所有的台。

在普通的美国家庭中,男人通常想要拿着遥控浏览频道;女人则通常选择一个频道从头看到尾。

有意思的是,许多专家说频道冲浪可以看作一种对待现代世界的技巧。越来越多的人被要求在工作中的众多事情中转换他们的注意力,而这通常是坐在电脑前操作电脑。那些注意力时间有限的人,也是那些能在这个连生意都是在线完成的世界上生存的人。

Exercise 24

No one wants to look *silly*(傻的) or do the wrong thing at a new job. It is important to make the right impression — not the wrong one — from the very first day. You will face new people. You will be in a new place. It may be difficult to know what to do. Here are several tips to help you make it through the first days at a new job.

1. First impression can last forever. Make sure you make a good one. Before your first day, find out if your new job has a dress code. If so, be sure to follow it. No matter what, always be neat and clean.

2. Get to work on time. Employers value employees who come to

work right on time. Give yourself an extra 15 minutes to make sure you arrive on time.

3. Pay attention to introductions. One of the first things that your *supervisor*（主管）may do is to introduce you to co-workers. These co-workers will be important to you. They are the ones who will answer your questions when the boss is not around.

4. Ask plenty of questions. Make sure that your supervisor has told you what is expected of you. If he or she has not told you your job duties，ask for a list. Set daily and weekly goals for yourself.

1. The underlined word "tips" in paragraph 1 means ____.

　［A］small sum of money 　　　　［B］small but useful advice

　［C］special piece of news 　　　　［D］small piece fitted to the end

2. A supervisor may be the following EXCEPT your ____.

　［A］employer 　　［B］boss 　　　［C］co-workers 　　［D］manager

3. According to the passage，how to make a good impression?

　［A］By following the dress code.

　［B］By introducing yourself to your supervisor.

　［C］By arriving 15 minutes early.

　［D］By asking for your job duties and setting goals.

4. It can be inferred from the passage that ____.

　［A］it is difficult to get a new job

　［B］your co-workers will show you what to do

　［C］it is necessary to get well prepared at a new job

　［D］the more questions you ask，the better you can be

☺ **答案与分析**

1.［B］。词句理解题。由该词所在句的前一句（It may be difficult to know what to do）及下文列举的 4 条建议可知，tips 应当是指"小而有用的建议"，即平时我们所说的"小贴士"。

2.［C］。推断题。由第 3 条建议中的第二句的意思（主管首先做的事情之一就是把你介绍给你的同事）可知，supervisor 肯定不会是你的同事（co-workers），故答案是［C］。

　　3.[A]。细节题。建议中的第 1 条即是如何给人一个好印象,其中倒数第二句说 be sure to follow it,而 it 指的就是前一句中的 a dressing code。

　　4.[C]。推断题。文章对于上班第一天如何给人好印象提出了建议,包括按规定着装(第 1 条)、准时上班(第 2 条)、注意介绍(第 3 条)和多询问(第 4 条)。这些都是为了让读者对上班第一天如何工作做好心理准备,所以作者的意思当然是做好准备工作很必要,选[C]。其余三项中,[A]关于工作是否难找文章中没有涉及;[B]是文章中明示的信息;[D]是随意放大了第 4 条的意思,该条只是说多问,并不是说问得越多越好。

　　没有人想在干新工作时显得很蠢或者做错事情。工作第一天给人正确而不是错误的印象很重要。你会面对新的人群。你会处在一个新的位置。也许很难知道该做什么。下面是几条小贴士,它们能帮你顺利度过刚工作的那些日子。

　　1.第一印象是最持久的印象。确保你给人的是好印象。在第一天上班前,弄清楚新工作是否有着装规定。如果有,一定要遵守。不管如何,总是保持穿戴干净、整洁。

　　2.准时上班。雇主们都看重那些准时上班的员工。给自己多留出 15 分钟,以确保准时到达。

　　3.注意介绍。你的主管首先要做的事情之一就是将你介绍给你的同事们。这些同事对你会很重要。他们会在老板不在时回答你的问题。

　　4.多问问题。确定你的主管已经告诉你对你的期望。如果他或她没有告诉你你的工作职责,你应当要求并将职责列表。为自己设立每天和每周要达到的目标。

Exercise 25

　　AWL is well known for its dictionaries and English language teaching materials. Some readers have written in to ask us for the latest information on high quality books on English, so here we introduce two texts that aim to improve spoken English *fluency*(流利).

　　Let's Speak (*Beginner*) — by Bev Dusuya, Naoko Ozeki and Kevin Bergman, ISBN: 962001359X.

　　Speak Up (*Pre Intermediate*) — by Bev Dusuya, Naoko Ozeki,

ISBN: 0582228050.

"Teach the students about your culture and help them talk about their own. "How often are these worthy goals kept from being achieved by the limitations of your beginner level learners? Students at all levels want to talk about culture.

Topics include food, shopping, sports, fashion, the roles of men and women, health, music, and many more.

These are all chosen from *surveys*(调查) of over 15 000 students about their own interests in cross cultural communication.

Let's Speak and *Speak Up* share a special but excellent way that allows all students to take part in.

The series has questions which start thinking and help collect opinions about personal topics. Conversation practice is provided by using models of basic exchanges on the topic. Also, the cultural information presented in the series comes in the form of interesting, *relevant*(相关的) facts and ideas from other countries through Listening Tasks and Culture Quiz exercises.

Team activities in books provide lively problem-solving games to enable sharing and comparison of cultural values.

Let's Speak is fit for entry level students of all ages. *Speak Up* provides the needs of higher level beginners, offering the same careful listening and speaking help, but with slightly more opened discussion.

For any information about AWL's books, please get in touch with the following address:

Beijing Addison Wesley Longman Information Center

Room 2306, FLTRP Beijing

19 Xi San Huan Beilu, Beijing 100081

Tel: (010)68917488,(010)68917788 ext 2306

Fax: (010)68917499

Email: zrh@public.bat.net.cn

1. **Which of the following are mentioned about the two books in the passage above?**
   ①publisher   ②titles   ③content   ④writers

⑤prices　　　　⑥pages　　　　⑦book number

[A]①、②、④、⑥　　　　　　[B]①、②、③、④、⑦

[C]②、③、④、⑤　　　　　　[D]②、③、⑤、⑥

2. The two books have in common everything EXCEPT ____.

[A]the same interesting topics

[B]the same level of learners

[C]proper ways to excite the learners to talk

[D]right kinds of activities for cultural communication

3. According to the passage, you can have at least ____ ways to be connected if you want to know something about AWL's books.

[A]two　　　　[B]three　　　　[C]four　　　　[D]six

4. The passage above is probably taken from the ____ section in a newspaper.

[A]Education　　[B]News　　[C]Bookshelf　　[D]Advertisement

答案与分析

1.[B]。细节题。文章开头即提到两本书都是由 AWL 出版的,故选①;由第二段"Let's Speak ..."至"ISBN:0582228050"可知,选④、⑦;文章主要介绍两本书的内容,故选③;而两本书的书名也提到了,因此②也应选。

2.[B]。细节题。由 Speak Up provides for the needs of higher level beginners 一句可知,Speak Up 合适更高水平的读者。

3.[C]。推断题。由文章末尾可知,要更了解 AWL 的书,可通过写信、打电话、传真或发送电子邮件共四种方式与其取得联系。

4.[C]。主旨题。文章讲的显然不是教育和新闻,故排除[A]、[B]。因文章只介绍书而并未劝说读者购买,所以排除[D]。

同步译文

AWL 因其词典与英语教学材料而著称。一些读者写信前来询问有关最新的高质量英语书籍的信息,所以在这里我们介绍两本旨在提高英语口语流利程度的教材。

《让我们说》(初级)——由 Bev Dusuya, Naoko Ozeki 和 Kevin Bergman 编著,国际标准书号:962001359X。

《大声说》(预备中级)——由 Bev Dusuya, Naoko Ozeki 编著,国际标准书号:0582228050。

"把有关你们的文化知识教给学生,让他们讨论自己民族的文化。"你们初级水平的学习者如何经常达不到这个很有价值的目标? 各种水平的学生都想讨论文化。

主题包括饮食、购物、体育、时尚、男女地位、健康、音乐,以及更多。

这些都是在对 15 000 名学生对文化交流的兴趣进行调查后得出的。

《让我们说》和《大声说》两书都有一种特殊而优秀的方式让所有学生都参与进来。

这个系列有一些问题,可以启发学生思考并有助于收集对个人问题的观点。用模拟方法就该话题进行基本的观点交换来进行对话练习。而且,本系列中的文化信息是以有趣的、通过听力练习和文化测验练习了解相关事实与观点的方式给出的。

对于集体活动,书中以生动的解决问题的游戏进行,使学生能分享、比较不同的文化价值观。

《让我们说》适合于所有年龄的入门级学生。《大声说》满足的是较高水平的初学者的需要,提供同样细致的听说帮助,但公开讨论稍多一些。

要了解 AWL 的任何信息,请与下述地址联系:

北京爱迪生・韦斯利・朗文信息中心

北京外研社 2306 房间

北京西三环北路 19 号,邮政编码:100081

电话:(010)68917488,(010)68917788 转 2306

传真:(010)68917499

电子邮箱:zrh@public. bat. net. cn

Exercise 26

Getting a new PC is one thing. Keeping it running smoothly is quite another. While a personal computer should continue to perform well for years, users know that system unsteadiness does exist. Yet you can reduce it to the smallest amount by following the tips below.

First, put in as little software as possible. You will have fewer software-related problems and a system that is easier to manage.

Second, you should ensure that you have as much memory (RAM) in your PC as you need. If you run Windows 98, your computer should have at least 128 megabytes(MB) of RAM or more. You can also get by with 128MB of RAM if you use Windows NT or Windows 2000, but these operating systems will run much more smoothly if you have 256MB of RAM or more.

Third, make sure you buy good hardware. No-name products may be cheaper and sometimes just as good as name-brand products, but name-brand products usually become well-known because of their steadiness. It's wise to buy products from famous companies because Windows will more often support the hardware that you buy. If you are starting out with computers, it's also a good idea to buy ready-made systems from major *manufacturers*(生产商). They are likely to have been tested thoroughly with your operating system, and you will generally experience fewer problems.

Fourth, do prepare for disaster. No matter how well your system runs when you get it, the day will come when it will need to be replaced. Hopefully, you will replace it because technology has become outdated, but you may need to replace it also because the hard drive crashes or you begin experiencing problems that no one can figure out. That's why it's important to copy your important information regularly. Whether you use a tape backup device or a CD-ROM drive, it's important to make a regular backup plan and stick to it.

1. **What does the underlined word "it" (in Paragraph 1) refer to?**
　　[A]System unsteadiness. 　　　[B]A personal computer.
　　[C]To perform well. 　　　[D]Getting a new PC.

2. **If you want to use Windows 2000, but your computer only has 64MB, what will you have to do?**
　　[A]Change its RAM for at least 256MB.
　　[B]Put in good software in your computer.
　　[C]Enlarge its memory to at least 128MB.
　　[D]Buy another new computer to match it.

3. **It can be inferred from the passage that ＿＿＿.**
　　[A]your computer will save the important information when its hard drive crashes

[B]your computer might lose all the information it stores when it crashes

[C]you must not put in much software

[D]you'd better use 128MB of RAM if you run Windows NT

4. What would be the best title for the passage?

[A]The Tips You Must Follow

[B]How to Start Out with a Computer

[C]How to Use Your PC Better

[D]How to Keep Your PC Steady

答案与分析

1.[A]。词句理解题。很明显,由 it 所在句及前面一句话的意思可知它指代的是 system unsteadiness(系统不稳定)。

2.[C]。细节题。第三段第三句说如果用的是 Windows NT 或者 Windows 2000,有 128 兆内存也能将就。意思就是用这两种系统内存至少要有 128 兆。注意不能选[A],这一句的后一分句说如果有 256 兆内存会运行得更平稳,而不是说这两种系统必须得有 256 兆内存才能运行。

3.[B]。推断题。最后一段提出的建议是"为灾难做好准备"。而由该段内容可知,这里的"灾难"就是指电脑出现故障,甚至硬盘瘫痪或者其他一些不可知的问题,并且指出:这就是经常备份重要文件很重要的原因。由此可以推断,电脑出现问题会使储存的这些重要文件丢失,选[B]。[A]根据常识即可排除;[C]与第二段第一句不符;[D]与第二段不符。

4.[D]。主旨题。文章的第一段为主旨段,该段最后一句说按照下述小贴士去做就可以将电脑不稳定降到最低,然后文章列举了让电脑稳定运行的四个方面的建议。所以,最能概括全文主旨的是"如何让电脑保持稳定"。

买台新电脑是一回事,而让它平稳运行则是另外一回事了。尽管个人电脑应当能平稳工作好多年,但用户们都知道的确会存在系统不稳定的问题。但如果按照下述小贴士去做,就可以将系统不稳定的情况降到最低。

首先,尽量少装软件。这样与软件相关的问题就会出现得少一些,系统也容易管理。

第二,应当确保有电脑所需的内存(RAM)。如果用的是 Windows 98,电脑至少需要 128 兆(MB)或者更多的内存。如果用的是 Windows NT 或者

Windows 2000,128兆内存也能将就,但如果有256兆或者更多内存,这些操作系统会运行得更平稳。

第三,确保买的是品质好的硬件。杂牌产品也许很便宜,有时质量也和名牌产品一样好,但名牌产品通常是由于其性能稳定而著名的。买著名公司的产品很明智,因为Windows一般会支持这些硬件。如果是刚开始使用电脑,从大的制造商那里购买预装系统的电脑是个不错的主意。它们可能与操作系统一起经过了全面的测试,通常会少出一些问题。

第四,为灾难做好准备。不管购买时你的操作系统运行得如何好,总有需要更换系统的那一天。乐观一点来看,你会是因为技术进步了而要更换,但你也许会因为硬盘瘫痪或者有其他一些没人能说明白的问题而不得不更换系统。那就是定期备份重要信息很重要的原因。不管你用的是磁盘备份工具还是CD-ROM驱动器,制定一份备份计划并坚持进行都很重要。

Exercise 27

　　Cigarettes may damage more than just children's lungs. According to researchers, teen smokers are much more likely to become *depressed*(抑郁的) than their nonsmoking classmates. The findings contradict the widely held belief that teens often start smoking to deal with emotional disorders.

　　In a study published this month in the magazine *Pediatrics*, researchers tracked a group of young school children's behavior. "Smoking within 30 days of the start of the study did *predict*(预言) being depressed a year later," says Elizabeth Goodman of Children's Hospital Medical Center in Cincinnati. Teens who smoked were almost four times as likely to be depressed a year later as their nonsmoking classmates. Unexpectedly, the study also shows that nonsmokers who were depressed at the beginning of the study were no more likely to be smokers a year later than their happier classmates.

　　Though links between depression and smoking remain unclear, the study's authors say *nicotine*(尼古丁) and other tobacco *byproducts* (副产品) may change brain chemistry. That finding is supported by the fact that anti-depression drugs can be helpful in helping people give up smoking.

The study suggests that teen smoking is a serious mental health problem，the authors say. "Smoking isn't bad for children just because it gets them sick 50 years later," says co-author John Capitman of Brandeis University. "It has a bad effect on them in the near future."

1. The underlined word "contradict"（Paragraph 1）probably means ____.

　[A]point to　　　[B]try on　　　[C]work out　　　[D]disagree with

2. The study suggests that teen smokers are more likely ____.

　[A]to be depressed

　[B]to defeat depression

　[C]to be sick when they reach old age

　[D]to give up smoking when they become adults

3. Which of the following is TRUE to the research findings on teen smokers?

　[A]Sick children are not likely to find comfort in smoking.

　[B]Happier children are not likely to become smokers.

　[C]Smoking does not help children who suffer from depression.

　[D]Smoking is not bad for children because it makes them sick in the future.

😊 **答案与分析**

1.[D]。词句理解题。由该词所在句前面指出的研究结果（findings），即青少年吸烟者比不吸烟的同学更有可能变得抑郁，与该词后面指出的广泛持有的观点（belief）即青少年常常是为了对付心理疾病才开始吸烟这两者之间的关系来看，它们是相互对立的，所以 contradict 应当指"不同，矛盾"等义，故选[D]。

2.[A]。细节题。答案在第一段第二句：... are much more likely to become depressed ....。此外，后文中也多次强调了这一结果，如第二段第三句。

3.[C]。推断题。文章说明了一种研究结果，即青少年吸烟者比不吸烟的青少年更容易变得抑郁。而文章说，此前的观点是青少年一般是由于心理疾病才开始吸烟。由这两者的对立与对研究结果的说明可以推知，作者的意思就是吸烟会导致青少年抑郁而不是让他们摆脱抑郁。所以只有[C]对。[D]项根据常识可以排除；[A]、[B]两项在文章中都没有涉及，也无法由文意推知。

香烟损害的可能不止是孩子们的肺。根据有关人员的研究,青少年中吸烟者比不吸烟的更有可能变得精神抑郁。这一研究结果与此前广为认可的青少年常常是为了应对心理疾病而开始吸烟的观点不同。

这一研究结果发表在本月的《儿科学》杂志上,研究人员跟踪了一群少年学生的行为。"研究开始后吸烟30天就预示着一年以后吸烟者会变得抑郁。"辛辛那提儿童医院医疗中心的伊丽莎白·古德曼说。那些吸烟的青少年后得抑郁的可能性几乎是他们不吸烟的同学的4倍。令人意外的是,研究还表明在研究一开始就有抑郁症的不吸烟者一年后并不比那些比他们快乐的同学更易成为吸烟者。

尽管抑郁和吸烟之间的关系仍为未知,但研究者说尼古丁和烟草的其他副产品可能会改变大脑中的化学成分。抗抑郁药物有助于人们戒烟这一事实支持了那一研究结果。

研究表明青少年吸烟是一个严重的心理健康问题。"吸烟并不仅仅是因为50年后会让孩子们得病而不好,"布兰德斯大学的合作研究者约翰·卡比特曼说。"吸烟也对他们不久的将来有着不好的影响。"

Exercise 28

　　The conditions in which zoo animals are kept have become greatly better over the last ten years. For example, one change for polar bears has been to feed them with live seafood and frozen vegetables.

　　The value of *zoo-breeding*（动物园繁殖）program is questioned for the reason that some *species*（种类）, such as the African elephant, do not reproduce well in *captivity*（圈养）. Some zoo opponents, people who are against keeping animals in the zoo, fear that the result of breeding programs may be new species of "zoo animals" which are used to living in captivity, not in the wild. They say that the money spent each year on zoos around the world（about £ 250 million）would be better spent on protecting animals' natural ability of living, such as the Tsavo Rhino Sanctuary in Kenya, where the black rhino has been brought back from the edge of death through careful management in the wild.

Perhaps there is a choice. The zoo condition and the natural wild-life have long been thought of as *opposites*(对立). But it might be more productive to think of developing zoos so that the conditions in which the animals are kept are similar to their natural homes. In other words, rather than being against zoos, the answer may be to change their nature. This can only help to make zoos a nice place for wildlife protection.

Zoos co-operate with each other in order to make their breeding programs successful. Animals are passed from one zoo to another in order to prevent inbreeding — breeding from closely-related animals. If animals that are closely related to one another mate, there is a danger they will produce unhealthy babies.

1. What does this article mainly talk about?

　　[A]Animals' food change. 　　[B]Conditions at the zoo.

　　[C]Zoo-breeding programs. 　　[D]Keeping animals nature.

2. The underlined word "rhino"（Paragraph 2）refers to ＿＿.

　　[A]a kind of wild animal 　　[B]some African people

　　[C]an unusual plant 　　[D]an effective method

3. What have people done to help produce more healthy baby animals?

　　[A]Checking animals' health all the time.

　　[B]Making animals stay close to each other.

　　[C]Having animals changed among the zoos.

　　[D]Building larger zoos for the mother animals.

4. We can infer from this article that zoos should ＿＿.

　　[A]be built like an animal's natural home

　　[B]find a better way to treat animals

　　[C]give up their animal-breeding programs

　　[D]send all the animals back to nature

😃 **答案与分析**

1.[B]。主旨题。文章主要介绍的是动物园里圈养的动物生存环境、繁殖条件的改善及人们在这方面所做的努力,因此最能概括全文主旨的是[B]

项。其余三项都只是文章提到的部分内容。

2.[A]。词句理解题。rhino 在这里是作为前一句中"保护动物的自然生存本领"(protecting animals' natural ability of living)的例子,由此可以推知它肯定属于动物的一种,故答案为[A]。

3.[C]。细节题。文章最后一段指出,动物园之间进行合作,将不同动物园里的动物相互交换以防止近亲繁殖,这样做的目的当然是为了让动物生出更加健康的小动物。其余三项在文章中都没有体现。

4.[A]。推断题。由第三段第三句话可以推知作者认为应当将动物园里动物的生存环境保持与其野生环境相同。其余三项都无法由文意推知。

同步译文

过去10年来,动物园里动物的生存环境已经大有改善。例如,对于北极熊的一大改善就是已经给它们喂食新鲜海产品和冷冻蔬菜。

动物园繁殖项目受到质疑的原因是有些物种如非洲象在圈养环境下繁殖得并不好。一些动物园反对者,就是那些反对将动物饲养在动物园里的人担心,繁殖计划的结果会是繁殖出一些新的"园中动物"种类,它们习惯于被圈养在动物园里而不是在野外生存。他们说,世界上每年花在动物园里的钱(约2亿5千万英镑)还不如花在保护动物的自然生存本领上,像肯尼亚的萨沃犀牛保护区,通过在野外的精心管理,已经将那里的黑犀牛从濒临灭绝的边缘上拉了回来。

也许有一个选择。动物园里的条件与自然的野生环境一直被认为是对立的。但考虑改善动物园里的条件,让动物们生活在一个与其自然环境相同的环境下也许更有效。换句话说,答案也许是改变动物园里的条件而不是反对动物园。这无疑有助于使动物园成为一个保护野生动物的更好的场所。

动物园之间正相互合作以使他们的动物繁殖项目得以成功。动物们被从一个动物园中转移到另一个动物园里,以防止近亲繁殖——近亲动物进行的繁殖。如果近亲动物相互交配,它们就有产出不健康的小动物的危险。

Exercise 29

　　The past fifty years or so have seen the gradual disappearing of animals from this earth, fishes from the sea, trees and plants from the land.

Many factors result in this unpleasant *phenomenon*（现象）. Among them, hunting is the main factor that endangers wild life. Some people kill wild life for sport. They take pleasure in collecting heads and *hides*（兽皮）. Yet others specialize in commercial hunting like killing whales.

Apart from this, the rapidly growing human population threatens wild life on land, too. Towns expand and roads have to be built, so forests are burnt and trees are chopped down. It seems that man needs every inch of land within his reach, so he moves on to the natural habitat of wild life. Tigers, lions and leopards slowly die off without the food and shelter that the forests provide.

In addition, rapid *urbanization*（城市化）means industrial expansion. Very often, poisonous chemicals, industrial wastes and oil are dumped into the rivers and seas. Fish and birds are threatened.

Man depends greatly on animals for survival. He needs their flesh, hides and furs. Thus, man cannot do without wildlife; or he himself would become extinct. The public should be made aware that it would be better to shoot the animals with a camera than with a gun. In this way, they can preserve and help wild life to continue living rather than to remove all signs of it.

Man must learn to farm the sea as he does the land. He should control the amount and the frequency of his catch. He should allow fish to breed and *multiply*（繁殖）before netting them. Man also needs to build forest reserves, and to pass laws prohibiting the killing of animals, especially those that are already rare. To keep the present animal kingdom, the least that man can do is to clean the seas and rivers and to prevent pollution.

The cycle of nature is such that it forms a vicious circle. The insecticides and *pesticides*（杀虫剂）that we spray on crops can kill the birds and animals that feed on them. When man eats these poisoned animals, he himself can die. We must therefore test the chemicals to be used before they are sprayed or it might mean the death of man!

1. The author's purpose in writing the passage is to _____ .

[A]explain how important wild life is to human beings

[B]call people's attention to serious problem of pollution

[C]explain relationship between wild life and human beings

[D]call people's attention to the protection of wild life

2. Which of the following is NOT true according to the passage?

[A] The growing human population threatens wild life because people take land from animals.

[B]Some people devote themselves to killing animals for money.

[C]People can preserve and help wild life to continue living by shooting the animals with a camera.

[D] Fishes are threatened by poisonous chemicals，industrial wastes and oil.

3. The phrase "natural habitat of wild life" in Paragraph 3 refers to ____.

[A]forests　　　　[B]trees　　　　[C]land　　　　[D]shelter

4. It is implied that ____.

[A]hunting should not be permitted in order to protect wild life

[B]man needs land more than wild life does

[C]if wild life disappears，so will man

[D]man has little knowledge of sea farming

5. The last paragraph is mainly about ____.

[A]the importance of wild life to human beings

[B]how the circle of nature is formed

[C]how animals are gradually disappearing from the earth

[D]how to solve the problem of pollution

答案与分析

1.[D]。主旨题。文章前面四段说明了野生动物正在灭绝的原因,第五段讨论了野生动物与人类的关系,最后两段讨论了如何正确对待野生动物,所以文章的主旨和作者的写作目的就是要唤起人们对保护野生动物这一问题的注意,选[D]。

2.[C]。细节题。[A]对应于第三段第一句;[B]与第二段最后一句相符,其中的 commercial hunting 指为了金钱而捕猎;[D]对应于第四段最后两句。只有[C]项对应于第五段最后两句但与原文意思不符。

3.[A]。词句理解题。该短语所在句的前一句说的是森林被人类焚毁、树木被人类砍伐;而后面一句则说老虎、狮子、豹子等因为没有森林提供的食物与藏身之所而慢慢灭绝。由此可以推知,这里说的(人类侵占)野生动物的栖息地指的就是森林。

4.[C]。推断题。[A]、[B]、[D]三项都与文意不符,也无法由文意推知。只有[C]项综合了第五段的意思,根据常识也可推知其正确。

5.[B]。主旨题。通读最后一段可知,这一段集中讲解自然循环过程中最终危害的是人类自己,呼吁人类改变这个恶性循环,因此正确答案是[B]。

同步译文

过去的五十多年见证了地球上的动物、海洋中的鱼类和陆地上的森林植被逐渐消失的过程。

许多因素导致了这一令人难受的现象。其中狩猎是危及野生动物的最主要的因素。一些人将猎杀野生动物作为运动。他们以收集兽头与兽皮为乐。然而另一些人则专门从事商业性捕猎活动,比如捕鲸。

除了这些,人口的快速增长也威胁着陆地上的野生动物。城市扩张,必须修路,因此森林被焚毁,树木被砍伐。人类似乎需要其掌握范围内的每一寸土地,因此侵入了野生动物的栖息地。没有了森林提供的食物和藏身之所,老虎、狮子和豹子慢慢灭绝了。

而且,快速城市化意味着工业扩张。有毒化学品、工业废物和油污经常被倾入河流与海洋。鱼类和鸟类都受到了威胁。

人类极大地依赖于动物而生存。人类需要动物的肉、皮和毛。因此,人类不能没有野生动物,否则人类自身就会灭绝。公众应当认识到用镜头拍摄动物要比用枪射杀动物更可取。这样他们可以保护和帮助野生动物继续生存,而不是将它们存在的迹象全部清除。

人类必须学会像耕作陆地一样开发海洋。应当控制捕捞的次数和频率。在捕捞鱼类之前应当让它们养育繁殖。人类也应当建立森林保护区,制定法律禁止捕杀动物,尤其是捕杀那些珍稀动物。为了保护现有的动物王国,人类至少应当清理海洋与河流,防止污染。

自然循环如此,以至于形成了一个恶性循环。我们喷在作物上的杀虫剂和农药可以杀死以作物为食的鸟类和动物。当人类食用了这些有毒的动物时,人类自己也会死。因此我们在喷洒前应当先对使用的这些化学品进行检测,否则就可能意味着人类自己的死亡!

Exercise 30

Every Wednesday and Friday *the Moscow Times* publishes Russian and international job *vacancy*（空 缺） announcements of leading companies, information on business education, training courses and MBA programs in Russia and abroad.

Contacting Job Opportunities

Marina Khloptseva, Job Opportunities Director

khloptseva@imedia.ru

Tel：+7 095 232 - 1768, fax：+7 095 232 - 9175

Rates

The number on the right is the maximum number of words allowed in the advertisement.

1 square	$ 275	30 words max
2 square	$ 550	60
3 square	$ 825	90
4 square	$ 1110	120
10 square	$ 2750	300
12 square	$ 3300	360
15 square(1/2 page)	$ 4125	500
30 square(full page)	$ 8250	1000
1 square：W = 49.8mm, H = 58.7mm		

Special placement of ads costs an additional 30% above the price of advertising space.

The advertising module "ear" is at the top of the page next the heading. The size of the module is 30mm × 60mm.

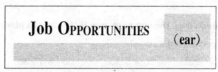

Minimum quantity of "ear" placements — 25 times.

25 placements	$ 2500
50 placements	$ 4500
75 placements	$ 6000
100 placements	$ 7500

Mailbox Service

The Moscow Times provides mailbox services for clients who want to receive and to collect CVs using fax or e-mail in regard to an advertisement placed in the newspaper. The service costs $ 50.

Mini Resume

The Moscow Times offers people seeking employment the opportunity to publish their own resumes.

Rates

| Textual advertising | $ 15 |
| Display advertising | $ 50 |

Deadline

The deadline for handing in advertising materials for Wednesday's Job Opportunities is 2:00 p. m. on the Monday prior to publication; for Friday's issue, the deadline is 2:00 p. m. on Wednesday prior to publication.

Job hunting on www. careercenter. ru

Placing banner advertisements in the Job Opportunities section allows you to create a link to your company site or link site guests directly to the information about your current vacancy.

＊All prices exclude taxes *stipulated*（规定）under Russian Law （from 01. 01. 2002 *VAT*（增值税）－ 10％ ）.

1. **How much does the company pay if it wants to place an ad with 500 words with special replacement?**

   [A] $ 4 125.　　[B] $ 5 363.　　[C] $ 1 238.　　[D] $ 500.

2. **What is the purpose of writing this text?**

   [A]To persuade more and more people to buy the newspaper.

[B]To help people understand the newspaper much better.

[C]To offer people seeking employment some information.

[D]To provide information on business education.

3. Which of the following is NOT true?

[A]All prices include taxes stipulated under Russian Law.

[B]All prices do not include taxes stipulated under Russian Law.

[C]People who place ads have to pay additional 10% for taxes.

[D]From 01. 01. 2002 Russian VAT is 10%.

4. It can be learned from the text that the deadline for handing in advertising materials for Job Opportunities should be ＿＿.

[A]every other two days before the publication comes out

[B]2:00 p.m. on either Monday or Wednesday prior to publication

[C]on Friday afternoon before the publication comes out

[D]2:00 p.m. on any day before the publication comes out

5. What would be the best title for the text?

[A]Job Opportunities   [B]The Moscow Times

[C]Job Hunting   [D]Job Vacancy Announcements

 答案与分析

1.[B]。推断题。根据第一个表格可知,一份 500 字的广告费用为 4 125 美元,然后根据表格下面的一句知,特殊布置的广告要加收 30% 的费用,那么一份 500 字,需要特殊布置的广告费用应为 4 125＋4 125×30%＝5 362.5 美元。

2.[C]。主旨题。文章列举各种表格、数字说明求职与招聘广告的价格,目的当然是为了给求职者或者用人单位提供一些相关的刊登广告的信息。

3.[A]。细节题。[A]与最后一句中的 exclude(不包括)不符。其余三项都是这一句的不同的说法。

4.[B]。细节题。在"Deadline(截止时间)"一条下,文章明确表明有两个截止日期:周一和周三。

5.[A]。主旨题。文章第一段是主旨段,表明是介绍《莫斯科时报》上发布的求职招聘广告的相关情况,因此[A]"工作机会"最能概括这一主旨。其余三项都不能概括文意。

同步译文

每个周三和周五《莫斯科时报》都刊登俄罗斯和国际上一些重要公司的职位空缺声明、俄罗斯和国外的商业教育信息、培训课程及 MBA 课程。

联系就业机会

Marina Khloptseva,就业机会主管

khloptseva@imedia. ru

电话:＋7 095 232−1768,传真:＋7 095 232−9175

费率

右边的数字是广告中允许的最多字数。

(表格略)

特殊布置的广告在上述广告面积的基础上加收 30％的费用。

报花广告模块位于页面顶端相邻标题的位置。报花模块的大小是 30mm×60mm。报花刊登最少为 25 次。

(表格略)

邮箱服务

《莫斯科时报》为那些想要通过传真或者电子邮件接收和收集关于报纸上刊登的广告 CV 的客户提供邮箱服务。该项服务的费用是 50 美元。

迷你简历

《莫斯科时报》为寻找工作的人提供刊登简历的机会。

费率

(表格略)

截止时间

周三版《就业机会》广告材料递交的截止时间是出版前的周一下午 2∶00;周五版的截止时间是出版前的周三下午 2∶00。

在 www. careercenter. ru 上求职

在《就业机会》上刊登横幅广告可以让你为公司网址建立链接,或者直接将网站访客链接到贵公司的空缺职位信息上。

＊所有价格都不包括俄罗斯法律规定的税额(由 01.01.2002 增值税法规定——10％)。

Exercise 31

Events

Israeli(以色列的) Paintings

Israeli artist Menashe Kadishman will hold a *solo*(个人的) show entitled "Flock of Sheep" from November 26 to December 20, at the China National Art Museum.

On show are 550 colourful paintings of sheep heads.

His works have been *displayed*(展出) in many important *galleries*(画廊，美术馆) over the past 30 years. They may be seen in the Metropolitan Museum in New York, and Tate Gallery in London.

Time: 9 a. m., November 26 — December 20.

Place: China National Art Museum, 1 Wusi Dajie, Dongcheng District, Beijing.

Tel: 64012252

Russia Ballet

The Kremlin Ballet from Russia will perform two classical ballets — *Swan Lake* and *The Nutcracker* — at the Beijing Beizhan Theatre.

Set up in 1990, the theatre *boasts*(以…而自豪) a number of first-class ballet dancers. Most of their performances are classical.

Time: 7:15 p. m., December 5 and 6 (*Swan Lake*); 7:15 p. m., December 7 (*The Nutcracker*).

Place: Beizhan Theatre, Xiwai Dajie, Xicheng District, Beijing.

Tel: 65003388

Folk Concert

The Central *Conservatory of Music*(音乐学院) will hold a folk concert to *commemorate*(纪念) the late musician Situ Huacheng.

On the programme there are many popular folks such as *Moon on the Bamboo Tower*, *Celebrating Harvest*, *Deep* and *Lasting Friendship*, *Golden Snake Dances Wildly*, and *Children's Holiday*.

Time: 7:30 p. m., November 25.

Place: Beijing Concert Hall, 1 Beixinhuajie.

Tel: 66055812

1. If your child is very fond of dancing, you may take your child to ____.

　　[A]China National Art Museum　　[B]Beizhan Theatre

　　[C]Beijing Concert Hall　　[D]1 Wusi Dajie

2. Which of the following is true?

　　[A]The folk concert will last three days.

　　[B]The ballet *The Nutcracker* will be put on once.

　　[C]The Israeli paintings will be displayed for a month.

　　[D]China National Art Museum lies in Xicheng District.

3. If one calls the number 65003388 on Dec 8, he probably want to ____.

　　[A]go to the folk concert　　[B]visit the Art Museum

　　[C]watch the ballet　　[D]none of the above

 **答案与分析**

　　1.[B]。推断题。由题目中的 dancing(跳舞)可知参加的应当 Russia Ballet(俄罗斯芭蕾舞)这一活动,因此去的当然是 Beizhan Theatre 了。

　　2.[B]。细节题。[A]与"Folk Concert"中交代的时间不一致;[B]与"Russia Ballet"中时间部分中的后一个相符;[C]与"Israeli Paintings"中时间部分对于时间跨度的说明不符;[D]与"Israeli Paintings"中地点部分的交代不符。

　　3.[D]。推断题。本题关键是看清题目。题目说,如果一个人在 12 月 8 日打电话 65003388,他很可能想去干什么。由电话号码可知,这是"Russia Ballet"部分中交代的 Beizhan Theatre 的电话。但该演出的时间是 12 月 7 日,所以 12 月 8 日打电话的目的就不得而知了,故答案应选[D]。

 同步译文

活　动

以色列油画展

　　以色列艺术家 Menashe Kadishman 将于 11 月 26 日至 12 月 20 日在中国国家艺术博物馆举办一个名为"羊群"的个人画展。展出的是 550 幅色彩缤纷的羊头油画。

　　在过去的 30 年中他的作品已在许多重要的美术馆展出。可以在纽约的大都会博物馆和伦敦的 Tate 美术馆见到这些作品。

　　时间:11 月 26 日至 12 月 20 日上午 9:00

　　地点:中国国家艺术博物馆,北京东城区五四大街 1 号

　　电话:64012252

俄罗斯芭蕾舞

来自俄罗斯的克里姆林芭蕾舞团将在北京北展剧院上演两部经典芭蕾舞剧——《天鹅湖》与《胡桃夹子》。

该剧团成立于 1990 年,以拥有许多一流芭蕾舞演员而著称。他们表演的大多是经典剧目。

时间:12 月 5 日、6 日晚上 7:15(《天鹅湖》);12 月 7 日晚上 7:15(《胡桃夹子》)

地点:北京西城区西外大街北展剧院

电话:65003388

民族音乐会

中央音乐学院将举办一场民族音乐会,以纪念巳故音乐家司徒华城。

节目单上有许多广受欢迎的民歌,如《竹楼上的月亮》、《丰收颂》、《友谊地久天长》、《金蛇狂舞》和《儿童节》等。

时间:11 月 25 日晚上 7:30

地点:北新华大街 1 号北京音乐厅

电话:66055812

Exercise 32

I was walking along the main street of a small seaside town in the north of England looking for somewhere to make a phone call. My car had broken down outside the town and I wanted to contact the AA. Low grey clouds were gathering across the sky and there was a cold damp wind blowing off the sea which nearly threw me off my feet every time I crossed one of the side streets. It had rained in the night and water was dripping from the bare trees that lined the street. I was glad that I was wearing a thick coat.

There was no sign of a call box, nor was there anyone at that early hour whom I could ask. I had thought I might find a shop open selling the Sunday papers or a milkman doing his rounds, but the town was completely dead. The only living thing I saw was a thin frightened cat outside a small restaurant.

Then suddenly I found what I was looking for. There was a small post office, and almost hidden from sight in a dark narrow street next to it was the town's only public call box, which badly needed a coat of paint. I hurried forward, but stopped in astonishment when I saw through the dirty glass that there was a man inside. He was fat, and was wearing a cheap blue plastic raincoat. I could not see his face and he did not even raise his head at the sound of my footsteps.

Discreetly(谨慎地), I remained standing a few feet away and lit a cigarette to wait my turn. It was when I threw the dead match on the ground that I noticed something bright red <u>trickling</u> from under the call box door.

1. **At what time was the story set?**

[A]An early winter morning.   [B]A cold winter afternoon.

[C]An early summer morning.   [D]A windy summer afternoon.

2. **Which of the following words best describe the writer's impression of the town?**

[A]Cold and frightening.   [B]Dirty and crowded.

[C]Empty and dead.   [D]Unusual and unpleasant.

3. **The underlined word "trickling" (last paragraph) probably means ____.**

[A]rushing out suddenly   [B]shining brightly

[C]flowing slowly in drops   [D]appearing slowly in a red color

4. **Why didn't the man raise his head when the writer came near?**

[A]He was annoyed at being seen by the writer.

[B]He was angry at being disturbed by the writer.

[C]He was probably fast asleep.

[D]He was probably murdered.

答案与分析

1.[A]。推断题。由第一段第三句中的 a cold damp wind、该段最后一句中的 a thick coat 可以推知天气很冷;由该段第四句中的 It had rained in the night 及第二段第一句中的 at that early hour 可以推知是在早晨。结合这两个方面可知应选[A]。

2.[C]。推断题。文章第二段描述了作者对所处城镇的印象。由第一句与最后一句可以得出 empty(空无一人)的印象,而第二句中明确出现了 dead

（死寂）一词,所以[C]项最准确。[B]项明显不对;[A]中的 frightening(恐怖的)在文章中没有体现;[D]说"异常和令人不快"也没有根据。

　　3.[C]。词句理解题。由该句中说作者是在"扔火柴到地上才注意到"这一点可以推知该词所表达的动作幅度不会很大;又由该词后的 from under the call box door 可以推知它表达的是一种流动状态。结合这两点可知应选[C]。

　　4.[D]。推断题。由第四段最后一句对电话亭里的男子的描述及文章最后一句,尤其是作者注意到电话亭门下流淌着一种亮红色的东西可以推知男子应当是死了,亮红色的东西应当是血。

同步译文

　　我走在英国北部一个海滨小镇的大街上,想找个地方打电话。我的车在镇外抛了锚,我想联系汽车协会。黑压压的云团在空中聚拢,每当我横过一条小街,从海边吹来的湿冷的风都几乎把我吹倒。夜里下过雨,雨水正从街边光秃秃的树上滴落。我庆幸自己穿了一件厚外套。

　　没有电话亭的影子,在这样早的时间我也找不到人来问。我本来以为能找到一家已经开门卖星期日报纸的商店,或者是一位正在到处转悠的送奶工,但该镇完全一片死寂。我见到的惟一活物是在一家小餐馆外边的一只又瘦又害怕的猫。

　　突然我发现了要找的东西。有一个小邮局,它的旁边——在一条又窄又黑的街道里几乎让人看不到——是该镇惟一的公用电话亭,上面的油漆已经脱落得差不多了。我赶紧跑过去,但当我透过那脏兮兮的玻璃看到有一个人在里面时,我惊讶地停下了。那人很胖,穿着一件廉价的蓝色塑料雨衣。我看不到他的脸,听到我的脚步声他连头都没抬。

　　我很谨慎地站在离电话亭几英尺远的地方,点了一根烟,等着轮到我。当我把灭了的火柴扔到地上时,我才注意到从电话亭的门底下淌出了一些亮红色的东西。

Exercise 33

　　Before World War Ⅱ, Chicago, Illinois, standing at the southern end of huge Lake Michigan, had the *reputation*(名声) of being one of the toughest, most lawless and *corrupt*(腐败的) cities in the world. It earned its ill reputation largely from those who sold strong wine during the days of 1919 to 1933, when a law forbade Americans to make or sell strong wine in any form.

Chicagoans have a great pride in their city. They say it is of great importance to the nation than New York. It is the center of American *commerce*(商业) and transportation. O'Hare Airport is the busiest airport in the world. 44 million passengers pass through it every year, and there are 2 000 takeoffs and landings every day.

Chicago is also a great inland *port*(港). It can send goods by ocean-going ships all the way to Europe — via the Great Lakes and the Saint Lawrence Seaway. It can send goods by *barge*(驳船), through waterway and canals, to the Mississippi and down it to the Gulf of Mexico.

1. **Which of the following *diagrams*(图解) gives the correct relationship between Lake Michigan, Chicago and Illinois?**

   LM — Lake Michigan   Ch — Chicago   Ill — Illinois

    [A]   [B]   [C]   [D]

2. **According to the passage, Chicago is more important than New York because ____.**
   [A]Chicagoans love their city more than others
   [B]Chicago is the center of America
   [C]Chicago is an inland port and has O'Hare Airport
   [D]Chicago lies at the southern end of Lake Michigan

3. **44 million passengers each year and 2 000 takeoffs and landings prove that O'Hare Airport is ____.**
   [A]the only one in America
   [B]the biggest one in the world
   [C]the busiest one in the world
   [D]the most well-known one in the world

4. If we carry goods to Chicago from Mexico, we probably go through ____.

[A]the Gulf of Mexico → Mississippi → Canals → Waterway → Chicago

[B]the Gulf of Mexico → Mississippi → the Great Lakes → Chicago

[C]Lake Michigan → the Saint Lawrence Seaway → the Gulf of Mexico

[D]Waterway → Canals → Mississippi → the Gulf of Mexico

答案与分析

1.[B]。推断题。由文章的第一句话可知,芝加哥位于密歇根湖的最南端,所以[A]、[C]两个图解明显不对。而由英语的习惯表达可知,芝加哥放在伊利诺伊之前,前者为小地名,后者为大地名,且前者是包含在后者范围之内的(事实上,伊利诺伊为州,芝加哥为市),所以正确图解就是[B]。

2.[C]。细节题。第二段最后三句说明了芝加哥人认为芝加哥比纽约重要的原因。将四个选项与原文一一对照可知[C]对。[A]在文中没有说明,[B]是取了该段第三句话的部分内容,[D]只是说明其位置,不构成原因。

3.[C]。细节题。第二段倒数第二句首先说 O'Hare 机场是世界上最繁忙的机场,接下来的一句则列举了一些数据,当然就是为了说明"最繁忙"这一点。

4.[A]。推断题。文章最后一段说明了由芝加哥发出的货物到达墨西哥湾的路径(芝加哥→水道和运河→密西西比→墨西哥湾),而题目提问的方向正好相反,所以答案就是[A]。注意该段第二句说明的是从芝加哥到欧洲的路径。

同步译文

二次世界大战前,伊利诺伊州位于密歇根大湖最南端的芝加哥市有着这样的恶名:它是世界上治安最差、最无法纪和腐败横行的城市之一。它得这样一个不好的名声,主要是由于那些在 1919 年至 1933 年间贩卖烈性酒的人,那时美国制定了一部法律,禁止人们酿造和贩卖任何形式的烈酒。

芝加哥人则对他们的城市充满自豪感。他们说,对于美国来说,芝加哥比纽约都还重要。它是美国的商业和交通中心。奥黑尔机场是世界上最繁忙的机场。每年有 4 千 4 百万乘客通过这个机场,而每天则有 2 000 架次的飞机起降。

芝加哥也是一个大内陆港口。它能通过大湖地区和圣劳伦斯海道将货物由远洋轮船运送到欧洲。它能用驳船运送货物,经由水道与运河到达密西西比,再往下运至墨西哥湾。

Exercise 34

Rembrandt, one of the greatest artists of all time, was born in Leyden in the Netherlands. His family ground its own grain in a windmill on the city's wall. As a child he liked to sketch the sun coming in through a tiny window and making a streak of light on the inside of the windmill. He carried this interest in light and shadow through life. His paintings often show one hand of a person in the light and one in the dark.

Many artists travelled to faraway lands. Rembrandt always stayed within 50 miles (80 km) of his home, although he lived to be 63.

Much of his life was spent in Amsterdam, then the richest town in Europe. In some of Rembrandt's paintings we see the rich clothes and jewels worn by people of that time in Amsterdam.

During the first ten years of his career he was a famous and fashionable painter. Then something happened which ruined him. He became so poor that he had to sell all his furniture and even his rich velvet clothes. To make matters worse, his wealthy wife died, and her parents took the money she had left to him.

This was what happened to ruin the sale of his paintings: the Amsterdam Civic Guard had paid him to paint a picture of them. Since he liked light and shadow, he painted the men as they were leaving the armoury at noon to go on duty. The men still inside were in such deep shadow that their faces could not he recognized. These men were very angry. The men in the sunlight of course showed well. But their satisfaction did not make up for the anger of the others. The picture is one of Rembrandt's best. It is called "The Night Watch", although it was painted at noon.

Even poverty did not keep Rembrandt from painting. He married a girl who had been a nurse to his son. They had a daughter. Since Rembrandt was too poor to hire models, he painted his wife, his daughter, and with the help of a mirror, himself. He painted the poor, the lame, the blind, and the sick. He dressed them in Biblical costumes, as was often done in his time.

Other Dutch artists of the time painted lovely cloth, dishes, and other such things simply because they were beautiful. They painted pictures of rooms with handsomely dressed people in them. Rembrandt was greater because he painted people so that we can tell how they felt and thought. He painted their personalities, not just their clothes.

Rembrandt worked hard all his life, becoming a better and better artist. The world stopped paying him. The people of his time stopped honouring him. But he was far greater than them. He was a great artist working on art problems ahead of his time.

1. Rembrandt's interest in light and shadow started ____.

[A]when he first saw a windmill

[B]in his childhood

[C]in the first ten years of his painting career

[D]just before he painted "The Night Watch"

2. How did he become very poor and have his fame ruined?

[A]He spent his money foolishly on rich velvet clothes and expensive furniture.

[B]His parents-in-law took away all his money when his first wife died.

[C]He painted only the poor and the handicapped who could not afford to pay him.

[D]He painted a picture which angered a lot of people.

3. Why were some of the civic guards represented in "The Night Watch" angry?

[A]They could not be recognized in the painting.

[B]They were badly painted in the painting.

[C]They did not like the light and shade effect.

[D]They wanted to be painted at night, but the picture was done in the day.

4. Why does the writer say Rembrandt was greater than the other Dutch artists of his time?

[A]He could do without hired models for his paintings.

[B]He represented the poor and the handicapped in Biblical costumes.

[C]He painted people in such a way that their personalities were revealed.

[D]He developed his interest in light and shadow.

5. Where did Rembrandt live most of his life?

[A]In Amsterdam.　　　　　　　[B]In Europe.

[C]In Leyden.　　　　　　　　　[D]In a small town.

 答案与分析

1.[B]。推断题。文章第一段第三、四句指出:As a child he liked to ... through life,即他在孩提时代就对光与影产生了兴趣,并终生保持了这种兴趣。所以答案就是[B]。其余各项都与文意不符。

2.[D]。推断题。文章第四、五两段指出了他变穷和使他声誉毁坏的原因。第四段谈到他变穷(没有交代原因)及使他更穷的原因(他有钱的妻子去世),而第五段才说明使他声誉毁掉的原因:This was what happened to ruin the sale of his paintings ...。综合这两段的内容,可知答案是[D]。

3.[A]。细节题。答案对应于第五段第三句:The men still inside were in such deep shadow ...。

4.[C]。细节题。答案是第七段最后两句,其中明确说明了作者这么认为的原因。

5.[A]。细节题。文章第三段第一句明确交代说:Much of his life was spent in Amsterdam.

同步译文　　历史上最伟大的艺术家之一伦勃朗出生在荷兰的 Leyden。他家在城墙上的一个风力磨坊磨玉米。从小起他就喜欢描绘从一扇小窗户透进来并在磨坊里形成一道光线的太阳。他终生都保持着这种对光与影的兴趣。他的油画中常常出现一个人的一只胳膊在光中而另一只在暗影里。

许多艺术家都到很远的地方去游历。尽管他活到了63岁,伦勃朗却总是待在离家50英里(80公里)的范围之内。

他一生中大部分时间都是在阿姆斯特丹度过的,那时它是欧洲最富有的城市。在伦勃朗的油画里,我们看到了那时阿姆斯特丹人穿戴的华丽服装和珠宝。

在他职业生涯中最初的10年里,他是一个有名的、时尚的画家。然后发生了一些事,毁了他。他变得穷困潦倒,不得不卖掉所有家具,甚至卖掉华丽的天鹅绒服装。更糟的是,他那有钱的妻子去世了,她的父母拿走了她留给伦勃朗的钱。

下面这件事让他的油画再也卖不出去了:阿姆斯特丹国民卫队花钱请他为他们画一幅油画。由于他喜欢光与影,他把那些人画成中午正在离开军械库去执勤。那些还在屋里的人处于很深的阴影之中,以至于他们的脸都难以辨认。这些人很生气。那些画在阳光下的人当然表现得很好。但他们的满意弥补不了其他人的怒气。这幅画是伦勃朗最好的作品之一。它的名字叫"夜巡",尽管它是在中午画的。

即使穷困也没有让伦勃朗停止画画。他与一个曾经当过他儿子的护士的姑娘结了婚。他们生了一个女儿。由于伦勃朗太穷,雇不起模特,他只好画他的妻子、女儿,并照着一面镜子画他自己。他画过穷人、跛子、瞎子和病人。他给他们穿上《圣经》中的服装,这在他那个时代是很常见的。

那时的其他荷兰艺术家画的都是些可爱的服装、餐具及其他诸如此类的东西,只是因为它们很漂亮。他们画的是有穿着漂亮服装的人的房间。伦勃朗比他们更伟大,因为他的画能让我们了解到画中人的感觉和思想。他画的是他们的性格,而不仅仅是他们的衣服。

伦勃朗一生工作勤奋,成为了一个造诣越来越高的艺术家。那个世界不再付酬给他。他那个时代的人不再尊重他。但他比他们都伟大得多。他是一个超前于他的时代、致力于艺术问题的伟大艺术家。

Exercise 35

You've no doubt heard people say how much they "need" a holiday, when what they really mean is that they want one. Certainly, people working under pressure feel a very strong desire to escape from work and become less tight during their holidays, and experience a changed *environment*(环境). For this reason, holidays away from home are now seen by most people as necessary to their quality life.

However, work for many people today are office work and mental, rather than physical, tasks. These people may seek much more energy-taking activities while on holiday, rather than simply lying on a beach.

Once people become used to going on holiday, taking holidays becomes a habit. Even in a *recession*(经济萧条), for many people the holiday is one of the last things to be given up, and indeed many workers have chosen to spend some of their last pay when being laid off on a holiday, perhaps to give themselves a "lift" before facing a *gloomy*(暗淡的) future.

Perhaps we don't like to admit it, but most of us also enjoy showing off about the places we have been to, and the lovely tans — dark skins we have got. The idea of tanning, however, is becoming less attractive than it was. So many tourists are now able to afford holidays in the sun that tans have become quite common; and although we join a tan together with health (and it is true that a certain amount of sunshine gives us a feeling of being healthy), it has been fully shown that sunshine, especially when received over a short, focused period of time, results in high danger of skin problems, as well as drying out one's skin and leading to more lines on your face later in life.

1. More and more people choose to have holidays because they ____.

[A]hate working indoors all the time

[B]want to get away from work

[C]love enjoying the beauties of nature

[D]become rich and want a better life

2. When office people have holidays, they often ____.

[A]lie on the beach and enjoy sunshine

[B]spend more than they can afford

[C]think about their work on the beach

[D]choose to do more physical exercise

3. A holiday may ____ when one has to face some difficulties in life.

[A]cheer someone up　　　　[B]help someone find a job

[C]be the last thing to given up　　[D]bring good luck to someone

4. At the end of the passage the writer tries to tell the readers ____.

[A]the importance of getting sunshine

[B]the bad effect of being on holiday

[C]the result of getting sun-tanned

[D]the healthy look of being tanned

5. From this passage we learned that some people can not live without ____.

[A]a tan　　　　[B]a job　　　　[C]a pay　　　　[D]a holiday

 答案与分析

1.[B]。细节题。第一段第二句指出了人们想要度假的原因是 the desire to escape from work,即摆脱工作,其中的 escape 就是[B]中的 get away from。

2.[D]。细节题。第二段第二句指出,坐办公室和从事脑力工作的人在假期里会寻求需要更多精力的活动而不仅仅是躺在海滩上。只有[D]项中的 physical exercise 属于该句中的 more energy-taking activities。

3.[A]。推断题。文章第三段指出,由于度假成了人们的习惯,所以就算在经济萧条时期许多人也不肯放弃度假,而且事实上有许多人把失业前的最后一部分薪水花在了度假上,这样也许是为了让他们自己在面对黯淡的前景之前振作一点。由此可以推断,度假是可以让人精神振奋起来的,故答案是[A]。其余三项都不合文意,根据常识也可以排除。

4.[C]。主旨题。本题考查的是段落主旨。通读最后一段可知,该段谈及了日晒已经变得很平常、适量日晒的好处及不当日晒的坏处等内容。因此,能全面概括这些内容的只有[C]项。

5.[D]。推断题。文章通篇都是谈论度假及与度假相关的一些情况,所以应选[D]。此外,在第三段第二句中有 the holiday is one of the last things to be given up 一句,也说明了假期对他们的重要性。

你无疑听到过人们说他们多么"需要"一个假期,实际上他们的真正意思是他们想要一个假期。当然,在压力之下工作的人们都有远离工作、在假期里变得不那么紧张并体验一种不同环境的强烈愿望。由于这个原因,如今大部分人认为离家度假对他们的生活质量来说是必不可少的了。

然而,如今许多人从事的是办公室工作或者脑力劳动,而不是体力活。这些人在度假时也许会寻求需要更多精力的活动,而不是仅仅躺在海滩上。

一旦人们习惯了度假,度假就会成为一种惯例了。即使是在经济萧条时期,假期也是许多人最不愿意放弃的事情之一,而且事实上许多工人选择把失业前的最后一部分薪水花在度假上,也许这样做是为了让他们自己在面对一个黯淡的未来之前振作起来吧。

或许我们不愿承认,但我们中的大部分人喜欢炫耀我们去过的地方和可爱的棕褐肤色——我们拥有的褐色皮肤。然而,把皮肤晒黑的主意已经不如

以前那样诱人了。如今那么多的游客能够在太阳底下度假,因此棕褐肤色已经变得很普通;而且尽管我们将棕褐肤色与健康相提并论(一定量的日晒给我们一种健康感,这是真的),但已充分表明日晒,尤其是短时间的集中日晒会有出现皮肤问题的高度危险,还会使皮肤过度干燥,导致日后你的脸上出现更多皱纹。

Exercise 36

Many animal and plant species have become *extinct*(灭绝的) and many more are in critical danger. Finding ways to protect the earth's wildlife and *conserve*(保护) the natural world they *inhabit*(居住) is now more important than ever.

Dodos:

The dodo was a classic example of how human caused damage to the earth's biology. The flightless dodo was native to the Island of Mauritius in the Indian Ocean. It lived off fruit fallen from the island's trees and lived unthreatened until humans arrived in 1505. The easily controlled bird became a source of food for sailors and was attacked by animals introduced to the island by humans such as pigs, monkeys and rats. The population of dodos rapidly decreased and the last one was killed in 1681.

Rhinos:

The *rhino*(犀牛) horn is a highly prized item for Asian medicines. This has led to the animal being hunted in its natural habitat. Once widespread in Africa and Eurasia, most rhinos now live in protected natural parks and *reserves*(保护). Their numbers have rapidly decreased in the last 50 years, and the animals remain under constant threat from *poachers*(偷猎者).

Giant Pandas:

The future of the World Wildlife Fund's symbol is far from certain, as few as 1 000 remain in the wild. The Chinese government has set up 33 panda reserves to protect these beautiful animals and made poaching them punishable with 20 years in prison. However, the panda's distinct black and white patched coat fetches a high price on the black market and determined poachers still *pose*(形成) one of the most serious threats to the animal's continued existence.

Whales：

The International Whaling Commission is fighting to ensure the survival of the whale species. Despite the fact that one third the world's oceans have been declared the whale *sanctuaries*(保护区)，7 out of 13 whale species remain endangered. Hunted for their rich supply of oil，their numbers have decreased to just 300. *Collisions*(碰撞) with ships，poisonous pollution and being caught in fishing nets are other major causes of whale deaths.

Tigers：

The last 100 years has seen a 95% reduction in the numbers of remaining tigers to between 5 000 and 7 000 and the Bali，Javan，and Caspian tigers are already extinct. The South China tiger is precariously close to disappearing，with only 20 to 30 still alive. Like the rhino horns，tigers' bones and organs are sought after for traditional Chinese medicines. These items are traded illegally along with tiger skins.

1．It is implied that ____．

　　[A]the dodo lacked the ability to protect itself from other animals

　　[B]sailors to the Island of Mauritius lived mainly on the dodo

　　[C]the dodo used to be a strong animal that liked fighting

　　[D]the dodo，pigs，monkeys and rats were the natives to the Island of Mauritius

2．Which group of the following animals has already ceased to exist according to the text？

　　[A]The dodo，rhino and giant panda.

　　[B]The rhino，whale and South China tiger.

　　[C]The rhino，panda，whale and tiger.

　　[D]The dodo and the Bali，Javan，and Caspian tigers.

3．____ can serve as a cure for certain diseases．

　　[A]The whale's rich oil

　　[B]The panda's black and white patched coat

[C]The rhino horn and tigers' bones and organs

[D]The dodo's delicious meat

4. Which of the following statements is NOT true?

[A]The number of South China tiger has reached crisis point.

[B]Many animals are threatened with extinction as a result of human activity.

[C]People hunt for the endangered animals for high profit.

[D]The whale is the representing mark for the World Wildlife Fund.

 答案与分析

1.[A]。推断题。由"Dodos(渡渡鸟)"下面对这种动物的介绍中的一些描述性词语可以推知这种动物缺乏自我保护的能力,如 flightless(不能飞的)、easily controlled(容易控制的)、was attacked(受到袭击)等。

2.[D]。细节题。由第二段最后一句可知 dodo 这种动物已经灭绝;由最后一段第一句可知 the Bali, Javan, and Caspian tigers 三种虎已经灭绝。综合这两个方面可知答案是[D]。

3.[C]。细节题。文章提到 medicines(药物)一词是在"Rhinos"和"Tigers"两个部分,说犀牛角、虎骨和虎的器官都可入药,所以答案是[C]。

4.[D]。细节题。[D]与"Giant Pandas"部分第一句话不符。世界野生动物基金会的标志是大熊猫而不是鲸鱼。

 同步译文

　　　许多动植物种已经灭绝,还有更多的动植物种正处在极度危险之中。如今找到办法保护地球上的野生动物、保护它们生存的自然世界变得比以往更加重要。

渡渡鸟:

渡渡鸟是人类给地球上的生态造成危害的经典例子。这种不能飞翔的渡渡鸟是印度洋上毛里求求斯岛上的土著鸟类。它们以岛上树上掉落的果实为食,一直未受到威胁,直到1505年人类到来。这种容易被捕获的鸟成了水手们的食物来源,受到了人类引入该岛的动物如猪、猴子和老鼠的袭击。渡渡鸟的数量急剧减少,最后一只渡渡鸟于1681年丧生。

犀牛:

犀牛角是一种极昂贵的亚洲药材。这导致了这种动物在其自然栖息地被猎杀。曾经在非洲和欧亚大陆广泛分布的犀牛,如今大部分生活在受到保护

的自然公园和保护区里。在过去的 50 年中,它们的数量大幅减少,而且这种动物仍处在偷猎者的不断威胁之下。

大熊猫:

这种是世界野生动物基金会标志的动物的前景难以确定。仍存的野生大熊猫只有 1 000 只。中国政府已经设立了 33 个熊猫保护区,以保护这些美丽的动物,并对偷猎者处以 20 年监禁。然而,熊猫那种独有的黑白相间的皮毛在黑市上奇货可居,决定了偷猎者仍然是对这些动物继续生存的最严重的威胁。

鲸:

国际捕鲸委员会正在为保证鲸鱼物种的存活而努力。尽管世界上三分之一的海洋已经被划为鲸鱼保护区,但 13 类鲸鱼中的 7 类仍濒临危险。由于它们含有丰富的油脂而被捕捞,它们的数量已经减少至只有 300 条了。与船只碰撞、有毒污染物及被渔网捕捞是造成鲸鱼死亡的其他主要原因。

老虎:

过去的 100 年见证了现存的老虎数量减少了 95%,减至了 5 000 至 7 000只,而巴厘虎、爪哇虎与里海虎已经灭绝。华南虎正濒临灭绝,只有 20 至 30只仍活着。与犀牛角一样,虎骨与老虎的器官被用于传统中药。这些药材与虎皮一起被非法交易。

Exercise 37

　　The business of on-line shopping so far has been disappointing for the pioneering *retailers*(零售商) who are already offering their services. The problem is that *consumers*(消费者), who say they are interested in the services, are mostly "just looking".

　　The Internet offers, among other things, "an electronic mall" with hundreds of retailers selling everything from computers to soaps. As with anything on the Internet, it is highly *decentralized*(分散) so reports of sales are not always correct. But many of the reports are disappointing.

　　But it is far too soon to announce the end of electronic retailing. One reason, say researchers and service providers, is that consumers are only beginning to understand the possibilities of the new technology.

On-line shopping allows consumers to research their purchases and communicate directly with the seller for product service and support. The new services also promise *visuals*(视频,图片) of quality goods equal to those on television.

Today, not many consumers have equipment in their homes capable of receiving such visuals and information. But Kingsley & CO. says that electronic shopping business will reach $ 4 billion to $ 10 billion a year in the United States by the year 2008. That means just 51 percent of the US homes will have the technology needed to make on-line shopping work, says George Sampson, director of Kingsley & CO.

In the end, the success of on-line shopping may turn on something as simple — and as difficult — as changing the public's idea of how to shop. "The problem with consumers," says Mr Sampson,"is that it is very difficult for them to recognize whether or not they want a product until they have already tried it. "

1. By "an electronic mall" (Paragraph 2) the writer refers to ____.

[A]the pioneering small businesses

[B]the business meeting through a computer

[C]visuals and information a computer offers

[D]a number of shops offering services through a computer

2. On-line shopping in the US has not been doing well mainly because ____.

[A]consumers only want to do research on some products

[B]consumers are not very familiar with the new technology

[C]consumers are not willing to spend money buying the equipment

[D]consumers only want to get some relevant information about the product

3. In on-line shopping, consumers are able to ____.

[A]do their own research on any products

[B]meet the seller on their television at home

[C]see quality goods on sale in all big companies

[D]see the products and the relevant information on their computers

4. The underlined word "that" (Paragraph 5) refers to ____.

[A] Kingsley & CO. 's estimates about on-line shopping in the US

by 2008
[B]consumers having the right equipment at home by 2008
[C]consumers' interest in electronic shopping business
[D]the present on-line shopping business in the US

答案与分析

1.[D]。词句理解题。由该句主语(the Internet)可知,an electronic mall 是由网络提供的;而由后面说明其内容的 with hundreds of retailers selling ... 可以推知,它指的是网络上一个聚集了众多零售商的虚拟商场,故答案是 [D]。它的字面意思是"电子商厦,电子购物中心"。

2.[B]。细节题。文章第三段最后一句指出,研究人员与服务提供商说电子零售业业绩不好的一个原因是消费者才刚刚开始了解这一新技术提供的可能性,也就是[B]的意思。

3.[D]。推断题。第四段说明了在线购物的优点:一是消费者可以仔细研究要购买的东西,并直接和卖家联系;二是消费者可以看到与电视上一样好的商品视频或图片。综合起来,就是说消费者在电脑上可以看到商品的样子与其他相关信息。

4.[A]。词句理解题。由上下文可以看出,that 指代的就是前一句话,即 Kinsley & CO.公司对美国在 2008 年前电子购物业营业额增长至每年 40 亿美元至 100 亿美元这一估计。

同步译文

对于那些已经在提供服务的先锋零售商来说,在线购物的情况迄今为止一直令人失望。问题在于那些说对这些服务感兴趣的消费者主要还"只是看一看"。

除了其他一些东西,互联网还提供了一个由成百上千家出售从电脑到肥皂等所有东西的零售商组成的"电子商城"。与互联网上的其他东西一样,这个电子商城高度分散,所以销售报告并不总是很准确。但许多报告令人泄气。

但要宣布电子零售业务的终结还为时太早。研究人员和服务提供商说,原因之一就是消费者才刚刚开始了解这一新技术所带来的可能性。

在线商店让消费者可以仔细研究要买的东西并直接与提供商品服务和技术支持的卖家联系。这些新的服务措施还提供与电视上一样的高品质的商品图片。

现在家里有能接收这种图片和信息的设备的消费者并不是很多。但是 Kinsley & CO. 公司说美国的电子购物业务到 2008 年将达到每年 40 亿美元至 100 亿美元。那意味着 51% 的美国家庭中将拥有进行在线购物的技术设备，Kinsley & CO. 公司的主管乔治·萨姆逊说。

最终，在线购物的成功也许取决于像改变公众购物观念这样简单——同时也很困难——的事情。"消费者的问题是，"萨姆逊先生说，"在他们试过一件产品之前，他们很难确定是否需要这一产品。"

Exercise 38

People in the United States honor their parents with two special days: Mother's Day, on the second Sunday in May, and Father's Day, on the third Sunday in June. These days are set aside to show love and respect for parents. They raise their children and educate them to be responsible citizens. They give love and care. These two days offer an opportunity to think about the changing roles of mothers and fathers. More mothers now work outside the home. More fathers must help with child-care.

These two special days are celebrated in many different ways. On Mother's Day people wear <u>carnations</u>. A red one symbolizes a living mother. A white one shows that the mother is dead. Many people attend religious services to honor parents. It is also a day when people whose parents are dead visit the cemetery. On these days families get together at home, as well as in restaurants. They often have outdoor barbecues for Father's Day. These are days of fun and good feelings and memories.

Another tradition is to give cards and gifts. Children make them in school. Many people make their own presents. These are valued more than the ones bought in stores. It is not the value of the gift that is important, but it is "the thought that counts". Greeting card stores, <u>florists</u>, candy makers, bakeries, telephone companies, and other stores do a lot of business during these holidays.

1. Which is NOT a reason for children to show love and respect for parents?

[A]Parents bring up children.

[B]Parents give love and care to children.

[C]Parents educate children to be good persons.

[D]Parents pass away before children grow up.

2. What do you know from the passage?

[A]Mother's Day and Father's Day are both in May.

[B]Fewer women worked outside the home in the past.

[C]Not all the children respect their parents.

[D]Fathers are not as important as mothers at home.

3. Which do you think is right about "carnation"（in Paragraph 2）?

[A]It only has two kinds of color.

[B] It refers the special clothes people wear on Mother's Day or Father's Day.

[C]It's a kind of flower showing love and best wishes.

[D]People can wear carnations only on the second Sunday in May.

4. What do you think "florists"（in Paragraph 3）do?

[A]They sell flowers.

[B]They make bread or pastry.

[C]They offer enough room for having family parties.

[D]They sell special clothes for Mother's Day and Father's Day.

答案与分析

1.[D]。细节题。文章第一段第三、四两句指出了父母对孩子的贡献，也就是孩子们爱戴和尊敬父母的原因。对照四个选项，可知只有[D]没有提及。

2.[B]。推断题。由文章第一段第一句后半部分知母亲节与父亲节分属于5月和6月，故[A]不对；由该段第二句及全文内容可知文章没有提及是否所有孩子都尊敬父母，故[C]不对；由第一段最后一句可知[D]不对。而该段倒数第二句说"如今更多母亲外出工作"，由此可以推知作者的意思是以前没有那么多母亲外出工作，故[B]是正确的。

3.[C]。词句理解题。由第二段第二、三、四句得知，carnation是人们佩戴的一种东西，并且有红色和白色的carnation。联系常识，不难推知它是一种花。[A]过于绝对，文章提到两种颜色，但并没有说只有这两种颜色；[B]不对，文章只是说人们在母亲节戴这种东西，没有提到父亲节也戴，并且文中用的是可数形式（a red one）而服装是不可数的；而[D]也过于绝对，在母亲节穿戴并不等于说只有在母亲节才穿戴。

4.[A]。词句理解题。用排除法。文章中提及了 flower，所以选[A]。[B]指的是文中提到的 bakeries；[C]中的 family parties 在文中没有提及；[D]中的 clothes 在文中也没有涉及。

同步译文

　　美国人用两个特殊的日子来向父母表示敬意：一个是母亲节，在 5 月的第二个星期日；另一个是父亲节，在 6 月的第三个星期日。这两天被挑出来用于向父母表示爱戴和尊敬。他们养育了孩子，把孩子教育成为有责任感的公民。他们付出了爱和呵护。这两个日子提供了一种考虑与父母互换角色的机会。如今有更多的母亲外出工作，更多的父亲必须协助养育孩子。

　　人们用不同的方式来庆祝这两个特殊的日子。在母亲节，人们佩戴康乃馨。红色康乃馨代表母亲健在，白色康乃馨则表明母亲已经过世。许多人参加宗教活动向父母表达敬意。这一天也是许多父母过世的人扫墓的日子。在这两天里家人一般在家里和餐馆里团聚。他们在父亲节常常举行户外烧烤。它们是充满乐趣、温馨感和记忆的日子。

　　另一个传统是送卡片和礼物。孩子们在学校自己制作卡片或礼物。许多人自己制作礼物。这些比在商店里购买的礼物更被人看重。重要的并不是礼物的价值，重要的是"心意"。贺卡商店、花店、糖果店、糕点店、电话公司和其他商店在这两个假日里的生意都相当红火。

Exercise 39

"In real life, the daily struggles between parents and children are around these narrow problems of an extra sleep hour, an extra TV show, and so on," said Avi Sadeh, psychology professor at Tel Aviv University. "Too little sleep and more accidents," he said.

Sadeh and his colleagues found an extra hour of sleep could make a big difference. The children who slept longer, although they woke up more frequently during the night, scored higher on tests, Sadeh reported in the March/April issue of journal *Child Development*.

"When the children slept longer, their sleep quality was somewhat weak, but in spite of this their performance for study improved because the extra sleep was more significant than the reduction in sleep quality,"Sadeh said. "Some studies suggested that lack of sleep as a child affected development into adulthood and it's more likely to develop his attention disorder when he grew older. "

In earlier studies, Sadeh's team found that the fourth graders slept an average of 8.2 hours and the sixth graders slept an average of 7.7 hours.

"Previous research has shown children in elementary school need at least 9 hours of sleep a night on a regular basis,"said Carl Hunt, director of the National Center on Sleep Disorder Research in Bethesda. "And high-school-age children need somewhat less,"he said, adding the results of insufficient sleep could be serious.

"A tired child is an accident waiting to happen,"Hunt said. "And as kids get older, toys get bigger and the risks get higher. "Hunt also said too little sleep could result in learning and memory problems and long-term effects on school performance.

"This is an important extension of what we already know. "Hunt said of Sadeh's research. "Adding sleep is as important as *nutrition*(营养) and exercise to good health. "

"To put it into reality,"Hunt said, "parents should make sure they know when their children actually are going to sleep and their rooms are conducive to sleeping instead of playing. "

1. What is *Child Development*?
　　[A]A new story.　　　　　　[B]A popular book.
　　[C]A periodical magazine.　　[D]A TV programme.

2. How many researchers are exactly mentioned in the text?
　　[A]One.　　[B]Two.　　[C]Three.　　[D]Four.

3. The underlined phrase "conducive to" (in the last sentence) could be replaced by ____.
　　[A]helping to happen　　　　[B]influenced by
　　[C]full of　　　　　　　　　[D]acceptable of

4. Which of the following statements is NOT true according to the passage?

[A]There are some daily struggles between parents and children because of having nothing in common with extra rest time.

[B]The children who sleep longer are weak in their study.

[C]Lack of sleep as a child has a great effect on his development into adulthood.

[D]In general，children in elementary school need at least nine hours of sleep a night.

 答案与分析

1.[C]。推断题。由其前的修饰语 in the March/April issue of journal 可知，Child Development 是一本双月刊杂志。issue 指杂志等的"(一)期"。

2.[B]。推断题。文章中提到和引用了 Avi Sadeh、Carl Hunt 两个人的话，对他们所做的研究和研究结果进行了说明。

3.[A]。词句理解题。由该短语后面的 sleeping instead of playing 可知，这里是否定后者(玩耍)、肯定前者(睡觉)，并且它们共同修饰主语 rooms，由此可以推断，其意是卧室应当"有利于"孩子睡眠而不是玩耍，故应选[A]。其余三项代入该句中都会造成句意不通。

4.[B]。推断题。由第一段第一句话可知[A]是正确的，父母与孩子在额外的休息时间等问题上达不成共识；由第三段最后一句话可知睡眠不足会影响孩子的发育，故[C]是对的；由第五段第一句可知小学生一个晚上至少应睡 9 个小时的觉，所以[D]也是对的。只有[B]与第二段第二句话不符，该句说睡眠时间长的孩子尽管在晚上老醒，但考试时得分都要高一些，也就是说学业成绩好。

"在现实生活中，每天父母和孩子之间的争吵都是围绕着一些狭隘的问题，如多睡一个小时、多看一会儿电视节目等等。"Tel Aviv 大学的心理学教授艾维·萨德说。"睡眠太少会更容易出意外。"他说。

萨德和他的同事们发现，额外多睡一个小时会有很大的不同。萨德在第 3/4 月份的期刊《儿童成长》中说，睡眠时间长的孩子尽管在夜间老醒，但考试成绩都较好。

"孩子睡眠时间较长时，某种程度上他们的睡眠质量不高，尽管如此，他们的学业都有进步，因为额外的睡眠比睡眠质量的下降更重要，"萨德说。"一些研究表明孩提时睡眠不足会影响成长发育，而且孩子在长大后更容易出现注意力方面的问题。"

在先前的研究中，萨德的小组发现四年级学生平均睡 8.2 个小时，而六年级学生平均睡 7.7 个小时。

"以前的研究已经表明通常小学生每晚至少必须睡 9 个小时，"位于 Bethesda 的全国睡眠不适研究中心的主管卡尔·哈特说。"高年级孩子需要的睡眠时间稍少一些。"他说，并补充说睡眠不足会很严重。

"一个疲惫的孩子肯定会发生意外，"哈特说。"随着孩子长大，玩具变得越来越大，危险也越来越高。"哈特还说睡眠太少会导致认知和记忆问题，以及给学业成绩带来长期的影响。

"这是对我们已知问题的一个重要延伸，"哈特这样评价萨德的研究。"增加睡眠对良好的身体健康与营养和锻炼一样重要。"

"为了实现这一点，"哈特说，"家长们应当确保自己知道自己的孩子何时真的想睡，确保孩子的房间有利于睡眠而不是有利于玩耍。"

 Exercise 40

JAMES AN COACHING COLLEGE

What is the main purpose of James AN Coaching College?

Quite simply, we are here to help students with:

⊙ HSC Exams: Years 11 and 12

⊙ Selective School Test: Year 5 to Year 10

⊙ Independent School Scholarship Exams: Year 6

⊙ Opportunity Class Test: Year 3 and 4

⊙ School Certificate Test: Year 10

The college provides expert tuition for students wishing to gain the highest possible marks in all examinations from Year 1 to Year 12.

We also help students:

⊙ excel in all subjects

⊙ have a head start

⊙ get motivated to succeed in their studies

⊙ increase their self-confidence

Through face-to-face teaching students are taught to perform well under examination conditions.

The Teachers

⊙ Highly qualified teachers from Selective Schools and Independent Schools.

⊙ James AN: Principal and co-author（合编者） of *Maths Tests for Selective Schools and Scholarship Examinations* and other books.

⊙ Other textbooks authors

Our teachers set high goals for themselves as well as for their students.

Courses And Subjects

HSC COURSE/YEARS 11 & 12

Subjects: Maths 2, 3, 4　　　Units: English, Physics, Chemistry

SCHOOL CERTIFICATE COURSE/YEARS 9 & 10

Subjects: English, Maths, Science

JUNIOR HIGH COURSE/YEARS 7 & 8

Subjects: English, Maths, Science

SELECTIVE SCHOOL/SCHOLARSHIP COURSE: YEARS 5 & 6

Subjects: English, Maths, General Ability, Creative Writing

OPPORTUNITY CLASS (OC) COURSE

YEARS 3 & 4　　　Subjects: English, Maths, General Ability

YEARS 1 & 2　　　Subjects: Maths, English

HOLIDAY REVISION COURSES

Special holiday revision courses are offered during each vocation.

Who can benefit from James AN Coaching College?

Students of all abilities!

We have helped thousands of students achieve results beyond their wildest dreams in the HSC and Selective School/Scholarship Tests. We'd love to do the same for you. All serious students will excel in their studies.

1. If you are a student of Year 7, what subjects can you take?

[A]English, Maths, Science and Creative Writing.

[B]Maths and Physics.

[C]Maths，English，Physics and Chemistry.

[D]English，Maths and Science.

2. Which of the following statements is NOT true?

[A]The teachers from Selective Schools are highly qualified.

[B]The teachers are authors of some other textbooks.

[C]The teachers set high goals for themselves as well as for their own children.

[D]The principal and co-author of Maths Tests for Selective Schools and Scholarship Examinations and other books is from James AN Coaching College.

3. The test for students of Year 12 is ____ .

[A]HSC Exams

[B]Opportunity Class Test

[C]Independent School Scholarship Exam

[D]School Certificate Test

4. Students are taught to perform well under examination conditions through teaching ____ .

[A]special holiday revision courses   [B]face-to-face

[B]self-confidence   [D]all subjects

5. ____ can benefit from James AN Coaching College.

[A]Students of all abilities

[B]Thousands of students

[C]Students from European countries

[D]Students who want to go abroad

😊 **答案与分析**

1.[D]。细节题。在"JUNIOR HIGH COURSE/YEARS 7&8"下的内容可以看出课程有 English，Maths 和 Science，所以答案是[D]。

2.[C]。细节题。将四个选项与"The Teachers"下的内容进行对照，可知只有[C]中的 for their own children 与原文中的 for their students 不符。

3.[A]。细节题。文章一开篇就指出："HSC Exams：Years 11 and 12"，说明 12 岁的学生进行的是 HSC 考试。

4.[B]。细节题。在"What is the main purpose of James AN Coaching

College?"部分的最后一句中明确指出：Through face-to-face teaching . . . 。

5. [A]。细节题。文章倒数第二段一句话回答的就是上面的问题 Who can benefit from James AN Coaching College，故答案是[A]。

同
步
译文

JAMES AN 辅导学院

James AN 辅导学院的宗旨是什么？

很简单，我们旨在帮助学生通过：

⊙ HSC 考试：11 年级和 12 年级的学生

⊙择校考试：5 年级至 10 年级的学生

⊙自主招生学校奖学金考试：6 年级的学生

⊙实验班考试：3 年级和 4 年级的学生

⊙学校结业考试：10 年级的学生

从 1 年级到 12 年级，学院为那些希望在所有考试中取得最高分的学生提供专家级的辅导。

我们还帮助学生：

⊙优异地掌握所有科目

⊙有一个领先于别人的开端

⊙激励他们在学习中成功。"教育＝成功"

⊙增强他们的自信心

通过面对面的教学，学生们将学会在所有考试条件下表现良好。

师资力量

⊙有着来自择优学校与自主招生学校的高水平老师队伍。

⊙ James AN：校长，《择优学校与奖学金考试数学测验》及其他一些书籍的合编者。

⊙还有其他教材作者。

我们的老师为自己和他们的学生树立了很高的目标。

课程和科目

HSC 课程/11 年级和 12 年级：

科目：数学 2，3，4；单元：英语，物理，化学

学校结业课程/9 年级和 10 年级：

科目：英语，数学，科学

初中课程/7 年级和 8 年级：

科目：英语，数学，科学

择校和奖学金考试课程/5 年级和 6 年级:

科目:英语,数学,总体能力,创造性写作

实验班(OC)课程:

3 年级和 4 年级科目是:英语,数学,总体能力

1 年级和 2 年级科目是:数学,英语

假期复习课程:

每个假期都提供特别的假期复习课程。

谁能从 James AN 辅导学院获益?

所有不同能力水平的学生!

我们已经帮助成千上万的学生在 HSC 和择校或者奖学金考试中取得了他们根本意想不到的成绩。我们愿意为你做同样的事。所有认真的学生都将在学习中取得好成绩。

模拟考场一

第一节　完型填空

阅读下面短文,从短文后所给各题的四个选项([A]、[B]、[C]和[D])中选出能填入相应空白处的最佳选项,并在答题卡1上将该项涂黑。

One day mother rat and her babies were out in an open field. They were playing and having a good time when ___1___ a hungry cat came on the scene! It hid ___2___ a big tree and then ___3___ forward through the tall grass ___4___ it could almost hear them talk. ___5___ the mother rat and her babies knew ___6___ had happened, the cat ___7___ from its hiding-place and started to run ___8___ them.

The mother rat and her babies all ___9___ at once. They hurried towards ___10___ home, which was under a pile of large stones. ___11___ the baby rats were ___12___ scared that they could not run very ___13___. Closer and closer the cat came. In no time the cat would be upon ___14___. What was to be done?

The mother rat stopped running, ___15___ round and faced that cat, ___16___ "Bow! Wow! Bowwow!" Just like ___17___ angry dog. The cat was so surprised and ___18___ that it ran away.

The mother rat turned to her babies, "Now you see ___19___ important it is to learn ___20___ second language!"

1.　[A]naturally　　[B]suddenly　　[C]nearly　　　[D]certainly

2. 〔A〕on 〔B〕between 〔C〕by 〔D〕behind
3. 〔A〕crawled 〔B〕jumped 〔C〕looked 〔D〕climbed
4. 〔A〕before 〔B〕when 〔C〕until 〔D〕while
5. 〔A〕Before 〔B〕After 〔C〕Unless 〔D〕Other
6. 〔A〕where 〔B〕what 〔C〕which 〔D〕when
7. 〔A〕jumped 〔B〕started 〔C〕jumping 〔D〕starting
8. 〔A〕over 〔B〕through 〔C〕after 〔D〕against
9. 〔A〕fleed 〔B〕flied 〔C〕fled 〔D〕flee
10. 〔A〕to 〔B〕for 〔C〕its 〔D〕their
11. 〔A〕Because 〔B〕But 〔C〕Therefore 〔D〕Although
12. 〔A〕as 〔B〕much 〔C〕so 〔D〕very
13. 〔A〕freely 〔B〕hardly 〔C〕soon 〔D〕quickly
14. 〔A〕ahead 〔B〕down 〔C〕that 〔D〕them
15. 〔A〕turned 〔B〕walked 〔C〕jumped 〔D〕ran
16. 〔A〕saying 〔B〕said 〔C〕shouting 〔D〕shouted
17. 〔A〕a 〔B〕an 〔C〕their 〔D〕that
18. 〔A〕pleased 〔B〕excited 〔C〕frightened 〔D〕worried
19. 〔A〕so 〔B〕why 〔C〕what 〔D〕how
20. 〔A〕our 〔B〕their 〔C〕a 〔D〕an

第二节　阅读理解

阅读下列短文,从短文后所给的四个选项(〔A〕、〔B〕、〔C〕和〔D〕)中选出最佳选项,并在答题卡 1 上将该项涂黑。

A

Americans have contributed to many art forms. And jazz, a type of music, is one of the art forms that were started in the United States. Black Americans, who sang and played the music of their homeland, created jazz. Jazz is a mixture of music of Africa, the work songs the slaves sang, and religious music. *Improvisation*(即兴演奏) is an important part of jazz. This means that the musicians make the music up as they go along, or create the music on the spot. This is why a jazz song might sound a little different each time it is played.

Jazz bands formed in the late 1900s. They played in bars and clubs in many towns and cities of the South, especially in New Orleans. New Orleans is an international seaport, and people from all over the world came to New Orleans to hear jazz. Jazz became more and more popular. By the 1920s, jazz was popular all over the United States. By the 1940s, you could hear jazz not only in clubs and bars, but also in concert halls. Today, people from all over the world play jazz. Jazz musicians from the United States, Asia, Africa, South America, and Europe meet and share their music at festivals in every continent. In this way jazz continues to grow and change.

21. It took about ＿＿ years to make jazz popular in the United States.

[A]20　　　　[B]40　　　　[C]80　　　　[D]120

22. From the text it can be inferred that ＿＿.

[A]the American people are all jazz lovers

[B]jazz is sung by African blacks when working

[C]jazz may become more and more popular as time goes on

[D]New Orleans is the place where jazz was first performed

23. The best title for this passage is ＿＿.

[A]American Art Forms　　　　[B]The Birthplace of Jazz

[C]The Development of Jazz　　　　[D]The Music of Black Americans

B

Everyone wants the best for a baby. A mother wants her baby to have the best in the way of food, toys, clothing and equipment. Her value judgements on prices may go wrong when it comes to buying for a baby, particularly the first one. Factory producers and *advertisers*(广告商) recognize this, and exploit it to the full. Far more is spent in buying push-chairs, special milk, and special powders for small babies than is necessary.

The child himself watches television, a particularly strong *influence*(影响) on small children. Looking at them as they watch television, and then watching them react to products afterwards, suggests that young children accept the television advertisements as well as the guidance offered by children's programmes, and find both equally attractive. The child comes early in life to the feeling widespread in this country that if something is said on television it must be true.

For this reason much Christmas gift advertising, and advertising for sweets, food and washing powders, is specially designed for children because of the effect their repeated <u>nagging</u> can have on their mothers. By exercising in this way they become *consumers*(消费者) at an early age and as a result, with present-day pressures, choosing and buying goods and services will remain an important part of their future lives.

24. According to the writer, a mother spends more than necessary on ____.

    [A]Christmas advertising   [B]special powders

    [C]television   [D]sweets

25. The underlined word "nagging" most probably means ____.

    [A]repeated demands   [B]baby powders

    [C]TV services   [D]children's programmes

26. Which of the following statements is best supported by the text?

    [A]Children like both TV advertisements and children's programmes.

    [B]TV programmes often advertise the best products for children.

    [C]Mothers encourage children to buy products advertised on TV.

    [D]TV advertisements provide the best advice to choose gifts.

27. The best title for the text could be ____.

    [A]Mothers and Babies   [B]Children as Consumers

    [C]Giving the Best to Babies   [D]Choosing Goods for Children

C

It was 7 a. m. in Kyoto, Japan, and the taxi company had just called a second time to say they couldn't find my house. Once again I spelt out directions even a blind person could follow. I glanced impatiently at my watch, and waited. Only two hours remained until my flight left — and it was an hour-and-a-half trip to the airport.

Outside, heavy rains were pouring down. My house was so far north in the city that buses pass only three times a day.

The telephone rang again. "Terribly sorry," began the man at the taxi company. Then I realized that the taxi company, flooded with calls, could only offer in-city runs. I had heard this happens when the weather gets bad. I shouted into the phone that I had a plane to catch and I would meet the taxi outside my house.

Standing in the wind-driven rain, I looked up and down the road. No taxi. A car went by, driver and passenger staring at the crazy foreigner in the *downpour*(瓢泼大雨).

Finally a white car appeared and pulled to a stop. A young man threw open the door, waving for me to get in. Shaking with cold and anger, I climbed in.

In the most polite Japanese, the man said he was called Mike, with whom I had spoken three times that morning. He had left his post in the office and raced here in his personal car. He apologized again, but did not explain why a taxi would not pick me up. Delivering me straight to the airport, he refused the 2 000 yen I pressed into his hand.

A few hours later, as the storm-delayed 727 took off, I opened the newspaper. On the second page my eyes caught the headline of a short article: "Taxi Strike Begins This Morning in Kyoto."

28. Why did the writer call a taxi early in the morning?

[A]There were few taxis in town.

[B]He was unable to find the airport.

[C]He wanted to catch a plane.

[D]All the buses stopped because of the rain.

29. What was the reason for the taxi company not being able to pick him up?

[A]The taxi drivers refused to work.

[B]The writer didn't give the correct address.

[C]More people were riding in taxis on rainy days.

[D]The taxi drivers didn't like to drive long distance.

30. The writer got to the airport _____.

[A]by getting a lift in a passing car

[B]with the help of Mike from the post office

[C]by riding in Mike's car from the taxi company

[D]with the help of a taxi driver sent by his company

31. We can learn from the text that the driver is _____.

[A]quick-minded at taking actions

[B]warm-hearted toward people

[C]unfamiliar with the road

[D]a self-employed driver

D

As more women in the United States are working now, more are finding it necessary to make business trips alone. Since this is still new for many, some tips are certainly in order. If you are married, it is a good idea to encourage your husband and children to learn to cook a few simple meals while you are away. They will be much happier and probably they will enjoy the experience. If you will be eating alone a good meal, choose good restaurants. In the end, they will be much better for your *digestion*(消化). You may also find it useful to call the restaurant in advance and state that you will be eating alone. You will probably get better service and almost certainly a better table. Finally, and most importantly, get fully prepared what you will need in your travel as a businesswoman; this starts with lightweight *luggage*(行李) which you can easily carry even when fully packed. Take a folding case inside your suitcase; it will be very useful for dirty clothes, as well as for business *documents*(文件) and papers you no longer need on the trip. And make sure you have a *briefcase*(公文箱) so that you can keep the papers you need separate. Obviously, experience helps, but you can make things easier on yourself from the first by careful planning, so that right from the start you really can have a good trip.

32. For whom is the author most probably writing this text?

[A]Working women who have no time for cooking.

[B]Husbands and children of working women.

[C]Working women traveling by themselves.

[D]Restaurant managers who serve working women.

33. By saying that "some tips are certainly in order"(Lines 2～3), the author means that ____.

[A]some advice for the trip is necessary

[B]some small changes are useful

[C]business experience is helpful

[D]careful planning is a must

34. What does the author suggest working women with families do?

[A]Attend cooking lessons with your family.

[B]Prepare simple meals for your family before a trip.

[C]Encourage your family to have fun while you are away.

[D]Help your family to learn to prepare food for themselves.

35. Why is lightweight luggage important for travelling businesswomen?

[A]It provides space for dirty clothes.

[B]It enables them to travel easily.

[C]It can also be used as a briefcase.

[D]It can be easily folded when packed.

36. What is the main idea of the text?

[A]Business trips are more difficult for women than for men.

[B]More women are finding the road to success in American business.

[C]Good business trips result from careful preparation before the trip.

[D]Careful planning of household affairs makes most businesses successful.

E

The research was done by a Dr Griffiths in England. He compared the behavior of 15 regular *gamblers*(赌徒) with those of 15 non-regular gamblers before and after they gambled. Both groups had increased *heart rates*(心率) during gambling because it was exciting. But the regular gamblers' heart rates went down almost straight after the game, while the non-regulars remained excited and had increased heart rates for longer.

When the heart beat increases, the body produces chemicals called endorphins which make you feel good. Dr Griffiths thinks that regular gamblers lose this good feeling soon after a game and need to play again quickly to regain the pleasure.

He has also discovered that regular gamblers have different *psychological reactions*(心理反应) from non-regular gamblers. In an experiment where regular and non-regular gamblers thought aloud while playing, regular gamblers had far more unreasonable thoughts. In their minds they turned losses into near-wins. Dr Griffiths thinks that nearly winning gives the gambler <u>a high</u> in the same way that a win would do.

Based on Dr Griffiths' research, doctors suggest that one way to help regular gamblers to give up gambling is to give them beta-blockers — drugs that stop them getting a high in the first place.

37. Dr Griffiths' research helps you find out ____.

    [A]which group of gamblers played the game better

    [B]a chemical to increase gamblers' heart beat

    [C]a way to help gamblers give up gambling

    [D]when gamblers should be given drugs

38. How did Dr Griffiths discover the gamblers' feelings when winning and losing?

    [A]By examining the different chemicals in gamblers' bodies.

    [B]By asking the gamblers to speak aloud their feelings.

    [C]By asking the gamblers to discuss their ideas.

    [D]By testing the gamblers' heart beat.

39. The underlined words "a high" probably mean ____.

    [A]a feeling of happiness   [B]a reasonable thought

    [C]a great expectation   [D]an exciting idea

40. According to the text, what do we know about non-regular gamblers?

    [A]Their bodies produce less endorphins during the game.

    [B]They don't consider losses in a game as reasonable near-wins.

    [C]Their bodies have no reaction to beta-blockers.

    [D]They have faster heart rates during the game.

模拟考场二

阅读下面短文，从短文后所给各题的四个选项（[A]、[B]、[C]和[D]）中选出能填入相应空白处的最佳选项，并在答题卡1上将该项涂黑。

The 1990s saw great changes in the way people communicate. People could send mail without going to the ___1___ , and go shopping without leaving home. ___2___ like email and download became part of people's vocabulary. The cause of this great change was the ___3___ .

The idea for the Internet began in the early 1960s in ___4___ . The Department of Defense wanted to ___5___ their computers together in order to ___6___ private information. In 1969, the ARPAnet (an early form of the Internet) first connected the ___7___ at four American universities. One computer successfully ___8___ information to another. In 1972, scientists shared ARPAnet ___9___ the world. They created a ___10___ to send person-to-person messages using ARPAnet. This was the ___11___ of email. Over the next few years, there was a lot of progress made in the world of computing, ___12___ most people were not using the Internet. Then, in the 1980s, personal computers became more ___13___ . In the early 1990s, ___14___ important things happened: the birth of the World Wide Web in 1991, and the creation of the ___15___ Web *browser*(浏览器) in 1993. The Web made it ___16___ to find information on the Internet, and to move from place to place ___17___ links. The Web and browser made it possible to see information as a website with pictures, sound, and words.

Today, ___18___ of people connect to the Internet to send emails, visit websites, or store information on servers. ___19___ are now an important part of our lives and are changing ___20___ we learn, work, shop, and communicate.

1. [A]post office   [B]supermarket
   [C]department store   [D]the office
2. [A]Expressions   [B]Phrases   [C]Letters   [D]Words

3. [A]computer   [B]Internet   [C]server   [D]browser

4. [A]America   [B]England   [C]China   [D]Canada

5. [A]put   [B]get   [C]connect   [D]leave

6. [A]have   [B]take   [C]reach   [D]share

7. [A]computers   [B]colleges   [C]telephones   [D]lines

8. [A]worked   [B]found   [C]posted   [D]sent

9. [A]to   [B]in   [C]with   [D]for

10. [A]place   [B]way   [C]path   [D]direction

11. [A]beginning   [B]finding   [C]creating   [D]using

12. [A]but   [B]and   [C]or   [D]because

13. [A]practical   [B]familiar   [C]expensive   [D]common

14. [A]two   [B]three   [C]four   [D]five

15. [A]new   [B]rise   [C]advanced   [D]modern

16. [A]easier   [B]harder   [C]slower   [D]cheaper

17. [A]circling   [B]seeking   [C]sending   [D]using

18. [A]tens   [B]hundreds   [C]thousands   [D]millions

19. [A]Emails   [B]Messages   [C]Computers   [D]Browsers

20. [A]how   [B]what   [C]when   [D]why

第二节 阅读理解

阅读下列短文,从短文后所给的四个选项([A]、[B]、[C]和[D])中选出最佳选项,并在答题卡1上将该项涂黑。

A

George is a young man. He does not have a wife, but he has a very big dog, and he has a very small car, too. He likes playing basketball. Last Monday he played basketball for an hour at his club, and then he ran out to a car. His dog came after him, but it did not jump into the same car, it jumped into the next one.

"Come here, silly dog," George shouted at it but the dog stayed in the other car.

George put his key into the lock of the car, but the key did not turn. Then he looked at the dog again. It was in the right one. "It's sitting and staring at me," George said angrily. But then he smiled and got into his car with the dog.

21. George ____.

    [A]has a wife   [B]has a dog

    [C]has a car   [D]both B and C

22. What did George do last Monday?

    [A]He bought a small car.

    [B]He played football with his dog.

    [C]He played basketball at his club.

    [D]He went out for a walk with his dog.

23. Which of the following is right?

    [A]His dog was lost.

    [B]His dog was staring at him.

    [C]His dog got into another person's car.

    [D]George got into another person's car by mistake.

24. From this passage, we know George's dog is ____.

    [A]clever   [B]honest   [C]greedy   [D]stupid

B

Many people are worried about what television has done to the generation of American children who have grown up watching it. For one thing, recent studies show that TV weakens the ability to imagine. Some teachers feel that television has taken away the child's ability to form mental pictures in his own mind, resulting in children who cannot understand a simple story without pictures.

Secondly, too much TV too early usually causes children to be removed from real-life experiences. Thus, they grow up to be *passive*(被动的) watchers who can only *respond*(反应) to action, but not start doing something actively. The third area for such a worrying situation is the serious *dissatisfaction*(不满) frequently expressed by school teachers that children show a low patience for the pains in learning. Because they have been used to seeing results of all problems in 30 or 60 minutes on TV, they are quickly discouraged by any activity that promises less than immediate satisfaction. But perhaps the most serious result is the TV effect of bloody fights and death on children, who have come to believe that it is an everyday thing. Not only does this increase their admission of terrible acts on others, but some children will follow *anti-social*(反社会的) acts that they see on television.

25. Because of TV, children have lost their ability to ____.

  [A]have ideas of new things   [B]understand pictures in books

  [C]read story books   [D]think in a clear way

26. What do school teachers worry about?

  [A]Children suffer from mental pains.

  [B]Children are weak at facing difficulties.

  [C]Children become uninterested in class activities.

  [D]Children spend little time learning unknown things.

27. When children see terrible killing on TV, they ____.

  [A]are frightened   [B]think it's real

  [C]become annoyed   [D]feel satisfied

28. The main purpose of the text is to tell people ____.

  [A]how to prevent children from watching TV

  [B]how children like frightening TV programmes

  [C]what bad effects TV programmes have on children

  [D]what teachers think of today's children

C

Last April, on a visit to the new Mall of America near Minneapolis, I carried with me a small book provided for the reporters by the public relations office. It included a variety of "fun facts" about the mall, such as: 140 000 hot dogs are sold each week, there are 10 000 full-time jobs, 44 sets of moving stairs and 17 lifts, 12 750 parking places, 13 000 tons of steel, and $1 million is drawn weekly from 8 ATMs. Opened in the summer of 1992, the mall was built where the former Minneapolis *Stadium*(体育馆) had been. It was only a five-minute drive from the Minneapolis-St. Paul International Airport. With 4. 2 million square feet of floor space — twenty-two times the size of the average American shopping center — the Mall of America was the largest shopping and family *recreation*(娱乐) center under one roof in the United States.

I knew already that the Mall of America had been imagined by its designers, not merely as a marketplace, but as a national tourist attraction. Eleven thousand articles, the small book informed me, had been written about the mall. Four hundred trees had been planted in its gardens, $625 million had been spent to build it, and 350 stores were already in business. Three thousand bus tours were expected each year along with a half-million Canadian visitors and 200 000 Japanese tourists. Sales were expected to be at $ 650 million for 1993 and at $ 1 billion for 1996. Pop singers and film stars such as Janet Jackson and Arnold Schwarzenegger had visited the mall. It was five times larger than Red Square and it included 2. 3 miles of hallways and used almost twice as Knott's Camp Snoopy.

29. We know from the text that the Mall of America is ____.

[A]near an old stadium

[B]close to an airport

[C]higher than the Eiffel Tower

[D]bigger than most American parks

30. Why are the pieces of information provided by Mall of America referred to as "fun facts"?

[A]They are largely imagined.

[B]They are surprising figures.

[C]They give exact descriptions.

[D]They make people feel uneasy.

31. What's the point of mentioning popular stars who had been to the mall?

[A]To show its power of attraction.

[B]To show that few rich people like to shop there.

[C]To tell the public about a new movie being made about it.

[D]To tell people that they have chances of meeting famous stars there.

32. We can infer from the text that ____.

[A]Japanese visitors are most welcome to the mall

[B]Canadian visitors would spend $ 1 billion at the mall

[C]Knott's Camp Snoopy was next to the Mall of America

[D]the Mall of America was designed to serve more than one propose

D

FILM *PREVIEWS*（预告）

In the Line of Fire

After his Oscar success as an aging cowboy in *Unforgotten*, Clint Eastwood plays an aging secret-service man in this action movie. He is Frank Horrigan, a devoted citizen who has strong love for his country and who believes that he was *responsible*（有责任的）for the death of John F. Kennedy in 1963. When a madman, played by John Malkovich, says that he will kill the present President, Horrigan is given the chance to <u>redeem</u> himself.

Sleepless in Seattle

A very interesting film from Nora Ephron, the writer-director of *When Harry Met Sally*. One Christmas, a little boy, who has just lost his mother, calls a national radio station to find a new wife for his dad, played by Tom Hanks. When a radio-reporter hears the program, she is sure that she has found the man of her dream and spends the rest of the film in an eager search for him.

The Firm

Tom Cruise plays a young lawyer, Mitch McDeere, who finds out that several members of his new law firm have died. When an FBI man finds out that the firm is run by the *Mafia*（黑手党）, Mitch is offered a job as an *undercover agent*（便衣特工）, who will pretend to work for one side while working for another. However, he refuses and thinks up a way neither to follow the FBI nor the Mafia. This is Tom Cruise acting the part he knows best — "The Great American Individual".

33. Who plays the major part in In the Line of Fire?

　　[A]Frank Horrigan.　　　　　[B]Clint Eastwood.

　　[C]John Kennedy.　　　　　 [D]John Malkovich.

34. The underlined word "redeem" probably means ＿＿.

　　[A]to show one's skills and bravery

　　[B]to test one's ability through a task

　　[C]to protect someone from being killed

　　[D]to make up for a mistake made before

35. We can learn from the second part of the text that Nora Ephron ____.

[A]worked for a radio station

[B]borrowed *Sleepless in Seattle*

[C]directed *When Harry Met Sally*

[D]acted the main part in *Sleepless in Seattle*

36. By the last sentence, the writer means that Tom Cruise ____.

[A]is a great American individual

[B]likes the part of Mitch McDeere

[C]is at his best when playing this kind of role

[D]admires the spirit of American individualism

E
Who Drew Circles in My Field?

In the summer of 1978 an English farmer was driving his *tractor*(拖拉机) through a field of wheat when he discovered that some of his wheat was lying flat on the ground. The flattened wheat formed a circle about six meters across. Around this circle were four smaller circles of flattened wheat. The five circles were in a formation like five *dots*(点). During the following years, farmers in England found the strange circles in their fields more and more often.

The circles are called "crop circles" because they appear in the fields of grain — usually wheat or corn. The grain in the circles lies flat on the ground but is never broken; it continues to grow, and farmers can later harvest it. Farmers always discover the crop circles in the morning, so the circles probably form at night. They appear only in the months from May to September.

At first, people thought that the circles were a hoax. Probably young people were making them as a joke, or farmers were making them to attract tourists. To prove that the circles were a hoax, people tried to make circles exactly like the ones that farmers had found. They couldn't do it. They couldn't enter a field of grain without leaving tracks, and they couldn't flatten the grain without breaking it.

Many people believe that beings from outer space are making the circles to *communicate*(交流) with us from far away and that the crop circles are messages from them.

Scientists who have studied the crop circles suggested several possibilities. Some scientists say that a downward rush of wind leads to the formation of the circles — the same downward rush of air that sometimes causes an airplane to *crash*(坠毁). Other scientists say that forces within the earth cause the circles to appear. There is one problem with all these scientific explanations: crop circles often appear in formations, like the five-dot formation. It is hard to believe that any natural force could form those.

37. In the summer of 1978, an English farmer discovered in his field that ＿＿.
    [A]some of his wheat had been damaged
    [B]some of his wheat had fallen onto the ground
    [C]his grain was growing up in circles
    [D]his grain was moved into several circles

38. According to the text, "a hoax"(Line 1,Para. 3) is probably ＿＿.
    [A]an attempt made to fool people
    [B]a special way to plant crops
    [C]an experiment for the protection of crops
    [D]a research on the force of winds

39. Which of the following may prove that the crop circles are not made by man?
    [A]The farmers couldn't step out of the field.
    [B]The farmers couldn't make the circles round.
    [C]The farmers couldn't leave without footprints.
    [D]The farmers couldn't keep the wheat straight up.

40. One explanation given by scientists for the crop circles is that they are made by ＿＿.
    [A]airplane crashes　　　　　　[B]air movement
    [C]unknown flying objects　　　[D]new farming techniques

模拟考场三

阅读下面短文,从短文后所给各题的四个选项([A]、[B]、[C]和[D])中选出能填入相应空白处的最佳选项,并在答题卡1上将该项涂黑。

Body language is a personal thing. It says a lot about a person, such as whether he ___1___ respect for others to whom he is talking, and whether he pays proper ___2___ to someone else's ideas. Think about your own body language. It is important to pay attention to it. ___3___, when you meet someone, don't stand too ___4___. An uncomfortable nearness is very ___5___ to the other person, ___6___ keep your *physical distance*(体距), ___7___ he'll have to keep backing off from you. ___8___, two feet will do.

Some of the ___9___ in which your body will tell the other person you are ___10___ carefully are:

Sit *attentively*(专注地) in your chair. ___11___ you *slump*(垂头弯腰地坐) down on your backbone, your ___12___ straight out in front of you, your body is saying,"I don't care what you're ___13___, I'm not interested."

___14___ the face of the person speaking and do not let your eyes *roam*(漫游) around. It's ___15___ to give the person speaking your ___16___ attention.

Keep your legs ___17___. Do not keep changing your position. Crossing and uncrossing your knees shows either aching legs or the ___18___ that you can ___19___ wait to get away. It is the way you may feel, but you should certainly ___20___ that fact.

1. [A]shows　　　[B]expresses　　　[C]passes　　　[D]proves
2. [A]effort　　　[B]attention　　　[C]thought　　　[D]care
3. [A]In fact　　　[B]At least　　　[C]In general　　　[D]For example
4. [A]long　　　[B]close　　　[C]still　　　[D]straight
5. [A]exciting　　　[B]necessary　　　[C]annoying　　　[D]shameful
6. [A]but　　　[B]yet　　　[C]still　　　[D]so
7. [A]and　　　[B]or　　　[C]when　　　[D]since

8.　[A]Normally　　[B]Especially　　[C]Gradually　　[D]Nearly

9.　[A]words　　　[B]meanings　　　[C]ways　　　　[D]rules

10.　[A]listening　　[B]looking　　　[C]sitting　　　[D]speaking

11.　[A]If　　　　　[B]Unless　　　[C]Although　　[D]Since

12.　[A]hands　　　[B]chest　　　　[C]head　　　　[D]legs

13.　[A]calling　　　[B]telling　　　[C]shouting　　[D]saying

14.　[A]See　　　　[B]Stare at　　　[C]Watch　　　[D]Glance at

15.　[A]exact　　　[B]comfortable　[C]acceptable　[D]polite

16.　[A]full　　　　[B]extra　　　　[C]equal　　　[D]real

17.　[A]straight　　[B]bent　　　　[C]low　　　　[D]still

18.　[A]reason　　　[B]purpose　　　[C]situation　　[D]fact

19.　[A]almost　　　[B]only　　　　[C]hardly　　　[D]nearly

20.　[A]cover up　　[B]talk about　　[C]think over　　[D]fight against

第二节　阅读理解

阅读下列短文,从短文后所给的四个选项([A]、[B]、[C]和[D])中选出最佳选项,并在答题卡1上将该项涂黑。

A

It was probably around 3 000 years ago that people first began making things to help them measure the passage of time. Having noticed that shadows move around trees as the sun moves across the sky, someone drew a circle and put a stick in the center. As the sun passed overhead, people could tell which part of the day it was by noticing which mark on the circle the shadow fell across. These circles were called "sundials". Later, they were made of stone and metal to last longer.

Of course, a sundial did not work at night or on cloudy days, so men kept *inventing*(发明) other ways to keep track of time. After glass blowing was invented, the hourglass came into use. An hourglass is a glass container for measuring time in which sand moves slowly from the top half to the bottom in exactly one hour. The hourglass is turned over every hour so the sand could flow again.

One of the first clocks with a face and an hour hand was built for a king of France and placed in the tower of his palace. The clock did not show minutes or seconds. Since there were no planes or trains to catch, people were not worried about knowing the exact time. Gradually, clocks began to be popular and unusual. One clock was in the shape of a cart with a horse and driver. One of the wheels was the face of the clock.

Today, scientists have invented clocks that tell the correct time to a split second. Many electric clocks are often made with built-in radios, which can sometimes be set to turn on *automatically*(自动地). Thus, instead of an *alarm*(闹铃) ringing in your ear, you can hear soft music playing when it is time to get up. Some clocks can even start the coffee maker!

21. In the first paragraph, the word "sundial" refers to ____.
　　[A]the shadow of the sun 　　　[B]the circle on the ground
　　[C]a tool to carry stones 　　　[D]a timekeeper

22. In what way was the hourglass better than the sundial?
　　[A]It could be used under any weather conditions.
　　[B]It could be turned over and over again.
　　[C]It was made of glass.
　　[D]It could last longer.

23. Besides telling the time, a modern electric clock can ____.
　　[A]answer phone calls 　　　[B]say your name
　　[C]start a small machine 　　　[D]cook different food

24. What is the best title for the passage?
　　[A]Clocks of Our Lives 　　　[B]What Can a Clock Tell Us
　　[C]Clock through Time 　　　[D]Clocks Change People's Lives

B

How men first learn to invent words is unknown; in other words, the origin of language is a mystery. All we really know is that — men, unlike animals, somehow invented certain sounds to express thoughts and feelings, actions and things, so that they could communicate with each other; and that later they agreed upon certain signs, called letters, which could be combined to *represent*(代表) those sounds, and which could be witten down. Those sounds, whether spoken, or written in letters we call words.

The power of words, then, lies in their associations — the things they bring up before our minds. Words become filled with meaning for us by experience; and the longer we live, the more certain words recall to us the glad and sad events of our past; and the more we read and learn, the more the number of words that mean something to us increase.

Great writers are those who not only have great thoughts but also express these thoughts in words which appeal powerfully to our minds and emotions. This charming and telling use of words is what we call literary style. Above all, the real poet is a master of words. He can *convey*(传递) his meaning in words which sing like music, and which by their position and association can move men to tears. We should therefore learn to choose our words carefully and use them accurately, or they will make our speech silly and *vulgar*(庸俗的).

25. ____ men invented certain sounds to express thoughts and actions.

　　[A]Because they wanted to agree on certain signs

　　[B]As they needed to write them down

　　[C]Since they wanted to communicate with each other

　　[D]Now that they could combine them

26. Which is true about words?

　　[A]They are used to express thoughts only.

　　[B]They can be spoken, but can not be written down.

　　[C]They are simply sounds.

　　[D] How they were first invented is not completely known to the world.

27. Which of the following sentences is true according the passage?

　　[A]The more we read and learn, the more learned we will become.

　　[B]The more we read and learn, the more confused we will grow.

　　[C]The more we read and learn, the more honorable we will be.

　　[D]The more we read and learn, the more numbers we know.

28. We can improve our speeches and writings ____.

　　[A]by using words at random

　　[B]by using words with care and accuracy

　　[C]by using beautiful words we like

　　[D]by using words which are grammatically right

29. Which of the following sentences is true according to this passage?

[A]It is by our experience that words are filled with meaning for us.

[B]Poets are masters of words but novelists are not.

[C]As meanings in words sing like music we should learn music in order to be a poet.

[D]Animals，unlike human beings，somehow invented certain sounds to express thoughts and feelings，actions and things.

C

Musicals，which developed out of British comedy at the end of 19th century，are stage productions that use popular-style songs and dialogues. They put together music and play，as well as song and dance.

In Europe，the US and Japan，the musical is a popular form of performing art. Musicals generally attract more people than do plays or *classical*(古典的) music concerts. However，most Chinese people are still not familiar with this form of art.

In 1987，the American musical "*The Music Man*"，a heart-warming story about a travelling salesman who tries to trick a small town into buying *musical instruments*(乐器)，was introduced in China. In 1990，"*Sunrise*" was put on stage in Shanghai. It is considered the first Chinese musical in China's history. But neither of these achieved as great a success as had been expected. This makes it clear that in China，musicals are still at their earliest stage of development.

By comparison，developed in many western countries for years，musicals have achieved great success on Broadway (in New York City) as well as in London's West End，both of which are famous for their musicals. The musical has become an important form of art in these countries.

30. What do we know about musicals in many western countries?

[A]They are not taken as a form of art.

[B]They are not as popular as concerts.

[C]They are used to teach performing art.

[D]They are highly enjoyed and welcomed.

31. The third paragraph tells us that ____.

[A]musicals are still new to Chinese

[B]musicals are difficult to understand

[C]the musical is not exactly a form of art

[D]musicals can't be accepted by Chinese

32. In the third paragraph, the phrase "put on stage" (Lines 3~4, Para. 3) means ____.

[A]written down in a book　　　[B]performed in a theatre

[C]made a success　　　　　　[D]shown in a film

D

The number of people in the world is growing. By the year 2 000 world population is expected to grow to 6. 2 billion. The fastest growth is in developing countries, where there is already a *shortage*(短缺) of food, housing, and jobs. Africa is the fastest-growing part of the world. In Kenya, for example, the population will increase 10 times in the next 80 years.

In Asia, a few countries have begun to reduce their population growth slowly. China still makes up about 21% of the world's population, but it has greatly slowed down its *rate*(速度) of growth. It is now growing at a rate of only 0. 8% per year. In India, however, the population continues to grow, and it is expected to be even larger than the Chinese population by the year 2040. The population in India is growing three times faster than in Australia, Japan, and the developed countries in Europe. In fact, European people are more worried about population *decrease*(减少) than increase. Eastern European countries are growing at a rate of only about 1%.

The best news is that, in general, population growth has slowed down — from 2. 08% in 1970 to 1. 6% in 1985. At the present rate, the earliest that the world could reach zero population growth is 2040. At that time, there will probably be about 8 billion people in the world. It is possible, though, that the population might not really stop growing until much later. With people living longer, the number of elderly will have grown by 15% by that time. Nearly half of the world's population will be living in cities. This is a situation that could cause a long list of other problems including pollution and a lack of food, water, housing, and jobs.

33. Which of the following is the best title for the text?

[A]Decrease of World Population

[B]Population Growth Has Stopped

[C]World Population — A Look Into the Future

[D]China's Population — One Fifth of the World Population

34. Among all the countries mentioned in the text, the one with the highest growth rate is ____.

[A]India   [B]China   [C]Japan   [D]Kenya

35. People in European countries are more concerned about the fact that ____.

[A]they do not have enough jobs for people

[B]many people from the countryside come to live in the cities

[C]the population in developing countries is not decreasing

[D]their populations are falling

36. Which of the following facts is best supported by the text?

[A]There will be a number of problems in cities in the future.

[B]The world population will stop growing in 2040.

[C]15 percent of the world population will be elderly people.

[D]Kenya will have the biggest population in the world.

E

Go ahead. Read this *leaflet*(传单). You don't have to watch the road the way you do when you drive the car.

CONGRATULATIONS!

By riding public transportation, you are helping to *solve*(解决) some of the major pollution problems in Boston.

1. AIR POLLUTION. *Motor vehicles*(汽车) are to blame for over 80% of the air pollution in the city. Eighty-nine percent of the vehicles in Boston are personal cars and fifty percent of them are often operated with only one person in the car. If people would use public transportation instead of their cars, air pollution levels could be greatly lowered.

2. SPACE POLLUTION. Thirty percent of the land in *downtown*(市中心) Boston is devoted to cars. Where there are *garages*(车库), there could be gardens. Where there are *highways*(高速公路), there should be homes and

places to work and play.

3. NOISE POLLUTION. Studies show that people today show a greater hearing loss with age than ever before. Much of this is due to general traffic noise.

The cost of a personal car is high to its owner. The average person pays about $ 2 000 per car per year in fuel, taxes ... and what's more, we pay in death from car accidents, in poor health from air pollution, in loss of hearing from noise pollution, and in the damage of our city by the ever increasing number of highways.

HOW YOU CAN HELP:

1. Do not drive in the city.

2. Use public transportation.

3. Support laws for improving public transportation.

For further information, call 876—7085. Please pass this on to a friend.

37. The main purpose of this leaflet is to ____.

[A]give information to people who are planning to buy cars

[B]discuss the major causes of pollution problems in Boston

[C]give suggestions to people suffering from pollution-related diseases

[D] persuade people to use public transportation instead of their own cars

38. How much percent of the land in downtown Boston is taken up by streets, garages and highways?

[A]30%.   [B]50%.   [C]80%.   [D]89%.

39. We may infer from the leaflet that ____.

[A]loud noises can make people lose their hearing

[B]many people in Boston can only afford cheaper cars

[C]pollution by cars costs $ 2 000 per person per year in Boston

[D]people in Boston don't have gardens because of the need for garages

40. According to the leaflet, better public transportation is very effective in reducing pollution because ____.

[A]the city will have more money to deal with pollution problems

[B]buses and trains do not produce dangerous gas

[C]there will be more places for trees and grass

[D]fewer people will drive their own cars

模拟考场四

第一节 完型填空

阅读下面短文,从短文后所给各题的四个选项([A]、[B]、[C]和[D])中选出能填入相应空白处的最佳选项,并在答题卡1上将该项涂黑。

One bright summer day, a number of little boys and girls were out walking with their teacher. They walked two by two, singing happily.

In their walk they came to a 1 over the river, and they turned to go across it. They had just reached the middle 2 there came a great shout behind them. The teacher told them to stop, and she 3 and listened. When she 4 the cry "Mad dog" she knew 5 was happening. Before she could do 6 , she saw the dog running to the bridge.

"Children," said the teacher, "keep 7 the wall of the bridge. Don't 8 or cry." Then she went and stood before the boys and girls 9 the dog would meet her first.

The animal came, its mouth widely open. The animal ran up 10 , and seemed to be going by, but when he had just passed the 11 , it made a *snap*(猛咬) at 12 of the little girls. At this moment, the teacher saw a man running up with a gun to 13 the dog. The children must be kept 14 until the man could come up. So she ran to the dog, and put her right hand into the animal's 15 . When the man came near enough, he shot the animal 16 . The dog had bitten her so 17 that the brave lady died soon after the doctors came. She had given 18 her own life to save the lives of the children. When people 19 it, they loved her for her bravery. They said, "The 20 of this brave lady should never be forgotten."

1. [A]garden   [B]temple   [C]bride   [D]bridge
2. [A]suddenly [B]where   [C]when   [D]and
3. [A]stayed   [B]stood   [C]sat   [D]turned
4. [A]considered [B]heard   [C]noticed [D]found
5. [A]that   [B]anything [C]what   [D]whether

6. [A]something [B]anything [C]nothing [D]everything
7. [A]close to [B]off [C]away from [D]out of
8. [A]talk [B]laugh [C]move [D]run
9. [A]as [B]so that [C]as if [D]so
10. [A]quickly [B]carefully [C]silently [D]slowly
11. [A]girls [B]boys [C]bridge [D]teacher
12. [A]none [B]one [C]each [D]no one
13. [A]beat [B]shoot [C]strike [D]drive
14. [A]happy [B]safe [C]alive [D]silent
15. [A]ears [B]lips [C]mouth [D]breast
16. [A]over [B]away [C]dead [D]down
17. [A]deeply [B]seriously [C]painfully [D]quickly
18. [A]out [B]off [C]up [D]onto
19. [A]thought of [B]understood [C]heard of [D]forgot
20. [A]idea [B]hope [C]deed [D]news

第二节　阅读理解

阅读下列短文,从短文后所给的四个选项([A]、[B]、[C]和[D])中选出最佳选项,并在答题卡1上将该项涂黑。

A

You want to know where the safest place for young children is in the car? *Experts*(专家) all say the back seat is the safest place for a child of any age. In the back seat, the child is farthest away from the force or effect of a *head-on collision*(迎头撞击), which can cause the most *injuries*(伤害). Just as important, the child in the back seat is removed from the passenger air bag, if there is any. If your child is under 8 years of age and weighs no more than 80 pounds, it is necessary to fit your car with a special child safety seat.

The child safety seat comes in three types or sizes: the first type is designed for babies from birth to one year of age, until the baby weighs about 20 pounds; the second size is for children between one and four years of age, who weigh between 20 and 40 pounds; the third kind is used by older children big enough to use the car's belt system. Moreover, all these safety seats must be fitted and held in place on the car's back seat. If your child does need your attention while you are driving, don't look back with only one hand on the wheel. Just pull over.

21. This text mainly discusses ____.

    [A]how a child can be kept safe while riding in a car

    [B]why the back seat is the safest place in a car

    [C]how a child safety seat can protect a child

    [D]what causes passengers the most injuries

22. This text seems to be written for ____.

    [A]safety experts　　　　　　[B]very young readers

    [C]parents of small children　[D]taxi drivers

23. The third type of safety seat is for children ____.

    [A]above eight years of age

    [B]between four and eight

    [C]weighing between 20 and 40 pounds

    [D]weighing more than 80 pounds

B

There are hundreds of TV *channels*(频道) in the United States. Americans get a lot of *entertainment*(娱乐) and information from TV. Most people probably watch it for entertainment only. For some people, however, TV is where they get the news of the day. But some new TV programs or shows put entertainment and news together.

This new kind of program in the United States is called "infotainment", which means information (info-) and entertainment(-tainment). These kinds of programs use actors to act out news stories, making the news of the day more interesting and exciting to people. The shows also use special effects.

An example of infotainment is the show "America's Most Wanted". The producers of this program get stories from real cases that the police have dealt with. In most of these cases, the police never found the person who *committed the crime*(犯罪). Sometimes they caught the criminal, but he or she ran away again. The people who make "America's Most Wanted" film it in the city where the crime happened. They use actors to play the parts of all the people in the case. At the end of the story, however, they always show "mug shots", or police photographs, of the real criminals.

24. The best title for the text would be ____.

[A]A New Type of TV Program

[B]TV Program for the Police

[C]America's Most Wanted

[D]Entertainment before Information

25. The purpose of the first paragraph is to introduce ____.

[A]news programs   [B]"infotainment"

[C]TV channels   [D]entertainment programs

26. One important difference between an infotainment and an ordinary TV news program is that it ____.

[A]reports news from where it happens

[B]shows the photos of real criminals

[C]uses actors to play the role

[D]announces news for the police

27. We can infer from the text that the producers of "America's Most Wanted" ____.

[A]also work as police officers

[B]hope to get money from the police

[C]hope the program will help the police catch the criminals

[D]often find it difficult to persuade people to act as criminals

28. In the program title "America's Most Wanted"(Line 1, Para. 3), "most wanted" probably refers to ____.

[A]criminals   [B]producers   [C]police   [D]actors

C

The banana "tree" is actually not a real tree. This is because there is no wood in the *stem*(树干) rising above the ground. The stem is made up of leaves growing very close together, one inside the other. The leaves spread out at the top of the stem and rise in the air.

Banana plants need a lot of care and attention. They must be provided with water if the normal rainfall doesn't supply enough. The area around the plants must be kept free of *weeds*(杂草) and grass.

About nine or ten months after planting, a flower appears on the banana plant. This flower is at the end of a long *stalk*(茎), which grows from the base up through the center of the stem and turns downward when it comes out from the top. Small bananas form on this flower stalk as it grows downward. Bananas really grow upside down. As the small bananas form on the stalk, they point downward, but as they grow they turn and point upward.

Bananas are harvested while they are still green. Even when they are to be eaten where they are grown, they are not allowed to *ripen*(成熟) on the plant. A banana that turns yellow on the plant loses its taste.

29. The first paragraph in the text mainly discusses ____.

　　[A]why the stem of the tree is wood

　　[B]how the banana grows on the stem

　　[C]why the banana tree is not a tree

　　[D]how the leaves grow out of the stem

30. The underlined word "it"(Line 3) in the third paragraph refers to ____.

　　[A]the leaf　　　[B]the stalk　　　[C]the stem　　　[D]the plant

31. According to the text, where do bananas actually grow?

　　[A]On the stem.　　　　　　　[B]On the leaves.

　　[C]On the flower stalk.　　　　[D]On the base of the stem.

32. From the text we know when bananas are harvested, they are ____.

　　[A]green and pointing upward

　　[B]yellow and pointing downward

　　[C]green and pointing downward

　　[D]yellow and pointing upward

D
Good table manners are back

Candlelight bathes the restaurant guests in a friendly light, the menu is about to be served. Some guests are prepared to eat while others are looking around with nervous glances. Which knives and forks should be used first, and where should you put the *napkin*(餐巾)?

For a while table manners were "out". Now men and women aged 30 or so are rediscovering the finer points of being polite.

Good manners give a pleasant *impression*(印象). But how do you eat "properly"? The golden rule is to act silently. You should not talk to someone with your mouth full. When eating a five-course meal — a frequent event during the holiday season — guests needn't feel frightened by the variety of knives and spoons before them: you work your way towards the plate from the outside.

Uncertain situations often can be mastered with common sense. For example, many unknown *salad*(沙拉) greens can be difficult to tell from one another, but you can cut them all with a knife. The napkin remains subject to special care. The correct way is to fold it in half and lay it on your *lap*(膝上).

If you leave your place, you should always place your napkin next to the plate. After the meal is over, both cloth and paper napkins are folded and not thrown onto the plate.

The proper table manners also can serve professional advancement. If a choice has to be made among several people for an important position, the employer may choose to lunch with them. Those who make noise with their lips certainly won't stand a chance.

33. How would you understand "table manners" in the title?

[A]Act properly while eating.

[B]Choose proper kinds of food.

[C]Eat with knives, forks, and spoons.

[D]Fold the napkin neatly all the time.

34. Guests who are unfamiliar with table manners often appear at dinner parties feeling ____.

[A]improper　　[B]regretful　　[C]uncertain　　[D]dissatisfied

35. According to the writer, what is important for good table manners?

[A]Eating quietly without making noise.

[B]Sitting still without glancing at others.

[C]Using knives and spoons one by one.

[D]Taking care to keep the napkin clean.

36. The writer wrote the text because he has noticed that good table manners ____.

[A]are completely forgotten by young people

[B]are brought back to people's attention

[C]are used when making professional decisions

[D]are difficult to learn and practise

E

Tales From Animal Hospital

David Gram

David Gram has become a familiar face to millions of fans of Animal Hospital. Here Dr Gram tells us the very best of his personal stories about the animals he has treated, including familiar patients such as the dogs Snowy and Duchess, the delightful cat Marigold Serendipity Diamond. He also takes the reader behind the scenes at Harmsworth Memorial Animal Hospital as he describes his day, from ordinary medical check-ups to *surgery*(外科手术). *Tales From Animal Hospital* will delight all fans of the programme and anyone who has a lively interest in their pet, whether it be cat, dog or snake!

£14.99 Hardback 272pp Simon Schuster

ISBN 0751304417

Isaac Newton: The Last Sorcerer

Michael White

From the author of *Stephen Hawking: A Life in Science*, comes this colourful description of the life of the world's first modern scientist. Interesting yet based on fact. Michael White's learned yet readable new book offers a true picture of Newton completely different from what people commonly know about him. Newton is shown as a gifted scientist with very human weaknesses who stood at the point in history where magic ended and science began.

£18.99 Hardback 320pp Fourth Estate

ISBN 1857024168

Fermat's Last Theorem

Simon Singh

In 1963 a schoolboy called Andrew Wiles reading in his school library came across the world's greatest mathematical problem: Fermat's Last *Theo-*

rem(定理). First put forward by the French mathematician Pierre de Fermat in the seventeenth century, the theorem had baffled and beaten the finest mathematical minds, including a French woman scientist who made a major advance in working out the problem, and who had to dress like a man in order to be able to study at the Ecole Polytechnique. Through unbelievable determination Andrew Wiles finally worked out the problem in 1995. An unusual story of human effort over three centuries, *Fermat's Last Theorem* will delight specialists and general readers alike.

£12.99 Hardback 384pp Fourth Estate

ISBN 1857025210

37. What is Animal Hospital?

[A]A news story. [B]A popular book.

[C]A research report. [D]A TV programme.

38. In Michael White's book, Newton is described as ____.

[A]a person who did not look the same as in many pictures

[B]a person who lived a colourful and meaningful life

[C]a great but not perfect man

[D]an old-time magician

39. The person who finally proved Fermat's Last Theorem is ____.

[A]Simon Singh [B]Andrew Wiles

[C]Pierre de Fermat [D]a French woman scientist

40. What is the purpose of writing these three texts?

[A]To sell the books.

[B]To introduce new authors.

[C]To make the books easier to read.

[D]To show the importance of science.

模拟考场五

阅读下面短文,从短文后所给各题的四个选项([A]、[B]、[C]和[D])中选出能填入相应空白处的最佳选项,并在答题卡1上将该项涂黑。

"$160 for a parking ticket! I'm calling city hall about this. There must be some mistake." Nick thought __1__. "Yes, sir, there is a mistake," said the man at the city hall, "__2__ I'm afraid the mistake's __3__. This ticket was for $20. However, the fine doubles every thirty days. It has been 90 days, so the __4__ is now $160. You will have to pay that." Nick had the $20 and he __5__ to pay the fine. But for some reason the ticket had gotten __6__ in his pile of papers and unopened letters.

Nick has always been a __7__ person. In the past six months, he had __8__ to pay his electricity bill, __9__ his jacket at the cleaner's too __10__ and had to pay for the "*storage*(保管)". A job *application*(申请) form he had filled out was never __11__ because it, too, was in one of his piles. "Get organized, man," his brother advised. "Plan what you __12__ do, do it, and then __13__ to be sure you've done it right."

Nick got a *calendar*(日历) with enough __14__ to write on. He marked important __15__ and times as reminders. "Nice job," said his brother. "Now __16__ you do what you're supposed to do __17__ you're supposed to." "That shouldn't be too __18__ with my calendar here," said Nick. "And read the small print on it __19__ you get a ticket," added his brother. "Or __20__ still, don't get another."

1. [A]happily　　　　　　　　　[B]angrily
   [C]disappointed　　　　　　　[D]excitedly
2. [A]so　　　[B]luckily　　　[C]honestly　　　[D]but
3. [A]mine　　　[B]yours　　　[C]ours　　　[D]theirs
4. [A]number　　　[B]pay　　　[C]cost　　　[D]total
5. [A]forgot　　　[B]meant　　　[C]refused　　　[D]remembered

6.　[A]missed　　　[B]covered　　　[C]mixed　　　[D]buried

7.　[A]patient　　　[B]careless　　　[C]wasteful　　　[D]tough

8.　[A]forgotten　　[B]required　　　[C]regretted　　　[D]considered

9.　[A]left　　　　[B]sent　　　　[C]bought　　　[D]washed

10.　[A]long　　　　[B]late　　　　[C]often　　　[D]early

11.　[A]mailed　　　[B]recorded　　　[C]taken　　　[D]received

12.　[A]have to　　　[B]used to　　　[C]would　　　[D]could

13.　[A]see　　　　[B]check　　　　[C]examine　　　[D]make

14.　[A]area　　　　[B]square　　　　[C]place　　　[D]space

15.　[A]accidents　[B]events　　　[C]dates　　　[D]weeks

16.　[A]take care　[B]believe in　　[C]watch out　　[D]make sure

17.　[A]where　　　[B]since　　　　[C]when　　　[D]that

18.　[A]late　　　　[B]bad　　　　[C]much　　　[D]hard

19.　[A]as　　　　[B]next time　　[C]since　　　[D]so long as

20.　[A]fairer　　　[B]easier　　　　[C]better　　　[D]happier

第二节　阅读理解

　　阅读下列短文,从短文后所给的四个选项([A]、[B]、[C]和[D])中选出最佳选项,并在答题卡 1 上将该项涂黑。

A

　　Now that man has actually landed on the surface of the moon, he has learned many new things about it. But one thing man knew before he ever reached the moon was that there was no life on it.

　　There is no *atmosphere*(大气) on the moon. The lack of air means that the moon is not protected from any of the sun's rays. The sun sends out heat and light *radiation*(辐射). Life on earth depends on heat and light. But the sun also sends out dangerous kinds of radiation. The earth's atmosphere protects us from most of them. On the moon, however, there is no atmosphere to stop the radiation. All the sun's rays beat down on the surface of the moon.

　　Because there is no atmosphere, the moon's surface is either extremely hot or extremely cold. As the moon circles around the earth, the side of it that is lighted up by the sun becomes very hot. The temperature there reaches more than 300 degrees *Fahrenheit*(华氏温度). This is hotter than boiling water.

The hot lunar day lasts two weeks. It is followed by a night that is also two weeks long. At night the temperature drops to 260 degrees below zero. This is more than twice as cold as temperatures reached at the earth's South Pole. Under these conditions, no form of life that we know of here on earth could exist on the moon.

21. Which of the following would be the best title for this text?
    [A]Why is there no air on the moon?
    [B]Why is there no life on the moon?
    [C]Why is the moon hotter than the earth?
    [D]Why is the moon colder than the South Pole?
22. The underlined word "lunar"(Line 5, Para. 3) probably means something about ____.
    [A]the sun   [B]the moon   [C]the earth   [D]the planet
23. How cold can it be on the earth's South Pole?
    [A]520 degrees below zero.   [B]260 degrees below zero.
    [C]130 degrees below zero.   [D]75 degrees below zero.

B

Why haven't I left yet? Everyone seems to be asking me this question now. Clearly their having to say goodbye as if it's the last time they're ever going to see me is beginning to wear out my friends. Some of the more unfortunate must have said goodbye at least three or four times. Much to everyone's delight, I will be setting off this Saturday, but getting all the necessary *visas*(签证) for the journey has been far from quick, cheap or straightforward.

Getting a Chinese visa was easy enough. The Mongolian *embassy*(大使馆) seemed a bit unprepared for me, or in fact any other tourist, wanting to visit the country in winter and it took half an hour of knocking on the door before I got an answer. The Mongolian visa, however, has a map of the country in the background that should come in handy if I get lost out on the grassland.

It was getting a Russian visa that had me wondering if I'd ever be able to leave. The requirements for the visa, especially for the trip that I plan to take, were a mountain of paperwork. I was required to prove, for example, where and when I plan on staying in each city and what train I plan to catch between

I've spent a lot of time preparing for this trip, but I still have no idea what to expect on this journey. The planning and packing has taken my mind off any worries I have so now everything is ready and I just want to get going. I'm sure I will meet some interesting people and see some wonderful sights, and the sense of the unknown makes it all the more exciting.

24. How do the writer's friends feel about the delay of his trip?
   [A]Grateful.   [B]Impatient.   [C]Delighted.   [D]Worried.
25. What made the writer start doubting the possibility of the trip?
   [A]Getting a Russian visa.   [B]The cold winter in Mongolia.
   [C]Inconvenient transport.   [D]Poor living conditions.
26. The phrase "come in handy"(Line 5, Para. 2) probably means ____.
   [A]be useful when needed   [B]be written by hand
   [C]be held in hand   [D]be easy to carry
27. How does the writer feel about the trip he is going to take?
   [A]Curious and eager.   [B]Patient and encouraged.
   [C]Worried but proud.   [D]Tired but hopeful.

C

Backpacks are convenient. They can hold your books, your lunch, and a change of clothes, leaving your hands free to do other things. Someday, if you don't mind carrying a heavy load, your backpack might also power your MP3 player, keep your cell phone running, and maybe even light your way home.

Scientists from the University of Pennsylvania in Philadelphia and the Marine Biological Laboratory in Woods Hole, Mass, have invented a backpack that makes electricity from energy produced while its wearer walks.

The backpack's electricity-creating powers depend on *springs*(弹簧,发条) used to hang a cloth pack from its metal frame. The frame sits against the wearer's back, and the whole pack moves up and down as the person walks. A mechanism with gears collects energy from this motion and transfers it to an electrical generator.

Surprisingly, the researchers found, people walk differently when they wear the springy packs. As a result, wearers use less energy than when lugging regular backpacks. Also, the way the new packs ride on wearers' backs makes them more comfortable than standard packs, the inventors say.

The backpack could be especially useful for soldiers, scientists, mountaineers, and emergency workers who typically carry heavy backpacks. These people often rely on global positioning system(GPS) receivers, night-vision goggles, and other battery-powered devices to get around and do their work. Because the pack can make its own electricity, users don't need to give up space in their packs to lots of extra batteries.

For the rest of us, power-generating backpacks could make it possible to walk, play video games, watch TV, and listen to music, all at the same time. Electricity-generating packs aren't on the market yet, but if you do get one eventually, just make sure to look both ways before crossing the street!

28. The first paragraph *hints*(暗示) ____.

[A]backpacks are convenient

[B]someday backpacks can generate electricity

[C]MP3 players and cell phones can also be put into a backpack

[D]backpacks hold things for people so as to free their hands to do other things

29. In near future people relying on battery-powered devices to get around and do their work don't need to give up space in their packs to lots of extra batteries because ____.

[A]their heavy packs can make electricity

[B]battery-powered devices will be improved a lot

[C]they typically carry heavy backpacks

[D]global positioning system(GPS) receivers and night-vision goggles work themselves

30. The electricity-generating packs are likely to be dangerous to us ____.

[A]while lighting his way

[B]when playing video games, watching TV, and listening to music, all at the same time

[C]while crossing the street

[D]at the time when creating powers

31. The backpack's electricity comes from ____.

[A]the gears with battery-powered devices

[B]the motion of the whole backpack while one walks

[C]a mechanism with gears

[D]an electrical generator

D

Have you ever thought about what determines the way we are as we grow up? Remember the TV program *Seven Up*? It started following the lives of a group of children in 1963. We first meet them as wide-eyed seven-year-olds and then catch up with them at seven-year *intervals*(间隔): nervous 14-year-olds, serious 21 year-olds, then grown-ups.

Some of the stories are *inspiring*(鼓舞人心的), others sad, but what is interesting in almost all the cases is the way in which the children's early hopes and dreams are shown in their future lives. For example, at seven, Tony is a lively child who says he wants to become a sportsman or a taxi driver. When he grows up, he goes on to do both. How about Nicki, who says, "I'd like to find out about the moon" and goes on to become a space scientist. As a child, soft-spoken Bruce says he wants to help "poor children" and ends up teaching in India.

But if the lives of all the children had followed this pattern the program would be far less interesting than it actually was. It was the children whose childhood did not prepare them for what was to come that made the program so inspiring. Where did their ideas come from about what they wanted to do when they grew up? Are children *influenced*(影响) by what their parents do, by what they see on television, or by what their teachers say? How great is the effect of a single important event? Many film directors, including Stephen Spielberg, say that an early visit to the cinema was the turning point in their lives. Dr Margaret McAllister, who has done a lot of research in this area, thinks that the major influences are parents, friends, and the wider society.

32. What does the text mainly discuss?

[A]New ways to make a TV program interesting.

[B]The importance of television programs to children.

[C]Different ways to make childhood dreams come true.

[D]The influence of childhood experience on future lives.

33. In the TV program *Seven Up*, we can meet _____.

[A]different groups of people at different periods of their lives

[B]different groups of people at the same period of their lives

[C]the same group of people at different periods of their lives

[D]the same group of people at the same period of their lives

34. What are the examples in paragraph 2 meant to show?

[A]Many people's childhood hopes are related to their future jobs.

[B]There are many poor children in India who need help.

[C]Children have different dreams about their future.

[D]A lot of people are very sad in their childhood.

35. Spielberg's story is meant to show that _____.

[A]going to a movie at an early age helps a child learn about society

[B]a single childhood event may decide what one does as a grown-up

[C]parents and friends can help a child grow up properly

[D]films have more influence on a child than teachers do

36. What does the writer think of the TV program?

[A]Interesting.　[B]Crazy.　　　[C]Dull.　　　[D]Serious.

E

"When one of the doctors *criticizes*(批评) me, I get defensive. I feel like a child again, being scolded, and I want to explain that I'm not wrong."says Viola, a nurse. This is a common *reaction*(反应) to criticism, but not a good one. There are better ways of dealing with criticism.

1. Try to be *objective*(客观的). When Sol was criticized by his new employer for not having made a sale, Sol's reaction was to feel sorry for himself. "I had put everything I had into making that sale,"Sol says,"and I felt that I had failed as a person. I had to learn through experience not to react like that to each failure."

2. Take time to cool down. Rather than reacting immediately to criticism, take some time to think over what was said. Your first question should be whether the criticism is fair from the other person's position. The problem may be a simple misunderstanding of what you did or your reasons for doing it.

3. Take *positive*(积极的) action. After you cool down, consider what you can do about the situation. <u>The best answer may be "nothing".</u> "I finally realized that my boss was having personal problems and taking them out on me because I was there,"says Sheila. "His criticisms didn't really have anything to do with my work, so nothing I said or did was going to change them. "In Sheila's case, the best way to deal with it was to leave her job. However, that's an extreme reaction.

You may simply explain your opinion without expecting an in-depth discussion. You may even decide that the battle isn't worth fighting this time. The key, in any case, is to have a reasonable plan.

37. When Sol was criticized by his employer, he _____.
    [A]argued bitterly with his employer
    [B]was angry and gave up his job
    [C]was sorry for what he did
    [D]was sad and self-pitying

38. According to the writer, you should take time to think about criticism because _____.
    [A]people may have a mistaken idea of what you did
    [B]you should welcome other people's opinions
    [C]people may discuss it with you in depth
    [D]you need time to understand yourself

39. When the writer says that "the best answer may be 'nothing'", he means you may decide _____.
    [A]to take no notice of the criticism
    [B]to argue with your boss
    [C]you need to change your job
    [D]you've done nothing wrong

40. The writer thinks Sheila can decide to leave her job because her boss _____.
    [A]didn't like her appearance
    [B]refused to change his opinion
    [C]made an unreasonable criticism
    [D]refused to talk to her about the criticism

模拟考场一·参考答案

第一节　完形填空	1. B	2. D	3. A	4. C	5. A
	6. B	7. A	8. C	9. C	10. D
	11. B	12. C	13. D	14. D	15. A
	16. C	17. B	18. C	19. D	20. C

第二节　阅读理解					
A	21. A	22. C	23. C		
B	24. B	25. A	26. A	27. B	
C	28. C	29. A	30. C	31. B	
D	32. C	33. A	34. D	35. B	36. C
E	37. C	38. B	39. A	40. B	

模拟考场二·参考答案

第一节　完形填空	1. A	2. D	3. B	4. A	5. C
	6. D	7. A	8. D	9. C	10. B
	11. A	12. A	13. D	14. A	15. C
	16. A	17. D	18. D	19. C	20. A

第二节　阅读理解				
A	21. D	22. C	23. C	24. A
B	25. A	26. B	27. B	28. C
C	29. B	30. B	31. A	32. D
D	33. B	34. D	35. C	36. C
E	37. B	38. A	39. C	40. B

模拟考场三·参考答案

第一节　完形填空	1. A	2. B	3. D	4. B	5. C
	6. D	7. B	8. A	9. C	10. A
	11. A	12. D	13. D	14. C	15. D
	16. A	17. D	18. D	19. C	20. A

第二节　阅读理解

A	21. D	22. A	23. C	24. C	
B	25. C	26. D	27. A	28. B	29. A
C	30. D	31. A	32. B		
D	33. C	34. D	35. D	36. A	
E	37. D	38. A	39. A	40. D	

模拟考场四·参考答案

第一节　完形填空

1. D	2. C	3. D	4. B	5. C
6. A	7. A	8. C	9. B	10. A
11. D	12. B	13. B	14. B	15. C
16. C	17. B	18. C	19. C	20. C

第二节　阅读理解

A	21. A	22. C	23. B		
B	24. A	25. B	26. C	27. C	28. A
C	29. C	30. B	31. C	32. A	
D	33. A	34. C	35. A	36. B	
E	37. D	38. C	39. B	40. A	

模拟考场五·参考答案

第一节　完形填空

1. B	2. D	3. B	4. D	5. B
6. C	7. B	8. A	9. A	10. A
11. A	12. A	13. B	14. D	15. B
16. D	17. C	18. D	19. D	20. C

第二节　阅读理解

A	21. B	22. B	23. D		
B	24. B	25. A	26. A	27. A	
C	28. B	29. A	30. C	31. B	
D	32. D	33. C	34. A	35. B	36. A
E	37. C	38. A	39. A	40. C	

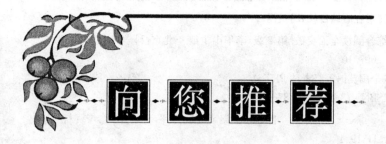

向您推荐

教辅类

词汇考点全面突破第一级	13.00
词汇考点全面突破第二级	18.00
词汇考点全面突破第三级	22.00
词汇考点全面突破第四级	23.00
词汇考点全面突破第五级	23.00
笔试题型全解与高分突破第一级	20.00
笔试题型全解与高分突破第二级	20.00
笔试题型全解与高分突破第三级	20.00
笔试题型全解与高分突破第四级	20.00
笔试题型全解与高分突破第五级	20.00

注:邮费按书款总价另加 20%

图书在版编目(CIP)数据

综合阅读全面突破. 第 2 级/李华山主编. -北京:科学技术文献出版社,2007.10

(全国英语等级考试 PETS)

ISBN 978-7-5023-5787-0

Ⅰ. 综…　Ⅱ. 李…　Ⅲ. 英语-阅读教学-水平考试-自学参考资料

Ⅳ. H319.4

中国版本图书馆 CIP 数据核字(2007)第 148691 号

出　版　者	科学技术文献出版社
地　　　址	北京市复兴路 15 号(中央电视台西侧)/100038
图书编务部电话	(010)51501739
图书发行部电话	(010)51501720,(010)68514035(传真)
邮 购 部 电 话	(010)51501729
网　　　址	http://www.stdph.com
E-mail: stdph@istic.ac.cn	
策 划 编 辑	马永红
责 任 编 辑	马永红
责 任 校 对	唐炜
责 任 出 版	王杰馨
发　行　者	科学技术文献出版社发行　全国各地新华书店经销
印　刷　者	富华印刷包装有限公司
版 (印) 次	2007 年 10 月第 1 版第 1 次印刷
开　　　本	850×1168　32 开
字　　　数	358 千
印　　　张	10.25
印　　　数	1~6000 册
定　　　价	15.00 元